The Wind Queen

Elizabeth Anne Thompson

A catalogue record for this book is available from the National Library of Australia

Publisher:
ASPG (Australian Self Publishing Group)
P.O. Box 159, Calwell, ACT Australia 2905
Email: publishaspg@gmail.com
http://www.inspiringpublishers.com

National Library of Australia Cataloguing-in-Publication entry

Author: Elizabeth Anne Thompson

Title: **The Wind Queen**/*Elizabeth Anne Thompson*

ISBN: 978-1-925908-25-1 (print)
ISBN: 978-1-925908-26-8 (eBook)

Front Cover: *Oil Painting by Greg Devenny - Mackay: Artist, Art Teacher, Owner/Director of Lavender Art Studios, Canberra ACT, Australia.*

For Greg and Abbey

The Chapters:

The Swallowtail Butterfly

This is a reflective story about a woman by the name of Elspeth Abney who lived in the Australian High Country located in the Snowy Mountains, New South Wales and her life, expressed in her very final moments of living. As the dying woman breaths in and out; transitioning through the sky gate to heaven, the story unfolds into a pictorial display of beautifying natural inferences. Elspeth's life memories are subtly sketched through memory nuances of the open plains and bushy scapes, a powerful bird of prey and other natural influences like the bush fragrances, wildflowers and the Swallowtail butterfly; but, more importantly, it is a poetic narrative about her fight against a jealous witch cognate woman.

Likened by many as a reclusive hermit who ate snakes and lizards, Elspeth lived in an old dark and dingy hut on the top of the mountain plains. The habitat was once a clean and crisp light wood dwelling; but, now, it was crawling with red back spiders. She was the most arid huntress of a woman that the snow gums or any man had ever seen — skin coarse and dried by the boiling sun, hair white, brittle and covered in lice. The aged woman's wrinkled body had a pungent smell of soured skin milk. But, once, some many years before, she had also been clean and crisp, young and spirited — full of glee and light, eating fresh fruit, herbs and fish. 'It is time to die and be done with it,' thought Elspeth, 'an old crone like me has nothing more to offer this world of cruel, hard cracked dirt, and besides, he has now been gone a long, long time, and it will be good to see him again, if only for one moment on the way to the next place, the next world and the next life.'

In the final hours of her death, Elspeth could see herself, young and beautiful, strong and diligent, skipping towards the sunlit trees. She had tanned legs and was wearing a yellow smock with a strawberry embroidered on the left shoulder, her cheeks pink and her white cotton blue-dotted shorts clung to her hips, her mind free and open. It was one of those days of blissful happiness and a time to rejoice in being alive. But, today, her body was weak and weary. Her sight was dull and her mouth felt and tasted like a mouldy blackberry. In a state of frustrated devastation and emotional turmoil, she sat in the shallow breath of her disintegrating bones, her beauty beaten by storms and scarred by the red flames of the fireplace. Elspeth could feel a sinking and a moaning within. Wanting to die and return to her yellow smock, she wanted to be free of her body. But, for some reason, she just lingered there in her solitary self, hating, despising and swearing about the storms and the flames. To be a decrepit old woman with only flashes in her mind of who she once was had become weary and tiresome. In wait now, she slept for a while and dreamt of the days she spent skipping in her grass sandals under the warmth of youthfulness. Asleep, lonely, and lounging in her creaky rocking chair, she was plagued by her grief and sadness. In her hut, at the foothills of death and isolation, Elspeth could see a faint figure in the light. It was him, and after so very long, Elspeth opened her heart and he gently and quietly spoke to it.

'Elspeth my darling,' hushed her male lover, and the father to her one and only son. 'There is a quietness in you and a deep gentleness of peace. There is a time to forget and a time to feel the warmth of my breath against your breast, alive with the papery colours of pink, cerise, yellow, and a light white. Lively papered flowers, in rich black soil will sing for our love, and call the silence of the high country to gather the prayerful people as witness to us and our specialness. The time has come to see the mountain roses and marsh marigolds in watercolour and made pretty by the clean air and streams of sunshine. It is the season to feel the light flow that made the flower patches of daisies look musical, and read like word pictures of late afternoon tranquillity.' Then, his figure immersed itself into her heart, filling it with more memories. Feeling a streaming light within his romantic poetry, it drew her closer within. The dilemma, however, to Elspeth's weakened mind and heart was that he was never actually a poet. He was instead a man of few words, a straight talker who loved to swear. The only words that he would say, of any deep meaning, were just before taking her. In a low gruff voice, he would say the words, 'Come here beautiful.' These few words would strike up a desire that neither of them could resist. That was the extent of any real expression of his deep emotions.

In her reverie, there were natural musical compositions and, standing at the gate of paradise, Elspeth could see herself as a small girl again. With her sweet little dolly Patti in arms, Elspeth could perceive herself, kissing and humming a sleepy lullaby to her pretend bub. It was a lullaby like no other. And, there her mother stood, draped in blue kindness, and a loving heart. She could see back into her early life and those days that were filled with long mornings of birdsong rendezvous and lots and lots of red jelly. As she sat there, surrounded by the musky smell of the barren hut, she wearily listened to the trees talking to the ground about her impending death. Her torso felt cool and hollow. There was no birdsong on that day. Murmuring to herself, she said, 'I can't feel my legs or my arms. My chest feels heavy and the little girl in me is disappearing, melting into my mother's blueness. I have no fear, only a sense of knowing that the end of my life is here. In the wilderness of my mind, in the darkness of my hut and in the loss of myself, I know that my life, in this time and era is now over.' Elspeth could feel the angel of death looking towards her duck feather filled cushion swaying chair, and the feeling in her chest slowly began to lighten. As her soul lifted gracefully from within, the wrinkles of her skin began to smooth out, her hair darkened from a course white brittle to a soft honeyed brown, her neck again was soft, and her body strengthened.

The angel came with a sternness of duty and a strong hand of fate. Elspeth knew it was time to face her deliverance with some regret. 'Regret is a part of life, and makes us wiser,' said the angel of death. And, then, ever so slightly the musical composition moved them both from the hut and into the valley of yellow light. Elspeth could see everything as clear as crystal. It was deep into the July Australian winter night, and looking back from the light, the hut appeared old and shabby. After years and years of hard and harsh weather, in these final years of her life, the hut had been completely forgotten. The old vintage style bath had rust in the bottom of it and the curtains were faded to a mildew grey. The clear salt and pepper shakers were grubby, the blue and red tops cracked and clogged. There were smelly, old, ragged jumpers and pants stuffed into the timber cracks and the door was now hinged at the top only. There was a feeling of separation, of loneliness and an emptiness in everything that could be touched. The glasses and crockery were grubby and there were parasites in and under the smelly old gas fridge. There were bits of dry bread on the bench, and some mushrooms that had been battered and not cooked. The battered mushrooms once tasted like fish when fried, and Elspeth often made them as a speciality for her European friend Krisika; now the fungi were crawling with weevils.

Krisika had stopped coming some many years before. Together, the two young women would take long walks through the open grasslands, stopping to admire the natural scenes and dramatized sunsets that, without depiction, realised them forming their love. It was Krisika's wild and almost desperate passion to orgasm and her mysterious other life that mattered little when she was with Elspeth. This deepness kept their love affair free and alive. Krisika had been adopted by a neighbouring family, she was a sad girl with strong eyes that held a firm but knowing look. Krisika was raised and nurtured by the well-to-do couple who were much older by the time they had adopted the baby. They did love her and decided to let the young child keep her own birthright name. By doing so, they decided her own name would help keep that natural attachment to middle Europe, where eventually, to their great sadness, she did return. She took with her the education she had received in Australia and her sexual passion that could not be lassoed by any man or any woman. It was as if Krisika had lived only to find the richness of her own culture, and the wildness within her would only be satisfied by the high art and ancient literary texts of old world Europe.

The hut, like Elspeth, had died a slow, slow death. There had been a breakdown in the daily routine, a routine that had once been filled with mellow meanderings and happenings that were intrinsically connected to changes in the dramatic weather patterns. Days spent smiling at the little ducklings waddling near the ponds and the sage aroma of spit-roasted kid goat, were shared as a delicacy between her and her many lovers. Now, Elspeth experienced a lonely death, a lonely life and was leaving a forlorn and broken-down hut. The shanty could be likened to the lovers she could never really commit to. The lovers, both men and women who had been besotted by her beauty, had wanted her in ways that Elspeth could not pretend to have wanted. The lovers were also left broken down and forlorn because they could never own a woman who belonged only to the bush, and compared to it, they were obsolete. The light took her back to the river gorge, not far from the hut, but far enough away to be secluded in the mysterious enigma of barrenness and sparseness. The depth of the large open and cool chasm overwhelmed her subconscious thought, and she began to feel the awe of the scaped ridge in her death belly — red rock and grey blue slate were stalked by the purple groove in the stone and made her sense an eeriness within. It was an eeriness that she could not understand. This uneasy feeling was shown in the reflection of the large pools of water.

The water reflected two clear faces swimming to the bottom of the slimy river bed. The gorge had a wisdom of its own, a wisdom that was entrenched in the last layer of rock — firm, hard, solid and ensconcing a foundation that was to be the invisible mesh, binding her and him together for all eternity. The feeling in her heart ruptured against the deep torment of the night, and against a cold torrent of tears that flooded the nearby fields. The meshed grasses had been their seal and imprinted the earth with the seed of their love. After much pain, they had been raised up to a renewed life. After searching and looking and waiting, they had finally seen their souls as one impenetrable being. Elspeth had borne a son, Mannus, a grown man now who had left his mother to become one with a world, a trying world that she never wanted to be a part of. In the slight rock of her death chair, she awaited his return and the river of his conception now washed over her. The daisy chain of her life was scattered like a string of pearls that she was always meant to wear but never did. As she sat in what had become her bereavement chair, there came a time of solitude, a shush that was opened by the cool winter sunshine floating through the latticed window pane. For a moment, there was no pain, and a sense of freedom that uncluttered her thoughts spoke through her body like an open book, bringing with it the quiet song.

The beauty of the birds, the beauty of the space, and the beauty of the sunny floral scape had often opened her intuition, protecting her and warning her of the unpleasant and hard things in life. They came in visions and gestures and sounds — echoes that she did not want, need, or look for. They awakened her awareness of the woman who despised her every move, her every action, her every word and her very being — a woman of deep-seated jealousy who completely hated Elspeth. In spring and summer, the flower pots had bloomed near the hut and the snow bush bride that Elspeth had planted when she had first come to the area swayed silently in the mid-day warm breezes. It sometimes brought with it a strange feeling that pervaded the hut. The feeling was difficult to interpret and brought with it a sense of listlessness and dissatisfaction. The snow bush bride, when in bloom, was gentle and soft in appearance. But in the middle of winter, it looked stiff, breakable and lost, like Elspeth in her later years of life. In her chair, she sat back, body facing the dim roof. She could feel something so low and sad that her warm heart began to sink down through the duck feathers onto the worn ripped linoleum flooring, which was greasy and cold like the distant pictures in her mind.

The pictures were depictions of lost boats, children crying and fragmented people who told sad, dark stories, filled with blood, vinegary wine, and would never be blessed by the purity of life's hand. She remembered the dense, dead feelings in her stomach and the pain against the torment of her thoughts and the cool water-coloured credence. The dying woman's now silky and softly drained hands reached for only the best and most beautiful, feeling the passion for ecstasy and love, saintly and blissful. In her longing, the deepest depths of the impending crisis and pain were ignited by the wanting of freedom, tranquillity, and gracefulness. Elspeth's thoughts became awakened by her individualism and the maudlin of her life's journey floated away. It was then that her true-life sentiment was revealed and could not be obscured in a pot plant. Now her soul had been cleansed by the remembrance of the fresh herbs and crisp cleanliness. The angel of death whispered into her ruby signet ring that her passions for a new life had already been exposed in the multiple orgasm, similar to the one that had borne her a son. The stone was a gift from her son's father, and a sign that after her death, she would be restored to her youthful strong and vigorous self, the ruby stone cleansing her of exhaustion and lethargy.

In the last hours before her death, the psalms of introit were quietly hummed by the angel and became submerged in Elspeth's body, mind and spirit, which began to ache and yearn in the renewed spiritual dimensions. Her body encapsulated the rhapsody of her perfections before the river of her life rose up to flood the streams, creeks, dams and open fields, destroying everything that had given her pain. For, in the last stage of her impending death, she did see all. The feeling in her heart ruptured against the deep ordeal of the night and against the cold torrents of the flooded fields. In tears, Elspeth was nearly dead. Yet, there were still flickering thoughts of the paper daisies singing in the past summer breezes. The daisies held the expressions of her life, like the seemingly purple suede water in the afternoon sands of her own family's early beach-front holidays and the pink horizons of expansive lavender fields. She also saw the white-tailed lizard that came every so often, shaped in silver haze next to the moon hovering high above the abandoned house where she had once lived. Yes, the white-tailed lizard, brought with it a clear message of change.

Elspeth could hear the summer singing from within the fragrant smell of her fresh, pressed and clean linen. It was as if each and every daisy in some way mirrored those unreachable personal aspects of her life. She looked into the shabby lounge room where her family of five had once shared so many Sunday roast lunches after the 9am morning mass, paint peeling off the walls and carpet bare to the thread. The meat had been succulent, tender and the gravy rich and thick. The Christmas pudding recipe notes lay on the long brown table surrounded by the familiar dark mahogany high-back, heavy chairs. The recipe handed down from the country kitchens and steamed with a hidden shilling of luck was the greatest treat for the family member who found it — a sign of many good things to come. Hovering above, Elspeth could see the old broken-down push-bike with the weather-beaten basket, that even as an elderly woman, she had ridden around town. The bike had given her a false sense of importance, even on a dull day. Although, the dullest daisies were the tears of her mother when she found that her husband had been having an affair with her oldest and closest friend. It was a friendship of childrearing, recipe swapping, flower giving and arm-in-arm walks on the beach. It was a friendship full of flowers. As time went on, and Elspeth matured, she knew that between people, at times, there were many secrets.

Friendship was not sanctified and the bittersweet taste of their forbidden togetherness won out over honesty. It was sad that her father, Jack, had also given her mother's best friend, Prue, those same papery daisies and often referred to her, in public, just the way that only a lover would. In those days, an affair was considered sacrilege to every human moral; sex was only meant for procreation. Pleasure in sex was not considered and everyone knew that it was a dirty fixation that was not to be enjoyed and never to be spoken about. Elspeth felt that shame again in her last moments of life. When she recalled a conversation that she had overheard her father having with Prue, she realised the pain and suffering in his devotional love for another woman. 'What can a man say to the most beautiful woman in the world, only that this is an affair of love, and need, but not honesty. It is sex, but not without meaning. You have fulfilled my life in ways that she never did, and never could have, and I always wanted to marry you and probably should have.'

People usually don't make polite conversation when they are having an affair. It is the unspoken language of the body that brings two people together who are attracted to each other, the meeting of eyes and those deep questioning looks. It is a longing to fulfil empty gaps and a need to feel something and someone different. 'My private life is separate to them and is an expression of myself and us,' replied Prue, with a sincerity in her tone and a voice that made him realise that there was never to be a real marriage, only a relationship that was cradled by the blissful sexual times they shared. 'I will never marry again, and even if we could, marriage would steal the only real happiness that I have ever experienced.'

The likeness between the two girls was uncanny. Looking into Liza's eyes, for Elspeth, was almost like looking at her own self. Both girls had a similar body frame, same shaped face and seemed to know, like twins, most of the time, just what the other was thinking. They were best family friends born eighteen months apart. Elspeth was the eldest. Their friendship was separate to everyone and everything else. When the girls were growing up, there was nothing outside their own places of fun, just Elspeth and Liza; countless family outings, beautiful days and dinners. Laying in front of the fire, falling asleep on the lounge together and drifting off to sleep with the sound of their parent's conversations — warm, comfortable and loving each other. These were the best times to remember, helping her to forget, some other, not so good things that had happened.

All those years without knowing, they had a blood bond. Liza had left James Creek when she was just seventeen, there was something pulling her away from the existence of her country life, pulling her in another unexpected life direction. 'I promise to write Elspeth, and will let you know everything that I do. I will write descriptions of all the places that I visit and mention all the people that I meet. I will come home twice a year, and we can once again go yabbying in the dam. To a fine dust powder, we will let the mud dry on our legs and in the summer holidays we will sun bake without our tops on. I will be home before you know it.' No letters came until years later. When the letters eventually did arrive, they gave no real advancement or insight into Liza's day-to-day happenings, but were three short stories that spoke about early life in Australia. Liza had become a historian and manuscript assessor and had seemed to have forgotten about the yabbies in the dam and those long, hot, muddy days.

Mannus looked into his mother's sunken eyes. They were now hollow circles with no glint of life left in her eyeball, iris or pupil. Mannus could no longer see her warm firm look, he could no longer see her guiding direction and he could no longer see the woman of strength that he had modelled so many aspects of his own ideals and life choices upon. Mannus could no longer see his mother.

The journey from Melbourne to the mountain wilderness had been a long and arduous one. Mannus had known for some time that his mother's health was declining, but no amount of encouraging or persuasion could convince Elspeth to leave the hut. Mannus wanted his ailing mother to move in with him and his family — Elsie, his wife, and baby Jules — knowing eventually that she would need to go to a nursing home. However, Elspeth simply refused to leave her hut and move into the city. News came from Krisika's cousin, Brenda, who was now the only person living near Elspeth. She said that the old woman had become close to death, lounging in her rocking chair and not eating a bite.

Brenda rarely thought about others. In fact, her greed and self-centred ways had always brought bad things into her life. She was always sick, tired, and full of negative stories about anyone she had ever met. But today, knowing Elspeth was dying, she thought to ring Mannus. Mainly because she did not want the responsibilities associated with the woman's death. Brenda had only ever looked in on the relationship between Krisika and Elspeth; she never understood it, and she envied their closeness. She envied their long walks and she never associated with them. Brenda never knew the intimate love that the two shared and would just run away when she saw them together. In her own small way, she wanted to be as far away from their fondling as possible. Their continuous fondling raised issues in her own self.

'Is that you Mannus,' asked Brenda, slowly and carefully when he answered the phone. 'Yes' Mannus replied, feeling weak in his legs as he connected the voice on the other end of the phone to his childhood.

'I'm coming as soon as I can,' and that was the end of the conversation. The end, he knew, had already come. Blaming himself, he instantly felt guilt for not spending more time with his aging mother, grief at the loss of his childhood and sadness about the life they had once shared.

Mannus had left his mother, but not the desire to one day buy the Seymour Homestead where she had worked, almost like a slave, for the rich owners for all those years. Mannus knew that for many a year, his mother was up every day before dawn, that she rarely had a day off work. That she had scrubbed, mopped, cooked and cleaned, doing whatever they had asked of her. For many merciless days, Elspeth, had sat waiting for Mannus to visit, pretending to herself that she did not care, pretending that she was strong and that she did not need anyone. Every day, after her morning cup of tea, when she was awake enough to focus her eyes, she would look out the window, across and down into the valley that led to the main road, just waiting to see something or someone in the distance — looking for him and them.

Mannus was now thirty-six years of age: a loving man, tall, dark and movie star handsome. He was a sophisticated modern guy wearing pointed leather shoes and seamed dark pants, taking much pride in his starched clean shirts. In his late teens, he had moved away to the thrill of an urban Melbournian inventive life, needing to discover who he really was. For many reasons he needed to be away from the hut and his nurtured but isolated existence. This existence, at times, had put him on the outer of modern living, and he wanted that erudite city arty Melbourne lifestyle. In him lay a genius, and a person who would one day rise up in the arts, considering even farming as an off-side occupation. Mannus had been shunned and not wanted, branded by some landowners before his birth as a 'loser from way back, one of them'. The homestead would one day be his and he could see his hand signing the contract, Jules running carefree in the open spaces, hiding behind the boulders and eating old-fashioned fly away cream-filled sponge cakes. Mannus had come back to the hut to lift his mother from her death chair and take her back into the gully, back to the place where he had been conceived, even though he had never been there and did not really know that place and its obscure secrecies.

'Can you hear me mother,' he gently cried, as he calmly and, with all his loving strength, engulfed what was now his mother's frail, aged and weary body. 'Why has God taken my beautiful Elspeth,' he wept into her lined face. As the last ounce of living life lifted from her body, he faintly heard her sigh. 'Back to your father, he is still in the gully.' It was time and Elspeth did have to go.

It was a strong stride that spoke of horses and her reverberating laugh that echoed amongst the gums. Each day, at sunrise, Elspeth would meet the flight of the Swallowtail butterfly. Together they would go, leaving the grey bush hut and following the streams that lead them down to the fields and into the haunting gully. Known to the elders as a place of disgrace, a place where the shunned and unaccepted would go to escape from the world. The gully and its alluring beauty called people to not only face their sins, but protected them from further transgression. It was also a place for secretive love making, love making that was naturally beautified by the organic forces of the terrain, the blue airstreams and the heavy and light rainfalls. The gifted ones could see the sea from the gully and no afflictions would be carried. The others rotted away to bare bone; they were the pariahs.

It was the oldest and coldest place on earth, hidden in the undulating mountains. It was where not many could live and not many were welcomed by the rawness of the land. For many years, Elspeth went to the gully, every day, and loved a man who she never invited back to her hut; the place where she alone had raised their son. It was never meant to be a family home and Elspeth's diverse personal needs inclined her to want to just be herself, independent and living without commitment to a full-time relationship. To know how to walk the gully and avoid the sacred rocks was sung in the hearts of the dark silk children, who had swum beyond the deepest waves. Only the gums knew just what she did out there all day. After they had been together, sometimes she returned with a rabbit strapped to her belt, blood staining her boots. At other times, she had a duck in hand, the feathers she kept to fill her bedding before the next snow. From her tender years, always pulsating gently above her, was the peaceful Swallowtail butterfly, lovingly fluttering and guiding her every steadfast step. And, with each step, loneliness flowed through the trees like a void in need of nourishment. The saplings had sensed her path. Her journey that had become laden with pregnancy, single parenting and great difficulties because of being invisibly pursued by the hate and jealousy of a cruel woman.

Much changed in the natural and uncultivated land and the seasons, like the four temperaments that could cool and calm the dawn and dusk in a trance moment: White and cold, irritable red hot, dry black wind storms and grey, thick clouds. Turning, they had seen her age. The trees had seen her turn from strength to weakness, and she lingered at times as her routine began to slow. The black sky lowered, and so did she, until she rarely left the hut. The trees watched Mannus leave the hut, which had already become a gravestone. Above, he could hear the wind starting to swell and the feeling of death at his back. The trees watched him carry his mother through the scrub, across the fields and down into the gully. As he walked, the ground under his feet felt as if it were directing him, guiding him and showing him where to go. The wind in the top of the trees suddenly became ferocious and wild, then, just stopped. Like her, the wind twisted and shaped his life. And, once again, the Swallowtail butterfly spread her wings and Mannus began his journey into his father's place of dwelling, Elspeth dead in his arms and his father's voice echoing in his heart saying, 'You are my son, you are my son and now you will meet your people. The people with whom you share the same blood. In you they will see me, and in them you will know me only through their stories of your mother's visits and my distance from the other world will you capture the essence of my life.

It was a world that was full of crookedness, full of nobodies and full of talk about a man who had lost his mind at war and his ambitions to drink. The talk was about a quiet man, who had an education, but no morals and a man who gambled his life and his possessions into an ego. It was an ego too big to trample down, too big for any other bloke or any other person. And, then, I left. I left because there was nobody who wanted me around and I wanted nobody around. I was a black man in a white man's body, a scared, traumatised and lonely man. I found your mother, who was also not wanted, a woman who was separated from her family, a woman who was an outcast because her beauty was such that other women became instantly and insanely jealous. One in particular, without a doubt, hated your mother and now it is time for you to know your mother's great sense of strength and wisdom. You need to know the inner power it took for her to overcome one of the cruellest witches in the world. It is true that the demonic one, this woman wanted only Elspeth's destruction. Your mother was poor, simple and intelligent, but the riches in her soul and the love in her heart were the greatest treasures a woman could ever behold. Elspeth was my other half and in our ostracism from them, we became one and had you. As you know, we never married or even lived together.'

Elspeth had moved from her family home, near to James Creek, to escape her father Jack who was a mean and hurtful man. Although he would never say so, the hurt came from impregnating his wife's best friend and seeing another man raise their love child. Securing a position on a homestead near to what use to be called Seymour, she was hired to cook and look after the house and two children of the people who owned the homestead. It was sometime in the early 1950s and Elspeth had turned 21 years of age. She was beautiful, kind with hazel green eyes and satin brown hair that swayed at her breast line. Elspeth had a smile that was serene and all-knowing in mystery. Elspeth knew the history of the district. She was born and raised as a country girl and she knew all the ways of how to live in the scrub. Elspeth knew the basic handed down traditions that were binding to the daily routines: How to white wash the fireplace, blacken the top of the old wood stove and how to cook scones, simple delicious scones that rolled off her hands like succulent warm jam dollops of whipped cream that melted onto the table. The only oven temperature guide that she used was to open the stove door and run an open hand through the heat. An experienced hand that could simply move through the heat, she knew just when the time was right to place the tray in the oven.

The owners of the homestead were a style of people different to those in the local area. Coming from the Sydney North Shore, they knew little of country life, but, they had money, education and were always well-dressed. Mr Clarence had original ties to an old noble English family, with Scottish lineage and he and his wife still possessed some of the family's old money: relics, heirlooms and furnishing, his wife was of a European background, well travelled and affluent. They were born into the upper class of society. Their family history of important Australian events dated back to the development of ferry services in North Sydney. They often spoke of the romanticism written in the family journals and the way new regulations had changed the face of private ferry business at that time, which was around 1919. They also spoke fondly of the foreshores that were transformed into beautified parks in a style of the Italian Renaissance because of the inclusion of the ferry rides between north and south Sydney. 'The Italian Renaissance is a far cry from the remote snowy region,' thought Elspeth. 'Why didn't they just stay in Sydney and spend their money and socialise within their own set'? Elspeth would never breathe a word of her private thoughts. Anyway, all that changed in 1932 with the opening of the Harbour Bridge because the ferries became almost defunct. Once again, she placed the tea cosy over the teapot; there was nothing romantic in her job.

Over the decades, the owners had lost their original commonality and ties with their own lands. They did not seem to understand the simple domestics or weather-driven life appendices that made country living different to that of following the hands of a clock. The owners of the Homestead were Mr and Mrs Clarence, accompanied by their two children, blooming Bessie and little Aidan. Very often, they kindly and warmly spoke of those important lineages, and frequently went on long picnics to the river, which was also a very relaxing pastime. Picnics in those times were often held by country people to celebrate their special family occasions, but were not as important or as significant to urbanised people. At these picnics, the Clarences almost always alluded conversations towards their other home and other life at Lavender Bay, which, to the local folk seemed fascinating, but completely and totally out of reach. The simple country folk had no comprehension of the words or meanings of the language used by the very sophisticated couple, referring to them as Sydneyites.

For the Clarences, picnics were a way of integrating with their new neighbours and an attempt to understand their values and ways of country living. However, they were not happy people and were often away for weeks on end. Sometimes they took their children with them, and other times they did not. It may have been their yearning to see the blueberries and heather which drew them to the clear silver mountains and glens of the snowy region or perhaps they thought they could farm highland cattle there. There was certainly a confronting obliqueness in the harsh Australian landscape and, although they would never admit to any type of insecure fearful feelings, the bush, its mystery and its all-pervading power was something which their money could not harness or hold mastery over. They were often terrified of the wilderness and the deep black nights, with no understanding that the bush was a much safer environment than a city. Few people meant less crime, less pollution and little problems. The only incidents to be afraid of out in the country lay in their silly imaginations. The bush, other than the odd brown snake, was a place of natural freedom. In its own way, the Seymour Homestead that was situated behind the six green and yellow leafed eerie poplar trees also had its own tragic story to tell.

It was a house of lush red roses and a garden of cockatoo trees, dropping in flight one at a time and two people who were not meant to be together in a union. This marriage was once a joyous contemplation and now a sad place of nothingness. Elspeth walked onto the veranda and glimpsed back into the night of horror. The Clarences had yelled, screamed and fought in the still quietness of the starry blackness. Gone now, their cruel words still seeped from the rustic wood and the old iron roof panels that were features in the sad, but elegant, house. These designs had lost their crafted texture to the rank, cruel ramifications of divorce. Loneliness, likened to the crone inside her miserable abode, was on the veranda that night. Elspeth felt life transforming and, for better or worse, the night time clouds of illusion became unmasked. When people disassociate from their attachments, things become much clearer. Things were definitely not good between the Clarences. It was so sad that after the unexpected death of their young son, Brian Clarence had almost immediately taken a lover. It may have been his deep grief or this person may have just been another in the long line of many women that he had swished off their feet, promising marriage, but never making any real commitment. Brian was a playboy and a womaniser.

Rosanna, a tall, fair-skinned, reddened brunette, was a distant friend of the Clarences and known in her own circles as a self-centred person. Visiting once a year to enjoy the scenery and the local agricultural show, Rosanna was a maths teacher, cool and calculated by nature. The first time Brian advanced his sexual desire towards Rosanna, the three adults were enjoying a Lavender Bay style dinner and reminiscing McMahon's point. It was an evening of perfect quintessential freshness. The sails of refined modern Australian cuisine conversed the emphasis of their conversation on seafood. That night, Brian was affectionate and loving to Angusina, but when saying goodnight, he sneakily pulled Rosanna close, pressing his chest into her breast and subtly squeezing her hand between his body and her stomach. Nobody at the homestead could foretell that their passionate liaison would, without a doubt, destroy Augustina. Augustina Clarence had cried for one full year before leaving. Walking out, she had left everything in the house that was personal to herself. Selected paintings and chosen pieces of crockery, ornate carvings, and all the small touches and possessions that once held sentiment and no longer had any meaning were all left behind.

Rosanna's Classic Estee perfume had lingered through the house. Brian's blind emotions had strangled Augustina's dignity. Throwing her emotions onto a hot iron, the whole experience of realising their affair had left her covered in the grave of her own flowery perfume.

That night, after dinner, the sky had hung heavy over the water reflection on the dam which was close to the old house. Augustina's arms and body began to ache. Somehow, in the water's reflection she could see them together, legs entangled and bodies moving against each other. Brian, with thoughts of Rosanna only, in the light of a candle flame, had lit a sensual, passionate dance. With every deep body movement, the promise of any future life with Augustina and his daughter Bessie were gone. Knowing her desire and need, Brian had carefully whispered the outline of a wedding ring into the centre of Rosanna's hand. The ringed whisper and the sexy intellectual Rosanna were far aloof from the fairly plain and ordinary type of woman that he had borne his two children with. Even Rosanna thought his proposal to be a lie. Or, perhaps she thought it was only her imagination, because when she looked into his deceitful self, her own dishonest persona was very transparent. They continued to convulse their bodies into a hot and fervent circular entwinement.

Augustina had wished his heart to fail, a lethal snake bite to gorge his eyes and the smell of vomit to follow him. She had wished this on him as he melted into what she had seen in the wet reflect as a den of black wickedness. Together, she had seen them lock their lower arms and sip champagne. At this point, Angusina's throat had become dry and her stomach knotted. By then, her death wish for them both had already gone to God for forgiveness. The light in Elspeth's eyes had seen death in the doorway that night, and like a woman who was half dead, she recognised death before it walked down the hall. It was pillared with greenery and steps to the heavens above. The lovers' pink tea roses were sweetly placed on a side table and Augustina's dead body was in a vase of his will to be done. They all knew the time to love and grieve. Augustina never went back to Lavender Bay and never let another man near her again. In some ways, she had become like the walking dead, her soul destroyed, her self-esteem and self-respect, along with little Aidan, gone, and her dreams of a life with Brian and her family, also forever lost.

Finally, death came to the marriage and the house was left standing strong in the day and night scapes, patched up by Elspeth's gentle care and yearning for a new day. It was a reminder that some things in life, full of promise, are best left to the imagination, and that the climax is only a release of attraction that melts naturalistic dreams into Chantilly black lace. Elspeth prayed that night on the veranda and her prayers were loosely answered. But, all those years after, the Seymour Homestead remained, in wait, for Mannus.

In the grey, slight stillness, a cool mist lingered as she sat amongst the dense coverage on the veranda. She knew someone else was there, just walking and smiling, like innocent fairies when they flutter from one hour to the next, in search of the sacred mushroom fruit circle, its root system meshed beneath the ground — the only gateway to fairyland. This was a quiet sound, a backdrop to the lost children's laughter that echoed out and across the valley towards the dead rocks to the quaint little farmhouse, cream in colour, that she had remembered as a girl. 'Is that you?' asked Elspeth, to the backdrop of his quieted voice. 'Yes Elspeth,' he responded, knowing that his spirit was only present for a short time. Whispering faintly, he beckoned her to come to him. 'Come to the valley and look for the gully. You will know where to find me. I am not far away from the large flat rocks that are surrounded by stiff briars and red berried bushes. Should I come humming a love song of no secrets, holding my left breast and carrying three lilies that signify love, honesty and purity, saying nothing of your escape from them.' Elspeth played with the delicacy of her own emotions and could feel his strong embrace, luring her to a secluded place where there was promise of a lustful experience. For this, she added depth of feeling to her words. The words were actually transposed from a novel that she had read. However, the novel was not about deep romance. It was about the blending of refined practical natural interactions in a landscape that had been untouched by human mistake and unblemished by pollution. It was a book about three people in another life: boy, father and friend. Many young men wanted to escape the birthday ballot, a ballot that said they must go to war. Finding a place to be free from conscription felt as far away as the moon. The idea of war was terribly wrong, especially for those who were of a placid nature. A place that seemed horribly frightening and a long way to go to wear a uniform, carry a pocket book and dodge booby traps and landmines. That's not to forget the other side of the banner, the expectation to kill if need be. Elspeth's lover, Mannus' father, did not escape the ballot, but knew of the valley and gully. On his return, he would escape to what some called, 'that cold old God forsaken place'. There, he would rest his traumatised mind and become invisible and forgotten. Mannus confided in Elspeth. 'There is shame in not wanting to fight. Some people frown and laugh. Out here, nobody cares, as most are running from something or someone.'

'No,' he responded. 'Come without a trace behind you, sneak through the trees and quickly camouflage behind them, squirm on your stomach and wear clothes that hide you in the long grass. Do not make a sound with any part of your body, and see the enemy before they see you. Remember, everything and everyone is the enemy'. 'Oh no,' replied Elspeth, 'is this the reason why your spirit visits me here, outside on the veranda? Are you speaking to me or your mates? Are you calling me to your bed or are you calling them to the war? Is this the war of cultures, power or nonsense? For above all, I am a woman, and it is us women, who will be bare and naked on the streets, and lost on dusty roads because of war, wars of men and wars of no love. Stay gentle, my love,' whispered Elspeth, knowing, as his spirit left the veranda, that a part of him had become emotionless in combat and thereafter.

Mannus' father, Cain Kennedy, had been at war in a country he did not understand and a culture that was so foreign to him that the dense, thick, Asian humidity seemed to patronise his presence — a place that was deeply enriched by the culture of the human spirit. Neither him nor his comrades were in any way aware of just what was being destroyed by the war, and in their complete youthful ignorance, knew no better.

Returning home to Australia, he felt psychologically unwell. Writing to a past acquaintance, Gareth Cell, he said, 'I don't think you thought that I would actually return from that hell hole, and now that I am back, I am going to write the truth of it all, the whole bloody truth mate!' Gareth went cold when he read the letter. You see, he was not conscripted to fight. Gareth was a father. He had a daughter, little Karris Bubbles, as her Grandfather, an old Sailor style of a man by the name of Berk Cell, who said he was originally from the long lost Southern Seas, had always endearingly called her. Gareth and his father were both criminals, they were on the run from numerous rapes and serious crimes, and found seclusion in the small country town out West where Cain Kennedy had come from. Somehow, inadvertently, Cain had met the criminal family. Cain, in his writings, would eventually expose these crimes. Gareth had laughed at him, knowing how much he had loathed the idea of killing and played on his fear of death. Cain had always intended to expose the crimes, which he found out about through a cousin Napper. Napper knew how bad the two were. There were broken marriages, abandoned pregnancies, and stolen possessions, including a string of illegitimate children they had left streaming from the bottom eastern side of Australia and along a broad stretch of the coast. A diversion out west was the best way to escape the trail of their destructive behaviours.

There was also another person involved with raping woman, and that someone was also exposed in Cain's writings, along with some of the roughest, foul-mouthed women in the whole country. They would all hang their heads when they were called to stand in front of the great counsel. The good, clean and honest, of course, would all be ushered straight to the throne of their next life. That other man was known only as Tubber. This was Australia, and by 1970, the protests against the Vietnam War had begun.

'The lights were low; the streets were dark,' wrote Cain. 'All of a sudden, bottles started to fly, cars were driving on the wrong side of the road and people were scared, really scared mate. There was one guy running with a girl on his shoulders. There were beer cans everywhere and the police on his back. I was right there behind them, when all of a sudden, he threw her down on the ground and ran in the other direction. It was bordering on dusk and women were scampering around looking for their kids. There was no help but the protesters went on. They went on and on to the sound of sirens. The girl, only seven, was trampled in that rally, ending up with a broken pelvis. The man who threw her down was in support of the war. Every dog has its day though, and five years later, he was jailed for paedophilia and arson — nice type, like you mate.' Cain only ever sent that one letter.

But, before he died, he wrote a very long book, exposing the crimes and sent it to the editor of the Sun Herald for publishing and a review.

After a long period of fighting, his poor state of mind had made him an outcast in his own home town. He found refuge in the backwoods, in the gully with the exiles, others who had left the cities and went to what they called the out world. It was in the gully that the outcasts created a new way of living and their lives became like a story within a story. Reality and fiction blurred the lines of truth, creating a natural style of living, a secular world filled with destroyed and lost people. Everyone had their own tale to tell, some were wealthy, others poor, some friendly and looking for company. Others, like Cain, were completely reclusive, not wanting any interaction, any comfort or any interference. Swirling around in his mind were stories of the Lady of the Realm. There she was at the foot of Sam Mountain — Ba' Chua Xu, always guiding and protecting with a wider message, for all Asia to know. It was about all that comes from domestic harmony: wealth, happiness and the celebrations of maternal messages, which were born from stone and the wise actions towards community. The stories were told to him by a woman with whom he had spent three nights with in the village of Vinh Tu. The three-day rainy season celebrations were in response to her prayers and were watched over by the other poignant female deities.

When the Mekong Delta opened its waters, the lonely, but powerful protector who was steeped in scholarly acquisition defeated her enemies with a strong ethnic and political stance. On those days, she was hailed and worshipped her for divine fidelity, a very pretty delicate woman whose cascading waters he would never forget —a real healer of the relics of war.

Before they had met, Elspeth already knew Cain Kennedy; he had been her heart spoken guide when working in the house of high demands. He was her secret escape and she had made him real when he was invisible. The man in her private conversations was no more than a figment of her own desires until the time came when she finally met him. Cain was a good looking, physically strong man. He was wild with passion and carried a gentle will. After the blood of war, he had arrived in the mountains to try and live as a down-to-earth man of personal redemption, not wanting to be a recovering soldier, solidified by the fear of death, wounded by his tormented mind. Cain was in need of casual love and companionship, but not marriage. Cain wanted much more than marriage. Or, so he had told all his mates in the scrub.

Living alone in a shanty shack on the other side of the river, deep in the gorge country and well out of sight, he knew of a girl who for some time had been working on a homestead as a domestic. Cain knew she was deeply lonely and in need of someone like him. Having visions of Elspeth, he had to find her. The visions became very intense,. Her face would shadow in moon beams and the smell of her body was familiarised by the rippling water that was made fresh in the mossy running creeks and alive in the taste of the edible bush flowers. Elspeth, he knew, was only beautiful, and his desire to impregnate her drove him inconspicuously to every door, to every sale yard and to every local gathering. Finally, there she was, planted by goodness at the Clarences' annual summer picnic. Cain's first sight of Elspeth was of a peaceful girl bending over to pick up a lamb —gentle, calm and unimposing. Cain immediately knew the girl of his visions and could clearly see Elspeth working under their steely eyes and under the judgement of their class values. The resonant and beautiful Elspeth had been setting tables, surrounded by the venom of jealousy — the bad woman's jealousy.

On that day, Cain had been employed by the Clarences to give pony rides to all the children. He was known as the odd jobs man and nobody questioned who or where he had come from. Cain did a fair day's work for a fair day's pay. That was all that most cockies looked for when they were employing people, except for one other thing — a good, clean, open face. A good, clean, open face was the best reference, and a shady or terrible character was easily spotted, as deceit and vice stood out in the company of the pure, good, hard-working people. Cain spoke to Augustina and knew, as men do, what other men want. 'The day is clear and blue and the beer is good Mrs Clarence'. Cain was gentle with her; his heart felt low because he knew that Rosanna was a 'very done up type of a woman,' with her clean-lined classy clothing, her pristine heavily applied make-up and snappy haircut. She did not blend in with the countryside at all. All this was very much out of place amongst the rest of the ordinary praying, clean women at the picnic. Augustina was a woman of great personal respect. She loved to dance and sing but held no particular gift in either area. She was a sound person, loyal to her friends and strong in her values. Everything about Rosanna signalled sex to men and she attracted exactly what she wanted.

'Yes Cain, a perfect day. The ponies look well-groomed and the children so sweet riding them. The eucalyptus scent is refreshing, just glorious after the rain. Have you seen Brian'? That was the end of the conversation and the very last picnic before Rosanna's red lipstick pillowed Brian's penis and her alluring sexual drive stole him away. Behind the back of every man, woman and child at the picnic, the two silently moaned within metres of the unsuspecting leisure party. Only Cain had spotted their clever departure, and a cool departure it was. There was a hill covered in briar bush and there were running tracks for the children to play hide and seek. In a ladylike manner, Rosanna had left the party to go elsewhere. At almost at the same time, Brian had ran into the bushes to play run and tap with the children. Rosanna gave Cain that sensitive and available look before applying her lipstick. 'Run, run,' thought Bessie. She ran faster and faster, almost gliding in and out of the briars. 'I don't want Daddy to catch me'. Hot, hot, the sun was so hot and then she stopped dead cold. 'Daddy is that you'? she cried. 'Bessie go away,' grumbled Brian. Seeing them together, Bessie began to scream. Her tears drained down her hot cheeks. Her childhood stopped on that day. There were no more innocent pony rides and everything became very sad. Heads dropped, people picked up their baskets and Augustina's family was publicly destroyed, humiliated.

Rosanna said nothing and Brian said nothing and everyone knew. It was the end of the Clarences' marriage and confirmation that the reflection in the dam water the night before was not Augustina's mind just playing tricks on her. Again, she wished them both dead, and on that day, did not seek God for forgiveness.

The days were boring and the house big. In her work as a domestic, Elspeth had seen things, heard things, and found out about things that others did not know. Isobel Jones was the head housekeeper and supervised Elspeth. She was an old, wise and kind woman with large breasts and a serene smile who was comforting to Elspeth. Isobel had warned Elspeth that because she was so beautiful, many, many obstacles would be placed in front of her, saying that many people would try and make her life miserable. Talking to Isobel Jones and listening to her wisdom, in the end, had helped Elspeth a lot.

'Elspeth,' said Isobel, 'you must work hard for your board, and the sky will open up to you. Do not overlook anything and your time here will be bearable'. Isobel's gentle voice took on a firm stance. Elspeth instantly knew her place. 'Yes, to working hard,' she thought. 'But, how can some have so much and others so little?' asked Elspeth. 'Well,' said Isobel, 'domestics are treated poorly in this country; they are not always respected. Domestics are still considered of a lower class and backwards in thinking, deemed ignorant and of little worth. We are not equal. The class system that came with the transportation of many poor people from England and white settlement has seen many people uneducated and still struggling to earn a living outside domestic and general farm work. Generation after generation, many have still not been educated. I had always wanted to be a school teacher, but there was never any opportunity for me to do so. With a sick mother, a younger brother to look after, and no father, I had no choice but to go into domestic work. However, my work in service has strengthened my faith, strengthened my resolve, and shown me a way far beyond the menial tasks of cleaning, because Elspeth, my dear, everyone has a purpose and life is more about a personal journey towards God and less about human class and status — trust me'.

As she turned and went back to her mop and bucket, Isobel gave Elspeth a beckoning look saying, 'Heaven waits, and I have many more things to convey to you, but all in good time my dear.'

Cain Kennedy knew that one day Elspeth would be free of her domestic duties and that he would love her as an equal. The homestead would be dedicated to her work, love, dignity and acumen. These attributes would destroy the class system and rise the beautiful girl to the top of the natural world. Drifting away in thought, comforting, the streams began to flood in a scape that was normally so dry. It was nurturing to sit silently, waiting for the cyclic dreaming to take her through the gully of spiritual dimension, a formation of bush charms. The twilight, which had closed the nuances of the day, had opened the antique doors of the house. It was now time and an eternity had passed. The streams, gleaming in the moonlight, mirrored something in her, more peaceful than the rest, like the quiet voice of Cain's calling.

Isolated from her own cultural roots, for reasons only God knew, Elspeth, in her work as a domestic, had formed kinship with the earth and the great eagle. The great bird that she likened to the lord dancing, held the universal power to all that was truthful and good, soaring oral stories in flight of lessons learnt. The bird was to become her guiding light and confidant. The quiet earth was a voice inside of her that diminished foul utterances and also told stories of life lessons in both her awake and dreaming states. Elspeth was called to follow the eagle's flight. Elspeth Abney, not unlike her lover Cain Kennedy, was a white woman who had also become a tarnished outcast. But the togetherness she held with the natural elements gave her deep purpose and a sense of natural belonging — a fitting that made her journey a savannah of prophesy.

Elspeth's grandmother, like most other grandmothers, had also loved flowers. She would often comment on the meanings of flowers, taking the messages seriously when coming across a particular variety at a function, and just like her own mother, was often choosing flowers that typified the reasons for celebrations and gatherings. Using her insight, Elspeth could see into her grandmother's last memories. These, she had placed in the heart of real kindness, in the centre of the absolute rose garden, the florae patch a homage to her remembrances and feelings. In turn, as she worked very hard day and night, in and around the homestead, Elspeth waited for her own absolution in flowers to be granted.

Just like her grandmother, the sweet and very pretty Elspeth was deeply intuitive. This deep wisdom kept her grounded and forthright. In the face of social stigma, the inner sight was her only comfort. She stood tall, slender and upright in nature, with hazel green eyes and gentle soft features, long brown hair and easily bronzed skin. Reserved and carefully spoken, Elspeth had already lost something of herself in the house. Some months after leaving her family, she went back in her mind and saw herself collecting all of her belongings. They had been thrown out to the back of the house. The old-world homeliness of the fig trees surrounding the abode and a blue and grey fairy wren card that sat on her three-mirror redwood dressing table were reminders that it was time to cook the evening meal, and that she would never return home again. She must try to never look back. Before leaving the veranda and her lover's whispers, Elspeth gazed out towards the disappearing mountain range. In the black of night, the ranges were highlighted in the strength of grounding power. She would use this power to transform her life into a song of freedom. Luckily enough, she did love cooking and, for now, she would bow down and walk through the antique doors, determined that one day she would find a simple hut. Always, she constantly dreamed about the hut, planning all her ideas about how it would look.

The outside landscape would need to be as perfect as the interior, situated on the open plain, but still positioned with an expanding view. It would be privatised by a long two paling fence and gentle rays of sun light. The river would be within walking distance. There would be an old mill grinder on the front veranda, a wagon wheel leaning on the wall, rabbit traps hanging from the ceiling and an old singer sower sitting in the corner. Even the small wood room would have handmade lace curtains. There would be beauty in the old, there would be peace in the waters, and there she would bathe outside in the scent of the Australian bush flower essences. The outdoor bath would be canopied by latticed wattle and the ginger, lemon myrtle. Holy mint and native thyme would all blend together. Just before she immersed herself into the fragrant water, Elspeth would brush her body all over with pepper bush. After all, it would be only a simple hut.

As Elspeth stepped off the veranda, a sense of quiet knowing swelled in her heart and she turned to look into the face of a woman who had sneakily been peeking at her through the keyhole of the back door. The closed door was situated at the other end of the wide and long hallway and was hardly ever used. The vestibule was hung with scratched pictures of vintage wine bottles, a poorly painted reproduction of a stone house on the Greek Islands and small candle lights that were screwed into the wall. The witch-like woman disappeared quickly into the depths of her shadiness, into the last reflection of her being. It was a dark selfishness, immensely sinful and very transparent. But, the nag's continual scamming to destroy Elspeth would come to no avail because Elspeth's sight gave her pictures and signs which over a long period of time, would help her to avoid falling into the deceitful one's well.

The corrupt woman came from the gorge country further up the river. Rising from below the waterfall that was furnished with varnished wattle and creepy bossiaea. The frightening woman kept company with other spindly bitter bush women, always wearing black, she disguised herself as halfway elegant. She often stood at the top of the fall on the granite tors. She spoke out in a loud deep voice about the weather and the lack of or abundance of water, and her plans to destroy Elspeth.

Speaking poorly of her in every instance, the depraved woman would deliberately lie about Elspeth's honesty, spreading venom in every corner of the shire. She sniffed behind her personal life, distorting, and making up untruths. All this was because she was afraid that Elspeth would upsurge and become more powerful and more successful than her. The occultist had not forgotten Elspeth's beauty, and at the beginning of time had made the promise that by hook and by crook, she would destroy the resonant beauty. And, what a nasty one she was when standing in the doorway, snarling, and smirking. A rounded stomach covered by a greasy apron, a broom in her hand, moles all over her face, ugly, unappealing and cold of heart, she was the meanest and cruellest of all the witches. People detested her; they stepped away, stepped around and ran at the sight of her. A cackle and a crackle and people knew that she was brewing a potion more lethal than any other. People knew not to approach her as she would engulf their souls and steal their memories. She was a dangerous entity not to be invoked, a dirty liar, and a manipulative evil, bold woman. Washing and scrubbing outside with no electricity and no respect or dignity, she bore nine feral grubs that ran around, speaking like their mother, in a base, crass tongue. Their words were demeaning, spiteful, and full of ignorant utterances. They were the evil one's offspring, the dim hands of darkness, and the lowest incarnates ever to be born — scruffy-looking deviates.

The Saddle Bag

There was a man, Neilson Grey, who lived not so far away from the Seymour Homestead. Pretending to own his land, everyone knew that he was a mean and difficult person. Neilson lived in the driest conditions and the land that he worked had a mostly nefarious feeling, similar to his miscreant and downing behaviours. Neither he nor his family would find the transcending golden road that meets the highest point of heaven and surpasses all that is shallow and lost. On twilight, early one spring evening, Elspeth was ordered by Augustina to go to Neilson's place of dwelling. The dump was shaded under a cluster of dark-rooted trees. She was to take the saddle bag that was his and return it to him. 'Do everything Neilson asks you to do,' demanded Augustina. It was then that Elspeth had the stark realisation that her life was not her own, that the only freedom she had was late at night when surrendered in private thoughts and prayers offered to the other world — a safe private world that nobody and nothing could penetrate. At that time, she gave no thought to the saddle bag, but was aware that Neilson was certainly not to be antagonized or trusted, especially if he smiled.

Those feelings subtly warned her to stay away from the man who often wore a black hat. Neilson walked in a guise to mask his own terribleness and Elspeth had heard whispers from others who worked in the house that he often played games with their children, locking them away in dark cupboards for hours on end. When they emerged, the children found that they saw everything differently and were no longer children of crayons or play time. Neilson's wife too, was also sometimes in the cupboard and wore the mask of a feral pig. Elspeth felt that she could possibly be the witch, the witch of many transient faces and personas, the woman who seemed to be everywhere, but nowhere. A woman who had no soul.

This was the woman, that for the next 25 years, Elspeth would need to stand up against. In her own way, Elspeth would need to fight the jealous one at every twist and turn. Fighting back and being strong would be the only way she could save her life. From that time on, Elspeth referred to the bad woman as only 'a witch'.

It was not clear at that time to Elspeth as to why Neilson had left the saddle bag at the homestead or just what was in it. There seemed to be distaste in Augustina's words when she handed Elspeth the bag. 'Take this to Neilson, don't stay long and don't look in the bag'. These words she directed, quickly, and with authority. Elspeth knew it was important not to meander or wander into the distant hills, which was really what she wanted to do. The gale tongue blew and blew across the plains and deep down into the early evening. It danced in black, yellow, and red — a symbol of death, a symbol of celebration, a symbol of revenge.

Elspeth walked past Neilson's bulls that were stationed in the paddock at the side and front of the shed. There he stood, blood faced and hard. More frightening than the bitter cold that swept right through her, he was the cruel face of the devil. 'I have brought your saddle bag', she stuttered her words, hesitating before she handed it to him. The thick, heavy leather had been sewn carefully by Berk Cell the tailor with a murky past who lived sneakily in the town. The small town was populated with a close cluster of people. Many families had lived in the area since the early days of gold digging. Overseas immigrants and countless family names, most were of ordinary class. Some found gold, purchasing large portions of land and establishing community services such as local shops, welfare groups, and even pubs. These people all went to town, shopping on a weekly basis, buying supplies and socialising on street corners before moving on to the next purchase or person to talk to. Most did not have the resources to buy land and lived in townships or in cottages on the outskirts of the pastoralists' plots. Mainly, the local folk were not immoral like Neilson and his wife. They were of the same ordinary stock — good hearted, God fearing, and forthright in their values, but not of blue blood.

The tailor was a friend of Neilson's, a calculated and shrewd nasty man who went about his business, chuckling to himself about getting away with doing nasty and underhanded things to innocent young women.

'Give it here, you rotten kid,' Neilson smirked, as he crankily snatched the saddle bag from Elspeth, his right hand wiping back across his forehead. It was a sarcastic, power related gesture, not knowing that the sweet girl in front of him held a secret that would open up in the gully, exposing what was in the bag and also exposing all his and his wife's brutal wrongdoings to the children, the innocents they had pretended to care for. The truth was always in the gully. The high iron shed doors squeaked slowly as the wind picked up the dust on the shed and the pungent smell of manure rose to the rusted tin roof, higher, much higher than the absolute. 'What will you do with your life?' A question with a double meaning, lacking any type of kindness, directed with the sole purpose of putting Elspeth right in her place. The piercing glare in Neilson's eye, demanded a nervous response from Elspeth, he then turned his back and the sky, once again, like him, blackened. The old witch-like woman looking into what could have been a crystal ball had watched Elspeth enter the shed and wanted to kill her immediately. In fact, everywhere Elspeth went the witch-like woman, like a dog on heat, sniffed her out, infiltrating every aspect of her life. The crystal ball under her hands had flashed pictures of Elspeth's every move.

The prying one peeked into her medicinal annals and vented her interpretation to a coven of bad mouthed women that she had set up against Elspeth. No matter where Elspeth went or what she did, the bad one was determined to undermine Elspeth's character and had planned to throw the young beautiful girl off the ledge above the gorge and down onto the hard-slate plateau. There she would spit on Elspeth and then run away. To hide her sneaky actions, the hag would change her person into that of an old, wise school teacher who was admired by all, a caring long-lost aunt who would arrive with gifts like a colourful rag doll and tennis racket, or as a social worker who came with good tidings, but was really a very shrewd, clever, and greedy businessman. This man would covertly set about trying to convince Elspeth to steal the deeds to Seymour Homestead from the owners, telling her they were needed to verify a company trust. The slate that the witch had intended to cast Elspeth onto was a deep sea green colour. It was the same slate that in the future, would line Elspeth's bush bathtub. It was the slate that Mannus had cut, finely glazed and finished for the privacy of his mother, who never read the newspapers or bothered with the witch's spit. 'Wash the front veranda, before you go from this place, you little bitch,' huffed and puffed the nasty wife. Elspeth silently attended to the task and with every flick of the broom she swept away the crackling magus' voice.

In those early days at Seymour, Elspeth reacted kindly, but was inadvertently controlled by the bad person's will. But, fortunately, the cleansing water streamed from the top of the gorge over the slate, flowing into the occultist's crystal ball. The water washed the words of warning: 'Elspeth is the strongest girl, your most painful cleansing – my most graceful dolphin.' This sign was a warning to the witch woman, that although at the time, she controlled the innocent girl with a degrading oppression, which had a similar negative effect to both radicalisation and sexualisation, Elspeth could always see beyond the mountain terrain and out to the sea, something the witch had no power over. To get away from Neilson and the witch as quickly as she could, Elspeth, wearing her khaki pants and old checker shirt, sprinted across the open fields and back to the homestead, leaving a trail of thick wet blood on the ground. It was the blood of her grandparents and those before her, the hard-working good people who had loved their little girl. They were there, standing at her baptism and witnessed to God their deep love for the little girl, a girl who should never have been near to such a violent man like Neilson or his bag drag witch of a wife.

She ran through the hottentot fig flowers that were often found in markets and church cake stalls. Those tiny lemon and pink softly spiky floras that were used to garnish children's heads in delicate coronets were sprinkled like a spring duvet pattern across the Australian Alps. The flowers closed at the end of the day and marked the boundaries between the wet and dry lands, like the boundaries that Elspeth placed between her and the past, knowing that one day she would move away from Neilson and similar people. Stopping to stand tall on the hill overlooking the homestead, she could also see the gradient streams of her life opening into rich, abounding rivers. Only the rain shadows in the lower regions were something to consider, as she slowed down and walked the rest of the way to the house.

There were bunches of dried wildflowers, delicate hoary sunray, hanging from the high ceilings in the big house. They were a decorative means of pleasure and prompts for artistic expression. The flowers brought forth discussion from those who appreciated sensitive and elegant feminine adorning. They were dry now, like the statues of Elspeth's early childhood and young adult friendships. The flowers had cracked under her boots, making each stride strong, strong enough to ride a cantering horse and to create stories in her mind likened to Irish mythology.

The flowers and the blood were the plot structures binding her story of hardship and love. The only help that Elspeth received in those days was from her own prayerful devotion. The prayers helped to find peace in her isolation and embellished her soul in the honey nectar of life's natural supplements.

However, a desolate and rough terrain she would have to meet. Even the mountains were a sketch of hazy paradise and the subtle purple landscaped tones seemed further away than ever that evening because the witch still needed to be defeated.

Early one morning, two old, established local women came to visit the Seymour Homestead. The women lived on a neighbouring property and were from the Parish of Wallgrove Country. One woman, by the name of Jane, was an academic who had always wanted to be a novelist. However, her creative scripts were rejected and her fictional writing a failure. The other, Barbara, was mysterious and aloof in her personality, spending most of her time buying and selling all different breeds of horses. They laughed at Elspeth, thinking she was a backward girl, who could probably not even read a recipe and would never be able to bake a cake. They had come to speak with Augustina about the new developments of the Country Women's Association. They had ideas about new campaigns to increase membership, which they hoped would raise awareness of the importance of rural women in Australia. Sitting at the kitchen table, Elspeth, whilst washing up, listened to their intellectual conversation, understanding every word of what they were saying. 'For thirty years,' boasted Jane, 'the CWA has always held a place of pride in our family. It is important that we take our work and fundraising further out and into the broader community. We must try to let people know that we are more than just a 'scones and tea' ladies group. People must be made aware that featuring at the Agricultural Shows with relishes and jams, including our examples of sewing are not the only things we do. We must educate the general populous more about our social service activities. People must realise that the organisation was founded, in many cases, by educated women. They, land holders themselves, were and are still a part of the active women's movement, working towards better conditions for all women in rural Australia'. 'I completely and totally agree', responded Augustina in a forthright manner. Although, by that stage, she was already packing her things to leave Brian, and her words, while diligent and forthright, hid her deep emotional stress, the indignity of her marriage breakdown, and her loneliness. Still, however, she wanted to be a part of the social and community work, which had also been familiar in her family. Being a supporting benefactor for the Mater Hospital in Sydney, she had already planned that Bessie would do her nursing study there.

It was Augustina's greatest dream to see Bessie rise up, and like herself, become a nurse. Although, Bessie had other plans. After the unsuccessful force of her mother's pushy wishes, her mother's desires had made her very unhappy. Eventually, Bessie became a florist and married a local guy who worked for the council as a rubbish collector. For years to come, Augustina never ever forgave Brian, and blamed him for what she viewed as their daughter's 'down turn in society', completely overlooking the fact that Bessie was well, happy, in love, and that her life with her husband was carefree, like a daydream. Bessie was secure, with good food, a stable income, kind values, and four beautiful children. 'However, don't expect too much Jane, as there is still much arrogance amongst people who do not understand the fragile social context of women and families living in hard boondock conditions. Intergenerational patriarchy is rock solid in some communities, and many women will never be given a voice or a choice.' Augustina's pessimism reflected her own personal pain, her personal story and the tragedy of her own family breakdown. 'My funny Aunt June,' Augustina went on, 'had a lot of stories about dozens of homemade scones, the first CWA conference that her mother attended in 1922, which, to my recollection of history reading, was held at the Royal Easter Show in Sydney.

That was the special day to dress up in hats, long gloves, suspender stockings, and pale-toned, pretty dresses, silk-lined and lovely. Easter was the only time many rural women went to the city. Aunt June said a lot of women attended the meeting, after which, quite a few local CWA Branches opened throughout Australia. Poor Aunt June died a slow cancerous death. She was dead and gone before any of us realised she was so ill. We were all left wondering just what had happened to her. Never formally joining the CWA, she always said it was because she had eaten far too many scones when she was growing up. But, for as long as I can remember, Aunt June worked on every CWA stall between here and God knows where'. The meetings were symbolised by loving gentle hands of great strength making jam drops, thick sweet raspberry jam drop biscuits, and peach blossom cakes laid out on rickety long trestle tables in quiet country town halls that marked the charity homes of the self-funded, non-political, not for profit groups of kindly prayerful women. Many were still cooking on those old wood stoves, creating the nostalgic recipes which would nourish, charm, and delight. Click, click, click went the light snappy sound of knitting needles and the knits in baby blue, pale pink, lemon, and snow white wrapped the tiny bodies of those without. The knits can still be found in maternity wards now, and hopefully for many years to come.

War-torn soldiers had meals prepared and in the depression, hundreds of hearts were lifted by food and clothing parcels. These are the familiar workings of many early Australian women. 'Cook on very high/hot for 2 hours', was the only instruction on some of the out-dated recipes. If the chimney was blocked from nesting birds or soot being built-up, the smoke would pour into the cold kitchen, choking us, and leaving a smoky smoulder feel and smell throughout the whole house. It took up to one hour or more to warm the stove and the food preparation was an event in itself, with beautiful garnishes and gravies and glazed fruit sauces. Everything was fresh and clean. When the stove was just at the right temperature, the aromatics of the cooking would seep through all the textures of the house, creating a homey feeling that brought a warm soft pink glow to our cheeks. The warmth of the cooking brought a really comfortable sentiment to our home. It was like being wrapped in a soft baby blanket', finished Augustina. There was an understanding between the three women, a certain commonality and an understanding of superiority which was not one necessarily of complete uncaring. It was just that their affluence was dominant and created a certain type of arrogance. No matter how much they worked to help the disadvantaged, they would never really understand what it was like to not to be able to read or write, to feel the hollow pain of daily hunger, and to suffer destitution at every turn.

Many underprivileged would never have control over their own destiny, and mostly, the affluent would continue to wipe their feet on the mats swept by the underclasses. 'Who is that little 'thingumgig' over there with the mop and bucket? God, where on earth did she come from?' Asked Barbara, slightly turning her nose towards the ceiling and dropping both sides of her mouth. The facial gestures suited her as she thought to herself, 'Has she ever listened to the art of Jazz, the bliss of Mozart, or ever sat in an Opera, probably not'. To Elspeth, they appeared to be snobby. They were not beautiful inside or out. 'Well her name is Elspeth Abney,' responded Augustina in her astute voice, 'she was recommended to me by Mrs Marlin from James Creek, and she has proven herself a worthwhile employee and gives a good clear shine to the windows. I don't suspect she will stay long and will probably find herself getting pregnant to some local boy, the farm hand or some other rouse about up here. Pretty enough though, she may in fact, at some stage, do something worthwhile with her life. However, I think not. And, I am sure that I did see her flirting with the priest at Mass on Sundays. 'Disgusting,' purported Jane in a low husky voice, 'oh well, as long as she continues to give a good shine to the windows and floors, you have nothing to worry about. You can always sack her if she does find herself pregnant. I would get rid of her after six months anyway. I like to keep my staff rotating, as after eight weeks or so, they do seem to become complacent with their domestic duties. When you are ready, just let her go on her own way.'

Cain knew that a pretty girl from a poor background may often be the target of lies and Elspeth, in her good spirit, had no awareness of their guttural meanness but did sense they would never speak to her. Cain also knew that Elspeth would be set up in low jobs and all the other girls from more established backgrounds would sit back and laugh at her downing positions. 'Well, they will never pray with me,' thought Elspeth, as she mopped the floor and picked up on a few words here and there. Actually, they never did pray with Elspeth and when it was time for the peace offering at Sunday Mass, Jane turned towards people in every direction, except towards Elspeth. With a quick almost cursory bow of her head towards the altar, Jane definitely thought that God despised Elspeth, when actually, in a funny sort of way, God could not stand Jane. 'Yes, she is just 'that Elspeth,' she has no real interests', said Augustina. 'She is nothing to write home about. I might give her a recipe book and see if she can read the damn thing'.

After that demeaning comment, they just kept laughing. Elspeth felt desperately alone. She looked away from them, across to the hills and the open fields, to see only what she wished to find within herself. Fragmented memories of the times she had spent with her tender grandmother held her thoughts as she poured them each a cup of tea. The elegant porcelain teapot, covered in delicate pink flowers and a touch of gold, was ever-present in her few possessions. Like her book of poems that, for comforts sake, she had stowed under her pillow, the teapot was a narrative compilation, sipping and waiting, demure and pleasant, alluding time and confronting in conversation. The bitter winds howled the morning conversation but little did the three women know that Elspeth was actually fairly well-educated and could certainly bake a cake.

The women left the table, taking the bunches of dried flowers. The flowers only grew in certain areas of the country and Augustina stored them mainly for her own use. It was considered, by some, as a highly suggestive societal gesture to give the brittle sweet prickly, yet pretty, posies as gifts. The two women were, in character, reminiscent of a couple of very bad and conniving step-sisters. But, what they did not realize was that Elspeth actually wrote her own recipes: garlic rabbit, tangerine duck, peppered fish with basil leaf, and her own variation of European palacsinta; those thin pancakes filled with fruits, cinnamon, and a light cream cheese. Off they went on horseback, back to their conversations and important plans to help the poor. Smiling at them as they saddled up, Elspeth knew the day of reckoning would come, that they would be left with only a small slice of cake to wonder about,no flowers to give, and just a pinch of salt to taste. In the end, Elspeth would buy a horse and name her Murrumbidgee.

Ribbon and chintz flowers papered the old walls. Looking out at the light changing landscape, Elspeth could see things of the past such as relics and icons of yesterday's ordinary happenings in daily life, a recorded copy of history that was interspersed across the property. There was the blacksmith's workshop, the only dead remains near the house, full of bits of steel and iron, rusted by the coals and lying in the rubble of small stones, jaggy rock, broken glass, a rustier pipe, and an old brown ceramic drinking bottle. Some fencing had become unfixed from the ground and was also rusting away in the far distance. The shell of an old car that had been burnt by a fire was nearby and the sounds of children playing echoed from within the wreck. Although it seemed to be alone, the jalopy was enveloped by the laughing of a now deceased family.

Cain's voice resonated down into the gully, up to the top of the ridge and, like a sheet being gently prepared over a bed, across the plains it gently hollered her to hear. It was cold, bitterly cold. Mopping and bed-making were a long way from the orange and red leaves that sat in the base of the bare branches, backdropped by the hush of water trickling into small cascades into a pool of liquid memories and his never-ending cry of love and desire for Elspeth.

Walking into the hall, the shadow of the red wine decanter imprinted her hands. The stylish grandfather clock was appliquéd with gold leaf patterns, like the one that sat gracefully in the center of the large decorative teak table. The clock hand stopped at 8.15am sharp, and by this time, all the dusting had been done and the floors were made ready for any visitor. The day's cooking was well underway and the morning tea of apricot slice was already baked. The music stand was placed next to the piano in the main sitting room, and upstairs in the tiny attic where the initial servants' quarters was discreetly located, Elspeth's soft blue cardigan hung in the cold air on the back of the small, white, painted timber chair. The pink chenille bedspread without a crease waited for her tired limbs to sink into the single bed. There she would dream of escaping from the house, with or without his beckoning.

Often, hymns could be heard coming from the little weatherboard church just half a mile away from the homestead. It was a reminder of innocent days when the world was simple and time was governed by natural law. Back then, there were many naturalists: artists, writers, and singers. However, mostly the days' duties were dominated by the Clarences' demands as they repeatedly inspected their financial records, looked for monetary gain in every situation, and only viewed human service in the same light as their trinkets or trophies. The tussocks were the audience members and they moved in devotion to the sound of the all-commanding and deeply resounding organ music that travelled across the seven mountains ranges and out to the ocean, a sea green monastery.

Elspeth sometimes just stared at the Stations of the Cross. Like so many other sweet little girls who, by fate and circumstance, had their virtuousness scattered to hell, she would always only look in from the outside, towards the affluent comforts that she would never know.

Elspeth's life path was similar to a character in a book that she had been reading. The story was set in the location of Seymour and her mind had swayed between prayer and a long journey when reading it. The church choir sang about love and all the community virtues, but Elspeth was not a part of that reputable worth. However, her inner voice was a notation of subtle bliss and like a fine pianist playing one of Chopin's exquisite Nocturnes, Elspeth floated away to the sea green monastery where, in her imagination, she sat and spun wool into threads of gold waiting for her imaginative prince.

Mrs Harrington, the local school teacher, was often in the church; hair swept up into a bun, starched, white, high-neck blouse, navy A-line skirt, flat black shoes, she noticeably stood at the back of the pews. Behind her permanent smirk, she wore a small gold cross. At a sideways glance, she murmured that she actually knew Elspeth from another local school.

The head of the church council, Mrs Harrington was a highly respectable community woman. However, she had a dishonest nature and secretly dreamed about young tender female flesh, making life hard for the attractive girls in the parish. 'That is your cross', thought Elspeth, 'for destiny reveals all'. Elspeth had seen Mrs Harrington's eyes glance over the young girls' breasts and buttocks. Elspeth knew that God's hymns had a strange and challenging way of revealing certain things, those sort things. Mrs Harrington would also have to walk the gully. Her dispirit could not be camouflaged by a certain type of cursory compassion that was not in salutation to Stations of the Cross. In the last judgement altarpiece, Mrs Harrington would find herself, laying on her stomach in the mud. The church offered a time of peace for Elspeth. Each week, she would pick up her little black bible, put on her best two-piece turquoise polyester suit, hat, and gloves. Going to church was important and dressing in a way similar to her grandmother, gave her a special feeling of being with her own blood. Most middle-class people attended a service in those days. It was a ritual and everyone was expected to attend. Elspeth knew God would take her to the place of deep prayer and sanction her from the hard affairs of the world. 'Dear God, thank you for my grandmother's sight', prayed Elspeth. 'You are welcome my dear,' whispered her grandmother from the other side.

Elspeth wondered again about Neilson, knowing in herself now, exactly what was in the saddlebag. She also wondered why he came to church; because as a human being, he definitely never considered anyone other than himself, and never God. The church was a place of hiding, a place to save face, and a place to carry his many, many great sins. ' Don't you know anything?' whispered one of the two women who sat behind Elspeth, in the church that day, 'you seem to have forgotten something?' 'What have I forgotten,' thought Elspeth, 'is it to be in the right place at the right time or to read the symbols that life has patterned into words, and light and other objects, that, when I look beyond the physical word, manifest into a greater being?' Turning politely, she looked straight into the woman's sullen and red face. 'I forgot only to leave', she thought. With deep regret, her thick, clotted blood began running down her legs onto her feet, through the floorboards, back into her gentle and dignified grandmother's hands — hands that were of a lineage from a convict woman of the first fleet, who was accused wrongly of criminality. It was when reading Liza's small bond book of letters that Elspeth found the answers as to why she had stayed working at the homestead for so long and had not left sooner. One was based on the convict's life — her voyage, marriage, children — and had many pertinent correlations between Elspeth's early domestic life and the uprising of women as they are known today.

The hand-written ink letters and paper incisions were crafted with silk edging and the front cover had been sewn in quilted satin fabrics of autumn colours — grey, purple reds and browns. The fabrics, like Liza's letters and thoughts, were not new. They were slightly torn and frayed between the seams. Beyond the stitches, the presence of a gum tree and flowers, beyond the presence, a spray of leaves, sunlit, glistened, beyond the spray, sky, blue in vastness, beyond the sky, a painter, skilled articulate in sensitivity, writing the spray of vastness in presence of today, tomorrow and yesterday's notes, were all written by Liza.

There was a sharpness in the saddlebag, one that cuts and cuts and cuts, until, finally, it uncovers blood. Words like the woman's would cut into the core of anyone's being. They were callous and cruel, not unlike Neilson. Elspeth had screamed that day in the shed, her head bled and her back bruised. Elspeth was silenced and never told a soul; she never looked at Neilson again. On that evening, when she went into her small room, a room that was never really hers, the cream lace curtains and little teak dressing table felt empty and she wanted to gather her possessions and leave. Instead, she put her head down and wept and slept. 'Walking the gully will be your freedom', she dreamt the words, 'you have been chosen to see the inner dreaming, to avenge the blood of our sisters, and to lead the rites of the ancient feminine passage.' 'Did I hear something?' thought Elspeth, as she kept sketching the dreams of her new life. Thinking she had awoken to the sound of hard feet, walking towards her, Elspeth had surpassed time. But, she was afraid and found herself back in the shed. Passionate sex with Cain in the gully had made her laden in pregnancy. With its winding passages and deep crevices, the ravine had penetrated her movements and eroticised her aching desires. Its small water holes and clasped branches had placed a spell on her womb. In nature, Elspeth had become succulent and her body had become translucent in the supple changes of life inference.

Lying on her chenille cover, he walked up to her, lifting his large foot above her womb. He gave a violent kick to her stomach, stopping within millimetres of her pregnancy, intent on shedding blood. Neilson had returned the saddlebag empty. 'You are cruel Neilson,' screamed Elspeth. 'Shut up you dumb bimbo', he had laughed in her face. In that instant, she had seen him in hospital with his infected stomach cut open. Awaking from her nightmare, she felt the need to swim. Elspeth needed to cleanse herself from the nightmare of Neilson, the man wearing the black hat who, in the dream, had become real. The streams and creeks had become vital to her reason for living and her future happiness rested in the palms of her own hands. These secrets she had learnt whilst giving the floors a double coated wash. Elspeth washed her face with the refreshing rain water, in prayer. It cleansed her skin, opened her inner thoughts and gave insight into her future and what it would be like living alone in the bush. The floor of her room for a moment appeared to be made of lapis lazuli quartz and star sapphire, reflecting past images and future promises. The depictions had been held in keepsake, from the day of her baptism for a bright and independent future. The nightmare held a comforting twist, for when being held in her mother's blue arms, the angels had prayed to the almighty, to protect her from all that is base, evil, and unworthy. The winged perceiver had always been present, even when Elspeth's blood was being drawn by Neilson and his ruthless wife. In the nightmare, Neilson Grey ran with the saddle bag into a rat hole, only to sit in the company of other such swine. It was time now and Elspeth thought more about a person she had encountered in the bookshop, but also wanted to forget.

'I know you, I saw you,' Elspeth was startled by the words and had not recognised anyone in the new township and her intentions were clear. As a part of her duties, she would go into the nearest town and buy the food for a fortnight and other essentials to keep the family. She travelled alone, often on horseback, and was never invited to travel with the Clarences. There was a clear distinction between house help and friends. Elspeth's relationship with the owners was purely of a business nature. Elspeth did the work and they enjoyed the benefits. Elspeth was honest but the tone of the woman's words indicated that she had done something wrong. 'I heard you were here Elspeth, but did not want to say anything'. Jealousy still lingered in her throat. The face was familiar to Elspeth, a face from another time, her early teens, and a time of brightness — a time of child's play, wonder and intrigue. Remembering the rip and the torrent of the sea, the three children were rescued close to the salty brown rocks. Elspeth was the one who had waved down the guard. They were staying with the woman's parents who had owned a villa that looked along the shore line; they were wealthy people. With firm thighs and dancing olive skin, Elspeth had come to visit as an unexpected guest, and the sea had swept her and the other two kiddies up.

Elspeth had loved the musical waves of the sea. 'I see', said Elspeth, remembering the woman's face that frightening day in the salty, rough waters, deep and black. The woman's face was well-crafted, but not refined. Casting her mind back to her teen years, Elspeth once again heard the small voice in her heart. It told her of the day they would recognise each other, a day when through the written word, they would reflect similarity but be moved away from each other through a different moral choice. This would be a time when Elspeth would live near to the earth in her hut. And, the woman who stood in front of her would work in a book shop. 'Books,' thought Elspeth,"were beautiful, shocking, necessary, brilliant, comforting, and sometimes unfortunately, cheap, rude, rank, distasteful, and more than disgraceful, not to mention boring. Elspeth picked up a large pictorial book of wildflowers and left the woman's annoying voice behind. Elspeth's reading of books was postponed for a while and she quietly awaited her chance for a different set of circumstances to transpire in the hut. Then, she would have more time to read books. For now, she only had time to enjoy a floral picture book. For now, she was so busy looking after the house that she barely had time to reflect on her last read book. A story written in the same area about an Aunt.

Elspeth left the shop and heard the ritual dance in the distant calling her. There she stood, the oldest and wisest woman in the land, moving her slowly towards the water, through the cool evening mist and now moonlit hills. The water streams always knew her poised position and the earth's circling was in motion. Down to the depths of the streams, Elspeth swam like a fish in a playful exultation, escaping her enemies and soothingly loving herself. Elspeth would never see the woman in the bookshop again and remembered her name as Lore Bott, a woman with sculptured dark brown ringlets and a lost song. It felt good to get away from those types.

Elspeth woke each day in the house that always seemed to be in need of order, and began to master the way of the household. She quickly had to understand the Clarences' personal routines, when, and how they wanted things done. She had to know the weekly schedule of meal preparation and exactly how the Clarences liked to have their meals cooked. The general courtesies and the way in which everyone interacted was also very important. Elspeth needed to quickly discern her daily duties and perform them speedily. Being a bright girl, this did not take long. Elspeth learnt to live in the solitude of nature, alone and with herself only. The trees had watched her mature and grow. As she worked, Elspeth became emotionally strong and full of determination. The ties to the dark side of her family were slowly cut down, and she began to consider other issues of importance outside of her daily domestic duties. As she heard the first sounds of the commercial wood logging, Elspeth felt the resolve for environment shelter. Way back then, in and around the early 1960s, big logging trucks began to make their way down the mountain's bendy dirt road and deep into the plunging forests. Around then, the first woodchip deals were made with foreign investors.

As she heard the felling of the gums and stringy bark beyond the river, Elspeth was saddened for the future life of trees. Elspeth began to look for answers from the sun, understanding that to cut down large masses of trees would bring immense difficulty to a person's life and the planets future health. Knowing that planting brings love and friendship, Elspeth grew many seedlings and with each venture to town would bring back grain, jars of dried fruit, and plant cuttings. She planted bulbs, seedlings, and cuts in her own small, private patch of garden. The garden was secretly hidden only a few miles away from the homestead, near a rock ledge that hid lush green grass. The patch was next to the flowing creek and covered with the branches of a heavy bush. Elspeth watered her hidden plot and when all blossomed, so did her joy, like her guiding Swallowtail butterfly. As the blushes of mauve spray bloomed, she silently awaited her own hut's garden. Elspeth had always felt protection from the foliage, knowing it carried water up to the sky. As a symbol of love for the land, the trees were also a healing power to the earth. The duties in the house became of secondary importance, as she began to think about other, more important issues to keep her mind occupied and to hunt away boredom. It was now all about living in a natural, free setting.

In those very early days when working in the house, Elspeth would wake to the sound of complete aloneness, stillness, and quietness. These silences were gathered in the early morning lingering of light. It was almost impossible for her not to be stirred or even aroused by the fragrances of the bush. On waking, she often pictured images of the high, blue sky line and imagined twinkling stars creating subtle images of candles and angel wings in the snow of the last winter. These imagined pictures spread from the front of the house and deep into the ridge at the back of the distant mountain gorge. The images spoke of Elspeth's destiny, a destiny that could not be stopped by the actions or thoughts of any man, or the cruel witch-like woman, no matter how hard they tried. They were cold and uninviting and at the same time mellow, vague, and in some places, only just present. But what the messages in the imagined images made very clear was that although Elspeth was working as a domestic, that she was sent with a clear purpose.

Often in the late afternoon, after the last sweep of the veranda and with those secretive messages grafted to her heart, Elspeth would stroll down under the red setting sky that was sometimes slightly overcome by black clouds. When walking towards the run-down shearer's quarters that was residence to some household help, with no expectation or warning, the scape would give way to a bright golden light that flooded onto the broken-down buildings and lit them up to look like a rich city. It was an old area of plain and ordinary people. It was a dilapidated place that in some ways was without soul. When the golden light flooded onto the wooden buildings, the ground that was not tarred or even gutted became a brilliant sonnet bed of streamed dusk. In the end, the smoked air surrounded Elspeth's walk all the way back to the house as the sun settled down under the hills. Then Elspeth, the servant girl, went on to serve another evening meal.

The cream vase of flowers was sat carefully in an arrangement of yesteryear fashioned cream agnes roses. Kendra Richards was a long-term friend of Elspeth's and the music teacher who taught piano to the wealthier families in the district. A quiet blonde girl, she had fallen totally in love with a timber framed painting. The picture depicted the symbols of matrimony from early settlement time. A stone being thrown into a river represented the union of a poor couple who could not afford a proper wedding. The waters of the river flowed around the stone and protected their life together.

Kendra was also in love with the door-to-door salesman who had left the painting for the owners to decide if they wished to purchase it for themselves. Also, he had clear intentions to seduce the teacher. Distracted by her feelings for the painting and the man, her music instruction had begun to suffer, and at that time, the Clarences had become more than dissatisfied with her music teaching. Kendra had been deemed lazy and inefficient by her employers. She had fallen for the painting which had hung above the piano. So much so that she thought it belonged to her and wanted to marry the salesman. This man was sulky and full of headaches. The painting, along with his tasteless jests, began to seduce the normally reserved and conservative music teacher. The allure of the seduction had stripped Kendra's self-respect, with the false promise that she would someday own the painting and be his wife. In the end, these false promises had cost her professional position and job. The salesman came to the homestead selling bric-a-brac and other products such as clothes, toiletries, and things that were still not readily available in town. During the 1950s and 60s, travelling sales people in Holden station wagons filled inside to the roof with all types of clothes, shoes, linen, cups, vases, handkerchiefs, baby clothes, modest bras, and even a touch of sexy underwear. They came from the cities to supply rural Australia with what was thought to be the best brands to wear.

The sales cars could be seen coming in the distance, driving along with flat tyres, and leaving a trail of dirt and dust behind them. Everyone became excited to see the travelling car shop and there would be a crowd waiting for service in the main street of small country towns. The rural women would often come together for lunch on the day of arrival and discuss, in detail, their different purchases. There was always slight competition between the women who would brag about who had got the best deals and products for their own kids. The overweight and uncouth man was the lover of Kendra but vowed never to marry her. Behind the doors and in the back of the station wagon he was the lover of many town girls. As he went from place to place, he was known as somewhat of a lady's man. Many married women snuck away with him while their husbands were off working in sheds and with their cattle. Crower was his name. Crower had laughed to himself after he and Kendra had a fling saying, 'She was a bit of a goer,' and then he went straight back to his wife for some home comforts: bacon, eggs, talk of his dead mother and his next departure in his Holden Station Wagon.

Soon enough, Kendra was replaced by another pianist, a woman with much experience but very little tact. The painting was purchased by the Clarences and was one of the possessions left behind after Augustina had left. Remaining friends with Kendra, their special friendship did become a little out of reach. Elspeth began to adjust to Kendra's absence and very much missed her gentle dove kindness. There was nothing sexual between them, only total respect and a complete understanding of the intertwining of both a professional and personal friendship. Elspeth completely loved Kendra and their friendship that spanned several decades was full of an unexplained togetherness. 'God, who are we anyway, what shapes our lives and makes us who we are in the breezes of life's sway,' asked Kendra of Elspeth as she packed her bags. 'It is not really our choice, but to seek within', replied Elspeth, dusting the piano. 'Those in the outside world do not matter and Crower never will. It is our own inside world that is always important. What really counts is that you cleanse your body of Crower's wayward strain. This will bring you into new self-freedom and you do not need to worry about them or this house'.

Kendra, along with her musical talent, left the homestead. In her imagination she took the painting of pain with her, which was grafted to her heart. A person of fine musical expertise had left the house. But really, it was he that was the disgrace, he was the shame, yes Crower was the bad one of false promises. Elspeth and the neighbouring farmers watched the piano teacher leave through the open scape, watching wisps of her blonde hair disappear. Those neighbours were not so talented and were left to their smirking. 'I want to see Kendra,' Crower stood at the door, an ugly pudgy red rash face', demanding, as his eyes quickly looked around, past Elspeth. 'No, she is not here', said Elspeth quickly, reading his secret swearing and bitter thoughts. 'A man with respect never swears in front of a lady', she thought, and covertly, it slipped. This swearing was another of his underhanded tactics. It was a hard word. Elspeth lent on the mop and bucket, a duster in one hand and with a sharp reply, she looked him straight in the eye, and, for a woman who very rarely swore spat out the words. 'Goodbye you, take your car of synthetic rubbish and go. Kendra is now sitting at her piano wearing mandarin silk and has a new piece of music to dance to.' The door slammed.

After this, it was some time until Elspeth and Kendra could again enjoy a long, deep, and honest conversation. Elspeth had also turned down Crower's sexual advancement. Knowing that her own mother had been betrayed by her best friend had made Elspeth think about the garden, life, and silk paintings, which, to her mind, were more important than any man or sexual act experienced behind a closed door.

As she glanced beyond the closing horizon, Elspeth saw the shadow of a woman weeding. She was not ignorant to the fact that some things are handed down, that the children of shadowed women would all be called illegitimates forever. Even the softest and prettiest girls, conceived before wedlock, were tarnished and branded as inferior beings by some in the conservative community. Elspeth went to the woman and helped her to plant the seeds. She waited in the garden, burying Crower's sexual invitation and his ugly face in the mud, which was where he belonged. Elspeth was not concerned about being branded a shadowed woman, and certainly would never have sex with pudgy Crower.

'Where is he', demanded Brian Clarence, in a stern and directive voice, a voice which had a feeling of dread hollowing through it. The

boy's father's heart went cold and the house was dead and still; it was already in mourning. Elspeth had finished picking the berries that were ripe and on the bush, ready for the blackberry pie, after which she had attended to the child on the request of his parents. They were soggily hung-over and could not stand the smell of their baby. They were too tired to attend to their son, asking Elspeth to clean him. It was their way of trying to keep Elspeth in that particular subordinate place. Elspeth just kissed his tummy and smiled at him. She attended to him with love. Elspeth, skilled and maternal by nature, had a natural affinity with children. This was Aidan Clarence and now he was nowhere to be found. 'Have you seen my son?' A face of desperation and piercing eyes looked at the young woman who had showed nothing but kindness to the often very hard people. 'Aidan was here with you today, before I went to town earlier,' replied Elspeth, alarmed, as the dark shade of the early evening could be seen outside and the depth of the dense brick walls were now speaking to her. The air had a bleak, black tangible feel to it. Aidan would not be coming home again.

'The dam, the dam, for God's sake the dam,' Brian's words sank into the bottom of the murky grey water. It was February and the long summer had replaced the freshness of spring with big black bush flies and serene long hot days of windy mountain terrain. All now lurked in the shadows of death. The smell of terror is all the parents will remember of their son. 'Let me show you his tiny footprints', called the streams to their bleeding hearts. Empty arms and no small child – no warning, no signs, no returning. The dreaming foretold that many young ones would be called to where the water deeply ripples, only to find that one would safely take them through the waters and into the playground world of animal stories. There they would remain until their parents arrived. There they would be taught how to survive on worms. 'A reminder', thought Elspeth, 'that we all must face our fate and a story of consolation, that hope is ever present. That the small human life lived on, even at the bottom of the drowning dam.'

Augustina stood at the top of the rocky-edged waterhole looking in, her black short hair and yellow dress reflected on the screen of the house door. An old wise man stood close by and, using his stick as his forecaster, he said, 'There is a baby's cry at the bottom of that water hole. The tracker dogs sniffed around the tracks for years, but we all knew that below the oldest and deepest hole there lay the cruel and matter-of-fact cry, caught by a rock and wearing a stained rag. It was a dilemma as to where the parents were at that time'. He then asked sternly, 'Are you the mother?'

There they sat in a circle, in the centre of the rippling water, rising smoke lifted up from above them and circled the house. They chanted and sang, they mourned and cast a ritualistic rock, the mothers' in union knew that one day their babies would return. These circle women were from the same ancient place as that of the old wise man — the place of black, yellow, and red rocks.

Brian Clarence was a good looking cultured man. His life in Sydney had been filled with the classics and education. He had slicked back hair and a smooth, clean face. An impeccable dresser of fine tweed and starched linen shirts, he had missed his lifestyle and often journeyed back to the city, only to find that his friends had moved on and places had changed. There was something in the isolation that did not agree with him. He was never attuned to the often hard, outdoor weather, and the smell of rum and beer were a permanent odour around is face, which was often left unshaven. Also, not being in love with his wife slowly and surely stole his interests and passions. He left his sports car and photographic magazines unopened and brushed off articles about his legendary golf heroes, Eric Cremin and Kel Nagel, even leaving his expensive Alexandra golf clubs at Rosebury. Although his wife was a religious fanatic and a bit of a judgemental person who could only self-pleasure, in the end, he needed not only her motherly support, but also her intelligence and cultured personality. However, he certainly did not need to be with a person whom he was just not attracted to anymore. But, after the death of Aidan and Brian's affair, Augustina was no longer present in the house and did not miss any of her beautiful belongings or him.

It was also after the death of the child that Elspeth eventually left the service of the Clarences. They had become very bitter and emotionally entrenched in deep grief. They were demanding and thought little of her or anything that she did. A failed marriage and grieving parents did not make for good bosses. In the end, even with her loving and quiet nature, Elspeth also came to despise them both.

To help cope with the difficult and demanding work, all the strange people to whom she had to get to know and work with, especially the nasty people like Neilson and his wicked wife who never seemed to give up stalking Elspeth. It also included dealing with the boy's sad death and saying goodbye to Kendra for a while. Elspeth, to defeat all of these hard things, and as a way to help get her through to the end of her working time at the Seymour Homestead, would put her mind into a total make-believe state, believing that she was a Princess of the highest order, who would someday meet a prince.

A Silver Lurex Thread

They rode together, the air stream inlay entwining their future hopes. They sunk deeper into love making. Through the gully, they danced and like a Prince and Princess, they were dressed in wedding garments. Wearing a lemon-lace dress with satin lining and yellowed lemon roses through her hair, she looked divinely tranquil. A silver lurex thread, which bound them together and forever, was spun by his mother's hand. He wore a love dream beneath her straddle. The horses moved along the track, beneath the grove next to the castle and into the shelter. There they kissed. It was a long time. Perhaps it was never since Elspeth had immersed herself in the freedom of the bush to dance the fairytale of a love trance.

On the outskirts of the wood land, the witch had waited for Elspeth's death, the call from the bush that Elspeth was dead. The witch had sat, along with some other hags who had watched Elspeth riding her dream horse, wanting her to freeze. They awaited her destruction. But, the long-awaited death never came. It was a death that Elspeth had banished by singing deep peace of the quiet earth.

Elspeth had seen through the material world and into the Prince's eyes. She bent down to say goodbye to him. It was a mellow melting of the spirit. It was a release from a clouded union. 'Well', thought the mean and nasty woman who was also often masked similar to a sly step-mother. 'Sometimes there are no goodbyes, she might just throw herself off the cliff and leave a suicide note — and her eulogy for us to snigger at. But no one will even care, because she will be gone and nobody, including me, will ever need to see her beauty ever again'. The terrible hag crackled and cursed in her ugliest tone, her narky teeth gapping at the front of her blistered lips. The creations that stemmed from her mind were grotesque and represented a sickness in her evil heart. The woman had a degrading and calculating mind and was behind the fall of many people. Her type of behavior was unfathomable. Her invasive and putrid looking statuettes spoke of darkness and evil, an evil that came from deep within her, similar to base unilluminated type drollery and certain faces that are chosen to represent certain characters too. It seemed that she always had a hidden agenda, either setting people up, telling lies, or looking into other people's gardens to fill up her detached daughter's chattels. 'Bad all round', that is how the homestead gardener had described her'.

A shelter for the high-country Prince and the Princess had long been prepared for by the Swallowtail butterfly's magic. Their coming together was potent and an almost fatal ride of lustful love. The ride was blessed in the light of a united butterfly's soulful candle. They rode the picturesque scene and from the high mountain plateau looked down onto the undulating and very steep valleys and crevices of the bush. There was an eerie feeling that outsiders felt when first encountering the enormity of the natural tree setting. Confronted, at first gaze, the unfamiliar bush setting would make newcomers feel that they may be squashed to death under an unstoppable falling tree. They were consumed by a deep fear that the remote scrub would completely swallow them up or that they would be lost forever in its hauntings. There were old winding tracks that were labored with dead grey trees, sticks and boulder rocks. Tree saplings often took on the gesture and optical illusion of something frightening. Like a camouflaged brown eastern snake that was difficult to see due to its various colourants, pale fawn, orange silver, yellow, orange, and black, or even a mad dog might lurk in a back gully. However, none of these things were of concern to the experienced bushman or wandering lonesome fella, who wondered why any other person would even dare to venture such terrain.

On those days, the dense bush scrub was wet, even at the height of the Australian summer, when mostly it was so hot and dry that all the flora and fauna were weeded down to a drought-looking state. Often, a late cool breeze would swish in and cool the temperature to lower than expected. There were communities living under the foliage. Imperceptible to the human eye, they would divulge themselves by turning from possums and honey ants to groups of warriors. They moved like women tip-toeing, halting at the smallest change of aromas, hunting without needing to glimpse and seeing everything before it happened. They witnessed the event's purpose and then either running or hiding, changed back into soil and leaf, or confronted the enemy with a cool clear look that would freeze the rival or rivals in an instant. At the front of the group was the most revered woman, a beautiful tall brown-skinned woman, purposeful in every twinkling. She had short, thick golden-brown hair and a warmth of wisdom that was blessed by the earth. She disguised herself by rubbing a deep black charcoal over her body, which hid her further from the onset of disease or being identified.

Amongst the native trees, burnt stumps and light misty blue mountains, the Prince had signified all that was respectful, wise, good, and wonderful. A monumental figure of moral values to aspire towards, the Prince played an imperative role in Elspeth's secret life, whereby everything that she touched turned to gold. In her imaginative world of play, they had lived together in a Manor Style House, looking out from the circular turret that acted as a bridge between two domains.

The two of them sat at the top of the golden spiral staircase with an ever-spanning outlook. There was a crest of thorns that hung above the top door, garlanded by natural fruits. However, as much as she adored her elusive Prince, she was aware that sometimes he would take pleasure in baskets of grapes, blonde, brunette, male, and female leafed garlands. In a wall picture, there was also the image the great God Pan, telling stories of his rustic and wild musical hunts. Big jars of all sorts were a part of the Prince's other life, styled by the hanging green sparkly clouds of heaven and a nanny feeding her kid goat in pretty pink flowers all streamed by gold. 'Another child will be born', said the Prince to the Princess. But then, before Elspeth left the depth of the bush to defeat her biggest enemy, the bush witch woman, the imaginative royal lovers of natural intercourse engaged in a rhythmical conversation about who they really were.

The ride had carried her thoughts towards the security of her hut, giving her strength and power to find her secret abode. Riding in ebullience, the wind pulled the sword from under Elspeth's long burgundy velvet cape and the dragonfly swarmed through the smoke of fire which she thought was coming up from the depths of the gully. The hidden people would reclaim the soul of their land — Elspeth was one of them. Imagining that there was another day of desert oak and dry ochre spaces — a barren spinifex — she likened herself to a black man in silver torrents of mauves, pink, and browns. This man had seen beyond many heads towards his amber dreaming. Elspeth had also walked in cinnamon sands, engulfed by distant still scapes, and inflamed by a lustrous gemstone. The waterholes, sun, snake, and moon beneath her gliding steps of tanned oak skin were a great spirited fire of love, and the melted sandalwood sunset and the desert oak in vast desolation quenched their entwining thirst. In reclamation of a single strand of topaz lotus thread, Elspeth opened her heart to the Prince.

'It was never ever easy', she confided, 'days, weeks, months and years went by. My mind was not my own and after so much pain, I simply buried myself in the shell of my own body. It was terrible really, not being able to express who I really am, not being able to grow up and being treated like a person of no worth. Me, a conscious sentient being with characteristics: sentience, matter, sensation, perception, and mental formation which all, like every other person, denotes birth, suffering, and death. Well, my darling Prince, I suffered, in every way and on every day. My unhappiness became like a thick, wet, soggy, dark grey blanket, sitting heavy on my ethereal and physical body. As a child, nobody knew just how unhappy I was because, on the outside, I was a happy-go-lucky looking kid. I was good at acting and good at covering up what it was actually like to be me. I searched inside day and night to survive. I searched in every 'nook and cranny' of my whole entire self. But, still, nothing could be found except the isolation, the shunning that I felt right throughout my young life. These isolations were to do with being rejected and the cool ostracises that were invisible, except to my heart'. 'Well, my life was nothing like yours', the Prince went on to explain. My parents filled me with complete joy. We had lots of family friends, lots of family parties and someone always seemed to be visiting us. Someone always wanted to do things with us like play tennis with my parents or cook us extravagant meals. The word 'popular,' to describe our family position is definitely an understatement, and it was hard not to be excited about the next great thing that was going to happen.

I think, even when I was young, through listening to adult conversations and hearing the news, that I was more than aware that sad things were happening out there somewhere, but that was it, those things were 'out there'. Sad things were simply just never going to happen in our world. Sadness and bad luck situations were all about other people. My world was full and filled to the brim with lots of good, nice things and people. The company of my parents, their affluent and really nice friends, and just thinking about fun sort of exciting times, put me in a privileged situation, and I never thought I would be anything less'. 'I only dreamt of that type of life', responded Elspeth.

They now walked the horses in a four-pace rhythmical pattern, along the sheep trail which overlooked the distant town. 'My aunt, who was a botanical artist, told me a lot of stories about who she described as 'The beautiful people'. She said that they were the people who were the very, very rich, and travelled the world enjoying music and the theatre. They were not royalty, but lived a life similar to royal people. That way of living sounded and felt like it was very, very far away and well out of my reach'. Again, Elspeth sighed.

The Prince went on, carefully considering his thoughts and own feelings. 'It was not until one of my friends became ill and died that I felt the drudgery of deep emotional pain. I was only 19 years of age, and after watching him suffer for several weeks without a clear diagnosis, and witnessing his young body disintegrate into nothing, the shock turned into a numbness that still raises its ugly head even now. There was a doctor by his bed, a doctor who gave his family and we few close friends, very direct counselling. In a wise and steady voice, he said something to the effect of: 'Every person is here on this earth with a burden to carry and nobody is exempt. Everyone has something that they have to come to terms with, a life lesson to endure'. I was not sure if it was he that was talking or a great master or even if God of evolution were speaking through him. But, I took it as a warning, that one day I would have to face something or someone or a situation in my life would change my world in an instant. It would be hard and frightening and be my testing ground in this world and give me great determination in the next. There was something else about my friend's death that made me consider my emotional life.' The Prince continued with caution. 'It is the feeling of guilt, a guilt so terribly painful, that often I cannot sleep and sometimes I cannot move from one thing to the next. And, after a long time of trying to cover up this guilt; it has become impossible to mask, because it surfaces in other ways. I will tell you about those ways and the reason for this pain another time.' The Prince's voice, by this time, had become solemn, his normally carefree and flirty disposition gone.

'Tell me now, lovely, how did you cope, you seemed to have managed gracefully.' Elspeth, without thinking too much, opened up to his question. 'It is so remote out here and the further out you go the more remote it becomes. This place is a long way from anywhere, a timeless place where nothing matters and nobody comes often to visit. It feels as if all forms of special life, are still in every corner of this quiet district. It seems as if God choose the good people that live here to work in harmony with each other and the environment, to do a good day's work for a good day's pay, to live without want and without regret or greed, and to have a set of moral standards and personal values above anything and anyone'. The Prince looked into Elspeth's face and dropped the horse's reins. It was a definitive moment that was captured by the witch who never gave up stalking Elspeth, no matter where she went of what she did. Not only did she have a 410 rifle pointed at her back, but the bag faced woman aimed it right in the centre of Elspeth's forehead. Elspeth went on, feeling the subtle, but clear unwelcome personal infringement. 'The people who live out here, the locals, refer to this old place as, 'out the back of bush' and it is 'out here, in the back of the bush' where I began to heal.

The people here were born to produce offspring of a sensitive and natural fibre. No questions were ever asked of me and no conversations about being or doing anything differently were ever entertained by, thought, or entered into on any level, at any time of the day or night. The only problem I encountered was that a bad-blood, jealous woman does not stop haunting my every step. The deeper I went, the more remote I let my heart, body, mind, and spirit sink into the clusters of trees and thick tussocks. I knew, the deeper I went into the natural bush, that the greater comfort would be found. A friend of mine questioned my fleeing into the bush, asking me if I was scared of being alone and telling me that I was running from myself and escaping life's realities and responsibilities. I quickly told her that being in the scrub was safer and that it was a matter of knowing how to not only walk the gully, but the whole scape.

I sought the bush comforts: spring flowers, spring dams and even dead tree trunks, ant nests, some rusted pieces of corrugated iron, or old beer bottles that were left over by the miners from the early 1800s. These comforts were all I needed to be sure that I was protected from other forces, my own insecurities and fears. I used these 'out back bush', icons to blossom up my life, to create one big blur of tranquillity and to sweep that tranquillity into every aspect of my life. Everything that I did, everything that I said had a kind of soft hushed whisper about it, because I tried to marry my voice with the soft aspects of bush life'.

Deep in thought, the Prince replied. 'Did you ever think about the outside world'? Going on, Elspeth explained. 'There was not one problem from the outside world prevalent in my enclosed, but densely natural and open situation: no war, no alcohol, no famine, and no threat of failure or anything that represented other ways of living. All these, in my mind were swept away by the natural forces and the elements and every changing scape. All was beautified in the foreboding light, a protective light. Wherever the outside pain was, it never touched me when I was surrounded by bush vegetation. However, when I was young, my family was my only discomfort.

I think my soul felt richer through this simple natural approach to life.' added Elspeth. 'They became the days of reckoning and disposing of anything that was not good for me. As my life became meshed in the protection of the environment, not one sneaky intruder could find his or her way into those clusters of trees. That is how I began to rise my way up against the awful witch hag — through keeping my own dignity and respect.' By this time, Elspeth's voice was likened to a flowing creek with a cold clear wind sweeping across the top of it. The Prince could see that she had become the land itself and this he could see was the very strongest position in her character. 'I don't care', thought the Prince 'about all these irrelevant and past gone notions. Elspeth, she is strong, wise, invincible and so very, very lovely. I will try and marry her anyway, and take her to my mother's castle. I want to lavish her with all that is good and fine. I want to lick every part of her skin and love her in a way that I can never love again'. 'There was something that did keep me going along and I have never mentioned a word of this to another person'. Elspeth went on to explain an amazing story, a story that the Prince conveyed to all his royal family and friends. They were impressed by the tale and wondered if they could tell a story so well.

'It was a discovery that kept my mind interested in things away from my inner self. And away from the stalker witch. It was something that had been lingering there on an open, slanting hill for a very, very long time and revealed itself to me. It was, in fact, a whole life portrayed in front of my everyday working routine. A whole family's life happenings, just staring me right in the face for all those years. A whole life of events representing early settlement right there at the foothills of the homestead. How I could have missed it all, I will never know. It is a deep question of observation, and in a way, it also brings up a lot of guilt because my father told me that I should always see — see everything and look at things differently. He demanded that I have a sort of a more in depth and questioning way of living and being in the world. I will question and doubt my absent mindedness for years and years to come. My biggest regret is not seeing that mine field of historical meanderings. The remnants, ruins, and relics of a family's past local habitation, were in the exact spot of the Seymour Homestead. On any still, silent spring day this scenario is very transparent. It is now as unblemished as any turn of past seasonal events. In my mind, I can see the wagon filled with only a few belongings, rocking and stopping over the rocky basalt terrain — the man, the woman, and the two children, ready for nothing that this old and isolated area had to bestow.

They had absolutely no idea of the ever-changing environment in the mountains: The harsh and freezing wind storms, the tragedy of isolation and everything difficult that awaited, and droughts, longer and more drawn out than the unrelenting poverty that could only be worsened by the unpredictable weather systems. There is nothing succinct out here. They were at the mercy of all things problematic; because of their lack of experience, unreal dreams, and high expectations of rich and prosperous stores and the ownership of much land. They were let down in almost every instance. Being naïve to everything about the bush and the vagrancies of the scrublands, they had no idea just how hard it would be out here. Slowly, when all dreams of any type of success had gone and the family were surviving from hour to hour, they did seem to become accustomed to the forsaken place, which eventually told them how to do things, how to make their day to day life somewhat bearable. Some very isolated areas, I heard were described cruelly by the man, as a fruitless barren woman, waiting for a babe in arms, waiting for those arms to be filled with the succulent love of breast milk. Year after year, in the depression, there was no homemade pink lemonade, cute smiles, lace bonnets, or delicate pastel knitted mittens. It is a hard place out here, and the land has a way of kicking those off it, those who are not of the exact same strand. Those who stay are strong, resilient, and with vision beyond the feelings of wretchedness.

Anyway, this is what I can now see at the old site and know to be true. There was a young, sophisticated but mature woman wearing a long, black skirt and a simple, crisp white blouse — nothing fancy. Also, she wore a small framed straw hat, adorned with a black silk ribbon. In her arms, she carried a baby wrapped in a white shawl. The woman looked like the reincarnation of mother Mary, never flinging or flirting, completely without error, with no bad influence or falseness in character, a prettified, stand out woman. When she was much older,

I saw this woman beautified by power and the enigmatic forces of own innate nature. This woman was the overseer of the hilltops where the wildflowers and kid goats played together. Then, there were old tree logs, grey, dried out and split in all directions, laying in a large neat circle, as they had done some 100 years before. There was a horse yard or perhaps the house fence. Sure enough though, it was, without a doubt, remnants of an old dwelling site. There was also a cottage of some sorts, which was surrounded by a half sunken stone wall. The rocks, which by colour could be determined as either being in or on top of the ground, were squared into a flat area of the hill. Earth stained rock had been lodged in the ground and the greyer, green side exposed to the atmosphere.

There was a fireplace, out house and a rusty tub that was probably used for multiple purposes like washing, bathing, and soaking. I found it rusted and mangled into a nearby barb wire fence. The cordless iron that was regularly heated in the fireplace was stuck in the ground between two rocks. A poor, hard situation, with no hope of ever really changing, the tell-tale signs of hard-ship were evident. It was as if the family were alive and voicing their problems right here to us today. This discovery opened my thoughts to thinking about early Australia and these thoughts consumed my days with stories that I made up from my imagination, stories that were titillated and tantalized by factual knowledge, things that I knew to be true about early Australian settlement and the future. All these amusements made my life bearable and interesting and stimulating. They helped me to forget that old demon witch who just never seemed to give up on trying to impede my every move. If I went to the shop, she was pushing a trolley behind mine. If I made a new friend, she was always whispering untruths. Staying good and stimulated by thoughts of early Australian life seemed to be a good way to live, and a safe place where she could not intrude.

As I glanced over towards the remnants of her home, I could hear the woman's thoughts in my mind. Her thoughts went something to this effect: 'This old land does things to you, it brings a sense of begetting bewilderment, and a found sacred sense of natural benediction. The isolation helps one to forget about anything other than the moment of truth and the Swallowtail butterfly. This old forgotten plate of land is only about what you can feel with your heart, see with your eyes and touch with your hands – what you know to be real within a captive and receptive imagination. There is no impression of stagnation or obliquity, and my experiences ground forces of the four winds into the soft, trusting eyes of the coming fawn and fallow deer. Those deer will be as new to this old world as we are, detecting movement at the greatest distance, but having little eyesight at dusk. Like us, they will suffer the stigma of being newcomers to this country. In modern times, they will be revered as being exquisite and wise, bringing only gentleness to the desolate terrain. When the sun is just about to set, it can be piercing to the eyes. Above the streaming clear blue sky, it sometimes, on the wings of a whistling and hustling wind, delivers a secret marriage proposal or message to any human or animal.

It sets motion to the end of a warm spring day that ends with soft purple mist, turning any proposal message into a myriad of mixed emotions, to be made peaceful by sleep in the clearing of the cool, starry still evening air.' 'It sounds like an amazingly very good way to amuse yourself Elspeth', replied the Prince. 'These strong images, ideas, and imaginings instantly bring to my mind the fact that you could be a great playwright. You should take it all one step further and evolve the characters and stories for the stage. You could rise yourself up amongst or even above the best Elspeth. This would be a very good way to move away from the witch's interference and share your ingenuity with the world. There is an audience out there for you, and this account of the lost family'. 'No' she replied firmly, sure of herself. The horses moved gracefully under the shade ready for the next leg of the ride. 'I am more than happy to be here in the shade of the tree and just continue to be a down-to-earth ordinary Australian girl. This is the best way for me to live my life. There is a great royalty in personal freedom. I am never bothered by an annoying person and my life is totally and completely my own, with the exception of the one jealous nag. I am free of façade and I never have to disguise just who I really am. I am totally and completely at peace with nature and God. I have no desire for public recognition'.

'Fair enough', said the Prince understandably, who had a friend in the theatre business whom he thought would like to meet Elspeth. Perhaps he would arrange a surprise match-making luncheon at the foreign tea shop or an afternoon tea at his dear aunt's house, who resided in a garden style home in the next parish. Meeting someone like him may be an unimposing way for Elspeth to try and move into a more cosmopolitan world, away from her much loved natural surrounds. A crush soda may or may not work. Elspeth would not be easily swayed, even by a millionaire theatre owner with a love for designer-made, purposefully lavish clothes. Many of his friends who loved honey, sugar, and unsavoury books would not be of interest to Elspeth. Those very successful types of artists would say that they have their own destiny and need to watch ill health and a lower soul transgression towards the fires'. 'Actually,' Elspeth went on, 'The foreign tea shop had an interesting history too. Our quiet, rural, and very respectable community was unaware for years and years what was really happening behind the shutters, behind the doors, and in the large back room at the back of the tea shop. Well, most were unaware, except for a few men who slipped out late when their wives went to sleep, saying that they had to attend to their livestock. The tea shop was located next to the run-down pub on the corner of Walt St. and that is why a lot of people never realised what was happening after hours at the tea shop. Card games and dancing girls, night in and night out — that was what was happening! People just assumed those slipping through the back entrance were pub patrons.

During the day, the metallic coloured milkshake containers reflected the glass mirrors behind the sterile servery. The spider ice cream soda pops and hard candy were in high demand above the chatting women, who often knitted baby clothes and gossiped about everything and everyone. They talked about what businesses had come and gone in the main street of late, who had gone bankrupt, and how much money they had lost — affairs of course. Mr so on, who owned the shoe shop, a well-respected man with a wife and baby son was, well, having private liasons with a merry widow who had four kids. They drank brandy every Saturday afternoon at the pub and she was totally under the illusion, that for sure, he would leave his wife for her. Although she had a respectable day job, every month that widow had a new man on her arm. Nobody was about to marry her.

And, then there was the retired solicitor, Mr Fist, who had a situation with a harlot woman. Those who knew what happened, said that he had fallen deeply in love with her, but could never marry or be seen in public with the disgraced woman. Mr Fist sat saddened in front of his legal papers for years and years and years. The legal man had almost died every night in his sleep, at the sight and smell of his wife. Then, there was a local girl, a dreary sort who wrote boring romance notes, notes without an ounce of literary merit. She had licked a big screen contract, and it was shocking just how jealous some others were about town that week. Oh well, that's life, and the gossiping went on and on and on and on.

Then there was the nun who wanted to be a film star or front-line singer. Nobody had ever laughed louder than the guys who were into very cool artists when they saw that nun trying to break in on the music circuit. So much did she wish to be a star, that she ran around all day and all night wearing performance dresses in the main street. However, she lacked the most absolutely important ingredients needed to become a successful female singer: Style, a resounding voice, and hauntingly beautiful words to share. She certainly lacked beauty. Most stars never wear their performance clothes outside of when they are actually performing, preferring to stay incognito. Similar to really rich people who never show their riches, they tend to get around in broken down old cars, wearing secondhand roses. The silly nun was only interested in self-proclamation, there was nothing prayerful about her person, only a deep, deep wish to be a superstar and nothing more. Besides, she was, without a doubt, in a relationship with another woman — a woman who looked very similar to her. The woman had long, thick, wavy, blonde hair, ordinary features and played the recorder. This woman was married, and every year, at the very same time, the two sexually infatuated women would secretly sneak off together, both wearing long drabby brown over coats and heavy black boots. With their hair full of knots, they would pretend to be going to a gospel reflection retreat. However, the only reflection they endured was the togetherness of a hot or warm bath. Not that I care about who sleeps with who.

The biggest gossip however, was about the man who was a widower. He was a reasonable type of bloke, middle class and established. Only days after his wife's burial, he started dating a very, very rich girl. This was such a horrifying situation, as his interest in her appeared to be succinctly financially motivated. It was sad for the man's deceased wife who had been a kind woman, and had devoted her life's work to the welfare of others. Everyone agreed that had the girl been in receipt of a welfare pension, that the man would never have even given her a second look — terrible. And, what about that poor, but very good-looking boy who had moved to the district from far away? All he had to his name was a small suitcase full of rags and a toothbrush. Well, he did have a distant relative who said that although the boy was poor, he did have some type of education, but for personal reasons, had fallen into bad traps. The traps for a short time had stripped him of some, but not all, of his dignity and virtues. The boy was just so very good looking that all the girls fell totally and completely in love with him. The jealously over his good looks were just so bad, that the boy was slandered in every quarter of the community, being made fun of and discriminated against in all circles. The good looking one was set up in base jobs, similar to Elspeth. He was smirked at, dumped on, and even accused of stealing.

There was one main offender in the discrimination case and that offender ended up on his own. A lack of real caring took him to a place of sad loneliness. The irony of this lad's good fate, however, was that he was very well-spoken, and never sucked his fingers whilst eating a meal, choosing always to use a serviette. The boy gave respect to everyone and was extremely discerning about how he acted in the world. When he grew up, they said that he used his education to help buy some decent clothes and shiny black shoes. Then, there was that single mother who had two kids. They were just two sweet boys with jet black hair and fragile personalities. Out of the blue and without any good reason, one took off. He just ran away, hating his mother, ducking at every intersection and avoiding any personal interaction. Stealing, lying, and telling his friends how, for years, he had been screamed at, pushed around, and forced to drink boiling hot cocoa were the reasons why he left his mother. To the outside world, she appeared to be a very respectable person, working in all sorts of community societies but his stories showed plain and simple abuse. The big bruises were covered by long sleeved school shirts and the boy seemed really alone in himself. Often, he would throw a tantrum and swear at all the other school kids.

Those knitting needles could sure gossip. A very pretty woman who was a cousin to the man who owned a tea shop came to visit. She had shoulder length brunette hair and prominent elegant facial features, visiting with no other intention than to slander the whole family. A rich woman who was very accomplished, she wore a black and red designer shirt and coat. Nobody from any house in the area had ever witnessed such an eminent style of clothing, impeccable and sweetly mouth-watering. In the beat of a drum, someone said that this type of clothing should be photographed and an article published about it in the local rag. Now, that would give some worn out and paper-thin aprons something to enjoy reading in front of their comfy lounge room fires. It would also scare off an annoying man nicknamed the dancing mosquito. Apparently, he had no real life purpose and had conveniently followed the woman to town, wanting to steal the woman's rich garments and cut them into rags. There was another man who was also involved with the out of towners. To try and impress the woman, he wrote second-rate songs about her. It is said that he was wanting to make it big in country town music circuits and attached himself to the two go-getters. The clothes, the woman, and the two men were all considered cheap extravagance in the rich community of prayers. Nobody was interested in the article. The man who owned the tea shop told his cousin and her slander to leave immediately, saying that she was a disgrace to his mother and demanded that she returned honourable status to the family by getting out of the area.

It was whispered by the gossiping ladies that there had been some unusual sexual liaison in the back of the shop between them, and that the rich woman was the instigator of a lusty and sickening sex scene. But, then again, gossip is gossip and people often make up stories to draw attention away from their own lust and desires.' said Elspeth to the Prince who just sat there sinking into deep silence after her long rapture. 'Well, then, perhaps you should stay a simple country style girl Elspeth,' responded the Prince, feeling that he did not want to create any more gossip. All was best left alone to her own imagined royal freedom. The horses, sensing his arcane thoughts, seemed, like the trees, to know more.

Riding down into the sleepy town one winter's afternoon, there was not a soul in sight. There was a small church and a dance hall that housed the yearly festival and, once, a long time ago, those very popular and playful Saturday night dances. Every weekend, a dance was held in a different town hall throughout the district and were known as a courting ground for the young single locals or an outing for young married couples. No beer was available, only lemon cordial and the variations of rock-n-roll jitterbug dancing exhilarated those who attended the evening function. There was lots of laughter, sweat, and unblemished rosy cheeks. At the dances, there was no distinction between the town and country kids, but there was strong competition between those who could and those who could not dance. It was not always the rich kids who had the privilege of private dance lessons, who could dance the best. There was a standout station hand boy, who was completely enigmatic when pacing and leaping the musical floor boards, swinging into the jitterbug. But soon, and for no reason, he did disappear. Some said he married an older woman and others said that he discovered he was adopted and ran away. Later, years after the boy's disappearance, there was a young girl living with her mother in one of the small communities. The girl bore a remarkable resemblance to the boy who had mysteriously left the dances.

'Some of my earliest memories,' Elspeth explained to the Prince, 'were that the timeworn community halls were cleaned and decorated simply with a few balloons. Sometimes there would be a band and other times we had to dance to a small record player or radio. It was always a fun time, dancing the jitterbug, a dance that was an American import and came into Australia towards and after the end of the Second World War. The jitterbug always made everyone feel sexy in a way. I think we all felt hot and erotic. Nobody could say they felt sexy, because it was against the social norm to feel that way. Dancing the jitterbug was sort of a way to have sex, without actually falling into the traps of deep seduction. It was a way of letting our hair down, in a time that was very conservative and most people, but not all, did exactly as they were expected to do. During the evening, and wearing those full-swing skirts, some girls left the hall to kiss and cuddle a boy who they thought might be nice to flirt with a bit. After they did, not one young man would ever dance with them again, or look in that direction again. They were considered naughty and impudent girls'. 'Do you feel sexy' laughed the Prince lightly joking. 'Sort of,' Elspeth joked back to his sexual advances.

That day, people, perhaps families or singles, snuggled away to warm themselves in their houses. The smoke-filled chimneys greyed the tanned yellowish atmosphere. It was the only sign that life lingered or was apparent inside those dwellings. There were mostly very ordinary homes, some slightly more modern than others, but many were weatherboard and falling apart at every beam, the dried paint work visibly peeling off the walls and doors. These houses were the backdrop in the still afternoon's picture and became witness once a year to the liveliness of the festival music. Just once a year, a fair few musical people descended on the town. Some wore unusual tie-dyed cotton coloured clothes and looked glazed in the eyes. They gave what would have been just another small conservative Aussie town new significance. The music gave a certain character that really jazzed up the sleepy and almost dead atmosphere. Fiddles, tambourines, and sausage sizzles filled the night campfires with home-made, mouth melting, pink and white marshmallows, all sung by the fire. These were the earliest signs of the hippy era, but at that time, nobody much understood flower power.

Diverting his attention away from sex, Elspeth went on to explain to the Prince about her former bosses. 'Rich they were, kind they were not, and the only way to survive their constant demands was to think about the gentle morning mists and the nature of my princely love dreams. In modern terms, I had to use my local streetwise knowledge to protect myself from their continual put downs. This streetwise way was hereditary within my genes, and I feel that somewhere in my ancestry, I am a descendant of Henry the 8th. I feel that I do actually have a blue vein in my birth line. Hence, my poor but sophisticated personality. I could see, feel, and touch everything with my mind's eye. I developed a deep sense of inner knowing and seemed to be aware of their every thought, feeling, and action. Even before they entered the room, I often knew what things those mean bosses would do, think, and say. I simply just knew and felt their discretions or indiscretions, mostly indiscretions. At times, I was full of sulk about my position and swings of lament and loneliness made me feel locked, closed in, and totally disinterested in my work. However, they never knew this side of me or my work, besides, I am half royalty anyway'. 'Agreed,' said the Prince, 'that King fathered many illegitimate children and the lines of those births seemingly purport royal attributes. I see now, my poor Elspeth, your natural intellect is cultivated by the seed of royalty'.

'Yes', replied Elspeth auspiciously. 'The healing properties of being royal by lineage are varied and, like me, were not acknowledged enough. Hoping one day be free of the witch and her projections, both negative and deleterious, was all that kept me going. I often had more than a single regret for staying, but, leaving was initially very difficult and I took many night walks under the full moon and clear night stars, looking for an answer as to the best and easiest way to escape. During those night walks and even in the brisk air of the mid-summer season, there was often a cover of fog that hovered above the ground. It was like a long hazy lake stretching far and wide, creating a fantasy miasma, an optical illusion that seemed to be waiting for the great sunrise to beam bright orange and red — streaming, far reaching layers of pastel silk scarves, crossways along the blackened mountain ranges before sitting high in the sky, well and truly above all'. The conversation with the Prince went on and the horse meandered through the open fields, leaving the township and moving towards the outskirts of the bushy woodland. Thinking of sex, the Prince gestured on towards the gully and over the other side of the ridge.

'To be looking and sounding so strong today Elspeth, you must have had a special guide with you, a guide who gave you the verve of these crude elements, which, in turn, forced any thoughts of them far away from you. Well, it is your life Elspeth, God given and with a tinge of royal blood line to exemplify. You are here, born on this earth for more reasons than the bold witch will ever know. Besides, when and if she does see or begin to understand those reasons, well, of course, it will be far too late, much too late. My insight tells me that somehow you will defeat her at every door and leave her and the hidden traps that she sets for you far, far behind. To sit in your solitary hut, bury yourself in a dark, dusty large wombat cavern or become an elegant very tall slender Y-shaped gum tree, will be your salvation away from her. However, you need to be careful because that witch has roamed this old country for longer than anyone, she can sever in an instant and laugh at what was and what was not, giving no thought to any consequences of such behaviours. Elspeth, your rich thoughts and carefully planned movements will outwit her mad insanity. My advice is, just wait now, for the greater space of yesterday's promises to be made clear in this world of scenic land. It is written, that in the right cycle of every epoch, symbolic goodbyes become apparent and real, with many differing meanings being understood.

And, that, with every closure, relationship to people, places, or things, special ones can see right into the passage of time, already knowing who the purple cloak belongs to, as it hangs alive and well in the cremation of the walking of the dead.' The clouds hung low on that day and the river rain droplets melted gently into the large pool of reflective water, a mirror image of water greenery, hardly ever seen in what was normally sluggish muddy, grimy brown water. The ducks and swans graced the lapping edges of the moss rocks and Elspeth knew that every word the Prince conveyed was absolutely true. Elspeth could see his words emerging from the water through the vibrating of what she thought sounded like a distant and vague didgeridoo. The Prince's manhood felt her youthful afternoon berry delight blossoming on the damp, thick, moist ground coverage. Like the native sound that the sunlight lit under each mossy rock, his hands of love whispered that his revealing of erotic love had begun its intoxicating power over Elspeth. Togetherness in the wilderness was at its most fulfilling that day as the horses gracefully ate long grass on the other side of the dam.

The clouds capped the sunlight as Elspeth lifted herself from under the Prince's warm, hot body to the sky. Most men get what they want when they are in need of a woman. Elspeth, although in some ways hardened to life in the bush and extremely strong-willed, did, for her own personal reasons, often give in to his suggestive and pervasive flirtations, knowing full well that because of her common background she could never marry a Prince. And, if she did, would never hold complete and full royalty in the company of those who were born and raised in aristocracy. The open private spaces and thick, dense, steel-blue grey mists that sat thick in the mid-mountain range saw the world at its happiest after their perfect union in orgasm. And when the circular didgeridoo vibrations opened her waters, the sheep trails that she imagined were lined with diamonds and pearls and led her dreamingly towards the hut. Each step along the trail of her life found a new experience. A new sentiment and appreciation which lead directly and beyond the dwelling into the gully of song. Riding again, on the paper trail that swept across the ridge, it was hard to see any open inlet into the deep gully. It was only an experienced eye that could see a slight dip in the rim of the landscape rock contours that were hidden by dead tree logs, low ground shrub, sticks, and twigs of many kinds.

These and other landmarks, such as the open downward slandered grass land that was ever so slightly backdropped by the bright yellow tops of the St John's Wort bush shrub and the upward echoes of the bird life chirrups that also denoted the entry to the crevice. Passing through the open hiatus there was a slushing and slight sinking of dampness under the horses' hooves. As the slow walk swayed their lower backs side to side and the big open sky lulled a lotus lament, a feeling of deep isolation crept in and Elspeth become fearful of being lost out there on the loneliest plateau. The Prince and Elspeth crossed over at the point where the bulrushes were parted because it was easy going on the other side of the arroyo. It had become hard to travel on the side of the creek bed that was becoming more and more heavily wooded as they slowly moseyed on down the range side of the slope. It was, in fact, a crossing for kangaroos mostly, and people had never before ventured to this natural long band of land. They were, by this time, deeper into the lunge of the escarpment than they had actually realized.

The Prince went on to explain, 'It is moist down here because recently there has been rain. However, some gum trees are dead because there has been too much rain. There has been a perfect amount of rain for some trees and they are healthy, flourishing, and not enough for others. As you can see, a fair few are dead and will not revive. Also, there has been a fire here too not so long ago, and you can see that some foliage is black rooted, but now, sprouting back with green growth sprigs and leaves'. Elspeth loved this simple side of the Prince. He was practical and often explained things to her in simple terms. Elspeth's response was of a spiritual rambling nature. 'I can see now and know that this land has rooted me back to the place of my origin, back to the fresh pure days and back to the starry almost indigo nights, when there was nothing here, and you couldn't see anything. Then, in the coolness of a whisper, everything spoke, everything had its own small but important reasons. Old rocks mangled in roots of fallen trees, deeply rooted branches that drew water from the artesian basin, wildlife of all kinds in perpetual abundance, hard sun-drenched patches of ground opposed the bright, beautiful, clear big blue skies —all with an encapsulated narrative.

We are here, my darling Prince. We are here with a purpose. The words of God and the essence of nature will stream into our bodies, hearts, and minds. Our presence here in this habitual crevasse will depict an honest picture of us. The sloping gully of this land, untraveled by modern man and trekked only by ancient wise people and animals will attune our souls to the birds. And here, in the scrub of instinctive density, will be the essential reality of who we are, where we have come from and where we are going. Life will only open up out here when our singing hearts are without doubt or question in total trust. It is then that we will be given extra life, replenishing breath, and here in every moment of our waking lives there will be continuing cradling birdsong and unadulterated solitude. Then, we will fully understand the deepest honesty of this forgotten place'. 'Ummm', replied the Prince, with absolutely no comment.

Elspeth just seemed to want to talk. 'There was another very poor family who lived on the outskirts of another detached country-side remote town, the Patterson's. Mr P worked at the local saw mill. He was clumsy in himself, and every so often, would slip and cut his hand in the wood saw. He was a nice enough bloke, but seemed not to know how to look after himself. They lived half in the bush and half in a destitute shanty, more of a makeshift hidden cottage. Mr and Mrs P and their six kids, who to this day, mostly all live at home or very nearby, were too poor to do anything much with their lives. I wanted to reach out and help them and often hoped that a change in their circumstances would come for them. Sadness would engulf me when seeing them struggle with living between the snaky ghostly bush land that was never ventured by any one and the hovel that they squatted in. It was all just so isolating and left me feeling hollow and void. I dared not approach them, and only looked from a distance when I went to collect empty jars from my mother's friend, Mrs. Carrol. My mother was always preserving fruits and never seemed to have enough jars. Apricot and plum were my favorite, but Mrs. Carrol was quite a doyen and tried mixing more unusual blends, adding tinctures diluted with clove and cayenne, imported and difficult culinary ingredients to come by in those outer days and outer places. Mrs. Carrol owned a large and very pretty orchard growing apple, nectarine, plum, and pear. The orchard was posted, netted, and protected without flaw. It flourished year in and year out, thriving, secured from the reddish, orange-marked pest of a harlequin bug.

The Pattersons had also made an attempt at growing an orchard. Theirs was next to a smelly old dam that had rubbish and rank smelly tobacco and beer bottles flung into it. The dam appeared to be littered with old, rusted drums and discarded bits of building attempts, such as nailed bits of wood and smelly salt meat boxes. Their fruits were rotten and the net half hung down into the sluggish dam water, riddled with bugs, smelly and disgusting. Nothing seemed to be cared for, although I never went inside that poor cottage, it appeared that the outside orchard typified what the family's whole life meant'. Elspeth's mood became reflective and she thought about some of her family's charity work, and conversations about the poorest of the poor who lived in seclusion from the rest of the community and wondered how much they really understood about this type of poverty. The Prince responded with water filled, far away eyes. 'I have never heard of anything so sad, so lonely, and so terrible. In no way can I relate to that type of living. Even if I try to imagine how these folks lived, I can only think of turning into a harlequin bug myself and that would be another story of change and deliberation because I am desperately trying to move out of my own life challenges. Turning into a bug could be my next eternal destination.

In some ways, the life of a Prince is similar to the life of a bug. I am in my prism of affluence and that too is often misunderstood. This is my personal burden, the cross on my back'. There was nothing more to say, just nothing.

'Mrs. Carrol's white garden home was full of niceties, freshly baked scones, Noritake China, crocheted doilies and the feeling of country style plushness. Everything had a perfectly prepared position and people in the locale said that she had not moved one item in over 40 odd years. Everything remained the same — bed covers, photos and all fixtures. Every day, she would clean everything to a spotless condition and nothing was ever broken or put away. To the front of the house, surrounded by pink and purple flower beds, was a large, round, three-meter-high thick stoned walled fish pond. The pond was shaded by a large blowy willow tree. If I had time, like the two fish gracefully swimming the butterfly dance, I would sneak a glance at the water shade ripples and lily pads. However, even then, in those early days, the witch's face would appear in the dim waters and would spook me away. When walking inside the house, the bay windows which opened to the back garden which was filled with antique and pale fuchsia. The pretty flowers would calm my nerves and sooth my paranoia of being sighted by the witch. The little path that lead to the orchard was marked by a fence that kept the house and fruit trees separate. It was a fairytale style of a house and one you would certainly appreciate.

Mrs. Carrol even told me stories, one I remember very well and wondered if she knew something about me that I didn't. It was about a girl who scurried around doing odd jobs, making beds, cleaning windows, and serving tables. There was a terrible woman with an evil streak who followed her every move and had even made a voodoo doll representing the hobo girl. Each coloured needle struck the girl's life with a bad luck scenario. Many serious events occurred in the girl's life. I can't help but wonder if Mrs. Carrol, who always appeared to be so nice and kind, was really the terrible woman, because similar things that happened to the hobo girl in the stories began to happen to me. So many tricky situations did come my way directly after visiting the white rooms at Mrs. Carrol's house. I remember feeling very sick inside myself, and wondered if my body was giving me warning messages to be on guard when collecting the jars and fruits from Mrs Carrol. One day on the way home, I slipped into a puddle and bruised my arms and legs very badly. There were little underhanded things that happened to me all the time after visiting Mrs. Carrol, but throughout it all, without knowing, I think that I must have been protected by my Swallowtail butterfly. I had a dream of the dolly being free of the needles, wearing a dress made of clover leaf and Mrs. Carrol being alone and crying'.

Elspeth went on, speaking as if she were filled with the elemental forces, which meant her words were naturally nourished from within. 'It was always the weather in the mountains, which, in all its many varied, differing exposures, was the saving grace in my external life. My life, was satisfactorily placed on the periphery of everyone else's world, at the edge of the bush and at the beginning of every season. Here's an experience I will now share on the last leg of our ride home. Out here, this weather, it throws you, this weather, it moves you, this weather, it wants to own you. The sweet smell of rain brings a slight sense of drowsiness and windiness rustles behind your rib cage. It challenges the mind and any type of normal thinking processes, pushing emotions and thoughts to the brink of absolute expression, making it hard for a person to hide what they are really thinking about. The body can become like an open book of poetic paragraphs and stanzas, with many colours of the words expressed in silent actions, similar to a game of charades, being totally inspired by the instantaneous wild weather changes in what are often described as disheveled and tempestuous conditions. And again, that sweet smell of rain can be followed by great hurling and burling gusts of winds.

The strong and beating sunlight that was once a hot day can be engulfed by moving brilliant silver-grey cumulonimbus clouds and the winds, all of a sudden, can push along and drop at the beginning of the summer afternoon storm. Although so isolated, like me, my solitary hut can withstand these unexpected gusty, fast-moving storms that are filled with immense emotions. In the middle of the Australian summer, in the midst of a blistering afternoon heat wave, a cool front can set in, rolling in from the south west. It can bring with it the promise of much needed relief from the stifling and completely unbearable heat. An electric blue storm can ignite the mountain tops and, as the dark sky meets the light sky, a sensational natural masterpiece will be born. If a cool low front meets the high heat, excessive gale force winds, heavy rain, silver streaky, crackling, lightning, and booming, gloomy, and shadowy thunder can engulf the hut, circling 360 degrees and powering overhead. The green in the tops of the trees becomes noticeably darker, whilst bright patches of blue sky let streams of God glide through onto the land. Just for a moment, the streams may look like a slippery dip for the pastoral fairies. It is impossible to stand up in such a storm; the body is knocked to the ground again and again'.

On that particular day, the Swallowtail butterfly wings grew larger. It was a visual motion that made the storm scape more majestic, coinciding with a drop in refreshing cool temperature. As soon as the storm rose, the mountains all around were barely perceptible. The haze and mist surrounding the squall were a thick, dense shield, completely hiding the whole entire range that only five minutes beforehand were clearly visible. The enormous, overpowering cloud that was also very beautiful, continued to drop large bouts of rain, until it was sunset. The balmy and still night set in, backlit by shards of thick golden lightning that made a jagged illuminated show all the way across the pitch-black rolling peaks and onto the outlying coast.

After riding and talking and loving, it felt good to be home and welcomed by the mountains and trees. Beyond the alpine baeckea and thickets, Elspeth could see a small girl waving and looking towards a young man who appeared to perhaps be her brother. Even from a distance, the boy seemed to emanate a sense of enormous power, strength, and knowledge.

This brother was fierce and fearless, standing anchored to the earth and perhaps chained, eyes fixed on her and hers on his. They became harder to see through the branched thickets and a dispirited dance swayed through their melting souls. From a distance, Elspeth saw his arms lift her up, and in one sensitive glide, place her in the dreaming space above. And, her elation was clearly only one of their delights, as they went peacefully gathering and hunting, similar to being in the communion of time. In this communion, sadness was accepted as just being a part of the term of a person's life and in death, along with all other emotions these were handed over to the next one born to carry. Like a person in service, who always knew her blood was eloquent, these two were from the chosen group of people scattered throughout the lands who would appear spasmodically in the open spaces, bearing a message for anyone who was willing to understand its meaning. There were many of these red, black, and yellow, ethereal gestures moving through the bush, mainly understood by those who could read the colours in the ever and instantly changing scape. In this case, the message was one of a home welcoming.

Change was coming and this was one of the last rides that Elspeth and the Prince ever took.

The Great Eagle

Elspeth knew that a grave digger was always there, not so far away, standing at the gateway holding a shovel with a changing body and face. It was the witch-like woman, and with every move, every thought, and every action, she continued to try and cut Elspeth down. She attempted to knock her off her own life direction by making an indecipherable, unheard of and off-beat comment, one that was meant to sound intellectual, but would often only be researched just before expectedly running into Elspeth at the town cinema or again at the corner shop. The bad woman's guises were many: one balding, one blond, one bearded, one male, one female, one rank, just to name a few. But, above Elspeth's every step, thought, and action, hovering in the high winded clouds, above the green mossed brown rock and open plain was the great eagle. With wings spread open and holding the force of the air streams, the bird hung above the disguised witch and, without fear, without anticipation, and with a stern presence, just waited.

Then, in a precise swoop, the bird opened the gateway to heaven and harnessed the force of the space above. It was a warning to the wretch that Elspeth was, in fact, a very strong woman. Elspeth would never be cut down by a mere bad force. The wattle, emu, and crow all knew that the spindled trees were the gateway to the graveyard and these particular trees, with dead grey roots reaching to the heavens and sky above, could be likened to an old, still woman of wisdom. The roots were a woman who held the ground firm with a knowing that life is a jigsaw puzzle, and with each placement of the pieces the deep-water holes and rainbows are only shreds of breeze in the delights of the mid-afternoon.

The red and purple regeneration in the tops of the gums that were mingled together on the hillside were a coverage leading towards the eagle's nest. Feathered, big, bold and strong, the blackish-brown wedge tailed bird instinctively fed its young, defending them and raising them to fly towards the historical graveyard that was situated up towards the large white boulders. This was not too far away from where Elspeth would leave her hut to take her morning walk. The large rocks were first seen below a coverage of thick scrub and bush land.

The boulders seemed to dominate that part of the earth and were anchored deep into the ground. They were sacredly placed, and when walked upon, a person felt as if there were a passage of eternity to find. The passage closes the gaps on all jealousy, turning regret to sadness and the feeling of sadness becomes a mask for wanting to be accepted and acknowledged by the greater things in life – respect, honesty, and integrity. The bad woman knew nothing of these qualities. Once, at the other end of the passage, the light was there to show the way. The eagle carried all its young to the boulders, a place surrounded by remnants of old bark, bush shrubbery, and twittering bird life. At this place, feelings and emotions would seep deep into the earth and a knowing of being close to the gate of eternal death or eternal life was instantly recognized. When a crisp damp air flow went through the florid and cherry colored tree tops, for sure, large gushes of water would soon resound through, down, and onto the grey-brown wood trunks. Every cloud of creational force would bring forward a storm of wild and wet natural corollaries. The utterly desolate avoided this place, for fear of being captured by the eagle and slipping into that eternal place of death, a place of no redemption for wickedness.

Every morning, the great bird, knowing the worst one's bad intentions, would circle the boulders, spreading her protective powerful wings and soar Elspeth's innocence to the sunshine, moving her away from the witch's cruelty. Hovering over the windy gliding road that led to the gate of the homestead, the eagle would fly above the work of the one great painter. All that was below the flight path was the painting, and all that was above was the palette. At some stage, the brush was thick with orange, brown and semi-tanned opaque paint and any chill in the air was refreshing to every stroke. It was a scene from the book of life that was gently caressed by the morning sky canvas, a canvas that was lightly touched up early each day with highlights of brightness, the colours dependent upon the season. Dust filled the cattle yards and the big, fully operational and noisy shearing shed. It was near the rusty out-building not far from the old white bridge and was nestled in the bare sparseness near a line of fruit trees. The shearing shed was a strong focus in the discussions between Isobel and Elspeth, and was of great interest to the then, young servant girl. The gliding road wound past a fallen over, empty, wrought iron water tank. Half mangled, it once bore the struggles of a winter drought. It had left the hand print of flat dry pasture that was situated amongst thick green dense grounds and healthy popular trees. A broken down ute, and a feeling of apathy were the leftovers of what used to be a hive of bustling and vibrant country life.

Hidden next to the gate, there was a flourishing vegetable garden and dancing light cut patterns into the majesty of this physical world of what the great artists depicted as 'country style romance'. These were the painter's final finishes on what may have been interpreted by the ignorant crone as artless scenery. The witch had no ability to see the world's afternoon delights or morning sunshine; all she could see was blackness. The eagle had predicted the bad woman's downfall, knowing that Elspeth had nothing to be afraid of. However, the bird, like the Prince, had also predicted the defeat would not be an easy one and that Elspeth would need to travel very, very deep inside herself to find the best way to win the war against her enemy. Also, Elspeth would need to follow a certain wildlife track, past the limestone rock and towards an isolated drum beat. This rock was near to where the angel of death sometimes lived and would occasionally appear. Elspeth would need to find the castle of rock vegetation. The answer would be there. Carefully, gently, and softly she would need to immerse herself in the richness of the master painters colours — fawns, red earth, white, black, and greys. These were the colours that grew in and around the castle of rock and dead trees. It was a naturalistic structure built by one with a chain around his ankle and a cross from the forehead to the heart and from shoulder to shoulder.

This type of landscape never lies. It creates only richness in its wake and diversity in its enormity, like pictures in still life and water colours that consecrate at every glance. The angel who lived in the castle had miracles to lay upon Elspeth. She held a portrait of the witch that she had etched into one of the big white boulders. The etching would be left behind after Elspeth's defeat and in understanding of the angel's message, the eagle landed next to the cherry tree that was fenced off near the natural castle — a sign of yet another grave. To easily find the trail and the natural looking castle, Elspeth would need to go back to the day when she was only visible to the trees, in her own garden at home, the days when she danced around seed pods, deodar, radiator, beef wood, and iron bark. These were amongst her earliest memories. There were also feathers, velvet soft green leaves, spiked wood, rocks, and twigs amongst the grasses. White river rocks that were a blend of the beginning and end of life, the regeneration of shells and clusters of wooden shapes molded the remembrance pictures of her life as a child. The wattle sprigs like baby's breath flora were sprinkled in the depths of a coloured sea green dried flower arrangement that hung on the white door of the house. It was now apparent to Elspeth, that the sentimental pictures of the past were closely connected to her being able to survive the evil occultist.

The house was never locked and was open to the resonance of all otherworldly conformations and connected to the great eagle. Even way back then, when the eagle was hovering above and protecting its young, the bird was also sheltering Elspeth too. In one well designed lunge, the Wedge tailed eagle's piercing talons, captured it's prey, not stopping to consider any childhood memories and being completely unaware of of any type of strange activity, but sensing danger. This was exactly what Elspeth would have to come to terms with doing to her biggest enemy. Devour her, and outsmart the tramp by trapping her away, or otherwise die herself. There was no child's play between the witch and Elspeth. It was downright hatred, right from the beginning. The witch loathed Elspeth Abney and the pretty one would need to use all of her inner personal power to fight back.

When there was nothing left to describe, when there was nothing left to see, except a sea of stratus fog cloud and a full round moon which reflected a mare of tranquillitatis that bathed Elspeth in soft rain. The night sky gracefully gave way to mid-morning, seeing the cockatoos lift from the earth in blue glory to a light sapphire sky, glazing above the deep, dark hill scape, shifting over the dead tree and gently landing one at a time on the bare branches. The morning light made the sparseness luminous, and also a clear view of the satin bowerbird and another dry mountain forest. Above the water, the pink, fresh, cool snow clouds hovered and the bleak, green gloom on the road ended. The ever-changing contrasts in the bushy highland only kneaded Elspeth's real love of the pretty things of nature further. A real vastness of beauty in the far-off lands and hills hard to behold was the only way to describe it all.

No matter how much or how hard the witch tried to divert Elspeth towards the dangerous underground cave that was situated below the wash of the seeping river, the servant girl stood strong and firm. This was the cave that nobody dared to go into for fear of the water above crashing in and flooding the hollows and cavities. Drowning would occur in a flash and nobody could withstand the flowing flood of freezing waters. Instead, Elspeth drank her billy tea and calmly and serenely let the harsh witchy elements that were meant to leave her frightened, terrified and isolated just wash over her.

As she sat back quietly against a tree, it was then, and only then, that she unknowingly began to prepare herself for the greatest prayer that she would ever surrender. Sipping the beauty, whilst taking in the denseness of the bush, Elspeth could hear the resounding cruelty that was only a shot gun barrel blast away, feeling she could have been any other woman in the world. Again, the witch used weapons to alarm and warn Elspeth that she was the absolute target of every type of wicked spell that she could possibly cast.

'There is always a struggle, thought Elspeth, between what is right and what is wrong, between the steeple and the dove and the human urge to become primal. To be allowed to be free, to feel that innate desire in watery, warm cherry and smooth body entrammels, deep within the sinews of the womb and heart'. Beating off the witch's inflictions of unfathomable grief, unhappiness, isolation, regret, and sadness would not be without an inscrutable, confronting, and emotional charge. This would take Elspeth to the depths of herself, to the edge of every facet of her personality. It would make her look at every thought and every action. She would need to use her perceptiveness and intuition to their full potential. This was a fight to the bitter most end. After this battle, Elspeth would never be the same person. Elspeth knew to survive, she would need to focus on thoughts of the lost gully, the natural mineral fresh spring waters that trickled down through it, and the formation of small swirling candle cascades.

Elspeth would need to feel the green moss and soft air, that, as a child, made her cheeks gleam a rosy pink health in the sunlight, always thinking of a time before the witch's dry air and choking, dusty words had tried to make her every thought debase any real richness. The witch walked on cracked grounds, iotas of her own greed. It was these cracks that she would finally slip through and her gluttony, which would, in the end, destroy her and her wicker. But when, where, and exactly how this would happen was not really clear yet.

At this point in time, Elspeth's intuition was not certain, to say the least, and she would need to wait a while longer for destiny to unfold. Elspeth's small child within would need to delight in reflections of paints, coloured chalks, black boards and near rhyming poems, needing a visual array of weaving patterns and a story book inclusion of ardor to keep her free of the witch's potent thick, brown muck. Gossip and greed were the old bag's only type of medicinal mixture. However, the one thing that the female demon was most afraid of was the great eagle's one big powerful swoop, knowing there was no shield from it.

Elspeth knew a lot about eagles, living in the bushland. She knew that the presence of an eagle was not to be shrugged off as being just another wild bird of the bush that was there, just flying high for no apparent reason. The bird of birds was to be respected, revered, and canonized by those who believed in the natural miracles of the earth. The great bird was already the owner of the mostly uninhabited territory and was in very close association with the oldest and wisest man in the world. She remembered the one who appeared in times of great need, yoked bare russet skin, carrying a totem stick, which turned into a wingspan of up to and beyond two meters. As soon as Elspeth spotted the eagle sitting in a bare branched tree high above the ground, she knew to be weary. It was always a silhouetted picture that outlined the bird from a far expanse that would halt Elspeth. Dead and cool in herself, she would know the witch was within the eagle's wind flight path. When the valleys were a purple misty amethyst, the eagle also often sat at the top of the rain gate and would lift its wings and breast, floating then to the bottom of what was dry bedrock. The people of the past could still be heard there, and their whispers and tears seeped up through the valley and meshed the grasses.

Out of the mud and out of the ether, Elspeth imagined that the bird would turn into a seraph, smiling, lovingly, and holding a bouquet of wildflowers in the will of heaven. A protection against the evil witch, the gentle subtle fragrance of the wilderness lingered in the mountain air reaching her every sense. To Elspeth, the flowers meant: seeker of marriage, sincerity, faith, devotion, aspiration, and surrender to the aphrodisiac. But, this expansion of awareness was really the eagle's enhancement of Elspeth's mental imagery, a secret guiding force for Elspeth to follow, leading her away and back to the safe haven of the gully. To get to the place of safety, was a choice between choosing to look for every natural sign and gesture that the bird winged in the motion of flight, or be swayed by the witch's fanciful and demeaning trickeries. The dams, which were often full of murky brown sludge, needed to be almost a clear green, and the living algae, growing from the bottom of the waterhole, seen the gliding bird's reflection glide gently onto the water. There was no sway between right and wrong. It was then that the bird flew with an almighty power and gracefully nested next to what was an early miners pit. The picture then became very obvious. The rough old witch would have to pass the gully of the dead or be piled on by an ever-growing bull ant's nest. Elspeth was on the right track and followed the eagle's signs.

Elspeth had everything and nothing to fear. Only reflecting on the natural appendences of life, the natural music of the storms passing, and the dreamy double rainbow with its coloured band of meaning. The ancient meaning of colours was seen in every speckle of the trees, every small and delicate wildflower, and every natural earth tone of the bush setting. Colours, Elspeth knew with all their light qualities and differing tonal arrangements and transparencies, could heal every aspect of the human body and thought, bringing forward exactly what she needed. It was a matter of knowing what colours to use, when, and how to extract them from the earth and for what specific use. Elspeth would extract the exact colour, transfer the light qualities and disguise herself in the face of her, knowing the unwise one would turn her face away from the beautiful light. The witch could never possess such inner contentment. To further deter the snarly one, Elspeth would call on the Swallowtail butterfly to help her walk the rainbow bridge. There could only be one way, the open gateway, which was the angel's road between heaven and earth.

Whilst Elspeth listened to the natural music of the bush, a coterie of starlings floated through the light air and squalling breeze. The disappearing rainbow stillness and fresh wild scape again became filled with brushing water clouds. The remote bush sounds could be sung alight the ancient colours and the depth of deep grounding, drizzly water twine protection. Bringing the almost silent sounds of the bush into the ecologies of Elspeth's natural state. Likened to a state of meditation, Elspeth sat back and asked for God's sign to help her transfer any fear of being killed by the dark one to be taken away, asking that the earth's magnetic field give her the answer when solving the riddle as to why the witch hated her so much. Elspeth also asked that God move her away from any other predators and that they, along with the witch, would all fall deep down into a devilish bog slush hole.

In the meantime, the eagle had everything in wing. Swirling and swaying above the witch's dark tree home that was masked as an innocent patch of daffodils, the greatest bird was free to master its attack on the wicked one. Moving with the rolling air, the great eagle made several open attempts to squash the witch's abode. These attempts initially looked like failures, but, in actual fact, were deliberate ploys to break the cruel one's confidence.

Gliding close to the base of the tree, swooping and lunging forward and backwards, with an effortless will that made exploring the area where the old sack lived easy. The eagle mastered the gusts of wind and in a quick motion flew to a point of high position above the shagged domicile. Knowingly, the eagle halted and hovered slightly, the big bird's open wings ready to fly in any direction. With its wedged tail tucked under, and slightly turning its head to make sure another predator was not on the horizon, in a mode of self-protection, the swoop met the ground and the unscrupulous one who had peaked herself out of the tree trunk to see why moving shadows were being cast on her tree home, knew instantly the shadow to be an uncommon occurrence, especially when the sky was blue and all seemed harmlessly well. The bird's surging force flung the old crack to the ground and the scare had worked. In a state of complete numbness, the ruthless female knew the fight to finally destroy Elspeth had become a death sentence for the bird, Elspeth, herself and perhaps the three of them together. After the warning was issued, the bird took flight, up into the open blueness and down into the bush, back to its eyrie nest on the high ledge of the canyon gorge shelf. The witch knew the bird would return. After all, she was the female huntress depicted throughout the ages in all cultures, the one of power and strength.

The bird also carried a history of spiritual defeats that are noted throughout the ages as being rational. From within the strength of its pinions, the eagle had always instructed man to be steadfast in his pursuit of truth. The only hope the debase woman had was to set a trap for the bird and Elspeth, similar to the offering of the poison apple, but the trick, it would need to work this time. What the brazen witch did not know or understand was that these outback surroundings were Elspeth's roots to the land. Every aspect of this hard-driven land was of no fear or consequence to Elspeth, and she would use every inch of the space to lift her up and beyond the witch's cruelty. The shameful one would be bested by Elspeth's strong knowledge that this old place would ostracise her malevolence, pushing her to that place of no return. Only the most pure and prayerful ones could stand against the harsh elements and live life in a peaceful way up there, in the coldest and oldest place on earth. The sullied one and her snipe friends were doomed from the onset by the eagle's great wing spread. Elspeth understood that the bird was just hovering back out of the wind, looking in and out from the rawness of the petrifying high ledge. Elspeth just knew that the eagle was only one species in a kingdom of wild fierce flock. Communicating to each other, they would all play a part in protecting the innocent Elspeth from the blood hungry one.

In one part of the land, just outside the old quarters that had been left to ruin, was another place where a man had died alone and forgotten. There was nothing there but dried-out, prickly thistle. At night, when the moon was full, a soft haze circle would light that patch of half alive, half dead thistle. Unattended by her caste of spells, the eagle had plans to catch the forsaken one. And then, swooping, halting, and bracing the coil twists of winds, she would encircle the bag, prodding with her beak and manoeuvring the witch to the briar patch, calling on the help of three magpies. The four birds would destroy the wickedness, pushing her to the brink of the grave road that lead to the dead man's half fallen down enclose. The eagle would work and move in a similar fashion to a matador, the strong swimmer, and the skilled golden combatant. Without hesitation, the bird knew that the witch would be engulfed and strangled by the thistle. But, before this could happen, Elspeth would have to do something very important.

Elspeth would need to discern the living history of the greatest bird in the whole land. She would need to move more thoroughly into the understanding of who the eagle actually was. To do this, she would have to call on both the oldest man and wisest woman in the district, who mostly resided in the next state at the bunjil shelter. It was by listening to their stories that Elspeth discovered why she was so connected to the eagle's direction, authority, and flight patterns of the open blue skies.

They came from the sacred cave that was painted with native images, and the meaning and real knowledge about the eagle. Unbeknown to

Elspeth, until this point in time, was the bird's immense historical power harnessed to protect the land. The bird most certainly had the power to defend Elspeth and journey her away from the harm of the wickedly woman. An understanding came through interaction with the two, who often walked over the ranges and wild patches to the greatest winding river. 'Initially, the bird was the deity creator of this ancient land', said the man, 'makin everything here, the rivers, mountains, trees, flowers, sky, animals and man. The creator deity of all, turning into a rainbow or a bat. A relation to the gliding possum, parrot, parakeet, and quail hawk. The eagle was not one to be tricked, set up or made fun of'. The woman of wisdom, who had sat above the waterholes, went on to explain that the eagle had also given charge of the winds to the crow. Saying that, when ordered by the bird, the crow and their relatives would open a bag of blowing forces so strong, that the winds of great potencies would sweep clear the lands of those like the bad woman, her husband, her coven and nine feral grubs. The bird would open its pinions and in one boundless rush of the wind, along with the crow, would clear the way for Elspeth and her good life in the hut.

After having this deeper insight into who the big bird really was, Elspeth's internal defence mechanisms helped her sweep away the murky waters of fear. Keeping a fresh green outlook, Elspeth knew that she could also smother herself in black charcoal and hibernate under the ground, in a snake pit or deserted wombat hole. There was also another rough, old, unexplored gully, a death trap to any inexperienced bush man who dared to travel there. The lush leaves and bush ant's nests long gone, there was no prettiness in that particular blind gully. But, in an instant, it would be the safest haven away from her. Waiting for the eagle to appear in the sky again, Elspeth would free herself from the soiled woman's desire to inflict destructive spell craft onto her innocent being, imagining the serenity of the crossing waves, and the distant sea gulls that themselves were present out of God's will alone. Maybe she would need to escape into that place.

There she would feel touches of painted blue sky, light winds and powdery snows that settled and covered the ground, melting into wet patches. In the background she could hear a drum that was played by the bush woman. The woman seemed to appear at the most unexpected and sometimes intimate times, knowing everything about the world of deceit. She was cool, calm, but not connected in herself with anything really very valuable. The drum, after a short while, seemed just a beat of resolution towards the witch's doom. Elspeth sat quietly in the sleet, cold, crisp clearness of another day, just waiting for the sound of a stream to trickle or a water bird to glide into the wetlands, flap its wings, and splash the dam waters. The bird's flapping and gliding wings were the only sound across the plains as the afternoon drew to a closure. Elspeth was a dreamer of very special things, and this was another reason why the witch despised her so. She detested Elspeth's beautiful dreamy life. The jealousy over the delightful, pretty envisages was unbearable to the degrading woman and she would begin to grit her teeth at the very thought of Elspeth's playful happy fantasies.

The sun clouds closed over the light, the breezes blew close to the ground, and this was the night of the red crescent moon. The dusty moon meant a few different types of things and when the snarly witch saw the crisp clear day was changing to a streaming orange red, it was clear then, that her judgement day was nearing very soon. Depending on a person's personality and position within their ever-changing life spanning pattern, determined what the seascape or glowing red actually meant. The red moon glow was poignantly, emotionally vital to each individual. It was the lamp between heaven and earth. Simply turned on, the lamp meant that a person's soul, pure and light, would reach out and protect vulnerable innocent life. Turned off, there was no bridge between the upper and lower worlds in a person's heart and no birth would come. Darkness and greed would lead from one destructive life to the next, and blood and sickness would run ruin, day and night, night and day. Miscarriage, loss, and sadness would strike those unlighted ones down.

Cleverness, alongside a cool and calculated approach, would need to be engaged by the witch to try and outrun both the great eagle and Elspeth. How would the witch cross the red homelands back to her tree house to hide and wait for the curse to be lifted? It seemed almost impossible, because she had already been injured by the eagle, and as her spells had begun to be wear off, was growing tired. Sleep might help, but, she had nowhere to hide now that the spiritual lamp was warm and aglow. There was another place that she thought may be a good place to run. It was a bit further beyond her own area. It was a place called Scabby Range. Scabby Range had an enormity of spookiness that may have been attributed to the fact that she was just a bit unfamiliar with the land. She felt uneasy, as if a black bird seemed to be guiding her past a fair few piles of timber that had been made ready for bonfires, strangely positioned ponds and dams that appeared to be unnaturally located right next to hillside ledges. The bird flew to where the witch thought there was a clear entry to the cavern, but it seemed to be an underground maze of crannies that found her scrummaging on her stomach further and further into the cold old earth. The holes narrowed and her mind felt as if it would explode. A mental attack with no spell to dissolve the torture, it was the accumulation of the witch's bad deeds that lead her to this never ending narrowing tunnel. 'You get what you give, and no one can escape life's natural turnaround spells'.

These were the words she had overheard Elspeth utter way back then, that night on the veranda when the Clarences had argued for hours and hours. But, on that night, the dishonest one did not realise that Elspeth's own mother drew the invisible sword against any intruder, the heart sword that all mothers possess to help protect their offspring from the worst demons of the world — a world that was harshly cold to those who were unprotected. The elements of the sword were pure love the messages had developed a language of their own. In Elspeth's case, only the great eagle could understand the messages that rose in the canyons of that night.

But, now, for the corrupt one, the cipher of the purple hills was locked behind the gate that lead on and through to the colossal high daunting mountain prominence. Scabby Range was suggested by numerous angled rock faces. Each jiggered face was an elusive entry point to the inner sanctum of safety that the witch so needed to reach. But, the eagle was already there, and Elspeth's plan not only to escape, but to trick the witch through clever deception, had already started to work. The first sign was the gentleness of the purple hills and this loveliness was appeased by Elspeth. That kind of love was totally foreign to the witch and panicked her so. The old hag had a feeling that her days were not only numbered, but all marked by total catastrophe.

After escaping the void, the witch awkwardly tried to get herself through a hole in the barbed wire fence. The fence caught her long black coat, scratching her hands and face, getting caught in her already knotted and bloodied hair. The nastiness in the rusted barb drew blood and the sight of the witch amongst all the natural beauty and reeked like stale urine. Right throughout all of the witch's tactics and deeds to destroy Elspeth, Elspeth had remained close to her natural love of nature and words. Painting pictures in her mind of pastel trees and soft grass under her feet, she embraced even the limitlessness of cold spaces. Seeing fields of lemon blankets surrounding gums, as hope of him and her, always dreaming, the silver lurex thread. Even on the day she said goodbye to the Clarences, Elspeth knew that the future would see the witch fall to her knees, knowing her life lesson and feeling a sense of the crone's nothingness. A pack of ravens would tear the malicious body to shreds of shard glass, and she would sink into the blackest thickest oiliest sludge. 'Evilness has its own demise', knew Elspeth. It was foretold by a mark, etched into the middle of her brow. It was a warning sign of danger, and welded into the witch's forehead by the protective birds; it was meant for all to see. In a kind of strong tranquility, the mountain spoke powerfully to her soul. It was a power that no man could ever climb, but a power that Elspeth could harness and use as a tool against the witch's visible and invisible discrimination, one that gave her the insight to be awakened to such cautionary signs.

At Scabby Range, there was another girl sitting inside the crag. Amongst many things, she spoke of the meaning of marriage. Retreating there, on her own for 12 years or more, she had been bestowed with many gifts of the spirit. People came from far and wide to seek her wise counsel. It was now time for Elspeth to ask for life direction. 'God can only marry God', said the girl who also had hazel eyes, 'and this evil woman who pursues your downfall is cunning and cruel, she is not to be antagonised. The best approach is to lead her to the biggest rock. Pretend you are going on a holiday. Once there, find a pool of water sheltered within the rock. At the bottom of the water holes, the gap opens and there is a space between the rock and earth. You will find safety there'. The girl spoke in riddles and Elspeth thought that the cool spring air was uncharacteristic of that time of year, or, it could have been just the chill in her words'. Would she eventually out run the witch, and be delivered by a lineage of roses from so many thoughts and feelings? Would she see through the people disguised as reasons in past pain or perhaps become half man, half woman?

This transformation would perhaps save her life and take her to the paradisiacal nature of the heart? It was a matter of deciding between fanciful thoughts and reality. No matter what happened, there was a death noted on every rock face of the elevation and with so much to decipher from that mountain girl within, it was just a matter of stepping forward through the mountain ash, to see exactly what might transpire.

She waited for the great eagle to grace the landscape and shadow the imprint of the master's paint brush, soaring from the great open wild wings and hovering over the waters of Sam's creek, which was the secret way to the impassioned lover's hideaway. As Elspeth awaited providence, there was a dim gesture in the water that made her think of the girl's purpose and why she chose to hibernate away and alone for so many years. The creek, which was also known as the serpent's rope wound, wove a narrative of despairing and fanatical love within her bloom. It was an escape from what she knew to be the truth. The truth was that no matter what happened, a confrontation would certainly occur between the witch, the eagle, and Elspeth.

'Why, asked Elspeth of the girl, why did you retreat here to this cold mountain range? How did you find such a place and what lead you out here?' The girl stared deeply into Elspeth's eyes and for a long time said nothing. It was damp and cold inside the mountain, safe from the witch but strewn with other ambiguities. To get out might propose a problem, as one wrong turn and Elspeth could find herself lost inside the caves forever. Bats and the linger of other deep earth energies were mingled with a strange sexual desire for a man. But, this could have been mistaken for just being a figment of her imagination as a masculine energy seemed to reach from within the walls of the cavern and warm her vulva. Elspeth sat there, throbbing, soaking. She just sat there, contented in the unexpected desire, feeling the natural urge to orgasm and waiting for the girl to answer her question. The girl replied, 'There was just one golden star in the sky that night, the last night that we were together. He was young and fresh and we often picked berries together. Shy and wanting of each other, we had become very good friends. The problem was that we were from different language groups and our love was hard to keep a secret. That night of the golden star, my uncle pointed the bone at my new young lover and the he left. For days, weeks, months, and years, I waited for him to return. All that I could see was that one golden star. So, I decided to follow it to this place'. I needed to see if I could slip in and out of dreaming with him. I knew I would find him again. This cold mountain place has become my home now and every night it is alight and awake with the golden star, the energy of him. I find another sign of his love, in the flight of groups of starlings, thousands of them that bring a swirling, twirling, meshing, and enmeshing black spotted message. They pattern and dance a windy morning not too high in the sky. Then, they come in close to the ground in large outsprays of zig-zagging loops.

This is rural Australia as not many see it or understand it. When walking here, to find the final resting place of the gold lunate, I took the opportunity to listen to the earth lair. It was then that I knew I would never return to my clan. I would stay here and wait. We are now on different sides of the river, my family and I. And, in the middle of the river, is a large wooden structure that is a maze of lost and dark hideaways. It is a scant, gloomy, grey-brown horrifying place that could break in any place at any time. It separates me from them. If you can entice the witch into that unsteady dim place, you will be safe. Never will she be able to leave, and never again will she bring you harm'. The girl spoke honestly.

'Those few memories keep me alive and well in my seclusion and aloneness. Somehow, I only need the company of the natural world to support my life. The clouds, the wildflowers, at times the desolate trees, the slimy water rocks in the creek, and the knowing that nature will give me everything is all sustaining. I will share these memories with you. We cascaded like renewed water, we seemed refreshed, cleansed and together, a warrior's cry. That summer, it was green after the rain, and lorikeets, hills, and mountains seeped up the nourishment of the wetness. In only a few short days, it would be dry again and time to embrace the daisies. The snow grass would be soft enough to make love on and for only a short time, both families had gone away walking'.

I loved the way his hand cultivated my mellow. It gave me a feeling of warm shelter, bringing forth stellar foundations from the sun and the moon. My happiness soared to the top of the world and into the great heights of the heavens. I was carried above the planet to the source of the garden which was actually the path to the great ones. As I ascended, I could see them standing together in a line of steel blue clouds and mountain shrub that hid any slithery hint of the red-bellied black in the mud. There were also hints of the colour purple to be seen in the brush of days ahead. I was in dreamy love and could not see beyond him and us.

Sitting back in heavy thought, her eyes then became misted and glazed, darkening like black paper. Through the mist's mysteries, the mountain girl said she would now uncover much of the day-to-day happenings of her young life, a life that was rooted in 50 million years of granite sedimentary rock and spread in snow gum, candlebark, ribbon gum, mountain gum, and the spiny echidna. As she progressed with her story, it became evident that both young women had much in common. They had both been servants. 'I left my clan early to go to a small settlement. The people there were not particularity rich, but needed help because the white man went away a lot on horseback to round cattle and sheep. They had three kids and one was sick.

Forming the early days was lighting the fire to boil the kettle and then straight onto copper washing outside. All this early work made the morning whitewash of the fire place and the blackening of kettles a hard place to start. Their sleeping babies woke on and off and needed attention, baking in-between, sweeping the floors, and making ready the picnic lunch. After serving lunch, the rest of the time was spent mending and darning socks. Custard was always the order of the day, and the vegetables needed to be ready for the roast. That meal could never be late for the routine was like the grassy creek, always running. The smell of the fresh bread made the kneading and mixing of yeast seem easy, and the new dawn seen much of the same. Monday was washing day, Tuesday sewing day, Wednesday all the shoes needed to be shined and on and on and on. Each day, on top of all the other jobs, I also had a particular chore to accomplish. Except for loving their kids, it was all fairly boring and very hard work.

It was one day, after all this almost punishing work, when walking to my home ground that I did meet him. It was at the place of glaciers and back tracks where the nature trails of common wombats, feral pigs, and goats run, near the sign of the orange blossom orchard, that I first saw him. I froze, thinking that he might be the type of man seeking a woman of gracility. But, then, he smiled at me, telling me that he had been staying in the bush for a year and had not seen another person for all that time, bar his employer. On that day, he had been mustering across rocky crossing, and taking the sheep down the Old Bobyean Road. Breaking the barrier, he then pointed out the quince trees, and asked if I wanted to sit with him on an old stone rubble seat, whilst taking in the view on the other side of the road. At that point in time, I did not realize that quince trees meant love and fertility. He explained that earlier that year, he had built a stone wall, and had since been busy filling hessian bags with rabbit skins, needing to be careful not to mix the coloured and grey skins because the coloured were the more expensive. Highly desired skins were needed for the making of rugs and slippers. I told him that I had only heard that rabbit could be cooked in numerous ways like garlic, lemon pepper, and tomato. These were exotic extrapolates in what were ordinary days, ordinary times, and ordinary people. I never cooked this for my employers. Again, he smiled, saying he would like me to cook some rabbit.

As Elspeth felt the girl's deep sadness and loss, she carefully moved the conversation away from the personal, bringing her own thoughts back to the first time she had heard that a local girl had left her family to live in the ranges. 'It was a long, long time ago, one late early summer afternoon. I was playing on a sand bank near the river's edge. The bank looked like the entrance to another field or place and I imagined that it was the unknown entry to where the great woman warrior sat.

The young warrior woman was extravagant, with kind ways and charitable giving. She was taking delight in the bees hovering from one Patterson's curse flower to the next. She cursed materialism for breaking all the goodness between future sisterhood, saying it would bring out the cruel feline qualities that matched war monger male rivalry. 'Interestingly enough,' said the girl, in my early seclusion, 'I did have those kinds of visionary thoughts, asking if on that late summer's afternoon, if the river's water had been muddied from a fierce storm the day before'.

'Yes' replied Elspeth, 'there was a lot of mud and I shared this with my aunt who gave me some very good advice'. Knowing about the runaway girl, she told me to 'Approach all problems from a position of love'. From that day, I knew I would need to find your mountain of wisdom, because I was not sure if I could approach the scheming witch from any position, let alone one of love.

The girl of the mountain gave her final advice. 'I can hear, smell, and feel the scratchy witch approaching. Likened to the muddy fierce storm, she is filled to the brim with hatred and jealousy; she detests you. That witch cannot face the truth of her wickedness and somehow likes being bad. You can combat her darkness by using life's natural ambiguities that are always subtly changing with the sun's light rays.

Use the early whispers of your own childhood bereavement, the sediments that are blown through the black willows, those draping branches of silk that line the river shore with gypsophila and are back dropped by the yellow-faced honey-eater and grevillea. These are all images and sounds that date back to early settlement. A time that did also hold hard women of no dignity. The witch is one of those women, and is not to be underestimated. This sorceress knows no beauty and will stop at nothing to destroy yours. She plans to strip your life and push you into a hellhole. But, if you can lead her to the river entrapment, she will have no opportunity to set you ablaze, aflame with trauma, afire with grief, or burnt with confusion — yes ablaze'. Finally, the base woman will be forever gone.

All the while, the eagle could instinctively hear the conversation between Elspeth and the girl in the mountain. Elspeth was tired, being left exhausted from the journey on foot from her far land to the high, and in some places, also nefarious hillocks. This eagle had set a course of her own. By opening her breathtaking annexes, the mighty bird, master of being airborne, lifted from the cave opening. For a moment, she curved her back and tilted her wings. A stillness in flight, this was just a slight pause, before her dramatic sky trip back to the night of the bad woman's curse. Unrelenting death winds, and cold compressed loud bangs, wishes of ill fate, the smell of dead rats soaking in dirty stinky brown dam water full of leeches, grubs, and rotting flies and other pests. The sounds of grinding teeth and the feeling of such demise was so strong that anyone who approached within half a mile was almost suffocated by the lack of fresh air. The sounds of the ground rumbled and the hauntingly made-up untrue stories about Elspeth lingered over, in, and out of the witch's abode. Degrading to Elspeth at every point, it was time now to put the long drawn out untrue stories straight. The terrible woman would not be returning to this place.

The eagle, with all her supremacy, sitting at the head of her convocation, called upon a group of crows to begin devouring the evil one's dwelling. Swooping and tearing, ripping and gashing, it was soon gone. Elspeth, although exhausted and tired, began to reminisce back to the day when she was free of the witch, back to the day when she was without burden and worry. Back to the day when she had no concern about the witch's vindictive ways. Quietly, her voice went on, 'Remnants of an old camp fire, directly opposite where perhaps 30 new deer or more had probably went bounding deep down into the bush after playing, grazing, and meandering on the high plains until mid - morning was begging the question: 'who had sat around that fire'?

The deer came much later and the track which was a pretty wildlife path used mostly by kangaroo, goats, and wombats. However, mostly feral pigs had found their way down into the bush. This was to escape the hunter who sometimes arrived with his mad dogs, and chased the wild life into a corner of the property. After which, he would shoot them down, dead and fast. It was the hunter who sat at the fireplace, a bottle of rum in one hand and a slab of meat in the other. He was no gentleman — light on foot, but heavy with grog. The man was a straight out cold man who drew the blood of pigs and later deer, sometimes for games' sake and other times to sell to the local butcher. When thinking they were getting away from the hunt, sometimes the pigs would run straight into his camp.

The black and the fawn, and the brown and the white deer had come in from Victoria and appeared early and left every day at exactly the same time. I was curious to follow them and see just where they actually lived out there. Their track was well worn and then suddenly hard to see. However, there was something in the invisible air that made me feel that the deer were close and looking straight at me. I walked lightly and quietly, following the trail from the top of the windy slope, down and across the fallen down barb wire fence into the lowness of the bush, past a long-forgotten pig trap, a sign that long-ago people had actually been there. The wind above seemed to be blowing far away towards another planet. There, in the calm, with rays of sunlight filtering in on the rejuvenating sapling, a steaming dampness was present after many, many inches of saturating rainfall. As I submerged myself further and further into the bush, I felt a great distancing from all. The bush is a world of its own and it takes a very brave person to embrace the sacredness of its almighty reign. In a way, the spookiness of the thick air and mysterious submergence of nature's energetics are hard to define, but present in every biological atom, and was almost too much for my mind to not only fathom, but endure.

A person in the deep heart of the Australian bush must be brave, must be strong. I do know stories of those who were of weak constitute and lost their sound minds in what the wise ones referred to as 'the back lands,' never returning home.

The wise girl listened, sitting like a stone in the damp, cool mountain cave, carefully asking the question, 'When were you first aware of her? Can you remember anything strange as a child or young girl'? Elspeth closed her eyes and went on, 'Even though there was some difficult struggles in our family, there was also a new discovery to be found in our humble home, so many wonderful, very simple pink fairy floss things to enjoy, the warmth of many summers, rainbow birthday cakes, family reunions, and gatherings of many celebrations. There were pretty pink dresses, many dresses, one in particular was lemon and stitched with a silver thread. I loved that dress more than any other. It was the time of lambing, the freshness of spring, and so many directions to walk and unearth.

There was one afternoon when I was about five years old. I decided to walk past the last fence line. It was then that I became aware of an unpleasant odour, really sour and rancid. Then, this low-looking type of a woman stopped and started to shout at me, smoke in her mouth. She shared with me that she had started to smoke, not as a teen, but in her adult years. Holding my nose to get away from the smoky fumes, I became aware that she had a deep hate in her eyes that could not be cried away. Instantly, I felt the need to be on guard. I felt invaded and contaminated by her presence. Again, she started to gargle the spit in her mouth. Fluey and heavy, the narky witch woman reeked of sour smell and that was what she projected onto me. I knew there was something very sinister about her and from that day, she seemed to be there in my life, appearing in many guises, many faces, many forms, and many experiences. A clear and straight answer came from the mountain girl. 'Yes, an evil entity from another world has attached itself to your pure life force. For sure, it has been following you with the view of destroying you. This plan has been in place since before you were born and for as long as you have been alive. Why you may ask, why me? The reason for this intruder breaking into your life is that a long time ago, a great sage blessed by the nature spirits came to save the world. In every epoch and time, the sage is born as a pure being and comes to save the world from the depths of despair.

The sage challenges the darkness and the darkness rages war against the sage; that is the reason why the witch follows your every step, day and night, setting traps and wanting you dead. I know by reading the pictures in my mind that you are a special one. I was also told this fact is true by a flame robin, a small flutter of bright red. For this, you need to be extra strong and let the great eagle guide you to a place of safety. If this does not work, then you simply must pray. You Elspeth, have been chosen as the blessed one of this era'.

THE PURPLE PASSAGE

Standing tall, holding a basket of succulent fruit, plump and ripe in her little arms, her eyes shone towards the white robe, the white robe that sashayed in the moonlit arid ravine, stark and desolate. Its movement called for softness to fill the long days as she slipped into the mantle. Just knowing that she would immerse herself in the Essene prayers of gentle joy returned any fearful thoughts from the darkness of the wicked jealous one. A blended pigment of grey, green natural tones was mixed with heavenly attributes, the togetherness of heaven and earth, the only recipe for a safe return. Elspeth reached for a piece of the fruit and offered its abundance to the water boy, who had escaped the eschatology, but would never return to the earth. The spirit of the Clarences' boy had followed Elspeth to every place that she ever went, loving Elspeth and her kindness.

The prayer to be saved from the witch's clutches began when she was in a trance, dream-like state, half awake and drifting in and out of an enlightened sleep. The effects of the prayer could only work when Elspeth was completely away from everyone and everything. To make the prayers work, Elspeth needed no interference from any other being and needed to have a certain isolated stance of mind, completely untouchable, both physically and emotionally.

This was the only way to offer her deepest sentiment to the source, the only way to find God's pure direction. Before embarking on any prayer, she would always whisper her perfect words of wisdom, Let God be in all that I think, say, and do.

Knowing that death, judgement, and destiny were all encapsulated within one seed, she kept her evening focus, both pure and powerful, fulfilled with the abundance of light and peace. In mystical knowledge, Elspeth deeply worshipped the dead sea. The lost caves buried the secrets of life and death, the secret of life and death that had seen every doer of evil and the rapist of the mother earth distraught to the bitter end. There was a lot to pray on. That evil woman's dark face, sly looks, and calculated decimation were dispelled by the fresh fruit of Elspeth's prayer. The innocence of Elspeth's plight lay protected in the rubble, written in the nameless, finely scripted cylinders by the guiding hand of the one shepherd who led her to a place of safe concealment. In future times, when deep admiration could be given, the writings would reveal the names of those real compassionates, those who would unveil the illusions of the material world.

The drowned boy, appearing in Elspeth's prayer dream, had trusted his own small inner voice, still, steady, and clear. He, like many others who had wandered into dams obscured by tall grasslands, did find a centre of calmness. It was the afterlife that illuminated a heart full joy of heavenly delights. Finding a good, kind soul to follow helped both ways.

Elspeth began to pray. But, first, she had to cast her mind back to her early days of praying, adopting her own rendition of sacred and enduring pleas, she could still see the great golden statue of Mary looking down at her and the smell of holy water on her brow. It was a dainty brass smell that poured into the wet mark. Elspeth thought this to be the best way to begin what she knew would be many, many nights of long prayer. The spiritual fight to ward off the snarl had only just begun.

Supreme blessings reign in the kingdom of the great dominion and the barren, hard, and desolate lands will flourish in the vegetation of loveliness, as divine favour will be bestowed on the poor, they will find riches in their mother's garden.

Pleasurableness will replace mournfulness and the earth will inherit the quiet gentle ones. They will know prophecy and their pain will be reconciled and soothed. And, with raging lust, a hunger and thirst for all that is right and good will also be purified. But, a man who spreads bad seed without love will never find that needle. His pain will be as wide as his indignity, and he will be recreated into the lowest life form again and again until he realises his bad mistakes. Merciful people will reap mercy by walking the crossroads of life at the sermon of the mount. Purity will always be likened to a simple clearness of mind, clean in every thought, and seen showered in the nature of God's summer glory. A gentle and peaceful face will be a sign that a blue lake of trust and faith has become a great sea of love. Like the small child of goodness that grows into the strong adult of high morals, only always to be called 'God's child', the persecution of righteousness gives hope to the visions of grandeur not easily attained. The breath will expel wicked tongues against the almighty ruler. And, along with the nasty one were those who laughed, scorned, and extended mental cruelty towards righteous people. The mightiest wind will blow them all away far, far away.

'This is my real name', whispered Elspeth, at the beginning of the next prayer, finishing her piece of fruit and standing in her white robe with a purple braid in her hair, arms open towards the etheric boy Aidan. The boy seemed intent on helping her to pray for serenity. 'I - yes - I am the purple passage, come swimming with me', said Elspeth quietly. The muddy waters drowned them both, and as night fell to morning again, Elspeth Abney slipped deeper into a state of invocation prayer.

It is with thanks that I open my arms and fingers in the formation of your great wings. And, my great eagle, I give thanks for your protection and unfathomable guidance. Without the guidance of your sagacious flight, I would not have the strength to combat the witch and her many deceitful façade semblances. I can now, with your help, and your native instincts, see into every planned attack that she has set for me. I can now hear her lies before they are told. I can now decipher the real voice behind any sweet, sugared stories that she concocts. I can now see and feel that through the act of prayer, and the potency of your power, that I will, one day, be free of that wretch.

I pray that one day, this day, or any day that you will rip away my entangled emotions and that any darkness that surrounds me, because of the witch's attempted attacks to destroy my life, will be, once and for all, gone. I pray that her worst nightmares will all come true — that her witchcraft spells vanish, and can never be invoked by her again. I pray that her coven of wicked women friends all get lost in the filthy pond that was made by man, and around the edges, set with traps. Also that, old rusted rabbit traps, boggy ditches and icy ledges give way under their rich black attire. I pray that they are all forever gone from the young and innocent, and that her jealousy creeps up behind and turns her into stone, a stone that cannot be cut by any sword. There are no prayers of forgiveness for her cruel vindictive ways. I pray that she will never again see the winter mountain ranges, graced with the whitest gleaming snow, which stretch across the scape. The ranges that look like a reclining side - figure of sculpted freeze, baring the enigma of time clandestine. May the secrets of the white mountains be forever closed to her. As hard as it may sound, I pray for her destruction in every waking moment and in every thought and action that I perform. And, may she never experience the real jewels of life. The finery that is like melting of body and earth into one stream of consciousness, that moment when one music note raises the body into a cherubic state. Again, she will never know those experiences.

In my deepest, longest, and alone hours, I surrender all thoughts of myself, my needs, wants, and desires to you Great Eagle. I trust, wholeheartedly that your strength, power, and might will protect me and release me from the grips of her hexes and incantations. In my heart, I form my own honest enchantments that, though your sprawling flight, above her evil ways, save my soul from the clutches of her bad intentions.

The intentions were shown to me in the hot, gusty winds, and cinder ashes of a firestorm that raged this land some years ago. This is a simple prayer to remove all these insults and terrors, as now uttered from my reservoirs, though your feathery annexes and into your piercing eyes; your predatory nature is to my advantage. My pain, in the shadow of the witch's putrid sloppy brew and continual stalking is as far and wide and as deep as any persons, a succession of losses so heartbreaking that no person could stand up in the torrent of their emotional havoc. Mine are more than the endless bleeding and the withdrawal of all senses. 'Please Great Eagle, remove this pain, remove this bag dag witch'.

I pray that she takes the hard lessons and that I never, ever, succumb to any of her tricks or elusive deceptive gestures. I pray that every twist and turn in your flying swings back around to devour her obnoxious, foul, and revolting evil self. I pray that all her ill intentions towards me permeate into her own life, that her fate is one of extreme bad ailments, that her spiteful, jealous tongue, as she hits the ground, will half fall from her mouth, and in turn will be swamped by bull ants and become infested with incurable infection. I pray that her death be long, slow, excruciatingly painful, and horrific in every way.

I open myself from the recesses within myself to the gratitude of your most powerful love. Within this state of deep gratitude, I give thanks for this life's journey, this time. Although it is hard to be grateful for the most painful things, I know that they have a purpose and that my ability to rise above her every sinister entwine and the stabbing dagger that she has pierced in my road will rise me up. These intentional snares will only strengthen my character, strengthen my tenacity, and solve the intricate detailed puzzle of my life pieces, the pieces of me that have been scattered to the squalls of human existence. In communion prayer with your great resplendent aura, I will continue on.

The desire to show my most sincere gratitude for your unending protection and assiduous indefatigability is something within me that yearns so high, that to fly into your wingspan, spread my imaginary branches around your breast bone, and to let your feathery fetters embrace my soul is my greatest wish. Within this prayer of gratitude is my every sense of knowing and being. And, even under the hardship of the coldest and most rancorous weather, no food, no light, natural or man-made, I will give thanks, in the knowing that without your eagle eyes, your precision sky sailing, and your guided winged eclipsed patterns, that I would never have a chance to return to myself, unharmed and only slightly blemished from the trauma.

I am so grateful to you, great bird of prey, for showing me the graces of the natural world, for leading me to the safety of the rocks, a hiding place from her never-ending glare of demise. For, in the midst of the agonising darkness, I am most grateful for your winged bearings towards the replenishing and refreshing river of life, the river source that will turn into a volcanic rupture, at even the smell of her pungent approach. I am grateful to you for giving me the strength to stand up against the surging winds of her curse and for giving me the insight to see. To see that it is only these natural graces that hold the answer to my salvation from her wickedness. For this, I am truly grateful.

I'm grateful for the protection that you show, sheltering me amongst the red breasted robins, the floppy platypus, and the soaring crane and that hoarded charmed possum's magic. All the natural Australian beauties are within my espy, an espy that is gladdened by the leaf, ground cover, the bucolic sunburnt waterways and in the distance, a very quick fox on a quest hunt for any spoor. From my observations, the untreated tints of the great bushland saturate my gratitude: olive, lime, khaki, jade, bottle green, avocado, and slush green permeate throughout cream beige, golden and milky butterfly yellow colourants. This is what you have given me, my soul sanctified in the natural love of the greatest piece of bush ever walked by any woman and any waterway ever swam by any man.

What this privation and continual stalking has done to me, is that it has made me look closely and deeply at every single facet of my actuality. The very small things that make me the person who I am, especially the things that I don't like about my persona. Behind me, at every table, at every rivulet and say, in every instance, is her wicked cry against my name.

All the same, I give gratitude for it all, knowing that this gratitude will lift me to that place of holy safety, that place where the doves and the gold in scripted dome are together churched in a sphere, circling the world. It is a fresh place where the great posthumous lanterns and ceramic pots, herb filled and gleaming with light, linger over the purity of love. No stalker can enter that divine place. Looking back in this state of deep reflection and gratitude, I can see now the real harm that the witch's continual and ever present invisible pestering has had on my life. The witch's smearing of blood over every path that I have crossed has almost shattered my will to live. For this, I am also grateful. To be in the hands of the dark one's wish and not be squashed by her spindled hand or be thrown into her hot caldron and brew of infection, laced with silver fish is a strong hold in my favour. From her guttural desire to paint me black at every door, I will rise in gratitude, clothed in white, silken gowns, fresh purple flowers in my hair, and fortified by purity. The purity of heart sets me apart from many others in this land of my birth. To stand apart, I was once told, would be a strength that would see me gracefully move through heaven's eye. Others would never see the haystack, let alone be given the honour to seek the needle.

The more she hates, the more gratitude I will show. I pray that the day when I waft past her and kneel at the throne of the great God will come sooner rather than later. For now, though, I will sit back and give gratitude for my innate abilities within this withhold of myself. I will not suppress my true being, rather, going into that place of self-besiegement prayer where I will beseech your every attention, o great bird. I will use these often taken for granted appendages in reading, writing, and discerning the meanings of words and place them firmly in the real, using words only to defend against every atrocity that she sets upon me.

Even on a day when the drabness of her saddens and blackens all cortex in my mind, I will show gratitude in action for everything that has happened. And, I give thanks to you, winged warrior, for counteracting her malicious manoeuvres. Taking this time, under the protection of your wing, has given me an interlude to look back and consider. Having time to discern, and now, have all revealed. The revelation that I can defeat the corvine with the dignity and grace of a classical dancer, will, one day, I pray, bring me to that glorified embellishment and finely embossed cathedra.

At my back, and with every step towards the freedom of light, I can feel the opening spread of your wings, stretching my arms and legs, opening my torso, strengthening my head and neck and pointing me in the direction of the sun. For this, I am truly grateful. To see and feel the light in your yellow and brown eyes opens my prayers to nothing more than you and your protective powers. Slowly, but surely, I know the time is coming when I can fully and safely express the depredation and pillage of my body, heart, mind and spirit — the damage that occurred whilst being pursued by the demon of that one jealous female.

In some ways, the patterns in my life are similar to yours, Great Eagle of superior flight. I pray that you will carry me on within your assume, and carry me through the dry plains of parched dust storms, beyond the stoniest grave, and past the trees that can often blaze a blistering inferno to the mountain of snow. That is where I wish to be, with you on that reign of snowy mountains replenishment, and snuggled safely up against a gum tree, munching leaf and being smothered in eucalyptus oil.

I offer my dream prayer of replenishment in gratitude of our emerging life patterns. And, fall to my knees, I will, night after night, to ask that the cross I bear in this world be flung far from your nest. For, I am sure now that the cross on my back is her. In my next prayer, I ask that I find the almost unattainable. I ask for that transformation — to evolve from human to bird.

And, after such a deep state of emotion and taking a stand against her wickedness, I will now turn my mind to complete peace. The peace, I know, will come when she is buried and long gone from the traces of my memory. I pray that no blemish of her abrasiveness rears its ugly face, which, in my mind is likened to a red, swollen, fiery balloon. I pray that the soft washes of fresh water cleanse the pores of my skin and flush any toxic residue of her presence from my sphere of encounters. Peace is not always so easy to obtain, and, after running from her at every point and gesture, above all, I crave peace.

I can only visualise flying to the most peaceful place in the universe without wings or an air path to follow, to find that inner sanctum of the loveliest things, where only the jars of flowery essences and healing herbs posy their spiritual kernels. I want peace and harmony, like nothing her inner or outer self will ever experience. With the stronghold of affections stemming down from the paradises above, I can see myself there, amidst the great ones of peace, the great ones of magnificent exaltation. It is not a place to laugh or scoff at, it is a place more blessed than any other, reachable only through the action of prayerful stillness of the heart. The heart that flames the purist in the perfection of God's softest thoughts. Is it my imagination or am I moving towards the place of the most spiritual? Can I serve the work of my master in any other way, other than being immersed in classical thoughts of things that are finer than any other? In idolisation, I surrender every aspect of my being to the greatest divinities and the spiritual entities of worship, to let the ether of the highest gather me in its enormity and spread my life to every corner of the consecrated province. This is my greatest prayer of amity. In that place of delicacy is the provision of many beautified truths. No lie or hardness can find that firmament of jewelled adornment.

The entry is guarded by the snakes that circle and your swoop that takes away any darkness leading me to the gouging river. It will never open its eye to the pigskin of a game player or the mad trickster of spells. It opens only to the most soothing of doves and the absolute clearest and tenderest of minds. It can only be an idyllic day that leads my imaginings and dreamings to that perfect picture of reality.

It can take the mightiest strength to find the deepest and quietest station. Wings lifted and a straight sense of knowing are collapsed into my fragile prayer for relief and saintly peace. In the wilds of my greatest desires and flush for serenity are directional calm aromas that give more than hope — that one day, I too, will fly into the spectrum of your flourishes. In very many ways, I will always know that for so many years, as close as I came to your pure streaming breath, it never entered my soulful yearning, for whilst under her continued persistent stalking, I could not breathe. For in her bleak utterances, I was blinded and became stark naked and exposed to the hollow eyes of the unknown and the unknowing. I can still feel her shuffling in my aura, talking about and around what was, and what was not, her continued handling of my mien, after a while, moulding a certain sour gummy stigma that will one day rise up, and wrap itself around her throat. It eventuated a coarseness that always belonged to her and not me. In the last silky prayer devoted to your feather plume, I know that it is now only a matter of days, hours, minutes, and seconds until I can ride that curl of lustrous barky ribbon, the band you dropped from the sky for me to follow. And, at the end of the stringy bark, I will wear that feminine crown of fresh wilderness florae.

There is nowhere more relaxed than being here, at the gate to those heavens. It is the only place that opens my eyes completely to what a world of peace and goodwill looks like. In just a moment, after arriving here in the bush paradise, a meditative state of freedom is fully experienced in my whole body, mind, and full self. I look across at the surrounding trees and walk down the noiseless undulating hills rocked with briars and ponded black rich soils. Absolutely nowhere else compares to this earthly compound. The sight of the fresh growing bush seedlings is a sign of hope, even when at times, it feels like much is unresolved and will never be known.

Peace, in this place, can only be attained through a series of long interchangeable flying prayers, that when landed in the source of purity, slowly, surely and carefully unpeel away the murky fibres of everything hard, that, over the years she has hammered into my soul. Through the deep silence of prayer, nail after nail after nail, each with a spikey rusted tip, will be pulled, extracted from every area of my life that she deliberately impinged upon.

And, like every fairy-tale ending, the sweetness in the goodness of righteousness will dissipate every strand of her obnoxious intrusions. These pure prayers of peace, I place in the hovering of your wings, knowing that the eagle spirit in my soul will fly above the storms and lies that she has invented.

I am just so tired, I am just so tired after her continual pursuance, but, I will rest my head against your beak, and from within me, continue to offer this deep, deep prayer. Although within my mind is her squawking and gore chatting, I will still offer a prayer of total and complete quietness. This will be a responsive prayer and within each devotional assortation, I will be open to your merging of my genetic intentions within your breast. The night prayer comes from within my deep-seated self. Even though it is dark, I will fly my own way to you, feeling protected in everything I do and everything I say. From within this position of bottomless entreaties, I will feel protected in the nest of our relationship, and wait for that all-knowing heart guidance from you. No matter where I go, and no matter how many times the witch of many personifications tries to embroil me in her bitter jealousies, I will keep close to your beak and know that your great wings are opening inside of me.

Tonight, I will focus my prayer on asking you, Great Eagle, to wing away any feelings in my body, that are ignited by any wrongdoings done to me by the foulest witch. I ask that you help me rise above the dark feelings that I know she wants me to experience. I ask that I can rise with you, my thoughts far beyond the depth of dark blackness and into a new pattern of flight motion high above her meanness. I will lay here until the next sign, that all is clear, and then move swiftly and with an essence of quickness away from the woman of poor standing. I will wait for your next quill sign. I ask you, as I lay here in the evening's blues and throws that you give me the strength, courage, wisdom, and insight to find your piercing, shrewd, and clever foresight. And, that every step I take is directly towards your launch into heaven's ways. I will place myself in your great speed and ask for safety as I move towards the open caverns, which below are alight with her hellish fires. I know that although you are the wild wilderness itself, that you are also a place of serenity, a place that I will need when crossing from this world to the next. I will go with your steadfastness and resoluteness which will carry me respectfully, into your haven. To make all this happen, I will beseech your calling towards me in every waking moment. I will ask the spirit to lift me to your awesome boundless presence and when there, I will my head before your plumages.

There will be no other, no other force like yours, and I will only place my heart feelings and prayerfulness in your strong winged love. No matter where she goes or what she does to me, I will rest my faith in your grandness and trust that I one day, will be free of her jealousy and terrible curse on my life. I know that in me are the seeds of the natural world. Your natural world and those seeds, when they are ready, will blossom and grow barriers of entreating flowers so that I can hide from her. The natural environment is also my protection and I will draw on the winds, rains, fog, windstorms, and fires to hold me unwavering in my encapsulated self. Safe standing on the ground, safe in the shadowy afternoon fading light that is cast by the ever-rising peaks and mountains, whereby you spread your great branched wings of love and place circles of protection for me to enclose around myself. I can only assimilate myself in the aura and essence of your pointed flair, knowing that you will pierce your beak into the centre of her black belly and ground her to death in the unloving space that she has created. I know that you will never show her respect or dignity and that your high flight, great one, will bestow many gifts on me, and that she will be torn from pillar to post when she realises that you and I are one.

I cannot live without your masterful guidance and grand winged designs that you have planned for my life patterns. I must have your strength penetrate and permeate my sometimes-unbelieving mind and tired, weary body. I can only see through your all-knowing and faraway eyes — those piercing eyes that undrape and unwrap every dark seeded thought or action that gets thrown in my way by her. I know that there are no optical illusions to be afraid of and with your sight guiding me to safer and higher ground, I will only see all that is good in every whisper. I will always trust your sight of utter faultlessness. Your innate qualities are like a fixed, etched gravure in my heart sanctuary, an image implant that will not be erased by any sneaky wicked spell. The bad scar she wears will be with her forever and she will never have the chance to infiltrate any aspect of my being again. The imprint of your life's flight, is far too powerful for her to destroy, no matter what tricks she plays on me. I can feel the flee of your delight, perched alongside of me, and as I stare directly into her face, she will wash away to the underworld of barbaric and torturous ones. I will never dwell in that place, the place where she finds refuge and only the very loathsome and deceitful go. The high ridge, I will be able to walk, no matter how many rocks lay at the bottom of the slope. I will open my chest and tilt my head towards the top of the rise.

Like you, I will spread my annexes towards the gorge winds and let your flight path lift me high above the rocky, thistly, and snake-driven barren place of that evil screwed Sheila.

The most perfect thing about having you, great one, as my sage, my seer, and my ever-divine guide and protector, is that I know you will always fly me into that special, private, and safe place. It's a place where everything is sanctified and full of purity, and the mystery of your greatness. Love is in every corner of that grand reach, which is centred in throw of the great dividing ranges. No maggot can find that sweet dwelling place. I will fling myself to that mountainous locality, which from the exterior and gazing towards, looks overbearing and overpowering. But, as I lift myself from the bounds of the snaky boulder path, I know I will rest there, right in the middle of the divide that will separate her from me. It will take time, but I know that when I finally rise above her sneaky, stalky jealousy, that all will be revealed and she will run, run, run. And me, I will smile at being defended by you, the Great Eagle of my salvation.

On that day and every day and every night, I will call upon you to remove any small underhanded act that she tries to covertly plaster onto me. I will ask that I am finally embossed with your ever-knowing and ever-seeing, so that nothing, absolutely nothing that the cruel crone does to try and force my life into the gouge of no soul, the place where she is called Lamia, the half serpent, half demonic woman, ever transpires. It is only through you that I will escape, drowning in my own blood from any wounds inflicted by her and them, her many personifications and those whom I call the bad ones. In the deep night shadows, I see your divine world of graceful birds. It sits high above the darkness of their unholy blood. It awaits me and the other silent victims of war and alike. This divinity in flight reflects divine hope, and in the bottomless nocturnal, my own spiritual struggle, that before I die will flood my breast, only to be released by your strength of power. I will open my hands and raise them to find your light, feathery heart.

As you, great eagle circle above and below, I will now put this great prayer of invocation and protection into play. I will outwit and outsmart the narky wicked one at her own game. I will be ahead of the hag at every turn and become untouchable. I will use my continual and unrelenting prayer to hide me from her sight, a sight that will be destroyed in the faces of the innocent and forever young.

O great bird of the Australian skies, I cannot pretend that I am not weary of her continual put downs and shaming of me, but I am determined to be strong. As I am not unscathed by her bad sorcery, I will use this greatest prayer to rise myself to the top of the world and leave her far behind. She must and will be left in the smallness of her contaminated mind. I beseech you, o magnificent bird, with all my might, to bring forward every great spiritual warrior. I know these guards will protect me from her continual inflictions. Every protective entity from each age and eon, I now need you all to come forward to rescue and release me from that cruel stalking creature. The seeds of these words which are derived from the great spring will now bloom.

Even in that tiredness, when my limbs are dragging the ground, the force of her hatred of me is stronger than the hugest groundswell sound of an impending earthquake. I will heed this quiet prayer of sanctity and pray even deeper into the night. This prayer, I know, will be reciprocal, as it is responsive by me and streamed to you, o greatest flying creature of the bush. You are one out here, one with the vastness of the night air and the coolness of dark sky, and I can sense that you can hear the prayer that is within me day and night calling from deep within for protection from her. The deep calling will draw me to you and in an instance of fear and terror, I know that you will open your wings and fly to me.

In everything that I say and in everything that I do, I will find a way to draw myself to you. I will find protection in the core of my relationship with you, and follow the guidance that you wing my way. I know all this to be true, deep within my being. I know that I can trust you to continue to move me forward and towards your great spiritual presence. No matter where I go, or who I see, you will always be within my deepest breath. Those great wings continue to open inside of me and the greatness of you sails me through the mid-air flows to the abundant and boundless rays of heaven's love. In every night prayer, I will focus my intentions on you, and only you, my feathered friend. I ask that you dispel the feelings of death that she bestows on me through all of her wrong doings and calculated nastiness towards me. The witch is no match against this prayer and your powerful flight against her on my behalf. And, I will, without doubt, rise high above the death feelings that she wishes me to experience. No thought of darkness or blackness will absorb my mind. I will take a new formation of wind and fly with you high above her callous ways, out above the bush and high above the winding rivers and gorges, to a place she will never find me. I will wait until the next sign that all is clear and move swiftly to the edge of the cliff face, away from the cruelty of the woman of poor morals and wait for your sign to leap forward off the edge to fly on.

When I stand on top of your perched hill and open my arms to your pull, I know that no matter how harsh the elements or how cruel her gesture, I will also be strong and free in your wind set. No matter how much slushy snow or how many rock faces will be there for me to struggle through and over, at the end of the longest day, you will always be there to nest my weary head. I will call on you in every moment, and find faith in knowing that you will fly to my aid at the most unexpected time. Swooping and staying in the thermal and hot air drafts, I know that you will use your strong aggressive power to scoop up the one deemed as the worst female ever, and fly with her to the outskirts of this country and dump her fair down a disastrous landslide, watching her clear extinction. On that day, she will have no escape and I will be free to soar in the thermal drafts. If the warm air becomes moist and rises into cumulus cloud, I will fly there too and completely rapture myself in the soft, fluffy clouds. In the meantime, she will be at the bottom of the well, at the farthest end of this world, never to return. Not today, not tomorrow, and not yesterday.

A broken skull will be her fortitude and for her meanness and greed, the foul occultist will not be able to remember who she is or where she has come from. The well will blind her eyes and she will never have sight again. There will be a coldness down there that will never see the light and bright sunshine. Making no right choice, she will wither under the treachery of her own bad and immoral deeds. But, I will continue to stand on the top of your perch, stretch my arms and, in my deepest prayer, call your flight to my relief. And, now my devotion to you, o one of focused flight, I will adhere to the beauty of your big, courageous earthly visions. What I see through your eyes will be the earth — plentiful, full of fairy dust, and the warm circles of wind that will rise me up towards that great purple passage of your powerful gliding strength.

No matter what obstacles are placed in my way, I will adopt your grand visions for me, visions to be free, and above all else, I will be able to write my capabilities and capacities of self-determination. Knowing that I will mirror my sights of the world with only all that is fresh and wholesome, I will adopt your great stance of discernment and high exalted freedom. My independence will soar with the speed of light across the top of the clouds and a long way away from her. Sparrows and ravens will feel my wing spread and powerfully generated lift off from the closest sphere of the ground. Large, fully flapping wings will generate enough midcourse to lift me to and above the gliding force of any ferocious storm, a storm that is exciting and challenging, but will not outweigh my swiftness of flight towards independence from the vile stalker witch. She continually sniffs around my garden of thyme and hides herself in cups of gossipy tea, adhering to writings of no real importance, except a consequence of chance.

Like you, I will test every interaction that comes to the door of my hut. I will disguise myself as a small bird in need of medicine, when really, I am the powerful one, giving no redemption for such wickedness. This will be the best way to test any person or creature, ensuring sincerity and self-protection from the evil doer. A good person will aid me immediately, and the evil one will try and cook me in blood and pepper. That nark, I know, will stop at nothing to hold me down in the depths of despair. I will use your inner awareness and long sightedness to avoid her at every single glance. I will be able to see through any façade that she endeavours to paint between me and what is real. Any poor illusion that she plasters in the minds of others will quickly fall away because of my adoption of your every eagle quality – knowingness of love, the realness of the best and most truthful things, and purity above her blackness.

All this, I will see through your protection of the natural and beautiful things in life. These things are like honey nectar, clear blue sky, green freshness of crystal blue waters, black soils of fertile grounds, and cow horns filled with the nourishment of the good rich loam. I will be like your young, when pushed over the edge of the cliff and caught time and time again by you, until the flight instinct has grown. I will endure any hard knock, until I too am ready to join you and the other eagles of flight. I will see myself sitting high on the mountain. The glacier lake below and clouds all around will conjure up your power before I fly.

I will gain my territory over and she will never have the vision for my own life direction that I model off you. I will use every essence of my mind to mimic the greatness in you, as to ward her off my back and down into another place of less fortune. Like the heavy goats that are much bigger than you, they will snatch her in the throat and graze her off the side of the hill tops. There is no defence against the mighty eagle surrounds that I dose myself with, night and day, morning and noon, and in every split second of time. I will fly directly into her storm and when the rains and thunder hit, I will not flinch or show fear. I will be as solid as a rock and drop the stone right in the middle of her dungeon. I believe that you have the power to ward off the dog that has been sniffing around my ankles for some very many years now. I have felt her pinch at every glance of an eye, and for so long it has been a cut throat, blood eat blood situation. For her to finally see that no matter what she does to me, she cannot rise up against the power of you. With your great domination of the sky and your redeeming spans of wakeful flight lay beyond the grave of her wishes for my demise. There, I can only find hope in each thought and prayer, hope that you will scoop me up from under her spell and, like your young, drop me from the cliffs, plunging towards the hard ground to teach me quickly to open my own wings, and fly to the other side side of the ravine.

This stand against her hate of me cannot be stopped or touched or moved. This great strength that I have invoked from your bird life into my humble human spirit is going to blossom into a life of peaceful freedom away from her and them, her conspirators. Once I am there, I will see in that ravine of heavenly escapes beautiful sanctuaries, lush flowery colourful gardens, jewels of all sorts to adorn my body, silken fabrics to weave into my skin, and fresh fruits and vegetables — exotic sorts that not even the earth can produce. I will continually replenish my body, mind, and soul. The bad woman will never be able to reach me. That way, I will remain in a place of natural, luxurious safety. It will be through the continual flux of this devotional prayer to the greatest and most powerful and most wise bird to ever fly this earthly plane, that I will be saved. Day in and day out, she will scuff around with a hung-over mind, no peace of beauty will be in her oubliette of sloth, and everything that she does, touches, or thinks about will droop and die. Flowers will sag in her presence, wilting away at the smell of her hog's breath. The sky will darken early on every day near to where she wanders in the shade and where she is not wanted or ever visited by nice and good ones. That bad-faced women will only find thorns and rotten carcasses to address her woes towards. But no matter what she does, the door to paradise that you have flown to me, will never open to her.

It will shut her out and I will be on the other side without worry or mishap. Like you, I will break my beak and pull out my waring feathers. Once they have regrown, I will be a new and fresh woman, inspiring to continue to move forward with my hymns to all of your life's winged journeys. I will model my life off every aspect of your being and within those prayerful songs, will stay young, protected and full of pleasure at the coming of your next flight. Nothing, no matter what she strips from me, will sway my faith in you, great bird of the nest. I am praying for my life, I am praying in every tender moment, that I will be able to relinquish myself from her clutches, that this happens before she realises just what I have done and how I have done it. The witch will not see the correlation between her continual bad luck and my rising up into the open skies of freedom and tranquillity. Not for one second will she be aware of my cunningness to escape the hold that she has placed on my life. Never will she suspect, that the unimportant girl of no consequence, and the person who it is whispered was little to know about, the forever serving girl, Elspeth, would draw on the magnitude of your bird velocity and divine prowess of greatness. Only to take flight and lift herself out from under those false elite notions and perceptions.

I will use your splendour, poise and great knowing of this most majestic land, and sparsely and uninhabited country to leave her far, far behind. On that day, like you, I will wear a feathered cape, and eagle accessories made of stone, stick, wood, and leaf. I will make a crown of thorn bush and wear it. Only on that day, will the jealous and creepy female realise that right under her nose, when she was busy making colourful spells and highlights, thinking that she was better than me, it was right there and then that I had actually outwitted her, right under the toned lavender skies, with my great eagle. The witch, to that very moment, will think to have been in a superior position above me, the young Elspeth who had once worked at the Seymour Homestead and served very many cups of tea to the witch of many guises.

I pray now, with my whole self, the blood life that streams from you into me and opens my heart to knowing the truth about the prosperity of just being myself without her. My heart tells me of prosperity and happiness outside the bloodiest pain that she protrudes and juts towards me through her twistedness. Once I rise myself above her and into your nest, oh how weary she will grow of my personal success. For this, I am prepared to wait. I am prepared to wait for the drag of the past to find itself suffocated in the off-shoot tunnels of the deep dead-end caves, the caves that once again, can only be found when squirming on one's belly, like a snake into the unforeseen and barred inner sanctum of the mountains strains. It is the most confining place in the world, where air is nowhere to gasp and claustrophobia can send a person's mind into a madness with a terror that will shrink the heart and thin, red serum in an instant. I will wait in that damnation, until there is hardly anything left of me to transition across the worlds to the seven gates. Through my prayer, I will defeat her every put-down of me, and will rejoice in every moment of my lone and silent suffrage.

I am prepared to wait until the last day and be left behind by everything and everyone. I am prepared to be left behind until you lift my life to its next sanction. I am not worried at all about being bruised by her less eloquent tongue. I am not worried at all about being scolded by the boiling water of her vituperation. I know there are many who can relate to these words. And, although all this is happening around, below and above me, I feel a sovereignty within me that will, with your help, fly me to a new throne. Beyond the hell of her projections and subtle insults.

Somehow, great pullet, I know that this is the time that you communicated through the pictures of your beak, feathers, and wings. That time is now here. It is here to bring serene magnificence and empower me to withstand the greatest difficulties that she can bring. The physical confinement of fear will not stop my prayer for your wings to shed a shadow over her, and lead me to your pronounced branch.

And, like some person who has chosen the path of scotch brew, she will be continually dehydrated by the intake of her own liquid poison. This too, will be her downfall, amongst the many other ladders that will be pulled out from under that woman, revealing the plunges in her horrific life's destiny. Things will go wrong, many things, but, under your guise, I, in faith, will never falter. I pray to be in your protective egg and once there, will wait to be hatched. I will make a dilapidated broken down, deserted, and isolated hut, my deliverance from everything not good, my protection in the wilderness. It will be a place of simplicity, where I will pray that those who need me and what I have to give, will find me there. I will open my heart to harmless enemies, strangers, and alike. They will find the woman of prayer, living peacefully in the bush with her inner sensitivity and kindness. A loving woman they had not guessed. My name will rise above and through the great sky gate of the heavens. However, one will not be able to enter. She is the one of greed, untruths, and no interest in amelioration. There, I will need little more than a few cups, a soft duvet, and books of spiritual dominion. I will live with natural things like love, and prayer will sustain my every need. I will see the goodness in every aspect of the countryside and see the highest in everyone.

That will be my bliss. I will wash in the river every day and in winter, I will slide down the snowy steep hillside on a heavy thick hessian bag without any fear. I will want for nothing, except a hut of contentment. For this to eventuate, I pray from every deep fissure within me. I will be happy to wear rags and not think about anything outside the basic needs of living and dying. I will seek guidance from your eagle eye, and when finally, in my last light breath of awakening, the soft Swallowtail butterfly's wings will ascend my soul, I will ask that I am raised above those terrible things and that I remain as strong as a mountain, and as firm in myself as any great woman.

But, mostly, now and in each prayer, I will ask to remain an ordinary person, sustaining the wisdom to survive against the odds, and anything that is and will ever be placed in front of me, anything that she deliberately sets to divert me from your airlift to the azure ether. And, without diversion from my life urges, and without pressing on another's calling and destiny, I will move forward, speeding on the wings of your nurturing, ingenious spur. In the knowing, I will be free and not bogged down by the tremors of mundaneness or unfulfilled by being too puffed up. And, in that speed of no haste, I will know that the dawn of each day is your rising in us all. I will take a sword and a pencil and make this spiritual statement an emblem on the door of my hut. In doing so, I will reclaim the greatest timetable ever written, my timetable that sets everything straight.

And, even in the harshest climate, that bends and weighs my mind, I will see the light of the sun and the silhouette of your black shape in its yellow full circle. It is high art in the motion of your perched stipulation. When I am called to the beacon of your plot, I will spree myself with mist and sit in front of your feathered chest, without trepidation and without concern, other than your directive knowledge towards how to find my hut.

The Hut

By this time, the winter had set in and the small snowflakes fell softly as they covered the foreground of the hut that sat tucked away and down into the foothills of the mountain range. They could have been mistaken for little white butterflies. The butterflies were gentle in spring and the snow drifts in mid-winter often turned into slush and bogs. These gentle snowflakes were a sign that for a few days ahead, the tracks through the ranges would be clear, but, then, the risk of being caught in blizzards was also near. Wandering through the high country, across the high plains, down to the rivers, and stopping at the known grave sites and natural springs, they wanted to forget the time of war, the cruelness, and the takeover of their lands. In all those tens of thousands of years of kinship, the original wanders would never have expected all that happened, or the greatest grief that occurred because of those extreme events.

Elspeth was also an outcast, and in time, her hut had become a refuge for the stolen and lost ones, taking in people who were running from danger, who were hungry, or who had been left behind by a world that was unwelcoming and not accepting of any kind of difference.

After leaving the service, her life was no longer owned by others, where every second of her breathing life had been determined by the

demands of house duties and the hard and unforgiving owners. At last, Elspeth could be free to be her whole and real self. However, after 17 years of complete ownership by the Clarences, her own self was somewhat of a stranger. At first, when living in her abode, she felt lost and very unusual in her new world. Elspeth felt that whilst in service for so long, she had been robbed of vital aspects of her personality. These inherently superlative qualities she hoped to find again in her old broken-down hut. She would restore both the hut and herself, but this would take time. She started nailing the broken windows, replacing the worn-out floor boards, clearing the roof cavity of the dead and live possums and rats. Ridding the putrid urine smells and the planting a fresh vegetable garden was both tiring and pleasurable.

Those early days held many and great difficulties, but it was the land and its natural resources that had supported Elspeth, both consciously and subconsciously, imprinting the signs of renewal in the everyday landscaped pictures. These continually ever changing magnificent pictures had been dropped from the eminent gallery above.

The pious pictures typified the grandeur of the greater things in life and softened Elspeth's emotions — her feelings of dejection, isolation, sadness, and the fear that arose in her soul when she could still feel the old cruel man in the shed, his revolting words of despise still running through her veins. And, of course, there was the demon woman who never seemed to give up pursuing the innocent bush girl. After settling in and adjusting to her new surrounds and for years after, the hut helped Elspeth to stay focused, free and happy — free to be away from them in a place of peaceful shelter from the outside world and all that represented discomfort and pain. It was a place of natural experience: Ancient, wholesome, and spiritual. It filled the spaces of regret, the spaces of forlornness. Nature never caused Elspeth any problems. In fact, after being bitten over and over again by the sneaky tongues and invidious jargons of untruths, she found nature and its elements better to love than any best friend. Elspeth found unadulterated kindness and nurturing in every hill, barrow, and twig. Fragile in simplicity, these natural things were familiar and comforting. There were magnifying experiences of organic lushness that meandered the days and nights in the hut. The extreme, harsh unexpected weather patterns were not of importance, and those experiences flushed away fear, removed any anticipation, and gave Elspeth a special insight into bush life.

'Sit for a while, my child', spoke the ghost voice. Elspeth was perched under a huge rock, and the peaceful women began to gather sticks, bark, and rock for the fire, as the men had not arrived. They awaited the caucus and readied for the night ahead. It would be filled with stars, crisp, cool night air and deep ceremonial communion. The giant boulders opened spaces to protect the little lizards and called people who traveled through the mountain terrain. Deep into the bush, it was the moss on the stones, and the bark that symbolized to a man that his woman was ready for him. With his spear, hard in place, he presented the food as an offering of his worthiness. Likened to the overwhelming feeling felt by a small child when entering the entrance of a large dark cave, Elspeth's breath, for a moment was taken by the mammoth granite structures that seemed to be balanced by the air alone, and serendipity was not the issue. The women seemed to understand Elspeth's presence and knew the day would come when she would blend into their everyday happenings, hunting for moths to cook in ash and then on rocks ground into paste for those deer skinned children who were tucked away under the shadow of the great rock. It was the nurturing women who made sleeping on the hard ground feathery and light. The unusual spaces between the communities on the open plains brought forward a unique difference in the people that Elspeth met.

The good shearer was uneducated in letters, but highly experienced at the cleanest clip, and a group of teenage school girls were carted along a track, hidden mostly by thick tussocks and grasses, up the school house, and later out and into the bush for afternoon teas. The shearer and the peaceful women knew the track well. Elspeth had heard that the shearer was invited to the old-school house to explain the importance of the track to the school girls, in a talk that went like this, 'the hard to see track has a secretive feel to it, remnants of an old bush fire, charcoal smoldering some decades before and windblown trunks and dense shrubbery and sticky leaf ground cover create an optical illusion that hide the track. If you did not have a bush eye or dream sense, you could miss the track. But the track is definitely there and has a purpose that may or may not reorder the stealthy, sneaky things that happened on the track some days, months, and many years before'. The girls were left pondering, like an audience who waited for an outcome or answer. The good shearer seemed to know that there was no reason or answer to the ambiguous unknown dimensions of the track. 'What appears to be a dead end is not a dead end, and when you think you have miles of straight forward walking and thinking in front of you, you may trip over a large stump. You must have your wits about you when walking around down there on that old track'.

There were other intelligent outcasts who roamed the mountains, but they could only be found after the mists of thick rain when no sign of rainbows could be seen touching the enclosed sanctuary and water lands. Rocks and burnt trees were also a sign of their presence, and the risen earth a natural taking in the windy hilltops. These were the ones who gave birth on hillsides, with each contraction moving the body length up the slandered gorge. Screaming to the open blue sky to release the pain of their forefathers, they delivered their babies in commune with the other children who ran around naked, soil in their hair, and a tin roof for shelter. They were happy and unpretentious. However, often they were turned away from every town store, only to stand in the fire, snow, rain, blizzards, and winds with all but wildlife skin to cover their bodies. They would liken themselves to the lush vegetation of spring thoughts, to river stones and to the ever-inner desire of owning their own home lands. That intention was always in the forefront of each and every action. They were said to come from the wombs of the less fortunate, like the one who scrubbed her clothes on washing board out next to the wood pile. It was also known by some, that she did cover up a serious wrong deed. There was a desperation in it all, and the rich town folk and productive farmers had no patience for them really. On bleak and often overcast days, the rain never ceased and the butterflies weren't there either. The old boulders and gum trees covered the tracks and footprints of the nowhere people.

Their white, stringy bark hair, aglow in the deep wet, they faded into holes already known to them, and the little birds danced on twigs, communicating the quiet stillness of the gigantic rock formation that was grey-green housing to the others that never ever came back. And, their ribbons, bows, and picnic baskets were almost archetype contours hanging in the clouds. The rocks scattered in the shapes of animals and kangaroos in open grounds. The children's laughter could be heard from an abandoned school house and there was contentment in the surrounds. But, the school girls were now forever gone.

The bush scrub, which was situated a little bit farther down from the round spring water dam, was like a completed extension of Elspeth's small boarded hut. It offered a lounge room plethora of uncontrollable and self-changeable natural treed rooms, depending on the time of day and season. The bush rooms became as much like her home as was the hut. They were prepared every moment by Elspeth's solitary self and offered a lifestyle that grew wise thought and strong emotion in herself. Taking different ones into the spaces of wildness, it became known that Elspeth's skills in determining the wilds where nobody would dare pass were definitely to be trusted. She read the weather tessellations by cloud, sky, wind, rain, wild life rustles, sounds and bird flight.

To come up with the concept of the treed rooms and extending her hut outside in the solid soil element, Elspeth decided as soon as she moved to the hut, that she would choose a piece of ground only half a mile away. This area was just a bit down from the quartz ridge. It was partly exposed and partly under the ground stretching in a horizontal rocky mineral outlay. Looking west, the ridge was a weaving mineral wave. Then with four sticks and four pieces of pink satin ribbon that she took from her glory box, Elspeth staked out the rectangle zone that measured 45 steps width and 95 steps in horizontal strides. The ribbon came from the glory box that had been given to her by her mother when she left home. Elspeth's mother realized that her daughter would never have a proper marriage. The dowry box was filled with all the special collectables that she had been putting together since Elspeth was only three years old. So far, the box had been a total waste of time, just sitting there locked away, in wait for a special wedding day that would never come. The baby bonnets, starched white linen, stitched initialed handkerchiefs, fancy decorated teaspoons, satin ribbon, two woollen blankets and a set of six crystal glasses all represented hope for a good future with a husband to care for: Old fashioned values that Elspeth did not entertain and did not wish to think about.

Staking the treed rooms with the ribbon symbolized much more to Elspeth about who she was — a strong human being set in the world of the great outdoors to withhold the rights and values of what it meant to be a real woman of integrity and forthrightness. For a few weeks, the ribbons that were tied to the four thick sticks blew in the wind, dragged the ground at night, a lingering extension of the hut. The treed rooms were partitioned into three clear sections and early on were enclosed with help from Fredrick the young homestead gardener who, together with Elspeth, built a picket fence. A gate at the top side near the limestone ledge looked like seating for those waiting to enter through the postern by stepping on the round rock that was mostly buried in the hard earth and became a mat. The mat opened into the lounge room area that featured an active ant's nest and a big gum tree with a dead tree that stretched long ways from its trunk. This became a chaise lounge style of a tree and a perfect furnishing for an outdoor room. It would rival the Clarences' elegant furnishings and Elspeth hoped they would never visit. The front area was mostly open to the south with a few bushy shrubs and a wombat hole on that other side. It was shaded by a huge overhanging tree. The tree was home to three large bird nests and situated outside of the additional nature extension.

This first section, Elspeth referred to as a replica of society's echoes. For she could imagine all those society people enjoying ant wine, crushed gum leaf soup and wombat poo mini toast! In her upper most room, she would only entertain the best of the best. Her sense of humor, although innocent enough, at times often did get her into trouble with some locals. They were at a loss as to why she lived partly in her hut and partly in a closed-off tree sanctum. Of course, Elspeth would always show respect to every man, woman, and child, no matter what walk of life they happened to derive from – everyone would receive gum leaf soup. The drawing room lounge area was a place for more important conversations to take place, a place to meet her imaginary Prince and find peace far away from the witch's clasps, piercing eyes, and unforgettable darkness. The middle-sloped area was connected to the upper and bottom treed room enclosures by the small animal paths, which eventually wound through the tall dense growth of lanky saplings. This was the designated kitchen area and also happened to have a nice round open space where Elspeth placed an old, heavy, wooden, oval-shaped table. She was given the table by the Clarences when leaving their service, along with a cosy wood heater to keep her toes warm on those early dew mornings, which would also see a bush billy brewing away for a few hours too. Open but private, that is how Elspeth described her new outdoor kitchen.

At the bottom of this area, there were two big open halls of natural habitat. This lower end of the treed rooms was a playground for visiting babies and toddlers. It was a kaleidoscope medley of exploration, and a relaxing picnic garden that was slightly privatized by cornered vegetation, including a large tree that was dominant in the bottom right side of the open sky casement rooms. This truly was a beautiful aspect to Elspeth's living domain, and it was all encapsulated by the curtains that were actually the slightly ascending hills in the not too distant ranges and the bluest of mountains. The hills silhouetted the picturesque extension that became a haven for Elspeth when finding comfort and peace, whilst leaning up against any one of the three mainstay tall trees. In this environment, and when feeling completely safe from the wickedness of her main enemy, including freedom from her work as a servant, Elspeth had the experience of becoming the bush itself. In this deep feeling of contentment and relaxation, the outdoor woman attracted many hidden proposals. A man's desire to be Elspeth's husband lay there, like ruins waiting to be acted upon. It was positioned, patterned in the earth for almost three decades. There were signs of strong masculinity in the marriage proposal that had been left in the cluster of rocks, sticks, and the dawn of wood.

For, to be a black woman in a white woman's body was like the embroidered stitches on the sea shells — red, amber, green, and yellow — and skilled eternally in the artistry of life's passions and pain, in the mixture of cultures, and the misunderstanding of a person's life passage. And, like a strong gust that symbolized the forthcoming storm, the placement of the dreaming in a circle and a fire lit at the bottom of the long thin branch were a calling to a woman of the same clan — a calling to come forward and read the sun signs. To read every natural piece of bark, every ray of light, and to pick up each and every stone, letting it tell its dreaming of the didgeridoo man who would shudder at the great thunder, and tremble at the sound of the storm. A storm that would trample down the vegetation and thrust them into a togetherness at the very last circle dance, casting off the old shell and replacing it with words, thoughts, and prayers, only to be encapsulated in the intimacy of lovemaking. Their expressions were like the images in the dated photographs that she spread across the floor of the hut — clouded images of fish and dimensions of spirituality. One was of Mary holding Jesus above the weather - board church, the other of a poor woman crying for her lost babe in the scrub. Elspeth was emotionally shattered at not being able to accept his proposal. She shed her tears and blood at the loss of what could never be.

In her dreaming, she knew that designed in all the colours of the rainbow were the instruments of peace and that there was absolutely no accident in the meeting of their destiny. The Blacksalle rained a lot in song that day, and the grey misty valley was surrounded by amethyst bare branches, the dancing billy goat weed, and mountains of elegant glandular pink bells. This was the place of the shadow people, a place of deep reverence, a place about birth, change, matrimony, and the circle of stones that the resounding pipe made, forming flurry winds and melting snow gums set in the bushland. The picture painted in the surrounding areas was one showing people of the past, some could be heard mustering on the distant station, others stamping the ground. The timeline of the ether and the smiling faces penetrated the mists as the hard work was never really finished. The knowing Murray greys stood serene and in their grey, fawn and brown coats and were drawn to the sound of the echoed scarlet red head and slate grey gang gang that flew to the sleet and snow melting in their path. They were nourished by the smell of comfortable home country life portrayed in the distance, like bacon and eggs cooking in the earth on the hot stone coals, not forgetting the slimline pines that were gutted by heat and drought where they used to live.

Elspeth returned to her hut, open to the circle of proposal stones and torn between their allure and her own providence and call. Reflecting on why they had met. And, what may have happened if she had chosen that ride. There had been a short and brief encounter between Elspeth and the didgeridoo man. Before they parted, the reverberating deep tubed music melted away in the background of their crossed cultural links. It made them feel like they were dancing a ceremony across the sill of secrets, and as they did, they became awake in the spiritual sleep of the day, afternoon, night and the next morning. The treed courtyard of their dreams covered their painted bodies. They left behind all of the spiteful witches who dwelt at the bottom of the cold wells. Their bodies were like plush warm velvet and shaped in the healing of black magic. Together, they came alive to the sound of wind chimes and amethyst butterfly wings. They were transparent in the heat of the long-scattered afternoon air coils in white, and they could feel the creation of silk satin blueness from the cloud silhouette. They remained aware of the witches and the death of their togetherness and no earthly marriage, only the intimate union of black magic.

The black man said to Elspeth's butterfly, 'All the while, I wanted you. And, as the years passed, my lizard woman, the proposal that I left on that first day of our meeting, next to the river in the open space, sat placed as it was, you never came forward to accept it, but I knew that you had read it. It will wait for the next dreaming to find you again'. These words of desire and human entreaty were of the wandering didgeridoo man. A man who had lost his didgeridoo music to the black girl, the girl who lived in a white skin. He felt her strand of black blood spill in his spiritual call to the eagle to protect her. Elspeth's response: 'It is a beautiful day for walking — overcast, still, and after the rains of our watering, very hushed. Everything is fresh, green, and shimmering. I can see, in your ebony eyes, some soft wildlife and the Swallowtail butterfly. On the slope behind the hut, there is a very old tree, the trunk is twisted and turned into a V-shape on the earth floor. Under the tree is a carpet of soft, green vegetation, and our wetness seeps into the greater depth of the cloud-cuckoo-land. There has been so much rain there, that even at the base of trees, woods that have been dead for centuries, these green shrubberies and new leaves are now sprouting on what were dead branches. Today, the kangaroo is here and everything feels completely beautiful in the nature of your reality and my keepsake of you'.

Elspeth went on again. 'I am here against the tree, looking at three others in the distance. One has been burnt with your fire, the other is another similar bare V-shaped, and the third is a very old-world-looking tree, with big strips of bark peeling off the trunk. These trees are standing amongst many others that have fallen down and are covered in moss. They are mangled together in branch thicket as natural bush statues, statues that could change into ceremony dancers at the call of a bird or gallop of the bushman's horse in the next paddock, a boundary to our coming together'.

It was so archaic out there, beyond the widest fields and gently undulating small hills where Elspeth had moved, the ancient grey rock face set as a natural trap, sat to evade those witches and that one in particular who was stark darkness itself. It was a place for the men who wandered towards the spring of the early birdsong to go down into the caverns underground. They waved to each other, as a knowing of a portending death. Spring, summer, autumn, and winter began to bear no meaning to their existence, as their spirits lifted from their tired limbs. The earth out there, no longer a mystery to them or Elspeth, had all the treasures of their lives illuminated in the fresh scent of the bush moss.

The ritual of rich earth, skin and fire became early dew happenings aside the tussocks and created memories of the grey rock marriage proposal and the trading of trinkets that also faded with each ceremonial step. A closure to life in this dreaming was denoted by skulls that were scattered throughout the ecosystem; it was the hand of God's disguised as haunting debris. They were left like his love etching that was under the tree, next to the river gorge, especially for Elspeth to find. The natural pattern could have been a modernistic card, reminiscent of rose petals and clear water that was never actually consummated or made nude by moonlight. Black and white textures caught the sunlight that streamed into the centre of the circular proposal and then lit the caverns. It showed those who did not know the path where Elspeth's hut lay, and saved those who had slipped through the silk dew drops. It illuminated how to find peace before reaching the climax of their withering selves.

Early in the mornings, when the fire had not leapt fully into the sky, it seemed like the bird song was a long way away from the rats at the bottom of the wet caves. They had escaped the blaze and terror of the haunting one. The morning star was still bright and to the east of the ground cover, long before the men had cast their sticks towards the rocks, looking for the signs of the ancestral tale that was a deep earth knowing. It was tomorrow that they would begin to make shrines of love and respect towards their loved ones.

These wanderers had not made it through the large crevice between the boulders and thought that they had been stolen by the rugged horseman that came through from another district. However, they had been herded by the three goats that had tumbled to the bottom of the slate gorge. This was after the roar of the fire had muffled the warning of the men's voices. The sounds of their cries were smothered by the black soil. It was rich, very, very rich black soil.

Elspeth spent long days walking through the passages of spring trees and twittering birds. There were hanging gum leaves of burgundy stems and the differing shades of green that made the landscape rich in its natural state. The trees became awakened by the knock, knock, and knock of the feeding kookaburra on the branch, which sounded like a nail being hammered at the back of the hut. Elspeth's companionship with nature and her resilience to the hard elements of the Australian bush, had blended her khaki jumper and torn brown pants into the core of the scrub and she felt like an earth idol. Elspeth was a mystery woman of another destination. A fire mist hovering over the steep cliff of another world and earth strings that played a sad melody of loss. Caring little for fashion and often shopping at the town second hand store, she looked perfect and beautiful in any attire.

There was no other as exquisitely looking and she could have worn an old brown sack; her beauty was beyond designing for. During those long days, Elspeth knew that in the awe of the lost valley, the highest of men were yet to be born, yet to be fed, and yet to fight between good and evil and between all that was and was not. She was protected by the lyrebird, snake, lizard, call of the birds and the deity of small things, like sticks and stones cradled in the sunshine. These men would bear a voice different to her own voice, which at times, spat venom. Elspeth made it clear to herself and the travellers that she did not wish to own the land, but was of it. To be of the land was to let it wash over her, to let it heal, to let it nourish and to let it pleasure her will. This concept of her positioning in the natural world drew down the wildness of the bush flowers. There was no rambling of nonsensical conversation, only a depth of presence that was good. The moss branches were a sign of rich vegetation and complete and total land fertility. In the back of the silent open and far away space in time, a master tree would loudly and with a series of thunderous creaks and cracks fell itself to the ground. That sound was like no other and it would send thwarting shudders throughout the dead quietness of the bush, freezing those on the beaten tracks, working in the fields, and washing dishes. This loudest and commanding bush noise made people stop and think about other more important things.

It was a time to remember him. Closed to the outside world was Elspeth's heart when living in her hut, but, every moment, no matter what the out-bush challenges brought, Elspeth forged a state of mind full of magnificent rainbow thoughts and total faith. The oldest trees that she would seek counsel from were the ones that were dead, but covered in thick green moss. Elspeth's mind and body became coloured in the healing essence of the bush flowers: The reddish Sheep Sorrel, amber and yellowish Billy Buttons that reflected the light, and touches of lilac coloured Round Leaf. Bush mint soothed her sometimes lonely heart. The soothing mint brought her mind to seek the openness of sunshine and the heat of the Mallee Boy Waratah brought change, to what was sometimes a death wish. To daydream the Casade Everlasting would slowly stimulate her imagination into a steam of colourants — puce, pink lemon, and myrtle grey — and the creation of the yellow Banksia, these colour fields of her existing life began to help Elspeth respond to the enthusiasm and vitality of the world. It was on those days, she knew, without reading a single word, or listening to any common gossip, that there was not one ounce of authenticity or grace in all of the witch's spell notes and certainly no beautiful flowers. In fact, the vile witch scurried among the bush flowers looking for poison to spike any crispy apple she could find.

The almost pastel chiffon colorants swayed in the hush, their wings spirited by bush perfume scents and delicately glowing like uncut sea pearls. They came with a message which would linger high in the candle bark trees. In time, their memos were clear. The trees knew Elspeth's every move and they expected that she would return to her calling, which was to live peacefully in her hut, with a butterfly sign fixed above in the cloud formations and evergreen days. A sign was displayed in the yielding wings of the acquiescent Swallowtail butterfly whose oak-leaved extensions, when open and spread in flight, moved Elspeth's every thought towards the great land of her destiny, to a place where her enemies could never go.

For many years, when living out there on her own, Elspeth felt the horrible desiccated heat and struggled the droughts. Hot were those days and dry were the terrible ripping winds. During some seasons, the dust bowls set in around the humble hut. In the stifling heat, Elspeth declared to herself that in older years, she would claim a habit and heal the needy, for she knew her discomfort was nothing compared to the suffering of many. After those annoying, bush flies and hot driven days, there was never a need to reason her future again. Summer snakes were a part of her everyday life, and ever-present hiding in rock piles. At any time, they could easily enter the flimsy shack.

Elspeth was sure that an old wise tale about a woman who did not offer a cup of tea to an unexpected visitor, and, afterwards was bitten by a snake, could possibly be true. The hearsay went that the venomous snake would eat her alive if she did not show hospitality to each and every stranger. The hot snaky days did rise fear in Elspeth and at times, perhaps an unspoken fear of being bitten herself. The tale may have also been the reason why the dark crows living close to the hut gave warning to Elspeth to also remember that from a past life, a snake in old religions was often used to fight evil and not to delve into tales that gave rise to unnecessary worry. Like the bush telegraph, stories that very often went from person to person, family to family or shopkeeper to customer, became all blown out of proportion. In the end, the stories were all made-up and held little truth of the real incident. On those fearful days of unexpected fires, strangers, snakes, and untrue stories. Elspeth enjoyed painting her hut and decorated the windowsills with small butterfly pattern, thinking of more peaceful times and the gentle designs that were reminiscent of classicism. All the while, staying close to the embodiment of her own Swallowtail butterfly.

Talking to nature filled the gaps when the passing visitors left for the other side of the river. That was a place that Elspeth would always avoid — a rocky hard path filled with sniggering old chinwags who drooled language and ate meaty, bloody flesh day in and day out. Never would she walk that way, never. Instead, her purified mind was always directed towards the talk of what happened in her Australian bush.

'I am here leaning against the natural tree statues. They have been coiled and spun by the natural changes and patterns in the weather. I can see that many of them are split by the constant thrashing of the gales and many scud showers. Some seasons they could not be lusher, they could not be more wet, each having their own symbolic etching which states an event from the past, present, and prediction of the future. These are characterised by all the shades of greys, whites, creams, blacks, and bush greens in the scrub where nobody would dare tramp a foot, except me — blooming me — with my ability to not only read the stars, but to know my blood lineage is highlighted, not only in the dead night twinkles, but in the hush of the oldest trees and twigs. There is a deepness in the curves and bows out here that cannot be discerned by many or perhaps any. The bush life had refreshed me, clearly making me stronger to reach the next day, next month, and next year — on my own if necessary'.

Elspeth was never lonely on the days that she spoke to nature, and often flung herself around a tree, sometimes falling into an erotic self-pleasuring that felt natural and beautiful, feeling the trunk between her legs and leaves on her lips.

But, what also kept her alive and interested in life, long before and after her young son was born, were all the stories that the travelers told. Keeping notes, Elspeth wrote many of the stories down; some were amusing, some very thought-provoking, and others were hard to understand.

A girl sat at the hut table, ragged, without much idea of speech, hungry, forlorn, and skinny. The blonde girl who pretended to be a longtime friend of Elspeth's said that her life had become all about sleeping, waking, and being rich in her imagination, even as she was poor every long, hard, scratchy day. It was about the balance of life and, in the end, who gets what. Saying that she had nothing, and that all the other girls had everything, the girl had not travelled at all and had been slipping from one relationship to the next, looking for security, but ending up alone after being used for sex. Finding out about Elspeth's kindness from a worried friend, the sad girl knocked on the door of the hut. It was early one morning and she appeared, standing in a stream of sunset. Elspeth noticed a slight bruising on her face. Elspeth's was coolly distant, wary, but still empathetic, knowing the girl might turn into a viper if she said one word that would raise an issue too difficult for the blonde to deal with.

Elspeth responded poetically, quietly, and offered her a cup of tea with a herbal infusion. 'The freshness of the day and the rituals of music that float from the days before either you or I were born, can and will open every sound from the sanctuary of nothingness in the surroundings that you have described. Try and emulate love from the cycles of seasons that are celebrated in the patches of daisies that gleam and glow in the light'. The window in the hut was ornately patterned with pressed gold and silver leaves, and the ledges were carefully constructed by the hands of a man who was a skilled mason. In small stones, the cross was subtly placed at the back of the frame and the four spaces around it illusionary in the depth of tonal grey panels that deepened into the thick wall that was covered in out-dated newspaper. In each paneled area, there was something to read. One was dark and black, and held a kerosene lantern in in the same shape as the frame. When lit, it carried frankincense turning the stone into wood and then it became invisible. Water was featured in the next space with an image of two pelicans, a message to the lost fisher people that schools of fish were near. There were always trees to paint, and the natural light was such, that when Elspeth peered through the third pane, an array of damp leaves gently touched her face.

Looking beyond, the didgeridoo man had reappeared. He was now standing on the edge of a rock, holding a girl in a pink dress. And, in the last space, two small speckled eggs sitting in the mason's hands. The young girl did not notice the beauty of the window panels, the black man outside near the rock, or even respond to Elspeth's very pretty words. Elspeth thought to herself, 'This is about love and loss. It is about letting the natural course of life and existence rise up from within. It is about praying that the gentleness of life defeats the hard and difficult ways. This girl, like most who come here to my humble abode, need care and understanding, for a time, anyway'.

Visitors to the shanty hut became more and more frequent as word spread that Elspeth could read people's faces, much like that of palm reading. In one glance towards a person's face, it was known that Elspeth could see into the reflections and happenings of a person's life. It was a reading of exactness, like knowing the precise time and the way in which a person would die. It was like a gentle shudder in her exterior body that opened Elspeth's heart of whispers, these whispers spoke of knowing. This gift of prophecy was often thought only to be held by a king or sage, not by a common woman. It was also a single sign that often spoke clearly, like a candle flame that could flicker any important moment.

The oldest farmhand from the homestead came once. il had been many years since Elspeth had seen him and he seemed deteriorated in body and mind since those early days, way back then he was a tall, strong, good-looking man, kind natured, and carefree. Hardy was the name he went by, but over the years, his marriage had broken down. He told Elspeth that he was under continual excessive financial pressure from his ex-wife, who pretended to be someone that she was not, and spent a lot of money in all the town shops. Many blue credit notes often arrived at his door, and he could not pay the remainder of all the debts. Ashamed, he hung his head. After she left him, his greedy wife went from one man to the next, looking for money and sex. It was a disgusting end and demeaning to a man who was not raised that way. Hardy expressed the lonely laments of the broken and once grand homestead and gardens. The tree house that was a deck across the back fence had fallen to the ground and seemed to shed tears on the final day of Mr Clarence's departure, who was the last to leave the house after the death of his son, his own marriage breaking down after being caught kissing his mistress by his one and only precious daughter, Bessie. Now, he explained to Elspeth that the homestead stood alone against the pending storms, and it was only the spirit of the birds who came of late, to weed and care for the gardens.

When the sleeting snow came down and settled on and around the house, it appeared to paralyze all the unsavory experiences that had happened when the Clarence family lived there. The settling snow softened the forever life-changing calamities.

Hardy was also still suffering aftershocks from hearing the body thud of the homestead horse trainer. This happened when planting bulbs in his last round of gardening duties. The man had fallen from his horse, and went through the ground into a state of permanent ice coma, saying it was similar to the feeling he had when looking at the empty wire bird cage, hanging slanted on the veranda, only to know that freedom came at a cost and no bird should be caged. Like the soul of the paralyzed man, the birds were captive, open and closed, alive but mostly dead. Elspeth was sorry for Hardy's personal decline, and could feel his pain. They sat together in front of the fireplace, stocking the wood, and watching the cinders spark into golden red. Elspeth related some soothing memories for him to ponder. Deep down, Hardy had always been in love with Elspeth, and now, in some short recollections, she brought his mind back to the day when the Clarences went to town and, along with Isobel, the three workmates decided to take a long afternoon stroll. They walked the road that stretched across and behind the homestead, looking down on the entire district.

'That day, there was a lot of wattle and Saint John's Wort in bloom. It was a magical glistening afternoon and it could have been any day, in any era. A timeless feeling permeated our walking and we were closed to the nonsense of the outside world. There were three deep black soiled wombat holes, just freshly dug, one marked by two crossed trees, the other opposite with a tree branch laying right down the middle, and the one a little further up the hill had a tree branch horizontal perched right in front. Do you remember that we thought the holes to be deliberately dug, almost purposely placed, one for daddy wombat, one for mummy wombat, and one for baby wombat? There were a group of very pretty gum trees with many flourishing seedlings growing beneath them. The shredded bark cracked, as we tried not to disturb the family of wombats. It was like every piece of earth surrounding the high road, the three holes, and the seedlings were untouched by human hand. No farming had occurred near that place, and little of the view had been seen before, other than through our eyes. The day was an artistry of illustriousness in itself. Holding the sky were two dominant lone eagles, all powerful one moment and instantly gone the next. From that one quick flight, leaving only the resonance and essence from the gliding and dipping hop, their powerful wings left us wondering just what the purpose of theirs and our carriage could be'.

The aging farm hand's eyes opened and his toothless grin widened with a brilliant smile. In this case, Elspeth's story of the past had worked, gladdening his low heart and easing his thoughts towards new jobs to be done. 'I do remember Aidan and Bessie when they were very young', said Elspeth. 'They played for hours in that tree house, him and her, looking out and watching the dancing horses brace the landscape against the cold winds of cry, the early bliss of spring and the scorching mid-morning summer heat, crossing the paddocks in their rustled leaf-coloured coats of golden shine and red. And then, they dozed in front of the fire of cracking hot coals and woods, warming their growing limbs, bodies, and faces until their cheeks glowed into a warm rosy red. The laughter and smell of food preparation would have been a comforting feeling and hopefully those memories will wash away the sad and confusing feelings over their parent's divorce. Settling her days, calming the night and bringing back that feeling of make believe magic. And, I know the horse trainer's accident was also devastating to the family, and all of us really. Life does throw up the unexpected'.

'The reality of Aidan's death was also almost too much for us to endure', replied the hand. After that small child's death, the heavy, heavy rains came and left the land and our feelings boggy, bulging with water that filled the thick, wet-logged tussocks - heavy were our hearts. After that, the sun became blistering hot, and our hearts sank lower into deep grief. After a while, the vibrant greens made us feel refreshed again, and I think, by then, the child had been found and carried from the dam to the highest cloud and shown the way, the truth, and the light'. The sad man carried the conversation and then stopped bluntly.

'Yes', responded Elspeth, besides what I refer to as the three-wombat hole walk, I have many other memories of the early walks that we shared, the three of us, the ones just shortly after I commenced work on that big station. Walking into the late afternoon, we became shaded under the same trees, knowing that the warm sun was placing different coloured bands across the hills. Blending and binding, mixing in the palettes of the soft, misty, pink, grey, and light blue afternoon tones. If we did not make it onto our next destination, the sun-soft sky would soon disappear in an instant. This would be beside the flowing creek cascade that we could faintly hear. We were keen to see the pretty reflection of the berry bushes in the water.

To do so, we would need to jump the messy scrub on the river bank, and the big twisted and burnt tree that was dead and beautiful looking, laying across the river in the shallow rock falls. Our walks were all linked to finding our fate in the moon-shaped fish, and not stepping on the dead bats that were left behind and had a lingering foul smell about them. Even back then, she was watching our every move, but more particularly, my every move. It was the deep fear of being locked into the long hours of demanding work that made those special walks so appealing to us. The fear of not being able to escape the never-ending drudgery of home, farm, and garden duties — not to be able to escape into the wilderness and not being able to experience the might and force of the land. This was simply incomprehensible to us. We knew that some city folk did see the country and a country lifestyle as nothing more than a dead existence. But, we, even in those youngish years, we knew it to be a life line that knots and knits nature and people together. That life in the country was replenishing and refreshing to any soul, a place where true healing can occur and a bit of good fun can be had. We knew that the earth can suck away any residue of human pain, replacing it with spring water, clean blood, the ignition of natural hormone release, and the rapture of everything innate and biological coloured — citron, avocado, boysenberry, and burnt orange.

However, way back then, we were just so inexperienced that we could never even think of the words needed to describe what we knew to be true. No, we had no mature discernment then, only the carefree spirit of the bushland to respond towards. And what about Isobel, our dear Isobel? She was too simple in herself to think in such complex terms, but had a wealth of wisdom that she shared with me in a way that no other woman could. There was no other woman like Isobel'.

'I agree', said the old man who was stimulated by the coloured and in-depth remembrance conversation that seemed to linger on for hours into the firelight.

Fluent in various languages, in the dead of night, a man came into the hut. Without knocking, his well-worn bush hat cast a sketchy shadow over the wall opposite the fireplace that had just expelled the last of the blazing fire and still red-hot coals that were burning into the last cinders. Elspeth knew straight away that it was Eric Fuller. Eric and Elspeth had once had a fling behind the half fallen down chook shed. It was a day that she will never forget. The lust they had experienced together seemed to override the neighbouring farmer's nephew, who was still a virgin, and never had experienced intimacy before.

Unexpectedly he had driven over the hill behind the burk, burk, burk burking of the hens. As soon as he saw the two naked figures enjoying their sexual liaison; steaming bodies and outdoor orgasm, he automatically reversed his tractor and slipped away without any judgment towards what he thought was a fun thing to do on a bright, sunny afternoon. 'After all this time Eric, what are you doing here, and why do you enter my hut so late and with the smell of rum on your breath? The pungent smell will make me drunk for a week', questioningly scolded Elspeth. 'Well Elspeth, there is a time when words cannot give the right answer, and I am here to...'

Eric's response took them back to the sound of the tractor and that day. Welcoming the morning sun with a sigh and a prayer that Elspeth did not understand, she wondered how interesting he found her now that she was in her mature years and way beyond her menstruation cycle. Eric finished the prayer and went on to say, 'Do you remember the day, before that atrocious storm, the whole landscape changed, and we began to tremor inside? In an instant, what was a peaceful afternoon became overwhelmed with the smell of rain. Boom, boom went the sky, as the clouds greyed darkly, and mixed into a terrorizing convulsion of lightning and quaking jolts.

Then, after the shudders of lightning that made us feel completely terrified, there was a lessening of rain and a warm softening in the air. After all of this, there was the most vibrant rainbow, a stretching half circle swathed the horizon, one end stretched down to the origination of the early settlement to where a little girl appeared waving. Surrounded in mauve, blue, and green, she appeared as a messenger from her dead ancestors. The little girl had a message about rainbows. Rainbows, we now know are more than a natural marvel, they are a divine phenomenon. 'I have come back again to show you the rainbow.

'Oh yes', replied Elspeth. 'The eagle seemed to know that we were coming, even though it was an unexpected visit that we had made to that habitation, it was one of those last-minute throws. The clouds were a 'blue, blue' and as I walked fairly close, the bird perched like a statuette on the bare boughs. It looked straight into my eyes, and, as I turned my head, we held each other's gaze. I took it as a sign of knowing the complexity of the changes ahead. Then, I had the feeling that there was an unwelcoming feeling and a fairly sordid thing may have occurred there before. Something hard was lingering in the air that day, but I took the eagle eye as a sign that everything would be all right. I had a strong sense, a very strong sense, that it would all be over soon.

I thought it to be long forgotten. I do remember the rainbow sitting across the sky, which turned into a light grey satin, showing us something about raw beauty. After the stormy and uneasy cracking thunderous feelings, there was a whispering wind as fresh and light as the sun, it streamed through into that divine phenomenon. The blissful rainbow then added to our wondering and reaches out to me even now; it is like an extension of my hut and twilights any unease that tries to penetrate my happiness here. The little girl is a nature spirit who lives in the bush, waving a smile at every move I make, just like my little dolly, Patti.' Another knock came just as Eric was leaving Elspeth. Their lips were swollen after the hours and hours of reminiscing and kisses and intimately rejuvenating their lost friendship, a relationship that proved to be still full of fun and a bit physical too.

The next visitor looked around with sorcery eyes. 'I am here to spill myself on the floor of your humble dwelling, to tell you the truth about how I felt about you back then, and even now sometimes. As soon as I am done, I will leave and never, ever darken your doorstep again. The truth is Elspeth, that I completely and totally despised you, everything about you repulsed me. I could see your untouched and unblemished soul, your beautiful silk hair and green eyes. Your beauty was too much for me to withhold in myself. Your beauty raised a jealousy in me that was out of control; it made me aggressive to everyone that I cared about. After years of hating you, the hate permeated out into every area of my life and I became bewitched by its cruelty. Do you see who I am? A long time ago, I vanished from your life. After these many years, do you remember that we spent time together working? I had to leave the homestead and try to forget that I had ever gazed into your face. I had to relocate myself and try and become like you. I had to find a job before my jealousy turned cancerous. I did little underhanded things to you. I had parties and never invited you. I spoke poorly of you to every person that I met on any road, day and night. Yes, I created a bad reputation for you; slowly I turned everyone against you. I did hate you and on some days still do hate you'. 'Oh yes, you did detest me', calmly responded Elspeth, 'I do remember you'.

After the visitor of hate left, Elspeth needed a break for a long while, accepting that not everyone is nice, kind, and gentle, but a certain strength is learnt from hearing the truth, the whole truth, and nothing but the truth. Actually, Elspeth really did not remember the aggressor so well, but did remember her mangy sulky dog. The animal smelt as bad as she did, and was also gruff by nature. Elspeth had another friend, who's name she had also forgotten. Eventually the woman trained as a professional dietitian consultant, and often cited Elspeth's poor background, suggesting that her good influence was very important in helping Elspeth's situation. However, the real intent for this person seeking Elspeth's company was one of attraction only; she was drawn to the beauty's breasts and thighs. Never on a wider social level did she ever mention her interaction with Elspeth. Actually, she had not really wanted to be associated with her at all. However, the attraction was not reciprocal and in the end, Elspeth had developed a dislike for the girl who was never her real friend and who dropped out of her course of food study. 'Things can go both ways', thought Elspeth and confidently left it at that, not needing the girl of hate or the pretend friend in her hut, her everyday life, or future.

After moving right out there, into the back bush and regaining her independence, the days moved and sprawled on, mirroring into each other, she took on an inner intellectual life. Letting the wilderness penetrate the waylays of her mind and bringing pictures of everyday pastures, filled with the horizons of long swooshing grasses which were slightly tanned and fear tainted by the quick fleeing fox. It was a place of inner stillness and contentment that could not be jarred by small peckings of doubt. She gave herself a lot of time to day dream and reminisce about a lot of differing and mesmerizing things, just sitting and sipping and waiting. Once time started to permeate her dreamy thoughts, Elspeth began her private conversations with the Swallowtail butterfly. This could be considered by some as her mind going mad, but Elspeth saw it as a letting go. Elspeth told her butterfly friend and constant companion, 'I am of good stock, stock that is a blue blood and finer than gold. As a girl, I was sprawled on the rock by the river's edge, not too far away from our humble family home.

On that day, I saw the black-bird, with the yellow stripe circle the water. The circular strands of life always have a sign of the beginning and end of most things. They are the signs that are often not seen until the end, and emulate each other simultaneously. The signs are not clear until matters are almost over. Most things end the way they start — innocent and good or frightfully bad. The signs are always there. I once read a story about a girl who turned her head to look straight into a book that was harshly shut by the wind on the day of her marriage. Towards the end of her married life, she went back to the place where the oldest pine trees once were, and where her love had proposed marriage; but the trees were gone. As she walked amongst the left-over tree stumps, she remembered the book shutting and as she looked down, there in her imagination, were the pages from a book; rustling around near to the ground. Shortly after that, her husband suddenly died. It was like the pages of their lives together had already been written. In the beginning, they would sit under the trees, amongst the amber greenery and forever kiss, just like the Prince and Princess. In the end, the book closed again. The fairytale of realities is always in circular motion, like you butterfly, flipping and fluttering, dancing a perfect pitched clip and resting your wings gently in this romantic relation'.

After her poetic thoughts and imaginings, she would feel the need to ground herself again, to find some practical traditional onward thinking. This approach was hereditary, built into her system from witnessing and being exposed to hard manual farm work. The work that seemed never to stop. Elspeth's father, for as long as she could remember, got up early every day, in fact, before dawn. Having a smoke before breakfast, he would sit on the black wood stove, drink black tea, eat steak and eggs for breakfast, and then leave the house. Sometimes, he would only return right at dusk. Other times deep into the blackness of the night, his torch could be seen from the kitchen window, the light flickering from side to side. He was up early every day, 5am sharp, never bearing anything that was unsavory. Elspeth's mother cooked, cleaned, and when short of a helping hand, would dress like a man and sweep the shearing shed floors, round up the sheep and pretend to be a rouseabout.

Out there, there was no room for grief or strong emotion. To show any emotion was considered a weakness. Neither men nor women from her local area hardly ever shed a tear. They were the backbone of the days and nights of hard methodical steadfastness, nothing flimsy or untoward. And, that would never change. Poetry was not known by many of Elspeth's relatives and was considered an uppity and bumptious thing. Poetry was only for those who were of high society books. Many were too busy doing shed or manual work and enjoying a day's yarn to think much about reading books. Straight to the point, black and white and nothing in-between, this bland upbringing was another reason why Elspeth desperately needed her hut. It was a different life out there. Elspeth knew that she needed to live alone in the elements and feel the wildness of unknown destinations and unexplained habitat to actually know the bush. A glance from above and a fancy note was actually only a token gesture. To smell, touch, breath, and eat from the land and its fruits — both sweet and sour — was the only way to embrace the wilds that continually shaped and mystified the hut's surrounds and beyond, into the bush valleys, across the river, and onto the other side of the range. There were other beauties to enjoy out there. The white roses and light, bright rays were often streaming in gold. The unclogged, clear smell of the bush and the dry soil were also there amongst the soft, lovely, fresh mists of the late, long afternoon sea breezes — a crispness that surged across seven mountain ranges about three hours before the sun set, settling into the high country all the way from the coast. And, the first morning breath painted a silent, still healing throughout her body. But, the most beatified experience, besides the still atmosphere, was the dream of her own destiny. It was knowing that, in front of her, dressed in a fine satin yellow gown, beaded in peridot, Elspeth one day would dress as the wind queen — a blessed monarch, from the other side of the horizon who had formed song, poem, and prayers to fend off life's cruel curses.

Living in the hut gave Elspeth time to really think about each and every encounter that she had ever experienced, with every person to whom she had ever been associated with, in any way, big or small. She saw the lesson of relationship and isolation, thinking clearly about suffering and affliction. She learned how to adapt her thoughts toward the different life phases that a person had and to communicate what interactions come into play to aid smooth or rough transitioning. Peace and love seemed to dwell all around her in the natural surrounds. But, this did not extend so much from people. Although she adored her visitors, the feelings of peace and love came from nature and nature alone. Through the natural experience of being in the roots of the countryside, Elspeth learnt to look for no one except herself. When in need of a man, Cain was the one who filled an orgasmic necessity, and the union which bore her a son. Elspeth also enjoyed her gentle female interactions, which the intimacies of, can be left to the imagination. But, it was nature that she craved the most. It was the hand of God's scape that Elspeth learnt to have a soul and true friendship with, and to deepen her faith into the reservoir of the earth, combating any small hurt or doubt. Like fulfilling herself with the brilliance of a bursting orange, she accepted her own humanness and fate, never really trusting anyone outside of her own self. The act of being in nature so much cultivated Elspeth's personality. So much so, that she became a woman of much prayer and sanctity.

In the last dreaming of her life's breath, the visions and floating images in her mind, opened up the murmurs of his loving notes, the notes Cain left under the rock close to where they had always met. In his final note, he explained that the process of expression seemed to ease the cruel pain of not being able to marry Elspeth, and that by living in remote seclusion, his pain had become masked, especially when the clouds were so low. He felt his anguish disappear into them. The dream calmed her into the valley of treasured trees, the trees that had foretold of the wind queen's arrival from the waters, standing at the helm of the prominent horse and cart that rose from the flow of time. As the seasons turned and the natural springs dried up, people who were once of the opinion that they were better than Elspeth actually became humbled by her personal force, a force which was greater than any other female, and could not be trampled down by any other might. The Swallowtail butterfly also appeared again that night, and in the mellowness, positioned herself right next to the wind queen, who, eventually, was known as the one shaped in clouds, cumuli, who drifted into the nocturnal realms of the unknown.

Elspeth recalled a conversation between a man who came from a neighboring property and a woman who he had given his utmost trust. The man was explaining just what he was doing on the hill, just behind the hut on a day when rain was all around. Except it was not raining on the very top of the hill, which is where he was conducting velum tanning lessons for a few youngsters from the local area. It was like a miracle, he went on about the velum and how it had been soaked in lime for several days, attached to the frame, and was ready for scudding. The velum was a new inclusion in the rich man's daily doings, and he was preparing parchment from the young calf skins to write letters to the trusted woman, who was not a lover but a close friend from the parish activities committee. The committee organized days out for families and were full of fun things for the youngsters to do. They had their own horse races, ate lots of light, cream-filled sponge cakes, and drank homemade lemonade. There were pretty girls wearing homemade dresses and ladies who again wore gloves and hats. They never thought about anything other than wholesome things. They also learnt about traditional country crafts, like the making of paper from vitulinum. They were taught that the rain was not to dampen the paper that was being made. The woman seemed to accept the man's trusted opinions and thought the activity an important part in the young people's personal development.

Normally, it was only the 'to do', who had such lessons. After that, the sky blackened and the full, almost golden moon shine radiated the outline of the clouds, the contrasts of the nights were cool, unpredictable, and closed above the hut. By this time, the dwelling was surrounded by a white picket fence and could be seen clearly, even in the darkness, like the eye of a cat, fox or any other animal that would catch the full moon light and flicker in the depth of blackness. Elspeth had placed tea candle flowers to light the path, but there was a feeling of worthlessness all around, a feeling that frightened her. It was a decimate time of solitude, and the flimsy rags that hung on the windows as curtains did not hide the obvious cracks in the wearing wood walls. It was then that Elspeth became acutely aware of the old woman of many changing faces, who was known to steep her body in the putrid aromas and who looked for things that were just not real. Scorning the sight of anything young and lovely and eating nothing but scraps, the obnoxious crone could have been a chook or pig and was sent by the coven to the windy plains, to find Elspeth and take everything away from the lovely one. The hut, her respect, her son, her lovers, and her dignity — she was sent to steal everything.

Elspeth, however, was too clever and tripped her up on the path because, in the dark, it was easy to mask herself as a friend from another town. Pretending not to be scared in any way, Elspeth offered the evil woman an apple tart, poisoned by disgust. It was meant to bring her to her knees. When she eventually died, the wind queen, from the previous dream, smiled a mirror image from the other side of the picket fence. It was as if, when the first rays of the sun lifted into the majestic fields, for the first time ever, the cruel woman was gone — for a while anyway.

Three black scanty birds seemed to fight the wind change, but lost the battle and war against the torrential gales and gusts that never seemed to give an inch. They were over powering and dogmatic, seemingly not to give up on that day. They shook, knocked, and deliberately damaged the backcloth. The strong winds were vivacious beyond compare, the birds never had a chance. The rainbow girl who had stayed deep in the bush to protect herself from a shadowy past, for fear of being exposed by the winds, was battered and bruised by life's tragedy; staying under the rainbow was the best place for her. Also, the winds seemed to conjure up faces of those who peered across from the other side.

The hut was positioned in the most isolated area on the whole range. Nobody except the man who owned the property, where the hut had been tucked away, amidst his other fairly extravagant home and sheds, knew of its location. It turned out that an long-time fishing friend of her father's died. It was there, at the funeral, that she had learnt that he had spent 50 years alone in the same old hut.

He had been a kind, considerate man who was never scared of the environment, explaining to his few confidants that living in the country was a good way to pass time. 'It is people who propose dangerous problems and not the trees, ants, or cattle. Country life is good for the soul'. The bush he said was like a church reredos and had always been a safe haven for a single gent. The tree became silhouetted in front of the deep grey sky and this day, when sitting quietly in her hut, Elspeth remembered the man who was known only as Andy, telling her years before, that peace was worth more, much more than any other thing in the world and that every tree could, and did have a branch piece of its own to convey. It was about finding beauty in absolutely everything, and that peace and harmony had all sorts of magical gifts and wonders to offer every human being. Elspeth, drifting off to sleep in the old timber rocking chair that once belonged to Andy, started to lift from with herself, initially it was just a few inches and then she could see into the eyes of all the visitors, past, present and future who had ever visited the remote site. Their hearts lifted and rose them up to the top of the world, rising to the top of the mountain, seeing and feeling the transitioning between soul and dark, between what was and what would be. And knowing, always knowing, that in cloud shapes and letters she would see into the next day positively, and with a purpose that would be inspiring to all women.

And, on that day and every other, she would be strong, beautiful, and very powerful, like rain storms and thunderbolts of lightning that strike proficiently hard and with absolute precision. Elspeth was just a farm girl at heart.

From the door of the hut, and when often sweeping the uneven dusty floor, Elspeth could see things that other people would not see, aware of the wild and, at times, savage cats that often roamed a large area and were extremely territorial. If cornered, Elspeth knew they would even attack a human being. A long time ago, the wild cats would attack and eat the koalas. But, from around the area that she lived, the koala bears were all shot out in the 1900s. The cats, however, remained a big-time predator, continuing to prey on snakes, lizards, little joeys, possums, and all forms of small marsupials. One quick snarly cat could often be seen preying on an old farmer's son who Elspeth had never met. Working on detached plot of land, she never really knew his name, but had observed him tending his sheep day and night, no matter what the weather would bring. Seeing him go from one side of the large land area that was territorial to the cat, their eyes had never once met.

The farmer's son knew that the feline lived in a hollow log down near the boundary fence, and that other cats lived under in the corner of the back shelter shed. The shelter was full of manure and the smell of damp sacks. Elspeth wondered why he never approached her. She wondered why he was such a solitary person and why he seemed to be only in tune with nature, his farming, and nothing else. Elspeth could feel him when he was working — shrewdly, distantly, carefully, firmly, sternly, without reproach and without invite, sexual or otherwise. The farmer's son was, without interest in anything other than his work at hand. And, the cat knew this. While the farmer tended his sheep, Elspeth looked towards his figure, waving in the wind to his dog, whilst the wildness in the cat took a turn towards a small eagle that had struck prey. The cat leaped and the eagle lunged for her. Then, after a scratching fight, the cat and the eagle fell into a pool of blood. After that, it was clear that the vicious cat had devoured her day's repast. Sweeping away 'the mind', thought Elspeth, 'can show small snippets of places and time, some bloodied and others a cool wash, like my incomplete book of poetry, that sits within the smell of mothballs on a dusty bench. I will now garnish it with a pressed four-leaf clover. It will be a sign to the other guests who may visit that modern thought did transcend old style language. But, my love of ornate brooches will never fall into the claws of the wild cat.

Each metaphor in the book, when related to forbidden thought and harnessed by a man can spell passion, eroticism, and the scented yearning of masculine milk. But, that old farmer's son seems not to be interested in these types of poetic notions. Feeding cattle, sheep, and remaining solitary seems to be his path, where mine is here in the sanctuary of my hut, with my poetry and notions of love and many ideas about other lovers'.

A Grave Stone

Elspeth felt the coldest feelings after deserting her outside world, a world that was already isolated. But, after many months, moons, mornings, silent and boisterous comings and goings, and living in her hut for a long, long time, she realized that real salvation can only be found in the deepest of solitude. Including the valley of hope that sat below the warmth of the sun and was of the deepest red. When in its brightest orange and fully ablaze, it encapsulated the steep descent of jagged rock that cast a shadow onto the other side of the river. The full heat of the earth would then call Elspeth back to her original gravestone and the other graves that she knew to be located in the local area. Each grave, with or without a head stone, had its own meaning.

A day came when Elspeth found a pottery vase full of hatred sitting near the angel wings on a grave. It was disguised as a gesture of compassion towards a dead child, a child that was buried under the seraph. But, on that day, Elspeth was guided by a sense of serenity and protection which brought her to the middle of the circular burial garden. Without hesitation, she picked up the ugly looking vase and glancing across onto the flat plains and the treed gully, a somber and cool feeling took over her emotions. In a moment she decided, just like that, to throw the vase away from the child and the roses. The small crock really did have a bad feeling to it. The dead child, Elspeth knew, was being cared for in the great heavens by the child's blood grandmother. In a way, that was only instinctual to those related to the dead child.

The ridge near the cemetery was recovering from the blaze and the little matchstick trees gave the impression of a soft slope. A visual array of earth coverage gave the imprint of a paradise that lay beneath the dirt, beneath the sticks and under the wounds of the fire shadow. Wattle and eucalypt mellow scented the ground and tufts of grass gave a sensation of honesty, an honesty that made being awake and alive feel real and free. Like the leaves and gradual opening of the caves deep below the earth, the water hushed similar to that of an artesian bore swelling in the underground. The passing cloud coverage above had begun redeeming the earth and the tiny blue bells in the distance signified more than flowers.

Standing over the gravestone gave Elspeth the opportunity to reflect on her early life and the very beginning of her adult relationship with the bad femme, that encounter outside on the veranda. It gave her the opportunity to ask again, just why she had attracted the witch into her life, knowing that every relationship is a mirror image of something inside each person. Was she placid on the outer and problematic on the inside or was the jealous one simply latching onto Elspeth's elegant and gentle ways? Was she trying to steal her personality and wanting to mesh into her flesh and bones, destroying all that was Elspeth, so that she could pretend to be her — in other words, the witch in character wanted to become Elspeth. The answer came in the loud kee-ow … kee-ow … kee-ow squawking sounds of 15 yellow tailed black cockatoos. Symbolizing rain, they came with a spiritual message of joy and no worry. The black cockies' flight meant that it was time for love, and hope, and the hush of the valley that marred the sea green sky and the merging of two that no one would see until the end, like the meaning behind some words that become out of date.

There was another grave in the valley. It was at the base of the windy road that moved up towards the grange and held glazed eyes that were set in the slate rock. It was the scene of an embattled heart. The base stones were a cluster of rocks that told of severe past pain and hurt. Looking in from a distance on the forlorn grave were red faces of nothingness, faces that never felt the small speckles of rain on their hard brows. They were friends of the wicked occultist, and even though they tried like all hell, they could not destroy that sacred place behind the broken heart of Elspeth, the innocent girl. The battle continued beyond the grave, as the light shadows faded, opening and closing like butterfly wings that, in the end, left a gentle feeling of love and courtesy behind the black cockatoos' squawking laugh. Behind the outside mausoleum, voices and memories resounded in the density of the stone crypts, of what was once the busy country area post office. In the beginning, it was the home of the bad one. The massive fireplace and large sweeping verandas were all reminiscent of early Australian dwellings. Inside, an eerie feeling clasped the throat of any person who dared walk into the house. With exchanging exterior rooms that would disappear and then return, it was a confusing place to endure.

The long-gone children's playful laughter hung high in the six poplar trees above the tin roof, an ever-present reminder that life is always drifting forward and calls children into the wider world, beyond what was known to be trusted and true. The early values of raising children like to be seen and never heard were of detriment to any child who mistakenly came across the frowning bad one. But, most of the children knew that if caught by the nag, she would lock them away in her own cupboard. Eventually, they all ran away back to their own gardens.

Elspeth knew to withstand her contaminated guttural utterances, she would need to stand strong in life and strong in absolute death, in order to have her name imprinted on her own gravestone and words that spoke of forthright diligence and uncompromising faith. To do this, a soul friendship with the self was needed first and foremost. She trusted only within and did not seek people outside her own self, for the outer natural world fulfilled her every sensory perception. It was the simple things that made her mostly outdoor existence feel nourished. It made her feel sweet and happy, inside herself and she enjoyed being in the Swallowtail butterfly's flutter. It was a sweet, cerise and mouth-watering joy being in nature. After so much time amongst the graves of those who had come and gone, Elspeth had no fear of death or dying and realized that life, looking in at the cowboys who smoked tobacco plant, or running the hare's circle before it found itself burrowed again in the hollow of a dead tree, was better than worrying about old age. Watching for the signifiers of the changing weather patterns was more interesting than being caught up in the beak-faced neighbors gossip, the tripe talk that tried to allude to her hopefully inevitable downfall. The nattering tongues were full of absolute nonsense, and Elspeth, like the Swallowtail butterfly, used her flippy, fluttery, butterfly dance to warm the shaded light on the gravestone and perfectly pitched her flight high above them.

Reaching her thoughts back to the women of early settlement, Elspeth thought to herself. 'They had no choice but to embrace the harsh currents of the wilderness and accept whatever fate was positioned at their feet. They had to wrestle with the fear of a snake bite, no food, loneliness, and sick children while the men went out on horseback for many months'. She looked at the wombats, pigs, kangaroos, and many varieties of birds, who, after some time, knew that Elspeth was of no threat to their livelihood. Early women would have felt these exact experiences too, and also knew that spread throughout the high plains were many gravestones of those who did not make it to the high peak of their own lifeline. There were many gravestones that related to the half-cast and full-blooded days — the stolen ones that were never supposed to be found.

There were lots of graves up there that had their own way of saying things, lots of different meanings and lots of cultural imprints to decipher. After many years of walking across the grave sites, Elspeth could read the meanings of those graves. And, with respect to those lives that they represented, she would fall to one knee and pray.

The small gulch was a lush fertile emerald wetland and the natural spring water rose from within the earth and was squishy and squashy under Elspeth's feet. The ground cover was saturated with a water source and small pools of black slushy soils were finished with tiny pretty wildflowers in dainty touches of red, purple, and yellow. The damp, leafy eucalypt enclosure moistened the aura of her being, as she looked up towards the relic graves that were found near the caves. The deep mountain holes were tucked away at the back of the crevasse, and had arisen and formed not from a tremor and constant swelling sea, but rather, small pools of underground stream water. Made black, sanguine, sepia, and cream yellowish, the caverns were cultivated by the ebb and flow of the fresh water and buried deep in the earth's surface. This had become a resting place of the sacred bodies for many tens of thousands of years. Out of site, and protected from the rains and sleeting winds, the bodies of high stature had ultimately disintegrated into skeletal bones, and had been placed into the chink of the levelled rock by their own descendants' chasm. They were never meant to be discovered, and the intrusion of bleached skin unsettled the beauty of the inner cave. The outer bones laid a curse on any hand who dare touch them. Elspeth never laid a hand on those bones. The rites of burial, she knew, were as much alive after death as they are on the day that the earth claims back any blood.

No salt of the earth type person could ever understand or read the clues that lead to the next tree, spider, or snake. This is the coolest and most difficult land and the very hardest to walk. When walking towards the opening, Elspeth spoke to her butterfly friend about the site saying, 'Those who do happen to reach its inner lush sanctuary, through the small rocky gaps, can easily slip between the large heavy rocks. These are the ones, the ones who will come forward with the next set of storytelling and in some cases, tremulous life lessons, no matter how hard. Pigment colours of the boulder hold the vital signs of what happens'. Deeper in thought, Elspeth went on to explain further. 'After the initial fire ceremony, the three bodies perished in the blank stillness of the black hole. The blankness could not be penetrated by noise, wind, rain, or sun. There seemed to be nothing in the grave for a long time. The big fish fossil on the exterior mainstay rock showed that the dead laid there, were actually from the sea. The one green tree gave them a fresh existence in the secluded resting place. Other signs of the carefully laid gravestone included the feeling of it being the last site. There were Swallow's flying close by and there was a resting ledge that was a baby's outdoor cradle also imprinted. Other fossils included rat and snake configurations and sea creature imprints such as a small fish, large lobsters, and sea horse'.

The butterfly lead Elspeth to and onto the next gravestone; it was where she stood and prayed. It was the resting place of her own dear grandmother. The story that lead to her heart breaking, but inspiring death. Positioned alone and near a lush garden of evergreen shrubbery next to the water fountain, at Raina's river of life, her grandmother's life dream of purity and freeness was expressed in a piece of blue stone. Small daisies graced the top of the headstone piece and a flowered daisy chain encircled a little angel of reverence. A collection of native banksia wildflowers and herbs were there always for Elspeth to grasp. *At Peace, I will be, as I sleep; And Awake, in Love, I will become, when you and I eclipse each other again.*

Like a lot of women, she experienced pain in early childbirth, with no support. Elspeth knew that many women struggled with the intense and intolerable pain of bearing children alone. Simply being pregnant and having a baby could mean death. Elspeth's grandmother carried the loss of twelve miscarriages and the death of a full gestation baby.

There was one consolation in the losses: After many pangs of deep heartache and physical depletion, she became so deeply experienced in pregnancy and childbirth, that an overwhelming compulsion to help any poor heavily laden single girl with no resources to have her bubby with dignity, became obvious and clear. It was her life direction to become the country area midwife and she did so for many, many years.

A woman of the stick, even if Elspeth's grandmother had access to the local hospital, she would very often dig a bush hole, cover it with fresh and soft grasses; adding red soil if she could. She encouraged the women to crouch down and give birth in a hole which had many benefits offered by the earth. In treed culture, the act of birthing was eased by the natural pull of the earth, comforting to mother and baby. It was a place for women only, and the laying of hands on the woman's body would help draw the baby from the dreaming into the earth experience. Easing the contraction pains, the inclusion of massaging black wattle, beach bean, and rock fuchsia mashed root infusions were rubbed with crushed nut and then washed with leaf. Also, the white woman's wives' tale, of boiling hot cloth and towels, over a fire, to then place on the birthing woman's lower back, were used in conjunction with steaming the baby and mother. Then, she rubbed both mother and baby with lemongrass and ragwort leaf to strengthen the spirit after the birth.

After a lot of years had gone past, some of those children born in the scrublands would knock on Elspeth's grandmother's door, seeking their own and new recollections of the reality and happenings of their birth place. Met with a gleeful eye, this confirmed that a happy spirit remained in the heart of the woman who had delivered them, for she knew, without being told, the name and age of each and every child that she had ever delivered. The grandmother's simple dwelling was made of weatherboard and nothing in the house was ever changed or moved in all those years. Everything remained the same. Every speck was immaculately cleaned. There were the same matching bedspreads, cups, plates, and every photograph was in its exact position for so many years. Elspeth's earliest memories were testimony to this. No updated furnishings were ever purchased. The cushion covers that she made looked flat through the perspex glass entry. The modest woman remained untouched by any demand to be anything other than who she was. The only thing that ever changed was her deepening faith. The staid, but welcoming feelings in the house made the visitors wonder about the midwife, her life, and what she had done to become so gentle, kind, and unassuming, with no thought towards materialism or self-gain. After her death, some would seek permission to visit the peaceful grave site and there they would feel the lapping of the water's edge.

Their own spirit seemed to somehow become fully entrenched into the blue gravestone, as they remembered the woman who used her own loss and pain to bring life and comfort to others who lived less than ordinary lives. They did not want to live in the shadows of the past, but rather celebrate their own reverence of being born into a hole in the earth which eventually would reclaim every thought, intention, and action that they would create, experience, and perform in the world. There was a common bond of fellowship between the returning souls, and the threads of their coming together became enmeshed in the alluring power of their dreams, ownership of place and a sense of being related to a particular totem within the barren region. In themselves, they could feel the sun lift them to the early day, like the eagle, flying with great speed to let Elspeth know that she should revere her grandmother's goodness in every piece of bark that she could find. She should exalt her work and character within the reach and realms of her saintly river retreat, and show the good, loving people, the hard-old yard hands, a gentle array of words that would span across the skies. The night stars flickered when her arms stretched towards the heavens. The day glimmers of sunlight leap into her heart, filling in with the promise of miracles.

Within her heart space, Elspeth always felt peace when meeting the babes her grandmother helped deliver, inviting them to always return to Raina's River and her Grandmother's precious blue water gravestone.

There was a yarn about a young white horse's grave site. It is said to be up at Dead Horse's Gap between the mountain ranges somewhere upon the open plains. It was marked only by the spooky feeling that a person feels when standing so high above the earth when the night winds blow, and a feeling of being able to ride the seas of life in any terrain. Being dead or alive becomes overwhelming; there was no holding back the elements of the powerful unknown. The brumby was not the bravest, strongest, or daring of the pack, but, it was the most graceful. It was hunted by a man who wanted obsessively to give the horse to his eight-year-old daughter Mona. The white star horse had fled the lower plains right at the beginning of winter, knowing that she may not survive, but feeling it was better than being caught in the clutches of a rich man's spoilt daughter who would treat her with nothing other than extreme hatred. The girl was known for her spiteful tongue and greediness. There was nothing ever honey sweet about her. The only hope that the creature of intuitive spiritual guardianship had was that the cherubs who often rode bareback would canter her to the next silver holy plain.

Needing to reach the top of the mountain ridge before the mid-winter snow, the brumby met compacted hard snow on the ground, frozen river creeks and trees like ghostly rivals. For at the gap, there were no friends to share in the heat of danger. It was a run that she would certainly not survive, considering that the snow had fallen early and fallen heavily. The slow, ascending trail was still visible at the bottom of the second ridge. The horse stopped and knew that not too far behind was the man. The putrid smells of his smoky beard and worn leather jacket were on the tip of the horse's nose, and for once, she gathered all strength with no fear. Up she went, with big strides of canter towards the icy trees which hide the plain on the other side. At the far end of the open snowy former glacier field, there was a limestone ridge and a beautiful monument it was, when lightly covered with snow. Flickers of shale grey green and blue were patterned into the ledge, which was a forerunner to a significant rock hill that protruded the landscape. The horse knew that a decision needed to be made at this T-junction of her attempted escape. To stop now meant she would be rounded up by the hunter who was also riding a fast brumby. The brumby was originally from the far south mountains, a big dark brown horse who had been trained to defeat no matter what.

The man was another pig hunter, and the cruelest of them all. He could not control his drink, and spent many nights sitting around campfires, bragging to others like himself of his greatest catch, the white star brumby. But, in the background of their conversation were the cherubs who held the life meaning of the white horse, biblical in essence, the horse sent to give an understanding of the true word. When she was young, the horse always knew that she was of ancestry to a pack let go by a man who owned a lot of wild horses, way back when he realized he had too many horses to look after, and did not have the feed or the men to support and rear them. This was before the time of the First World War. Running with the heart winds of the great mountain ranges as a young foal, she was never at peace with herself. There always seemed to be the fight and flight syndrome to cope with, forever fleeing from the dangerous hunters, forever trying to hide. A white horse can only camouflage herself so much amidst the snows, and even then, a soft snow of white powder fall was needed to just lightly tarnish the eggshell tone of her coat. When there was no snow, the other brown, fawn, and greyish chargers could blend into the natural scale so much more easily. These were the horses of the heroic bushrangers.

Over the years, the beautiful horse had suffered nasty gashes to her legs, paining hunger, when not being able to stop for verdure, and the loss of love and friendship because she was forever moving on. This, however, did not stop her from being determined to fulfill the role that she was born to perform — to be the great word of the open spaces. And, like the strong horse that she was, as the light snow gently settled on the shrubbery near the frozen water behind the mound, and all that could be heard were the sound of the Shrike-thrush, peeling bark off the snowy gums and singing, purr - quee - yule, the horse fled the earth to what is now her grave site, cantering straight through the hill of rock that brave horse went. The story goes that once inside the ice cavern, she grew wings and ascended the next leg of the journey, flying back to where she came from. It was whispered that the small graceful wise one could not lose her rights to be a wandering beacon of fidelity and upholding faithfulness to the ways of natural living. Living a life of emotional stability, untangled by the constant overseeing of any man's hand, and living by the energies of the earth were her goals. To be caught up and caged by a spoilt brat of a girl would have meant a slow death of indignity. Cantering towards a sure death was a better way to go.

At first light, it looked like a serene chapter from a fairy tale. There appeared to be a certain magic in the colours highlighted by first day. The atmosphere made every aspect fresh. Pretty pinks and golden hues opened the farm setting and the stirring breath from the wildlife that grazed the grasses included foxes, rabbits, kangaroos, wallabies and wombats moving around freely and without hesitation. The animals sensed that this was the place to be. They would move close to the house and the playful wilds in the distant morning mist and were undisturbed by anything. There were chooks too, clucking around the shed. Harmonious it was, but there was something wrong with the scene. There was no sign of human life. Looking through all the natural elements, there was no man, woman or child in sight. Beyond the horse yard, near the side post, there was an imprint in some shaded mud of a shoe. The old deserted farm house had lay abandoned now for some 50-odd years and why, Elspeth never really knew. It was a mystery that people from far and wide had speculated on for years. The tailor who lived and worked for many years in the township, said that the house was left standing by just one old man, a person whom he believed to be the last living relative of a couple of miners, who had immigrated from the potato fields of Ireland to strike it rich up at the now abandoned Kiandra gold fields.

Those two were lucky with their panning and found a fair few gold nuggets worth some many pounds. With one hunk, they purchased the house and settled there for a while. Later, one married and had two sons. The other never married but became the local minister. Later, after his religious studies were finished, the man of the gospels moved into the Church Monastery. The house which always had a golden glow was kept as 'fresh as a button' by the wife of the household. The two sons grew up to hear stories about how their father and his God-fearing brother had found nugget after nugget of gold. They purchased the house and a fair few other local opportunities, such as a couple of land portions and several thousand sheep. They were the early ones who had established the region's welfare and social community, but, every Friday night, off they would go to enjoy a cold beer or two or three or more, raving on about the early days and their mining explorations. Up in the now gnashed out fields, that so much resembled the hills and in winter, the freezing cold of Ireland, the similar environment was what attracted so many of their counterparts. These fellow ordinary Irish men were not only lured to Australia by the stories of large gold finds, but prospecting was appealing because of the many wide open spaces and grazing opportunities.

Over they came in their thousands; some found gold, many did not, but all were of the same class — mostly poor, uneducated, church going, and full of promise for a better life away from the Irish famine and depression that had wrought devastation and, in many instances, brought a slow death to many families. Scrubbing the earth with water and digging large open-cut geological forces, stacking rocks, and heeding all sorts of obstacles, the harshest and coldest wind storms and poverty that reigned in abundance was found here. The mixtures of cultures was often a confusing and difficult interpretation of the very beginning of the new integration of many societies. There were over 20,000 people working out there in those fields; it seems strange that they were missed, simply overlooked by some. It may have been that the people there were thought of as just gold diggers and not really immigrants. The Chinese and Irish were the most dominant nationalities, with Europeans and some Islanders crossing after that. They formed New Chum Hill Town at Kiandra and within the now isolated mountain patterns, fragments of their living can clearly be seen, such as old wheels, blacksmiths, and decimated hut sites giving direction to the earth's scars and tunnelling where sluicing had occurred up from the water course ways.

There were fights, tears of homesickness and devastation when the realization that gold bullion was not to be found by all. The mineral reefs, however, had another purpose, another meaning other than just the sign of prospective golden wealth. There were signs of steep topography and an indication that in years to come, those deep-rooted hills, after being raped, would become a treed graveyard. After a series of fires, the mountain ash resembled a ghostly huntress' web, a web of white deception that would be cast across the ranges and made any onlooker feel insignificant in its compelling and unnerving awesomeness. Nobody would dare fight that grave of death isolation. Elspeth knew the reef of scaring well.

But one of the saddest gravestones in the district was that of a young man, livered with growths in his young body. The carcinomas seemed to age him over night. The boy was a naturalist, a gentle pastoralist who had already lost both his parents in mining accidents. His site was left alone on the forsaken hill, that later others would trek hundreds of miles to find. It was a few miles to the southern side of the main range, hidden mostly by overgrown tussocks in summer and never seen in winter, as it was covered by the lofty and haughty hails. Where he came from was the highest flat plain on the prominence.

Difficult to grow anything or farm way up there, he still seemed to produce the finest wools and richest beef. The homelands that he cultivated were tastefully, but not boastfully decorated, and a large wreath always dwelt at the top of the stairs in the small cottage that he occasionally shared with the rich publican. A remembrance of the gentle push his father once gave him towards keeping his faith strong, the wreath was never taken down. No matter what outsiders brought to his calm and collected world, the young man was focused and never without conservative headlong rational. 'Why, why, cried his sad mate from near Currawong Station, who had ventured the route following the ravens from Delegate and up through the wilds of The Bundian Way towards the peak ranges, a place that he and his friend had gone exploring together years before. Both knowing one day, the secret track, that was a ceremonial trail between the mountain alps and the whales at Eden, would be the source of great interest to modern scientists and alike. Up he went, into the richness of the changing lands, high into the Bogong Country. On arrival there, he found his good, fun-loving mate had died, in pain and suffering. It was then that he told the Publican who was also there the secret of secrets. 'He was deeply in love with a girl from the other side of the district. She was the loveliest of lasses that he had ever seen.

But, it was just not meant to be, because his friend had become ill before he could propose marriage, and something else had stopped him too. He had heard that she also lay with women and had a type of independent streak in her blood that he was unfamiliar with. The woman was one he would not know how to tame'. To his mind, a woman so attractive needed protection from the harms of the world and was surely innocent of and to, the wicked ways of human desire. Surely, one so magnificent in looks would not delve herself into such places, places that he was raised to believe as being totally and completely forbidden. 'My friend, my mate, he confided in me that once he felt too weak to offer her the protection that she needed, and that all the bad things that he had heard through the mail were lies'. Elspeth just sat back and thought into his words. 'Dreams of purity are just that, dreams. Every person has their own way of seeing the world. At least the lad died with his dream'.

'What do you think, Elspeth' months after his burial, the lad's friend asked her quietly, as he tried to come to terms with his loss. 'I never met him, but knew of a goodness that came from his work on the land. I knew he was single and without a family, but thought him out of my reach. I am sorry for your loss and it is unlikely that anyone will ever grow pasture as rich and fruitful as his, or that anyone will ever again grow that fine wool either. I think, really I do, that he may have been touched by the grace of the high country up there, really I do. He was a special one whom I had observed a lot, but did not understand him or his personal feelings'. The Publican of few words said nothing.

In spring, only the five girls' hats were found. It looked as though they had been placed in a mushroom fairy ring, as if there had been a whispering fairy dance of secrets and songs that had been the sisters' last time together, before they fluttered to the next kingdom. There seemed to be more worldly and unaffected dainty bush fragrances in just that one area, the place where the hats were perfectly circled. The ribbons, silk roses, and twigs that adorned the hats were there, just quietly bending in the wafts of subtle warm air. The straw on the hats also seemed untouched, as if they had been tucked away under a ledge, away from the melting slushy snow. Elspeth had thought that perhaps the fairies had flown with the hats and then waited for the family to arrive. Nobody would ever know what actually happened to the girls wearing the snow shoes after they had left the care of their endearing, but not very intelligent mother. For what type of a mother would wave her five daughters off in the snow, with no trace of an adult to watch over them? It was said that the girls looked beautifully incarnate and perfectly embodied before they left. Icy rose cheeks and dressed in long handmade cream lace petticoats and light woollen checker skirts of differing colours in maroon, dark blue, and chocolate brown. Each had a flannel long sleeved short, light blue and a bottle green cardigan. All this was covered by heavy woollen coats with puffed sleeves, linen lining, and wide starched cuffs.

Fluffy white gloves, with matching scarves had seen the girls readied for the adventure of their lives. 'Take - this - all - of - you - and - eat - this - is...' the depressing mass was said by the Irish priest at the hut sight. The father of the girls and his family stood away from the mother, who was there alone, and was not wearing a hat, dying in herself as the plain wooden caskets were lowered into the ground. The grieving mother said that her five girls had now returned to God's womb.

But, what actually did happen the day that their loving, but not so thought bearing mother waved them goodbye? Well, the little lamb told the fairy who had gathered the hats and circled them into what was to be named as the circle mushroom gravestone. It was rumoured right across the top of the high mountains and into the fairy dust, that the girls had arrived at the high slope at noon, alone, and with no adult to look after them. They took their sandwich lunches from their pockets and sat on the two big icy rocks overlooking the skyline on the southern ridges. Smoke from the mountain huts filled what otherwise would have been a crisp blue clear perfect day.

The smell of smoke and haze was familiar to the young women and reminded them of what it was like sitting outside near the woodpile, waiting for their daddy, who never seemed to return home from his long drive. The twins sat on one boulder and the other three sat nested together, happy that their mother had trusted them. They had felt above anyone and anything in the whole wide world.

Then, all of a sudden, and out of the blue, the mountain began to shudder and move within. For an instant, the girls thought the loud rumbling sound may have been in their imagination. Then, to the left, they could see snow sliding, and in a direct swoosh of freezing air it swished them up, plunging them to their death and suffocating them, breaking the limbs of their growing bodies. It was quick, disastrous and the giving way of the mountains compacted snow shelves, did not allow the five, yet-to-mature voices time to scream, or even feel a hint of fight or fear. It was all in their imagination. They were waved off to their fate, gone forever to the circle hat mushroom gravestone.

Sometimes, on big long droves, for whatever reasons, the men just had to go. Sickness, injury or the one reason that was not discussed much at all was alcohol poisoning. There was always a man by the name of Jackey Jackey. He was the black run about and none of the other men had much time for him, holding a similar role to a shed rouse about. But, Jackey Jackey was a very smart one, and could work as a tracker, relaying the best way to move the cattle forward and into protected alcoves or natural holding paddocks, just in case of unexpected flood or blazing fire. Jackey Jackey could read the sky and the tracks, and knew the trees as markers, indicating when to stop, refresh, drink, and sleep. Jackey was always referred to as a 'Johnny come lately, or late starter at everything he did'.

He used bush medicines to heal and kept the men's spirits up by telling them all the dreaming stories of the Wulguru. A jack of all trades, every droving party had a Jacky Jacky. Being told by the head horseman what to do, all the time, his jobs on the trail were lowly and unfulfilling, but, never once did he complain, choosing instead to tobacco up his pipe and sit with himself and smile. Drawing in the knowledge that when it all came to a head, and the top horsemen were not sure just which way to go, how to quickly move the large droving team under the shade of the biggest and blackest thunder clouds, or where to find crystal clear water when thirsty, including how to hunt bush tucker when starving. They would quickly call on Jackey Jackey. Being left behind to clean up camp and then ride like the wind to catch the group, the droving hand about was also given the task of digging the grave of any man who suddenly died out there on the unbeaten track. The body would be wrapped in a blanket, still clothed and literally thrown in. The landing thump would mean that the corpse had found its resting place and those men gathered around would take off their Bushmen's hat and hold it with their left hand over their hearts.

That was it; no priest meant no prayer service. Then, Jackey Jackey and another helper would fill in the grave quickly. The next step was to build a simple grave timber structure to show of the rum death. They used four logs placed in a square around the hole dug and four medium size v-shaped tree trunks to hold four more logs to enclose the grave. It could stand one meter high or a middle log shelving would really make the mark of the man, three meters high. Then, a piece of plain wood with the man's first initial, full stop and surname would be nailed to the log above the man's head. A simple cross was all that was etched above his name. The next harrowing task given to Jackey Jackey was to ride 'bare back' in whatever direction, to find the widow of the man and give her the sad news about the death of her beloved spouse. He would tell her of the exact whereabouts of her late husband's grave. However, the grave was often so very far away, that she never had any hope of visiting the site to show her last and final respects. Instead, in what became the tradition of the drover's widow, a snow gum seedling would be planted near to the families dwelling. Each year on her late husband's birthday she would pick a flower, any flower and press it in a book of remembrance. The growing family would have a picnic by the growing tree and if a new marriage was to come, it would happen adjacent to the tree. The real gravestone was the snow gum.

On one of the few visits to the backwoods hut, Elspeth explained to her young granddaughter, some many years later and just before she died, the real meaning of the gravestones. 'My darling girl, one of whom I may not see to grow into the flourishing beauty of womanhood, it is important to read the signs of lives gone before you, to reflect on your relationship to them, to learn from them, no matter how poor, rich, indifferent or insignificant they may have been. Take heed of these old wise words and study the gravestones of many. From this you will understand the many varying chapters that a person's life can in script'. Elspeth walked the many gravestones and knew so much about the passing of those lives and never wanted these to be forsaken in what she knew would be a modern world full of materialism, disrespect, and the waste of a good many warm homely cups of tea. So, on she went. 'There are so many differing gravestones in the area to consider. Many, in my young years were integral to daily living and, in a way, helped people to get about their daily business, being referred to, in general conversations, as a way of capping time and acknowledging other events and historical happenings'. At the time, her granddaughter was only four years old, but nodded in understanding of every word. 'Yes, Nanna, love you'. Hence, the gravestone chapter of my life.

✧ ✧ ✧

A lure was set, a trap for Elspeth. It was disguised as a flourishing rose garden. It was well designed by the bad one's landscape architect. It had a clear, covert purpose, which was to lure the beautiful Elspeth into the middle of the garden bed. It was planned so that as she walked through the garden to admire the roses, the rich thick soil beneath her feet would give way. With that, she would plunge to her death, falling many yards below into a pool of lic- infested, warm water, putrid in smell and slimy with bat faeces. The garden was meant to be a grave with no escape and certainly no redemption. Death at the bottom of the pit was imminent. The garden was planted near the town hall, encompassed by a decorative style.fence. Over many seasons of cultivation, the garden had gathered such momentum, that it became the talk of many country ladies' luncheons.

But, after many years of living alone, Elspeth had developed extra sensory perceptions that were beyond clairvoyance. On the day that she decided to visit the garden, she soon glimpsed the top of the flowers and instantly she knew that something was very wrong. The gate that was normally shut had been left open, and there was an extra strong fragrance drifting towards Elspeth. This was a clear message from the flowers that something was terribly wrong. Heightening her sense of awareness towards the one single flower, Elspeth could see that it had obviously been placed in the centre of the foot path.

It had not fallen hard, there was no damage to the petals and it had a conspicuous feel about it. The witch was lurking and lingering on the other side of the town hall that sometimes posed as a cinema and other times a tea hall for flower shows. Elspeth decided to call upon some of her own magic. This was not black magic, it was a white dove prayer and, in a flicker, she would.once again metempsychosis herself into the great eagle bird, opening her great wings and keeping low to the ground, seeking out the wicked one. She hunted her scent back into the garden. It was fast, it was without hesitation and through the gate she ran, tripping over her black habit into the centre of the garden.

Thump to the bottom of the well. It was almost the last recollection in the gravestone chapter and pretty much the end of the evil powers that the witch woman cast out into the world of naturalness. The sinful witch who had gone to so much trouble to try and capture Elspeth by laying long thistle over the hole and covering it with the soil, thought for sure, and without a doubt, that Elspeth would end up being drowned in the bottom of a dirty well. Meaning for her to step into the soft black soil, she would never expect to be harrowed down by the big bird. The bird was clever and used the creepiness of the increasingly persistent winds to deliver the chase towards the garden.

Elspeth went on to recollect to a group of those visiting ladies' groups from the Cross, these women had come to hear about the earliest memories she had, living a busy life out in the back paddocks. These lovelies were from the Sydney Branch, and were really keen to try and help remote families who needed support with their children's educational needs by supplying books, pens, and school bags through their charitable funds.

'It was one of the saddest days, and one from my very earliest memories that I will never forget. I remember that there was an old saddled mare looking in from the next grounding at the ever-flowing stream of walkers. We were meandering through the wide treed path, that was a natural ecclesiastical sanctum. There was a troop of tearful young mourners, heads dropped behind the simple bare coffin that was carried by four young men, people that I had never seen before.

The ground was harder than ever on that day, and the cold winter and grey afternoon kept us rugged in our drab grey school coats, dark beanies, and stockings that caught burrs in the long tussocks and pricked grasses. All of us children were either of lower, middle class, or poor. There was only one girl of affluence within the walking group and she wore a long white crochet dress and an expensive white coat. Her hat and boots were matching and looked to shine. Who she was is something that I will ponder on until this very day. The myrrh that swung in the thurible chained our thoughts together; even though we were free after the longest requiem sermon in the world. The holy smoke was a reminder that God was everywhere and knew all our thoughts, words, and actions.

Again, that was a day I will never forget; it was the sorriest day around here. As a child, I think it was the first day that I had actually felt sadness. It was a grief so deep and thick and painful that it gored right into the pit of my stomach. It was a really terrible day, and there was a lurking feeling of decimation and hopelessness floating all around. It was very, very difficult to try and comprehend that a good man, a wonderful teacher, and the kindest soul that I had ever met was never coming back.

The stern Irish priest reminded us 50 or so youngsters that we should rejoice in life and think only of the positive things that Mr Bayshire had brought to our lives. He told us clearly to be aware that one day we would all die, so it was best for us not to pass judgement and be strong with no tears and no fear, unless we were hiding a terrible sin. If that was the case, we would need to confess the very next day after the funeral. After the service at the Cross Roads Church, and the long drawn out Requiem mass which held a sermon about purgatory and being absolute in every thought and action, we were all given penance before commencing the walk behind the coffin.

We needed to move in a line two by two, moving towards the cemetery across the other side of the river. We had to cross, single file, onto the small and partially broken wooden bridge. The unstable bridge was rickety and worn out. Especially frightening were the rotting wooden tree trunks that pillared the planks and railings. The deep and rushing river was running and washing below and there were no shallow parts in our area. It was then, as a child, that I first called on the real power of prayer. It was also the day that I really felt, if the bridge were to give way, that I could actually die. I would be swept away forever to the bottom of the cold icy Snowy River. I would most likely hit my head on a rock, scar my knees and elbows, and drown a frightful death, swirling and twirling until my body would be trapped under a deep, water ledge rock.

However, that did not happen and we proceeded, ever so slowly, behind the coffin of our much-loved teacher. Mr Bayshire was the best teacher who ever taught us, and he had died a mysterious death. In those days, it was rude to talk about people's medical conditions, and how or why they had passed away. Looking back on those very early days, Mr Bayshire was only a young man and much later on in years when reading his elegy now, I realise that he was just 36 years of age.

He was a young, fun, and genuinely loving teacher, who had taught us all so much. He was a gentle spirit and a great role model to all us young ones, whose gravestone is forever garnished with fresh mountain flora'. The Red Cross ladies did not clap. They just stared, as if in a trance, after listening to the aging woman in the rocking chair that hung as a gaunt shadow in the passage of their own thoughts.

It was said that God took them young – a very young mother and her two small children, one was four and the other, two years of age only. Alone, the three of them were at the whim of the isolated world. They lived out the back of Rocky Ridge, near the bend in the running creek in absolute poverty. Nobody, absolutely nobody, ever visited them. As both children were born out of wedlock, the three were inconsequential in the minds of the whole community. But, worse than being illegitimate, they were born to two different fathers. Both conceived after wild nights of consuming large amounts of distilled homemade brew at a singing shanty house. It was a shocking disgrace in the eyes of the most fearing, grace saving, and prayer abiding people. The young woman was referred to as the 'back creek tart' and her children, 'those two little toads'. Standing now is what is referred to as the fireplace gravestone. Whatever possessed the young mother, nobody will ever know. The chimney and ashes remain and a few blackened pots and three names scratched into the soot: Esme, Wander, and Ruth. There was a lonely black feeling of death that surrounded the burnt place. A man similar to a chimney sweep came late every night to try and cleanse the pain of the indignity of the woman's life, every night, climbing in, out, and around the damp, cold stone sweeping the resonance of the three saddened lives left to rot on the in the flames of the red combustion. But soon after, he did not bother going back again.

In changing times and before the three deaths, the woman had worked in the local store. The shop was sunk with the flooding of the town, and it is whispered it was there that her identity was fully realised by the town clerk. The clerk was a person of authority, who acted as an intermediate between the policeman and the judge. 'That person came to this area under a false name, she snuck in late one night, and lived in her sick dying cousin's back wood room, where she gave birth to her first brat. After about three months, the confinement became too much and she went out, got drunk with the inn keeper's son and fell pregnant again. The inn keeper's son was forbidden to marry the girl he was forever in love with'. The Clerk made a public announcement. The Judge was a hard man of no leniency and ordered that she leave the respected town with her illegitimates; nobody wanted them around here. For a while, there was an elder, a good aboriginal woman who would help the destitute girl and take her warm tea, another caring lady from the town church would bake scones, and flush them up with jam and cream. That was all those three had to eat, a Devonshire tea, except for a goat herdsman, who took one of his milkers and showed her how to milk. Unfortunately, that was not enough to sustain the uneducated woman and her babies. As winter began to set in, and the ground was icing with frost, there was no real comfort.

The woman had no skills to light a fire and it was a fluke if she even managed to get one started. As soon as the fire was blazing, smoke choking through the chimney, both small bodies were flung onto the coal. After that, the whole cottage caught alight and today the only remains are the gravestone fireplace hearth. But, then again, nobody really cared about the 'back creek tart' or her two little brats and some just snubbed their noses, shrugged their shoulders, and gave no thought to who the mother really was — all except for the eccentric town drunk.

A prominent news reader gave a moving broadcast, and spoke with a sincerity that will never be forgotten. Those two children never did experience hearing the rattling sounds of the small cold bottles of milk that were enjoyed by all the other littles for morning tea. They never knew the excitement of the first time their bank book was stamped by the teller at the Bank of NSW Wales. The bank was architecturally designed with the head office located in Sydney's inner city, Broadway. They were never to experience the first episode of Bellbird, Playschool, or Adventure Island. They had no fun or excitement to come home to.

One day, in years to come, she will stand on the town hall stage in the small municipality, that, some fifty years previously, had moved to higher ground to avoid a water fill. There, she will step forward from the past. In her heart, reciting the prayers of her father before her, baby in arms, wrapped in a new white shawl, with an edge sweeping the dusty floor boards, she will wear a crispy white blouse and long, slightly A-lined skirt, black shoes, walking as graceful as her grandmother's prayer in a flat straw hat with a black ribbon tie. From the steeple she will reign. And, she will rise, footings and all, out of the slimy waters, to remind those that sunk the town that there was not a word of truth in what they did. Although the spirit of the community was was moved away to further hills, the woman will send one of her disremembered daughters to reveal the place where one of the world's most sacred prayers will be offered. It will be a moving time of revelation, one that the simple people, the backbone of this country won't be able to dismiss. The substance of the town's essence that slowly filled under the waters had become a gravestone. All things of reminisce importance were gone, lost. It was the saddest time. Over a period the people looked on as abandoned trucks, old cars, sheds, and all the buildings in the main street slowly vanished under the newly formed water catchment.

After a few months, nothing could be seen, and some did not mind if a few small things were gone, like bad thoughts and feelings or memories of serious incidents. Luckily the church was moved on a truck and forgave small transgressions against the soul, perhaps a little white lie, or the knowledge of a possession that had accidentally been borrowed and not returned. But more so, the old church was a place for the town's sad, lost, and lonely hearts. It was a place of deep prayer that also held all the sentiments of the towns people's lives.

It goes that the church was quickly erected, but as much as the people prayed and confessed there, they never felt the same comfort sitting in the new location. They longed for their original place of worship. In the new church, there came a false man who conned and tricked the innocent folk, and some abuses occurred that in the end, all went up in flames. In the same month that the new church was burnt to the ground, all those years later, the drought in the area uncovered the remnants of the building. It is whispered that the girl in the straw hat, with her baby in arms, was also found amongst the rotting debris of both church site gravestones, but that was just a rumour. Both bewildered sites were then lavished with the placement of fresh wildflowers.

The Wildflowers

The spring and summer days were more than dreamy. The meadows had very pretty wildflowers, beautiful and lovely in every way, opening to the bright morning sun and closing in protection of the chill night air. Now, after such bliss and glory, the wildflowers were gone for another year.

However, after the flowers had gone, their blissfulness and pretty comforts seemed to remain as one. The bushes, rocks, and sapphire ridge melted and meshed into a solitary state. This was the ridge near the flower patches that, from a distance, looked like a white soft fluffy blanket with yellow touches of light brume. Nature beamed at its most brilliant in the early morning and in optical illusion, aspects of the view looked like statues blessed by the golden sun, radiating on the ground. It was an awe-inspiring view that caused Elspeth to stand up high, giving her the feeling of being celestial, but also grounded in the naturalistic realm.

Elspeth was earthed in herself and felt the flowery energy within shake away any illusions, opening her intellect and helping to follow her woman's intuition. It was the intuition that the early women of the country, in every second of their outdoor existence, had to trust and call upon. Living within the weather-beaten shelters and vast openness of the great spaces, they had little more than the wildflowers and their own intuition to help get them through any day or night. Then, within the yellow hills of the Australian bush, again came the bird song. It penetrated the silence of the light air. The tweeting songs lightened Elspeth's thoughts. It was unlike being in any other place on earth. Somehow, this particular area stood out, calling the familiar ones back to their own territory. It was as if the reason for living and dying was placed in each flower. Although it was an unusual way of seeing things, it was a place that could soothe every small feature, but break the back of a man who was stronger than an ox. It was a place where the superseded farm machinery that was pushed to the end of its turning in the earth, was left to rust away. Any who suffered such a breakage could use the bush flower essences to rise out of his spine and achieve great mountainous things, prosperous things like his owning a plot of land, a couple of horses, a billy to boil, and the flowered woman of his dreams.

Elspeth confided in her dear friend, Kendra, who visited the hut many years after her resignation. 'The Clarences will never know the beauty of the wildflowers. They will never know the fairy magic of the high country that floats through the air every time the flowers bloomed. They were too caught up in their materialism, upper crust friends, and socialising at every tick of the clock. They were simply too busy to see any of the daisies. For some reason, the beauty of the flowery hills was simply not seen by them. They were always too busy, making sure that they had everything needed to be the best. This was more important than the wildness of the paper flowers. Incredible as it seems, the reason why their young son drowned in the dam, only to be rescued by the girl from the purple passage, was because they were not interested in him as a human being. They saw him as another thing; that was all he was, just another thing. They had a possession that sometimes seemed to get in the way of their leisure activities. Often they shoved him away in a lonely room, when they were choosing a wine or talking about importing designer clothes. It was shocking, and when Brian Clarence decided to have an affair it was all too late. The young boy was dead and the family was left in ruins forever'.

'Well Elspeth', confided Kendra, in a soft voice of flowery overtones. 'People walk their own roads, their own way. And the Clarences, I know, were not particularly nice, good, or kind people and are now facing the backlash of their own behaviours, thoughts, and actions towards you and a number of other very good servants. I remember the shed cook saying there was a word that was known and understood by those who spent their lives servicing and bowing down to the needs, wants, expectations, and demands of others'. Elspeth soon remembered the conversation that had taken place in the flower beds. 'It took a certain amount of humility and humbleness to serve with grace, keeping self-respect, a respect that would never be acknowledged by them. The word was yes. Saying 'yes' to everything and never saying no. Saying 'yes' with a smile and a slight nod of the head. But, in-service circles, the word yes, meant something more. A servant needs to hide within their own self, learning the ways and wisdom of the heart, listening to the small voice of the heart was not hard when a person lived within themselves. After some time, working in-service, when no other door could be found to open towards an independent life direction, a certain acceptance of life's fortitude within the self was realised through following the small inner voice of the heart.

Walking back in time, through the wildness of the mountain flora, Kendra now explained that it was the shed cook who had also confided in her, the pretty blonde, heartbroken piano player, saying that one day, she knew the Clarences and others like them would have to lift their self-centred heads towards the servant girl, and one day see a powerful, strong, and brilliant woman. A woman who, with her own physical and mental integrity, would rebuild a ghostly, broken down hut. With her own hands, she would use a hammer and nail, repairing with the precision of the finest carpenter. Firstly, she would analyse its surroundings to see just what the real weather conditions were, and just what the hut would need to withstand every blizzard, windstorm, and heavy snowfall. With nothing in her purse except a needle and cotton, it seemed almost impossible that she would squat on her own, take possession of the abandoned hut and rebuild it almost from scratch, from its very beginnings. She looked around in every derelict shed and in every full rubbish tip and went to auctions to find the best deals from deceased estates, finding decorative teaspoons, a teak sideboard engraved with a rose inlay, and a half moon glass china cabinet. There she would find everything needed to rebuild the hut. And, moving her forward to do all of this preparation for her new hut were the ever changing and always to return wildflowers.

They had become her driving force. After the hut was ready, she would settle and live, find her lovers and feel the world between her thighs. All these words came true, and now Elspeth could see the pages of her life turning as she read the real meanings of the wildflowers.

The appearance of certain flowers throughout the year meant certain things to Elspeth's position at any particular time of the day. The flowers gave her signs of peace, patience, or even a warning. There was a certain strange elegance in the old brushwood sitting room, next to a rusted wheel, or an early shear's knife that was found by an unexpected traveller, perhaps another woman of sadness and regret; a person who had loved only one man and whose heart was pierced by the memory of the knife flirtations that he had wounded her with. She fell for a whimsical person who did not bring forth a flower to their relationship, but instead ran off with his mates to brag about his desires for other girls. Elegance was near to the wheel, and the knife was found close to a wild bush orchid flower, the flower that knew the history of the tousled flowers.

The elevation of the uncluttered and unspoilt scape was enhanced by the wildness of the flowers, the only markers of an earlier sub-continent terrain, a landmass that had broken millions of years before, leaving in its wake the prettiest flowers in the world. The high-country treasures, the yellow billy buttons, heart leafed iced plant, red olive plum, water primrose, and the simple field daisy, were just a few species that Elspeth mentioned in her response note to Liza's three letters that were never fully finished.

Elspeth knew that the wildflowers, in their thousands, were God's hidden gems to a world that would grow so fast, that many would never know their appraised beauty. Fearing the day that the people of the post, post-modern world would be so reckless, as to rape the world of the wildflowers. A post, post-literate world did not necessarily mean the most intelligent of times. Trust and faith, for the abundant future of the divinely spread flowers, was all that Elspeth could offer, going on explaining to Kendra, that, 'On higher ground there were hard bushes, grasping the large granite boulders. There are many rugged plants, looking like the old bonsai shape and giving a feeling of callousness. They are not attractive, but add to the rouge character of the thicket life up here.

The craggy looking wide climber clings to the heavy boulders, taking advantage of the night heat that emanates from the day's sun soaking of the rocks that could also be determined as sarsen. These big rocks seem to represent monumental praise and are a doorway to the other side, to a greater place. The enormity of the boulders, and the amount of heat during the night that they generate, gives the plants a micro growth to what appears to be a stagnant deep-rooted brittlebush of no importance. The summer months in Australia, January in particular, brings about a magnificent crescendo of wildness in bush flowers. But at any time of the year, for the seeker of flora and fauna, flowers can be found in the most unlikely areas of the high country. Surrounding the glacial lake, the wildflowers are scattered amongst the rocky flat ledge between the hills and peaks of the highest Alps, in what was referred to by the early settlers as the 'new world'. The florae draw water from the deposit of water pool that has an enchanted picture book look to it'. Kendra acknowledged the path of the flowers, long, winding, sweeping and, under a starry night sky, that there was a mood set that needed to be humanly experienced to really know, feel, and understand. Imagination could not conjure up the smell of the wafting aromas of the wildflowers at night. When the dynamic of the seasons and the weather patterns were aligned with a dusty mood that was right, the combination of a warm night and a collection of flora set the divine scent of the earth's cosmos with a density of perfume in the air. A scent that is wild, purposeful, and made by rare rudimentary forces. It is a still, mid-summer Australian night, that blends only with the sound of the crickets and frogs. There may have also been beasts of all kinds, but that can be left to the mind's fancy. Above in the blackness, there was a snake curled up between the kite and the Milky Way, and the starry night that was alive and awake with all sorts of activity, such as shooting stars and comets lightly exploding. The whole balmy aromatic night sky was set to the morning sunrise and the opening of the arrays of prettiness. 'It was the coming of the flowers that always kept me going, just knowing in my heart, that one day, I would open my eyes and be surrounded by the wildest flowers, each representing a holy thought, and ruling over evilness and the bad weather, that Crower had dumped on me', said Kendra honestly, as she recollected the pain of her departure from the Seymour Homestead.

Elspeth acknowledging what she had to say. 'After you left the house, it was the meaning of the flowers that also kept me strong in the face of the witch's continual stalking and invisible discriminations. It was also being amongst the beauty of the untamed, uncultivated wildflowers, where I found much comfort after so many years of following the eagle's flight towards the prayerful victory over my enemy of many witchery faces. The flowers seemed to reach out to me, they would grasp my contemplations, and scope of thoughts towards being set free from her. They gave my life resurrection after her indignity, that un scrupulous bore of a witch would have to sit back and now cry over me. The great eagle and the Swallowtail butterfly also helped me rejoice in the wild seeds that were planted in every life force. I missed you so very, very much Kendra, but, understood that you did have to go. Our good souls and the kind attention that we gave to everything in the house, our ever care and tenderness, could be likened to the wildflowers, harvesting of pure love. This love could not be broken by the cruel witch's intentions, not ever'. Elspeth rose the tone in her voice. 'We knew that we would be free of the winter season in the next life, but we were given a chance in this one to experience the cold, and then to melt into the warming sun's flourish — wild, pretty, free, and uncultivated was an absolute blessing. The nag bag, however, would freeze and be lost in the blizzards, but, not before her blood boiled over in the heat of jealousy and contempt towards me and probably you too'. The lives of the wildflowers are in God's hands. It was a purposeful planting, even though some seasons were dry and without nascent flowering at all, they always appeared'. Kendra responded quietly, 'No one, but no one can write the flowers like you Elspeth'.

'Without the wildflowers, the high country would have absolutely no meaning, no grace. It could not adorn the body of mountain flowers again with their flattering array of sprinkling opening and closing colours. The wilderness flowers gave an imperturbable glimpse into the unknown and unforgiving world up here. Being painterly planted by the hands of the earth's soul, they give an elusive escape of other treacherous things that are happening up here. Like the many small mites, grubs, and bull ants that live under the rocks, they pattern the steep hills and are lazed by the mauve tufted orchids, clustered in patches under the sun's rays. The flowers dismiss the creepy things in life and bring softness to a person's eyes.

The flowers balance the harsh elements of the ecosystem — sky, air, and differing types of grasses that the field mice run. Each day, I cry that the flowers will never leave. Like a babe in the womb, I want to tuck them away forever inside me, so they will never leave my body. The emergence of new life, this is what they mean. This old scape is in its sunny emergence; as soon as the flowers appear, they bring happiness on a sad day, and people feel beautified by the natural pigment colours of the land. I know that nothing, absolutely nothing will stop the coming of the wildflowers, not the driest seasons, not the raping of the trees, but the continued ploughing of the ground is a concern. There is no need to worry that the wild florae will dissipate forever. The wild flowers in his area are here for eternity'. 'O yes', gently smiled Kendra.

On those days, walking past the small mushrooms, in the middle of summer, the prettiest patches of flowers were scattered under the trees and made for perfect snow-white pictures to be painted. The patches of flowers, however, were also a place for the wild cat to hide. We were careful when stepping through the papered carpet bed, as the cat or snake on a warmish day could destroy the feelings of open happiness, reaching down into the papery patches was tempting but also a bit risky. The wildflowers, were just so very pretty, gentle, and serene: pink Australian bindweed, yellow mountain banksia, and honey caladenia. Exploring the beauties of the highland plant life was a never ending flowery excursion of hope and happiness. They brought forward a happiness that covered up the sadness of working a dismal day's work, for those of no appreciation of floriculture through experiential participation. The flowers will always be open to the big blue sky and the upper bush scape in the high region. They will remain to be the shedding of coldness, bringing peace and comfort, in late spring and early summer. In the scent of the daisy chain, picture by picture, they will paint with imaginative floral gesture, scape by scape, the great wastes of hardness and a history of pain will flourish in the letting go of the difficulties. They bring forward a manifesto, an original land bouquet of flowery terrain and hills adorned with delightful colour.

The flowers took away the foul witch's spell, and along with the butterfly and eagle, gave a struggling servant girl direction towards her own life in the bush. She was free of the witch's outdated and stubborn values, her big headedness and her lying seething ways. The adorable flowers simply brushed all that away.

Late in the day during one summer's shower, a man came to the hut. A stranger who was healthy, strong, and in need of company, he needed someone that he could share a few quiet moments, a long conversation, and find some commonality with. Meeting him at the back door, Elspeth could see him walking through the many yellow Billy buttons that were about three to four inches in height growing towards the hut, brushing each other in the wind. She knew that together they would end up dancing the array of cute button top flowers. Like him, they were playful in appearance, and brought a sense of entertainment and amusing thoughts, which backed right up to the shed and the rear of the wood dwelling. Gently grabbing the pretty young and now independent Elspeth, the outdoor guy strongly mounted her up against the back of the hut and spontaneously, under the steel, grey-blue sky, gave her an afternoon delight. The dwelling moaned at their outdoor binding and she flushed under his want and yearning. It was the flowers that he was attracted to, knowing that a woman of absolute beauty and intelligence would be close by. After that first time, he was a regular summer visitor. Some seasons they made love, other times, they did not. But, he always took a bunch of buttons home to his wife, hand-picked by Elspeth.

The flowers held some secrets that would not be divulged, unless they were drunk as an infusion like Saint John's wort. That flower would always reveal the absolute truth, an inner knowing that is suffered by some married women. It was an important flower to Elspeth and she took seriously the knowledge passed down from her grandmother who told her that Saint John's Wort would protect her no matter what. It was considered a noxious weed by the farmers who cut it out of the ground at any sight of growth. However, it was a special plant of protection and noted in many ancient books, for not only being a plant to help calm the nerves, but a plant to ward off evil spirits and badness. So, Elspeth planted it around her hut and when harvesting the angel-petaled plant, she would excrete the red serum from within its stem and leave it at the gate by the bottom of the winding road, placed in an elaborate glass with gold leaf grape colored engraving. The glass was placed in the center of a dried flower arrangement and was made irresistible to the bad one, who did drink from the cup, and then ran to the hills only to purge it from her anus and retch it from her gut. Elspeth turned a segment of the story of Snow White into one point of her own colossal canon of strategies set down to defeat the bad women of no interest and no comment.

Every bad wish that the witch had wished on Elspeth was warded off by the wildflowers. The flowers never grew near the bottom of the gorge which was under the burnt-out stump that she sometimes accommodated. That place was a den of heinous iniquity; it was a hollow domicile of no real feeling. It was a place laden with evil, devilish thoughts, and faces, hard and wrinkled with nothing of beauty borne there. The flowers and nature knew that where greed and wickedness lay is the path to demoness things. The pretty wilds would not grow in such places and, unlike Elspeth's pretty, clean, and well-attended hut, the flowers would never grace the coven place of the witch's cell. Those flowery graces were in every small heavenly pocket of Elspeth's beautified existence and the witch knew this. For this, she and her coven would seethe at the mouth, swearing and moaning in contempt at the magnificent hut and its impenetrable flowered surroundings.

In response, the witch decided to mask herself as a very attractive older woman who set up a cart of dried flowers at the top end of town.

An alluring stance she adopted, so as to try and seduce Elspeth. The witch had heard that Elspeth was attracted to both men and women.

With long, thick ebony hair, which was a totally different colour and style to Elspeth's, and holding a deeper wave, she wore a plain long tartan skirt, black boots, and a crispy cream blouse with a black silk ribbon tie at the neck. Without a doubt, Elspeth was lured by her very feminine characteristics, but was still not all that interested in being in love with her. There was something very trance-like that would happen around this person. The spell was a mixture of ideas about being born in the last epoch before enlightenment. Apparently, she was an advanced being and was drawn to the wildflowers to help save the poor. All proceeds, the sign on the cart, would go towards those affected by Thalidomide. The bad woman intended to give Elspeth a good dose after she had licked her cherry blossom. Yet, when approaching the cart of wildflowers, Elspeth felt that all too familiar warning, smelling out the seductress' semblance that was disguised by a bunch of wildflowers.

It was a calling from the great escape where the flowers were born and seeded. Just for a moment, they cast a shadow over the gentle face and exposed the jealous, competitive, and sinister person who had an ulterior motive right from the start. The shadow, taking away the flowers, the barrow, the clothes and the innocent pretense, left her only a snarl of belligerent envy. Thank God Elspeth did happen to glance more closely at the fading shadow and use all of her internal might to withstand her overwhelming attraction to the woman, who would burn her out with a single light lick.

Then there was the man who came to the hut carrying an arrangement of both dried and fresh wildflowers. The well-dressed man wore clean skin pants and designer boots. During the day, normally he wore a sweaty torn singlet, but when visiting Elspeth, he chose to wear an imported paisley-patterned shirt. The bunch was tied with a thick, blue satin ribbon, the ribbon a symbol of his status in the area.

He was a man who sat back and smiled at the Clarences and their strange, out-of-step way of living in the wilderness. A man of stunning looks, Cain was jealous of his position. A pastoralist who owned the largest landholding in the district worth millions, he was also educated. Totally intrigued by the pretty Elspeth and her firm decision not to take a husband, he was determined to win her heart and take her from the hut onto his own sheep and cattle station. The station was home to 20 horsemen, a large shearing shed and a good fine wool cheque every year. 'Elspeth', he thought, 'with all her independence and forthright ways, will not resist my marriage proposal, because no other bloke out here has anything to offer like me. Everything of mine will be hers, that is if she can raise herself out from that bloody old shanty that looks like it could do with a few nails and a new door. Elspeth can become the lady of my house. I will protect her forever and a day, and she can have her hair done in town every week, buy any dress that she wants, and prepare everything for us.

I know at first, she will resist all that I have to offer, but I will place a diamond in front of her, bearing a stone so expensive, that no other man could ever afford to buy such a rarity. If at first, she does not accept my offer, the large diamond rock will be kept in my safe, for her future consideration. I cannot understand why such a woman wants to fend for herself out there, on her own, night and day, chopping wood, building fires and stocking the soot every day. And not to say the least, raising her illegitimate son without support. In my house, she would be the most respected and revered woman on the whole plains, and she will have personal help. I know of a woman who is the best cleaner around here. She has another position, but I will give her twice as much to come to my Maura Homestead and undertake all the duties, similar to the ones I know Elspeth did so well for the Clarences. Those silly city folks, who did not fit in up here at all. They looked absolutely ridiculous trying to live out here in the sticks. They were just city slickers from way back. But, the old saying goes, you can lead a horse to water, but can't make it drink. If after one year of waiting, Elspeth still refuses my proposal, I will seek another, and perhaps try and find the pretty blonde thing who plays music. But, the ring remains in wait for my special Elspeth.

To remind her of who I am, I will tie the blue ribbon to the horses' rail, and hopefully one day, she will tie back her hair, carry my flowers, and leave that dilapidated old hut. That dive should have been demolished at the turn of the century. Surely, she will choose a life of comfortability, security, and warmth over that continual isolation. And, if that bull of a woman from the lower gorge, whom it is common knowledge, absolutely hates Elspeth, ever comes to her new house, I will personally take my high-powered rifle and shoot at her, as quickly as a running fox. I will deliberately scare that draggy woman until she runs to the next parish for good. As for Cain, her drop-out lover, well, I will look after his boy, and that will be the last of that. No questions will ever be asked. What I know, and really like about Elspeth, are things that make her different from the other women that I have met around here, including the women that I grew up with. Elspeth has so many qualities that would make for a damn good wife. I know that she does not interfere in our people's business. I have never heard any gossip from her lips and, as a real man, I know that she would be more sexual than any other woman that I have bedded. Also, that woman is capable of doing outdoor work, riding and mustering, understanding what is important when working the land. She's beautiful, but also strong. I know that she prays and I would respect this, for I am, at heart, a God-fearing man of the soul too.

Elspeth is caring, loving, a good cook, and, above all, honest. My money would be safe in her hands. I would have no hesitation to give her a signed blank cheque, for anything that was needed. Elspeth understands stock, she understands that at different times of the year, important animal husbandry tasks need to be done. It is a matter of knowing how to manage the stock, the land, the men, and balance the ledgers. Elspeth is perfect for all this, and she is just so endearing to people. Children adore her, and she is sweetness in every way. Elspeth's life is totally wasted in that God forsaken hut. The only thing that I am not sure about is her ability to be able to fully commit to just me and that is what I need — full commitment, no other lovers or sexual attractions. I have heard some rumours of her private liaisons, but these I find amusing, totally amusing. Little manifesting orgasms that occur indoors on her duck feathered bed, or outdoors in the reeds by the river, or against her hut. People talk out here and farmers just laugh. You see, seeing animals copulating is a part of the natural instinctive way. There is nothing wrong with sex. But marriage is much more. It is about having the company of a beautiful person, a woman who is distinctive in every way, a woman who has her own solitary self and her personal presence. Elspeth is adorned with no mistakes. She's a woman of great personal substance, a wife of experience, brilliant in all ways'.

From high up, Elspeth watched the man carrying the flowers that she had returned to him. Leaving, he rode down the road and disappeared into the next holding. Head low and eyes sunken with rejection, Elspeth had felt his pain, when saying no to all the flowers that he had offered. Although she was very, very attracted to him, she felt that it was not fair to let him slip his hand where she would have liked it to go. It would have been wrong to have led him on to believing that she would be his wife.

Standing on top of the sloping ridge, Elspeth could see across to the side of the highest peak. The little baw baw wild daisy flowers seemed to smile brightly at her, and opened happily and hopefully when seeing her face. The coolness of the air filled Elspeth's head and chest, refreshing her eyes. As she breathed in and out, and looked down towards the flowers, although isolated, Elspeth felt welcomed in their presence. The flowers dissipated any feelings of loneliness that she felt when standing up so tall amongst the high striking peaks of the mountains. Elspeth wanted to pick all the flowers and hold them close to her face and body but was too scared to do so, for fear of interrupting the fragility of this normal and natural place of growth. The contrast between the delicate flowers and the huge overpowering and overbearing mountain scape were almost too much to comprehend. The clouds, low in the grey-blue sky, were the main influences overseeing the pretty flowers, and again, more important than any man, rich, poor, or otherwise.

On that day, however, Elspeth relished being able to see those particular and commonly mountainous wildflowers. The prettiest ones beheld the landscape that was uninhabited, onerous, and at times deeply frightening in its aloneness and solitude. Not touching them, just leaving them to be honest, alive, and free was a blessing for them and Elspeth. It was then that it occurred to her that the answer to the loneliness that she had struggled to reach within herself was in no man or woman, but had been answered by the presence of the flowers. Their ferocity had been scattered in the floret patches and was embedded in the limestone rock faces and dry, swaying grasses. The answer, as to how and deal with being alone, and one that she had long awaited, was to be found in the flowers only, and no other human being. It was how to deal with being alone up there, everyday, especially in the early days. Initially, it was difficult for Elspeth to cope with and she developed a longing and yearning for real company and friendship that could not be satisfied or fulfilled within her own self. Being with strangers that she initially conversed with when working at the Homestead was really difficult for Elspeth, as they did purport a different style of language to hers. Some had that slow drool, and all they seemed to discuss were comings and goings of the weather, sheep, cattle, and the mechanics of land rovers.

Elspeth's family communicated differently to those in the new household. Some words and expressions sounded very different to

Elspeth's, and often left her with an inquisitive look on her face. All of a sudden, Elspeth could see the answers to her aloneness in the pretty happy faces of the wilderness flowers. In some ways, Elspeth felt chosen by the flora, and felt very drawn to their uncultivated position. Their simple way of spreading out across the open, unblemished ground cover was the language of the wildflowers that gave her the best company.

Elspeth began to feel blessed and nourished to be alone within the peace of the flowery existence, up there in the summer rye of the seasonal changes. It was a gift to see and behold those delightful little flowers. Elspeth felt, in some way, a part of them. Something inside of her was very similar to the flower sprays and settings in the sky high flowered patches. They were open and free, simple but glorious, gentle, but nonetheless hardy and full of life's love, thus, capturing an inquisitive look. It was like looking at someone whom you thought to be of no worth or consequence, and then, all of a sudden, finding that they have inside every hidden gem known to man.

The beauty of the white and lavender sprays encompassed the hard, rocky-hills terrain that was grounded in a mountainous panorama view. A view seated behind a natural cut in the hill formed a path that was softened by the flowers, softening the inner hardness of the rock. The path seemed to lead right to the peak of the hill and there was nothing quite like the view that was laid out before Elspeth's eyes. There was just nothing as beautiful as those swaying wildflowers. The scene conjured up a fairy tale vision of a perfectly-set table awaiting the Prince and the Princess of high peaks, waiting for them to eat a lavish lunch of edible flowers, grapella fruit wine, and summer-steamed vegetables garnished in light golden apricot oil, herbs, and ground pepper. It could only be the most majestic table in the whole world — natural, free, and blessed by the temperaments of the changeable scape and the golden sun streams that Elspeth often called the holy spirit or light of divinity. It was beautified by the bird life and low cloud descent and massive floor that needed discovering. People with those types of wicked problems could never find that place of the protected wildflowers and the scenery that danced between the heavens and the earth. Only an experienced guide would be able to wade through the various types of flowers, and maybe find the majestic caverns and towering summits that stretched above the open plains.

The dangers spoke about being footloose and alone on the high plate seemed irrelevant that day. The loneliness became imaginary and on that day, after just a few hours of being up there, Elspeth began to see being alone as a great gift towards freedom, a great gift to be found in every delicacy of the papery daisies. The wildflowers could be seen in this spot and many, many others.

The French ultramarine blueness of the lake on the other side of the rock formation was set in a green grass, snowcapped scene that was adorned by the hoary ray sunrise flowers. For a moment, Elspeth thought that there were three figures moving through the still picture, two women and a man. But, then again, it could have been her imagination, as instantly they were insignificant in the most creative scene ever recorded, in Elspeth's mind anyway. The lake looked inviting, cold, and more beautiful in every moment — a cool and watery masterpiece to behold, magnificent in its own place and timely appreciation. The flowers gave the scene all it needed to become a summery sight of the elemental forces of nature. It was meant to be that way. A large jiggered rock fixation sat behind stupendous flat floor rocks, adjacent to the lake. Each piece of rock was positioned to reach up from under the sea bed of a million years ago or more.

The formation gave rise to the artistry of the earth's plate. They were sharp forms of green-grey rock and appeared to look like it had been deliberately cut. But, then, full of characteristics that were both haunting and indescribable, they were not softened by the flowers, but spruced up by the yellow billy buttons and tufts of grass. 'There can never be enough yellow buttons', thought Elspeth.

Elspeth knew that the formation, was, in fact, the ore that Isobel had told her about. It was the stone cut by early man, by which knives and tools were made from. They were the best, sharpest, and most important implements used by the early travelers of these parts. On closer inspection, Elspeth could just see the backbone of a man etched out in the rock, an art form from so very long ago. The word goes that it was his high standard of knife cutting and bending over so much that eventually broke his back. The image showed his lazy counter parts — how not to cut the stone. The area of incisive razor-sharp rock and stone was the feature place up there on the limestone ridge, amongst the summer wildflowers and wintery snow falls — a place also only known to the elders.

The bare branched snow gums reached out into the cool air that could not be spun onto by long legged spiders. They were intended by the witch to make Elspeth feel desolate, destroyed, and abandoned. The flowers gave Elspeth so much grace and became such a sanctuary, so much so, that she could not be made to feel anything other than totally protected and happy to be up in the mountains on her own, away from them —the worst woman, Neilson, her dreadful husband, their nine feral grubs, and her equally bad friends. Powerful up there amongst the high wildflowers, the beauty and the florae saturated Elspeth's whole being in a feeling of peace.

The flowers just seemed to ease the pain, giving hope, and protection in every small way and keeping her safe from the woman's evil, conniving, wanting desire to see Elspeth dead, thrown over the cliff escarpment, or flung into the fire like an old iron. Instead, being surrounded by the unseen shielding aroma of the wildflowers, Elspeth grew so much in her own personality and character that she cleverly outsmarted and outwitted them all.

The crown vetch pink flowers could have easily been picked and looped around the top of the extreme boulders, and, when braced, would look similar to a tiara rhizome adorned with the blushing petals that Elspeth would sometimes wear when visiting Cain in the gully. These individualized the boulder that already, like Elspeth, stood on its own amidst the mountains. This was the place that Elspeth knew, with her renewed character and strength, was of no return for any old blunt woman who dared follow the innocent one. The brown and scratchy textured rock stood flanked by a smaller boulder of a similar pointy shape, a crown vetch in the foreground yearning to be placed at the bottom of the astounds indomitable rock wall, the whole area laced with pink serenity. The only other demands of the scene were the green grass and path that led to the other important features in the high altitude of the glorious and mostly untouched scape that was saved especially for Elspeth.

Elspeth continued to converse with Kendra. 'Living in the hut gave me that opportunity to experiment with the wildflowers for many varied reasons and purposes. Some days I would walk miles and miles and miles, in search of all various species of flora to do things such as make paint, brew tea, and blend my own medicinal tinctures and creams. I remember Isobel telling me about her love of painting and also my creative aunt who had actually told me how to derive paint from the wild flower plants. I would choose, say, three flowers in each colour range that I was planning to use in my pictures, like say pretty colour combinations of red-orange by using royal grevillea, shaggy peas and mother of millions. For lemon-yellow, I may have picked yellow billy buttons of course, including wattle of any description and yellow mountain banksia. The colour of purple and pink would be determined by variegated thistle, leafless pink, and purple broom. To explain further, I would choose three bright colour combinations and dry them out in front of the fire, on a hot rock, or hang them outside in the sun for a few weeks. The brightest colours would certainly make the richest powder pigments when dry. To get the clay pigment, I would crush dried flowers into a light powder and then bind the powder with egg white. Soon enough, a light paint would form, and I would be ready to paint many very soft flower paintings that adorn my hut. I would give pieces to friends and often expressed my secret sexual desires in the paintings.

I would never tell anyone other than you Kendra, but sometimes painting a picture after self-pleasure was better than having sex with some Johnny come lately who was full of beer and although good looking enough, was too smoky to even contemplate kissing. I simply cannot stand the smell of tobacco, and the slightest hint gets caught in my throat and I feel like spitting straight away. The paintings always depicted the life of the wilderness flowers. In fact, it always came back to wild bush flowers, beautiful in every way and expressing my own personality and desires so very well. I just can't seem to be tied to one person and, like the wildflowers, I must be allowed to be free to feel their prettiness amongst the many hills out here'.

I can only remember the first day that I decided to immerse myself in the essence of the bush and commenced making my own bush flower essences for healing. I made my own creams from the milk of the thistle bush by adding the flower essence and beeswax. I was so elated to extract and use my own tinctures. It was delightful to peer out from my hut, and find that all around me was all that I needed. The magnifique flowers were right at my fingertips to help make exactly what I desired. I actually used my intuition more than fact-finding to bind my beauty aids.

I was not afraid of being poisoned, and was drawn to the right flowers and plants to extract all that I needed by floating flower petals in the freshest of spring water and then adding a very small amount of brandy to distil and preserve the healing floral essence. What a gift it was to be free of my domestic life and commence making my own bush flower products. I was careful and never gave anyone a recipe or a drop of my own healing flowers. I only used these to look after myself and, as you can see, after many years, my skin is glowing and fresh from the daily bush extractions. I found Hawthorn that does grow locally. It is a very, very helpful plant to use. Some of these, I will tell you about later on at the end of our walk. However, because of the colour of the haws when ripe, I did also enjoy to make a red delicate and light jelly. Jams and syrups were readied too, and I would have to travel slightly down south to the upper side of town to find the flowery white plant with the small reddish shaped olive fruit. I also made a lot of fresh bush salad from the greened leaves.

The Hawthorn bush flower was so useful that I decided to bring large cuttings back to the hut and grow a bush for myself. It gave a good strong barrier to some of the wildest winds in the country and, when dried out, it was an excellent fuel to light a good strong fire. 'A good all-rounder', that is how I would describe the uses of the Hawthorn bush. In my early days living right up here, I travelled far and wide on foot. I discovered that the Ribwort leaves, when young, could be cooked or eaten raw. I did not like the bitter taste of the plant and preferred to boil the whole plant and extract a gold/brown dye. However, the seeds were useful to grind into a powdery addition for an unusual cake flour, or even cooked into a sago and eaten for breakfast. The Ribwort was a sign that grazing had occurred in the area, so there was plenty around here. Really strong medicinal uses come from the Ribwort, and I did apply it once to sooth a snake bite. Another time, it settled my irritable stomach.

'This all sounds so amazing Elspeth', said Kendra who had no idea the extent of Elspeth's intuitive knowledge of the uncultivated florets. 'When I was growing up, my eyes were not open to the mountainous buds, I just somehow did not seem to notice them, or, perhaps I was accustomed to their prettiness. But, through your eyes, learning how you put the essences of the petals to use is just so very beautiful. I wish now that I had also included the theme of bush flowers into my music. Maybe, just maybe, it is not too late to compose pieces to match your experiences. Perhaps we could collaborate and write some of the most authentic colourful and wildly mesmerising musical notations to complement your understanding of the nature and power of the flowers. This coming together would be the most rewarding musical experience of my life. I can see the raptures of the music drawing on the colourants and dainty spiritual essence of the bush like no other. Also, this would be a way to rekindle our special bond, a bond that has been slightly weakened after so many years of being apart'. 'Let's do it', replied Elspeth enthusiastically. 'I am ready to share so much of my flowery extractions and kernels with you'. She then pointed to the next of her explanations, the use of the Rubus Berry, describing that while the fruit was edible at just the right time, it was actually tea that she made from the young leaves and enjoyed the most health benefits from. It was a very good recipe for tummy pains and bloating. 'Who else, my dearest Kendra, could I tell such deep and polite secrets to'? Elspeth smiled into her musicians friend's face, a face that had now been washed clean of the pain and humiliation of falling in love with a 'two-bit' traveling salesman by the name of Crower.

The women, clasped arm in arm, continued to admire every small detail of the wildflowers.

'To me, the wildflowers speak many different languages. They have spoken to me through the little purple girl who whispered ground colours that spread across the open plains, and along the side of the long and winding tracks, and back roads — the ways that nobody actually knows about. They say that along with a clouded morning awakening of the sun, which is like the hand of the lord caressing a painting as the sunlight seeps into the cloud scape, gently bringing colour to the morning sky, the flowers are God's grace to the world. A statement of all that is lusciously natural, good and pretty, they are a source of abundance that bloom around trees and illuminate in the afternoon light. Having such a close association to the high country wildflowers did make me different compared to most other people. They enriched my life in ways that many will never understand. They nurtured my soul are a constant delight to my eyes, and are a natural cleanser to my environment. They opened and closed my senses and are a reminder, that in every moment, heaven is only a flower grasp away from my hand. When the sun is just about to set and it brightens and often pierces the eyes, the flowers speak of other things, like singing at a wedding under the clearest of the big blue skies. They are so fulfilling to admire and behold, that they can satisfy a person's desire to be needed, sexually or otherwise.

Also, through the hustle and bustle breeze, I avoided the slight glint of contempt in the worst one's eye. It was the day she tried to give me a small seemingly pretty box. But, it was a tarnished gift to try and sway me into her cunning plan of destruction, yet another new box of tricks for me to decipher. Luckily enough, on that day, the wildflowers helped me avoid that immoral sniggering woman who also wanted me, in the wind, to fall off my horse. Similar to the fairytale of Snow White, the wildflowers of protection and love grew me into a strong opponent against the sorceress, or any other woman who had bad intentions towards me and my life with the flowers.

I remember the jostle, flurry and strong emotions of one warm spring afternoon; the weather was both warm and wild. Sitting in front of me was the soft, misted, purple sky and the deepening of earth's shadows. I experienced a myriad of emotions when thinking that out here, in the heart of hilly, rocky, bushy Australia, and surrounded by the wildflowers, that I had actually defeated the darkest one who came up from the creepiest gorge around this area. The flowers strengthened my faith to do so, but not at first, without experiencing some trepidation and unease. It is the hardest thing to stand firm; dressed in a wild flower gown and be ready to rise above the base woman. The woman did nothing other than set good people up against each other, lie, stalk, and connive her way through life. She was a woman of no self-respect or dignity who also spent a lot of time drinking hard and heavy spirits, a sweaty alcoholic wave of smelly faeces encompassed her big, round, red face, as she approached me with a scorn that I could hardly endure.

But, then, the scented flowers wafted a gentle fragrant breeze into my heart and, on that warm afternoon, she began to dissipate right in front of my eyes. Another day, a summer day this time, I could see the eagle's distant flight. I had been enjoying a morning of relaxation in the hut and my young son was asleep in his cradle. There was no disturbance and I was happy. The eagle's flight was directly over a patch of daisies in the far-off paddock that belonged to a neighbouring farmer. The flowers were also bracing the side of a hill that sloped right down to the peanut-shaped dam. The waterhole actually looked like a small lake and then, in an instant, I could feel a dark change in the happy morning. The eagle was warning me to run and hide. I felt that the eagle wanted me to hide on the other side of the dam. The witch had arrived back from wherever she had disappeared to and had prepared a heavy brew that was filled with three pigs' heads and the additive of shotgun powder. These ingredients were lethal and set to make me turn around and run out of the district. The witch had set herself up with the slimy brew, and was well on her way with the sludge, sprinting towards my humble hut. Traipsing up from the back gorge, she had been simmering the slop and making it ready to throw and splash, not just on me but all over my sweet and innocent hut for a few weeks. The flowers on the hill would hide my fear, and help me deal with my complete disgust of her.

Her beaky pointed nose and steel wool grey hair were very unlike the softness of the sprays that opened to protect my life, and with them, bringing a wealth of nature to my doorstep. My desire to keep the floral fields awake and alive in my world brought forward that very strong desire to gather them all up and, like a new babe from the womb, put them there forever — yes, flowers on my breast, away from the blunt old crone. Thank God it was the height of mid-summer and that I could use the perfume of the flowers to throw her offguard. I spread some on the opposite side of my hut, to make her think that I was on my way back from where Cain lived. You remember, the gully of no return. But, in fact, I was on the way to the other side of the dam to hide below the bulrush and to wrap myself in the daisy chain of remembrances. There was the happiness in the timeworn landscape and those sprays that emanated the sunny life of the emergence of new growth. There was real life in every natural form, beautified by the natural pigment colours in the land, the ones that I used as a paint base. Like Christ and all the other great worldly saints, nothing, absolutely nothing, could stop the coming of the next round of wildflowers.

I knew deep in the seat of my heart that I had not to fear or worry, for they would return, like him, for all eternity. To further hide from her on that day and any other, I would quickly pick a bunch of flowers, make a tincture, and dowse myself with it before leaping from the hill covered in floret deep into the bottom of the peanut-shaped spring tarn. I knew that if I were to dive directly into the centre of the pool, I could slip straight through the mud and into the waters below. There was a small aerated cavern and I could sit there for a while and hide from that wicked, bold, snooping person. The witch would never know how to find that secretive place. I would think only of the small buds and the gentle things that came close to my simple hut, and were in need of my tender spirit. In my later years, the white deer especially knew when danger was present, and would sometimes send me a sort of telepathic warning that the traitor was moving around the hills, saying appalling things about me and laughing at every opportunity. The deer consoled me that not all was lost, and telepathically showed me how to find the cavern below the muddy waters. Under the root system of the flowers is where I waited for the hog's brew and shot gun powder to leave.

One day, after I had really settled into my hut, and had embraced the fact that at the same time of the year, and every year I would be surrounded by the wildflowers, I felt absolute abundance. The sunshine was beaming all around me, amidst the wildflowers and green scene, and I felt that this country side world would go on forever. But, then I remembered my grandmother saying that absolutely nothing goes on forever, and that it was God that played the final card in the abundance of life. Just at that moment, when standing in the majesty of life's natural serenity, an unusual sick feeling penetrated my body and thoughts. I was on top of the lightly covered florid hill and then, all of a sudden, I felt a hand in the middle of my back and tripped. Rolling down the hill, the beauty slowly started to evaporate in front of my eyes. The greenery turned to a dull grey. The sky, blue and free, became like a hung canopy sack that was moulded and dusty. The wildflowers became like steel statues and a hard rock face that yearned for grapes and herbal wine. Initially the day was clear, but on closing, the debris from what looked like pigs burrowing into the ground, had seen a sort of rooting of the earth. The normally mossy blanketed glove, that protected the fields, and brought insects, small wild life, and bunny rabbits had a raped feeling to it. My head hurt a lot, as I wondered who had pushed me to the bottom of the rocky hills.

In the remoteness, I could hear the voices of rough, gruff men speaking. I think they were the pig hunters again, and best friends to the coven women. There also seemed to be residue of a fire. The ash I had smelt burning in the last summer months. I did see a smoke rising, but this seemed to be a long way from my hut. The voices came closer and closer, and I began to fear for my life. I was so afraid, that I quickly had to think of ways to get away from them. If caught, I would have to succumb to their sexual advances, and try to endure a gang rape. I escaped by smothering myself and crawling along the lea with my body covered by the flowers. Then, I saw her, the small girl again from the purple passage, wearing a coat of berries. Although the clearing had been destroyed by fire, the pigs' gouging of the ground did not bother the girl. The men's voices were closing in around me, and I projected a pleading face of help towards the girl's gentle, brown eyes. The red berries perfumed the bush. Suddenly, the girl took off her coat and flung it over my body. The restorative essence of the berries had a sort of special magic to them, and as the men came towards my covered body, they did not seem to see me at all. Then, a great wash of heavy rain dropped on them and they began to run. They were all carrying wooden hand hammers and were grunting and burping. They were repulsive at best.

I seemed to be invisible to them, otherwise they were sure to have raped me. I'd have been bashed and bruised, flung deep down onto the flat rocks at the bottom of the boundless, endless deep, jiggered ridge. The berry coat made it so that no drunk or rough man would ever step there again. The best thing about the heavy rain was that it filled the gnamma in the flat rock. The gnamma are holes that collect water that seem to stay for many months to come. The holes are the natural etymological of the hard rock face, which is also plunged with many other signs and symbols. These scribed natural indentations, lands, and gouges were only understood by the oldest and wisest man in the world. The girl pointed to a small gold pot that had been left out of stock by the original miners who only ever thought about the importance of becoming rich.

Although, as you already know, most remained very poor, and had to endure the unfamiliar harsh environment of the unknown deep-rooted bush, the isolation that came in the darkness of the night gums, and the long of being alone with no one to talk to. At times, they did not and were not aware of the fact that they would need to harness all the shades, lists, gradients, and inclines of the bush. The desperate miners would need to master the anomalies of the outward scrubland to be able to survive. Mostly, the original miners and their families endured the dissident hardship of being out here, and developed an oppressive and sad look upon their faces. This sadness often took them to their graves wearily, without much interest left in life. But, I Kendra, I will take Isobel's advice and stay camouflaged in the wildflowers, until the next chapter of my life spreads open to talk of our flowery music'.

Talking to Isobel

'In those days, we all lived clearly and soundly by handed down old wives' tales, tales that were taken as gospel truth, no matter what. In addition, there were strict rules that were set down by our own parents or guardians of the households. None of us had any real type of education. We just lived from day to day. The routines surrounding exact meal times went: 6am breakfast, 9.30am morning tea, 12 noon lunch, 3pm afternoon tea, as country folk stayed outside late in the evenings, we mostly ate dinner late followed by a 10.30pm supper. Everything we did revolved around these eating times. We learnt everything about how to live from our mothers and fathers, and most children were either taught some spelling and writing at home, or, if they were lucky, and there was an old-school house nearby, then the children would possibly go to school, but only until the sixth grade. Some kiddies were sent to boarding school very young, or home schooled by a live in teacher. Children were seen and not heard, and adults were always right, without question. Wealthy children were educated by a nanny who also looked after all their personal needs. There was never any coming together of the rich and poor kids, unless there was a secret forbidden love, a love that was kept a complete hush by all the youngsters who knew what was happening. The secret codes were all kept in one glance, for fear that everyone who knew would also be punished.

These loves never found their way to the marriage alter. However, there were rumours that some childhood romances flourishing affairs well after the marriage vows were taken. Sexual intercourse could happen behind a shed or on top of a secluded hill. Gathering eggs could take longer than needed, and the kitchen hand knew exactly what to say when the eggs were late, murmuring something to the effect of, 'this morning we will have fried sausages and tomato, the chooks did not lay today'.

Isobel knew the ways of correct behaviour, behaviours which were founded on the characters and social position of the people she worked with and served. Isobel was careful when addressing each and every person, and knew her place in every situation. She was always polite, helpful, and diplomatic; being diplomatic was instinctive to her. She protected herself, the head service woman at Seymour Homestead, and other new or younger staff members like Elspeth.

'Let me give you an example Elspeth, as to how to move through your day without stepping on the toes of others. If the gardener has lost his shovel and asks if you moved it and you did not, instead of saying, 'No, I did not see your shovel,' say something like this. 'I think I may have seen it and let's have a look, perhaps it is in the shed or over by the spring'. Really, just help him find the shovel so he does not become frustrated and blame you for moving it. 'Always put everything and everyone else first, and try and see into what people are saying, and for what reasons they are saying it'.

'Never create an enemy or ill feeling towards other people. Ill feelings strike a person down in many severe ways and cannot be hidden through a fake smile or the pretence of goodness. There was a girl who worked here before you. She was very cunning and her every move was about self-indulgence and self-gain. But, people could see right through her deception and into her scheming and self-centred ways. In the end, she could only find a job making beds at the local bed and breakfast. Having had no real friends, people would say that she was just not a nice person, not caring. People would run and hide at the first sight of her face.

It was common knowledge that she was deceitful and cruel; anyone who stayed overnight at that bed and breakfast would end up with food poisoning, losing their best clothes, or being given the wrong directions. No matter what she did, she was always on the wrong side of life, simply because she chose to be. Life is about choice, life is about the sweet goodness of simplicity, and the natural feelings that come from within a person who is clean, living, and free of wanting — and being honest, of course'.

Elspeth listened to Isobel day in and day out. It seemed that at every turn she had the wisest advice to share. She had an innate ability to see into every situation and steer Elspeth towards very good things, towards the light of God. Isobel could see into the soul of a person. There was only goodness and honesty in Isobel and, after months of training, Elspeth wondered why Isobel cared, why Isobel showed her so much kindness. It appeared to be her nature, and personal way to be a good, kind, serene, and a gentle soul who acted with compassion, never thinking about herself. Over the many years of working in that hard place, for people who were extremely ungrateful, Isobel had seen just about every type of person and every type of situation. But, this did not stop her from turning bad situations into something good, positive and wonderful.

This was another skill that she imparted to Elspeth, saying, 'In anything not so good, you can always find a ray of light, a shimmer of bliss and even something supreme. It can be hard to find, but it will always be present, it will always be there'.

The other thing that Isobel did, was seek deep counsel and advice from within her own heart, from within her own self; listening to her heart and taking into firm belief her Christian values. 'Be still and know that I am God'. Listening to her heart direction, that small voice of absolute truth, always directed Isobel to the garden of fresh renewal. It was a place that nobody could penetrate, and only those of pure love and kindness grew in that garden. 'Create an atmosphere in your world that is tangible, an atmosphere that people just know is good. You can do this by seeing the best in people and taking a genuine interest in the small things that make their lives real and of value. When you are working, always pray. Pray for others, pray for yourself and pray for goodness and kindness to follow your every step. Pray for a pure existence and don't worry so much about religion. God comes in many forms, and means something different to everyone. You must accept this'. Elspeth mopped and listened and was unaware that Isobel was discreetly, subtly, and deliberately strengthening her character.

'I realised a long time ago that many people hide behind religion. They use it as a confine and hiding place, and a lot of wrong and bad things are done in the name of religion and its rituals. Know that the best way to overcome this is to enjoy the extremities of religious practise, find peace and comfort in say, the offering of the bread and wine and the gesture of peace, but have your own clear and personal values. Don't listen to doctrines about going to hell if you do something wrong. However, evilness is something to really consider and is different to making a simple mistake. Doing something wrong is a test and a lesson which will lead you in your own life direction. It is the way of purification. Every man has his own life direction and everyone is here with his own life lessons. No matter what social status he carries, every man has his own reasons to live, his own reasons for wanting to find heaven'.

So much wisdom came from within Isobel that even years after Elspeth had left the Seymour Homestead, she could hear Isobel's calming voice of restful authority blending and kneading every moral fibre of her thoughts.

'When we used to date, the young man would always be dressed to perfection and present at the young woman's front door with flowers. The flowers were a sign of newness. Sometimes he would bring a gift from his own mother, such as a freshly baked and often warm cake. The warmth was meant as a sign of welcoming and the way in which a commonality between the two, perhaps uniting families, was established. These were tokens of kindness and affection, and were a way of placing the young man in the light and position of goodness and trust. As such, it was common courtesy. As the relationship prospered, then, writing poetry was seen as a romantic gesture of great sincerity. At no point during the dating phase were sexual relations allowed. This period of time was never under 12 months. Eighteen months was given that agreed silent nod by the older members in the family. Absolutely nothing was taken for granted by both parties, and courtesy at all times was extended. A chaperone was present on most dates during the courting phase. Older brothers and sisters came in handy to fulfil this role'.

Isobel did have her own private life, and although working as a domestic, she was not actually from a very poor background. Isobel's father lost his job when she was fifteen. He had suffered a series of serious strokes, and soon enough could not work. Most of the family's savings had gone towards looking after him and supporting the large family of ten. It was a shock and very hard on Isobel, because being the eldest child, she had to leave school to support her mother and eventually ended up in domestic service. It was hard to believe that in just 12 months of her father taking ill, Isobel and her family's life had changed so dramatically. But, within Isobel, tucked away in a secret tattered box, in the back of her life, was her early education, which, one day, she had always hoped to resume, but never did.

When working at the homestead and over the course of 17 years, Isobel had held a discreet, long-term relationship with a man who often visited the homestead to discuss the politics of Irish immigration and the improvement of work conditions in the local area. The man had mirrored her own words and life as a domestic. This acknowledgment did not go unnoticed and Isobel opened her heart to him, quietly discussing her own employment concerns including no pay rise in 17 years and the discomfort and indigence of having to move from the worn-down unpleasant shearers' quarters, which is where she mostly resided, into the back shed when the shearers arrived to shear the sheep twice a year. Also, working 15 hours a day without a break or care from her overseer, the situation was not nice at all. However, what she poignantly noticed was that when required to work in the house after dark, no outside light was left on. No light meant no real interest, and it was difficult to find the gate or the latch. It was even more difficult to see the path ahead or negotiate the steps.

Elspeth never knew the exact extent of their relationship. Whether they were casual lovers or just very endearing close friends, the nature of their relationship was not that much of interest to her. But, what she did know was that the highly influential man was an artist and that he had a strong interest in all tones of colours including black ink wash nudes, Philippian narratives carved out of Lauan timber, and textured interiors that were always pleasurable and sexually exemplifying — all things elegant and beautiful. He liked many things, whether it be a soft silk crocheted doily, a long teak wood sideboard or reset antique jewellery. They were really good friends and he told Isobel many sustaining things about the development of early art in Australia. It was not just a quick textual message to ignite Isobel's interest that he spoke of. Each and every conversation had real substance and meaning, little snippets of educative importance to help Isobel cope while she cleaned, stimulate her mind. To bring her thoughts towards her own artistic endeavours, Isobel shared a childhood memory with Elspeth.

'Once upon a time, in a circular garden, I sat, just a small girl with wide, deep blue eyes and milky, unclear thoughts about the day. I was just a small girl sitting in the scented fragrance of my own mother's violets. A heavy perfume lingered throughout the afternoon's longest moments. Time is always slower in the world of a child. It was a day similar to many that I had experienced and I always wore a smart dress, perfectly ironed, and stitched with satin. My good, loving parents knew from the day I was born that there was something unusual about me. I never wanted to play sports and I was quiet in myself. I was not confident with many people or things. What I loved to do was draw. I wanted to see all things looking out from a piece of paper. I wanted to stay in that place where nobody can enter and feel myself in a way that nobody would ever really understand. That was the place where I wanted to draw my characters and forget anything else other than my drawings'.

It was this interest in art and the light in art that she shared with her friend. Isobel had learnt a lot about early Australian Art from her friendship with the man, asking Elspeth if she was aware of an early Australian Artist who died of a miserable cancer in his left breast and that he had been charged twice for forgery of bank notes. A Scot who had left many pictures portraying early Australian life and Aboriginals became a famous convict after sending many pictures back to his dear aunt who had raised him. 'Yes, really interesting', replied Elspeth, 'my aunt enjoyed watercolour painting too. I also remember her telling me some important things about early Australian Art'.

Isobel continued on with the talk. 'When I first came to the house some many years ago, it was owned by a council. At that time, it had been relocated from next to where the creek is now situated. It needed renovating before it could be resold and started up as a working station again. They were very different days and, as I was preparing meals, all sorts of unusual tales would end up in the kitchen. They would say that those in the house could hear wild brumbies cantering across our folklore and into the stories around the campfires. The wild brumbies, coloured from ebony to fawn, followed the pack lead, a great stallion. Across the majestic natural habitat, they cantered to their own destinations in open plains, by the water, or under the gums. The steel-blue background was adjacent to the wind that picked up their manes and scent, carrying it to the dingo's. At night, under the full moon and cloudless sky, the packs of wild dingos located the horses, preying on the young foals. They would run down the mare and foal, blood and innocence left to fall on the open ground. The rest of the pack had been enclosed in the deep crevice of the open cave, that slated entrance that resembled the arch shape of sacredness, and held a haunting feeling of an archangel hovering in the steeple above the chamber. The cavity was unescapable.

Their coats ashine with heat, and their eyes in terror of what would come next, they knew that the man was also on their track and they needed to go further into the bush. The horses knew of a kind man who would shelter them. Living by the river and being the best and most skilled of hunters, the horses knew of his secluded goat farm. The entrance was also hidden by two big boulders, with only a narrow passage which was right at the end of the gully. It was always in the gully, a trap, a vixen, or an ultra-vivid wind vortex that, if they were not careful, would trick the horses into galloping onto another plane where again danger stood in many semblances. To be sure that all was clear, the brumbies would first go to a secluded hut that was nestled behind the three clusters of trees at the base of the hills. The weathered grey timber was likened to the dead trees, and the rocks on the hill had a certain dispirited feeling about them. Isolation, fallen fences, and an old wagon wheel abandoned by the early settlers gave the impression that no one was there.

After leaving the safety of the night, the brumbies would move out of the cavern before morning to cross the several mountain ranges. As they huddled together, the water from the blue water hole sloshed under their hooves and they messaged the others of their impending visit. This finished their time of hope in white gum valley. They would wade the waters of the rivers, embracing the rugged tracks and thorns, in fear of the whip and steep foot of the drovers. Washing the tables and floors one morning tea, and over a cuppa, Isobel confided some important information to Elspeth. This particular conversation cultivated Elspeth's interests outside of just living and being. In fact, she was very moved by what Isobel had told her. The subject at hand became the center of her single life and parenting up until the day she died. 'There are just so many high country stories that I can tell you. My experiences out here have left me clearly knowing that this is very much a man's world. Many young girls were not permitted near the shearing sheds. It is the women who have always had to work long and hard to prepare the morning, afternoon teas, and lunches for the shearers. I encourage you, young Elspeth, when you leave this service, to stand strong in your resolve to fight for the rights of women in this country. And, also to marry in dignity.

Way back when the convict women were brought off the ships, they were lined up and the rich pastoralists or men just wanting a wife would walk the line and drop a handkerchief at the feet of the woman he was interested in. Soon after that, a marriage would occur. These women were considered the lowest of low, and if they were not chosen as a wife, soon they would be pushed into domestic service, where they were treated poorly — so poorly, in fact, that there is now an intergenerational line of women who have not been able to break that cycle of poverty. It would be so good for a young desired woman like you to challenge the idea written by some journalist way back when, stating that the bush is no place for a woman. Yes, I think his name started with an A, he set men high above women, giving them the status of 'true bushman - men of the nation'. Women were put under a man's thumb, right from the time we walked off those hellhole ships. To live independently, out here, and enjoy the mysteries and great natural gifts of the countryside, but, more importantly, to rise up against its dangers, will strengthen you in every way. You could do more than fundraising and really get yourself out to the meetings and make your hut a beacon point for the development of women's rights in this area. You can do this and become more powerful than those other two snobs who come by here on the odd occasion. Actually, those two do nothing towards women's rights. But you, you have promise to give.

There is an organization called the Union of Australian Women. Firstly, they work to safeguard peace. They work tirelessly to defend the rights of all children, with the main focus being on the right to life, happiness, and education. I was lucky enough to attend the first meeting in 1950, which was held at Radio Theatre in George St, Sydney. An important meeting it was, discussing all the important issues affecting women and children. Branches soon opened in other states. The first congress was actually held in Paris, 1945, where much was discussed about trying to help all women and children who had suffered extremity, in and after the war.

After being in service for so long, Elspeth did have a very strong interest in women's issues because she knew, first-hand, what it was like to be so oppressed. It was interesting that she also joined the SOS, Save our Sons, movement after seeing what had happened to her beloved Cain, who took a strong stand against the Vietnam War. Frightening it was, to take such a strong vocal opinion, knowing that legal action could be taken in relation to those women who lead the anti-war movement. Being gaoled under the Crimes Act was a real risk; nobody spoke peace. Important meetings were held in the hut and the topics went far beyond house-wifey type issues, like the consistency of cake mixes, placing nappies in the sun to sterilize them, or kneading pounds and pounds of dough.

The women involved wanted real change to nuclear testing and disarmament. There was a campaign launched against war toys and a call for world leaders to resolve their differences around a conference table. They worked with trade unions to have representation to help lower the cost of living. Elspeth's steadfast and firm connection to the land gave her the strength to raise her voice on these issues. She had leaflets, publications, and pamphlets designed, and information about conferences held disseminated. All over the world, fundraising was organised, including affiliations with other important organizations such as: Australian Council for Social Services and the International Children's Emergency Fund. This was to become Elspeth's life work. Her journey to and from the hut was filled with all the natural joy of the earth, sun, moon, and stars was also fulfilled with knowing that progress for the rights of women, children, and peace were well under way. However, this social work position was detested by the jealous woman, adding fuel to the fire, and even more hate towards Elspeth.

One of the most important values Isobel conveyed over and over to Elspeth was the need for her not to lose faith, no matter what happened in life. She encouraged her to adhere to the values of a Judeo-Christian way of living, explaining to Elspeth that she also modelled her life ideals off the famous a social worked who she greatly admired and was inspired by. Isobel really tried to help the young women who came to the homestead, steering them towards independence and ensuring that they had more than just the basic provisions needed to get by during the long and hard days of duties. Isobel ensured that the young women were genuinely cared for, respected in their cleaning jobs, and would often take on some of their allocated tasks just to make them feel equal and not dominated by her supervision of them. Isobel was the kindest of people, even knowing sometimes that a particular girl's ego might rise up, set her up, steal from her, and even try and take over her dictum. In this case, Isobel, in all her wisdom, would just move forward and give the girl a deep, knowing look that gave a message to the girl that it was time to retreat from that type of behaviour.

Of course, Elspeth wanted goodness, kindness, purity of love, and everything prayerful in her world. But, there were certain things that Isobel suggested that Elspeth just could not contemplate, things that she could not come to terms with, like the suggestion that although she should fight for the rights of women, she should also find a husband, settle down, and have children as soon as possible. The idea of being tied to one full-time relationship, forever, was not at all appealing to

Elspeth. But, she did listen very carefully to what Isobel had to say about the early men who established Australia. Substantiating the view that a Christian marriage and beholding children were the foundation stone of the country's economic, social, and political position of stability. Some of the earliest men who came to this land were all men who were of strong faith. In Isobel's book, the heart of progressive social development and achievement were also rooted in the Christian values of understanding, forgiveness, and sacrifice to God. Nothing more and nothing less. Elspeth did think that Isobel may have really wanted to be with that man she confided in, become his wife, and have children, but that never did happen. They were simply from different worlds, and Isobel, for all her good advice, never did seem to be able to break out of her domestic work. Isobel would perhaps never really appeal to such a distinguished man of literature. Anyway, not at that time.

Although Isobel and Elspeth did get on very well most of the time, and had a respectful love for each other, there was a day that Isobel questioned Elspeth very firmly asking, 'Where is your faith'? It was a strange day, and for some reason Elspeth had not expected the question, which had a slightly interrogational flavor and feel to it. Perhaps Isobel had picked up on the fact the Elspeth was very liberal in her way of thinking, or worse still, just for a slight moment, Elspeth thought that perhaps the witch had penetrated Isobel's psyche, dowsing in with a split-second injection of venom. Going on to say, 'a pure way of living and strong faith is what you will need Elspeth, to get you through the days of highs and lows, of good and bad, the most confronting challenge that life will throw up in your face. You need a good sturdy conviction to model your life's existence towards, such as the saviour, his persecution, and his excruciatingly painful death. Also, you need to imitate his ability to stay good, loving and kind, alas, even when there appears to be an enemy at every door. Without faith, surely you will fail. I do not know where I would be without my faith in him and would have been banished for sure to that place they call the Skull'.

In finishing that day, Isobel said a few more sobering words. 'I never feared God; I never feared purgatory. I just had faith in the principles of compassion, forgiveness, and trust that on the other side. Heaven has already prepared a place for my soul and I vowed when I was very young never to commit a sin'.

And, even so, Isobel, at this point, decided to convey one of the most important pieces of information to Elspeth that she would ever need to hear. It went like this. 'When you have a pure heart, a pure way of thinking, reason, and dignity in yourself, you will have the personal power to ask God to cast a light on areas of darkness and shadow. An answer to a problem will come in a way that you least expect, and it will be then, that you will be sure, absolutely sure, that you will have equality in everything you do. It may be something small that initially you may think of as being a coincidence, but, in fact, it is a sign to take a stand and protect yourself through delving into the deeper source of knowledge. It is true that God and good deeds are light and love'. Elspeth responded by saying. 'Thank you, dear Isobel, thank you for caring about me, and for giving me what I think could be very sacred knowledge'. Isobel just could not help but say, 'believe me, out here, there are those who are just never going to change. They will never see beyond the traditional ways set down by the formations of the cross, and so it should be. We must all take pride in this burnt sunny country, scorched and cracked for months on end, and glowing in the red and orange bright hotness. We endure blistering, hot, dry days that are made easy by understanding that we are not perfect, but can make good of things anyway. In the hot days, we are careful with water and, on the cold days, share a blanket with the less fortunate.

Although this may sound contradictory to my thoughts on women's self empowerment, you can manage both. Everything should revolve around a good, solid family life. All life directions and goals must focus on raising healthy children and having a successful marriage. These are the early values of this area and will remain so for decades to come.

The reason why these values and life positions will remain virtually unchanged out here forever is because there is very little outside the influence of the bush. Out here, hard work and 'bloody' — as the men say, 'bloody hard yakka' — is the way to go. If you put in the effort, you will receive good benefits. It is important to have sympathy for the Aussie battler, the person who has less in his or her life than you. The reason being, is that you never know when life will turn its tide on you, and take you down an unexpected hard path. One of the main, important life lessons is that here in Australia, every man, woman, and child must take responsibility for his or her own actions in the world, no matter what their upbringing or life chances are. Underpinning this is a call for total honesty. That's right. 'Fair dinkum, ridgy - didge, true - blue, dinky - di honesty'. But, getting way back to what I said before, about shadows and darkness, watch out for hoons, drongos, bludgers, and whackers. These are the people who will lead you up the garden path, throw you a few praises, and then lock you in a room and throw away the key.

We see those types around here from time to time, but they always end up on their knees, swinging off a bottle of rum or running away because they become completely transparent in the wake of the purity of an uncontaminated bush. They are completely confronted by it all.

'What other lessons will I have to endure, Isobel, before I am released from this life of service and drudgery? I simply do not know how you have coped for all these years, just doing the same thing day in and day out, week in and week out, year in and year out'. Elspeth asked this with a sense of knowing that it may take many years before she could be boundless and free of her own life's weavings and spinnings. Isobel responded with a brush in her hand. 'Patience and kindness, that is how I managed to get by, and by taking whatever came my way, praying when in deep trouble, and never letting them see my vulnerable side'. Elspeth went on. 'You seem to go on without faltering and you do seem content and happy with your life's journey. I just cannot see myself living here in the Seymour Homestead forever, where so much has happened over the years, much more than the Clarences' divorce and the death of little Aidan, God Bless that small boy.

I have often wondered if there was foul play in his disappearance. Did somebody come and take him away, you know, like lead him to the edge of the wallow and push the kiddie into that deep waterhole? I know he was saved and swept him to the other side unharmed by the purple passage girl. But, something deep inside is bothering me about that day. When they questioned me, I just seemed to know that there was much more going on. I have wondered about him a lot. Some say his grandmother was mad, and did go to an asylum. Is that true? Do you know anything about her,' asked Elspeth, with a shed of tear and a puzzled look on her face. 'Although not a grandmother myself, the work that I do has brought forward the need for me to draw on the maternal instinct of my own grandmother. I know that in native tribes, the grandmother is highly revered and that before any important decisions are made in the community, the grandmother's advice is always asked. In a similar sort of way, this happens here at the Homestead. Before any household undertaking is acted upon, I am consulted about the matter. This includes the smallest things, like the quantities of foods and supplies needed for the household for the next month — flour, salt, and sugar — and what to do, if, say, one of the servants, guests, or even the owners has a mental break down.

Believe you me, that does happen out here in the back roots of this long - standing farm and sacred land. Mental illness has been an issue for as long as I can remember, and a lot of very concerning things have happened due to people's mental instability. Treatments have included electric shocks, transcranial electromagnetic therapy, and also bright light therapy, which are mainly performed in Sydney at the hospital. Large doses of psychotic drugs are taken and some people even have a series of actual psychosurgeries whereby certain parts of the brain are operated upon. To answer your question, 'Yes, I did know Aidan's grandmother and I think she did have a few small problems, But, this was absolutely no reflection on Aidan, Bessie, or their father, Brian. But, what I know for sure, was that the family did need country respite to deal with the ongoing trauma they experienced when looking after their mentally unwell grandmother. I feel this was also a precursor to Brian's many affairs with guttural women like Rosanna. I also know that by 1963, most people will be walking around zonked out on valium. I know this will happen and have heard that the new drug is on its way and will replace chlordiazepoxide. However, it is interesting that these difficult behaviours were initially considered and deemed by those who know nothing of the taboo topic to be silly, attention-seeking, and nothing that a good, hard day's work wouldn't cure.

These insensitive and uncaring responses have actually resulted in both men, women, and even children being locked up unnecessarily in mental homes. In the asylum is where these poor unfortunates experience abominable conditions and treatment. Raydalmere is a place nobody ever wants to go to, a damn god-forsaken gruesome, ex-schoolhouse in Parramatta. A long time ago, I remember going to that mental asylum to visit an middle-aged hand who used to work here. He lost the plot and took a pitch fork and stabbed a horse to death. As soon as I walked into the overpowering front entrance, I could see, feel, and smell the bruises that seeped from the patient's deadened life forces. It was frightening driving in the bomb of a car that I had borrowed from dearest male friend Jimmy, who knew the hand well. As I pulled up in the semi-circle driveway, I had a black feeling drop into my heart. I felt a very oppressive feeling everywhere I turned in that place. Actually, Jimmy was very concerned that there could have been an issue with that hand. Anyway, when I got there, he was restrained to a bed, wearing a straightjacket over his heavy hessian shift-style dress. The first thing he told me was that a nurse had put battery acid into his ears, as a punishment for not eating the broth infested with pig's hair.

For God's sake Elspeth, no matter what happens here at the Homestead, keep your head screwed on straight, and never react to your menstrual pain. Nobody should know when you have your bleeding period. Just pretend it is not happening. Otherwise, you could be whisked away to a mental asylum like Kenmore at Goulburn, or even Callan, again located in Parramatta. Any person that I sense in my heart may be slightly mentally unwell, I always let them know about a doctor who left Raydalmere to start his own practice in Macquarie St. The medical man was criticized for his unorthodox attempts to make patients at Raydalmere more comfortable. I have heard that he uses hypnotherapy and better medications. I know that when he left Raydalmere, in his goodbye speech he said that conditions in Australian Mental Hospitals were 100 years behind other countries. I think he went on to help others who are addicted to drink too. Yes, he did establish a group for alcoholics that keeps people's names private. Anyway, enough of all of that, because it is all a bit depressing and we have a good floor or two to shine'.

Elspeth took the advice about not showing any vulnerability whilst working on the homestead seriously. No matter what she was feeling like on the inside, Elspeth would always pop on a smile, get to work, and never ever complain about her workload or any jobs that were dumped on her night and day. She worked consistently and knew that her fate was sealed by her calm temperament and the wisdom that she had gained from working under the direction of Isobel.

Some matters were not negotiable in Isobel's book. Isobel was strongly against older women entering relationships with younger men. Why, well, the conversation arose when Elspeth noticed that Jimmy did not look himself one day. Normally, he was such a happy-go-lucky 30-year-old guy, always joking around about how he toasted toast by lighting a match behind a fan, or that he was not of Anglo-Saxon origin, but was, in fact, half Islander and had family in the Himalayas.

He told one innocent joke after the next to make people around him feel at ease, that they could just be themselves in his company. Lately, however, James seemed to be carrying a load on his shoulders. Isobel burst out in a rage of anger, something she would never normally do. 'Yes, Elspeth, it is her, that terrible woman who bewitched our fun-loving Jimmy. It was Rosanna who came here and had an affair with Brian, but has also been sleeping with James. Besotted by her beauty, James could not resist her flirty temptations and has fallen victim to her desire. It is so disgraceful and it makes me feel like vomiting. I really feel it is just so bad for an older woman to bed a younger man, and these are the reasons why. Men need to develop in their own natural way. An older woman, with or without intention, does take the power role in the relationship with a younger man.

Also, her experienced sexual drive can become too much for a younger man to resist. It becomes a vicious cycle, by which, she is being filled by youthful sexual energy and the young man is being lassoed into her vagina, which eventually strangles his mind and burns away his innocent, youthful, life position. The unbalanced relationship steals away the young man's position on his life line journey. After a while, although he looks young, he begins to age more quickly than his peers. It takes a strong woman to ignore an attraction to a younger man. Instead of acting on the desire, she needs to look into her own world and fill it with what it lacks. This is the best action — to turn her back on the young attraction, not make it physical, and certainly not contextualize or intellectualize it. The older seductress is a demon who, if marries a younger man, can never actually match his youth. No matter what she wears or how much makeup she applies, she will always be an aging crone compared to the young buck'.

Elspeth was stunned by Isobel's frank account of this most taboo and extremely sensitive topic. But, she pricked her ears up and listened intently as Isobel went even deeper to condemn the sexual relationship between a younger man and an older woman.

'The saddest thing is that the relationship steals away the young man's right to father a child with a girl of his own age. After a while, deep inside, the man starts to despise the older woman whose sweaty menopause starts to make him feel sick, putrid, and repulsed. When he starts to mature, if he has any intellect at all, the man will see that in his youth, he was actually abused by the female sexual predator. Also, his desire to have a younger woman will find him being continually mesmerised by the idea of becoming a father.'

For the first time, Elspeth decided to challenge Isobel. 'I know of a woman who married a younger man. Initially, everyone in our community was totally against their relationship. The woman was separated and had three grown daughters of her own. I am not sure exactly what happened. They say her first husband was a bad drunk and gambled his money at the card table every night. They lived in a really run down, shabby house on the other side the district. The road to their house was mostly inaccessible. It wound the side of the gorged hilled country where the river, gouges out below. Big, deep holes in the road, along with boulders, made the way impossible to pass, especially when it rained.

The family had no electricity, no running water, and everything that they owned down there was worn - out and tattered. After many years of desperate struggles, struggles of all descriptions, the marriage finally broke down. The woman left the house and, at that stage, took with her the three teenage girls. Apparently, her drunken husband moved into a room in the local pub and was only ever seen stumbling along the main street. No matter what time of the day or night, he was always carrying a bottle of beer in his hand. Unkempt, unshaven, he was left to his own devices and could never hold an intelligent conversation ever. I happened to bump into his ex-wife in the hairdresser one day, and she began to tell me all about how her and a young Jackaroo fell in love. I assumed she had few friends, because I had only met her a couple of times and she confided in me that, after a while living alone, she joined the Church Choir. He was there too. The young Jackeroo explained to her that his mother had always taken him to the choir and, as an adult, he had kept up the weekly routine. He enjoyed the songs and, although not the best singer, singing always made him feel good, no matter what mood he was in. Some days were long and hard working on three various cattle stations and he was often tired. The Jackaroo had explained that singing made him feel as fresh as a morning bird. At first, she did not notice him really and had just let him talk away to her.

In the beginning, it was all innocent enough. She did not realize that they had become attracted to each other. It had been so long since she had felt any sexual feelings that, at first, she did not realize just what the feelings meant. The local and well-known Jackaroo was 17 years old, a very sweet-faced kid who wore a checkered shirt, heavy boots, and a tight pair of jeans, worn in the knees and dusty. And, then, overnight, they just seemed to find themselves in bed. It just naturally happened, it was not a forced or coerced situation. Together, they naturally fell as one. Elspeth went on to explain to Isobel how much she admired the pair, because although they endured public ridicule from everyone in the community, they seemed a lot happier than most married couples. They actually seemed to mix really, really well together. The Jackaroo taught his new lady, 20 years his senior, how to herd cattle, fire a gun, and all about the pending weather patterns. The woman cooked night and day for her young beloved, and they never seemed frightened to show their affection in public, always holding hands and peeking sweetly.

Responding to Isobel, Elspeth said, 'I would normally never disagree with one word that you say Isobel, but on this moral issue I have doubts myself after seeing the happiness shine out of those two. I am sure that it is up to the individuals and I could not see any crime in them being married'. On that day, Isobel stood her ground and responded fairly angrily by saying, 'Mark my words Elspeth, nothing good will ever come from that type of marriage, and succumbing to temptations of the younger fleshes will only bring a person many disasters in life. While on the exterior, the Jackaroo and the divorced woman of three girls look happy, behind the scenes there would be nothing more than deep emotional pain. The older woman will continually fret about getting older and older, and she will become intensely possessive and jealous of her young husband's every move. No good can come of it'. Isobel left the mop and bucket, walked out of the dining room where she and Elspeth had been cleaning and preparing for the next round of guests, slamming the door. Elspeth wondered whether or not Isobel had ever fallen for a younger man, her reaction being so intense. Thinking to herself, she said, 'Well everyone is an individual, meanwhile, out here in the country, every day, week, month, and year is the same, and people mostly adhere to strict church values. Well, on the outside looking in, everyone is just wanting to be good, and living by the book, so to speak. Doing things like having an affair with a very young man can only do the woman concerned a lot of social and personal damage. The woman would be damned in everyone's eyes forever and beyond eternity'.

She thought further on the issue. 'A silly woman once told me that if I were to marry an older man, I would always retain the feelings of youth, and that if were to take a senior man as a husband, I would always feel like a young girl. Another much more experienced lady said that it would not be wise to marry a senior man because, in the end, I would just end up looking after a geriatric husband. Mostly, women who marry older gents are only after the money. For me, however, none of this applies, because I point-blank refuse to enter into holy or civil matrimony. Besides, the earth provides plenty for me and my garden, which is always watered by me and will never wither'.

Elspeth, with her own openness to sexuality and her own ideas on the oppressive regime of marriage, was really not that worried about anything that people did in their own private lives. Initially, people were married firstly to the church, and then to their new husband or wife.

The law was the law, and the idea of doing anything outside what was expected by the church would be seen as heresy.

Entering again, Isobel was composed and without question. It is time to change the subject Elspeth, she said calmly and with her usual efficient standing. I have so many more very important things to tell you about and it is really imperative that you take good note of what I am saying. Out here, even though you have known this area from the time you were a young child, and you know every tree and spider, and every small creek and windy path, it is still so easy to become lost. Lost, yes Elspeth, lost and disoriented, especially near where the tree clusters look almost exactly the same. You may think you are going to a safe place, when walking towards where the men took huge portions of soil and rock from the hills, when mining, in the late 1940's. You could become light-headed and giddy. That is the place many have gone and have not returned. Some call it devil's corner and others call it the home of the forsaken. Walking way out there could mean a very long and exhausting day. It is where the allure of the natural, beautified, iconic, picturesque pieces of bush are just so mesmerising, particularly on the days that bring a pink and pretty glow to every leaf. As you drift off into the magical feelings of the shrubbery plants, wildflowers, and twittering birdsong, all of a sudden you can become disorientated, and, before you know it, you can't remember just what tree cluster you walked through to reach that natural spring. The ditch that is often filled with muddied waters has gone, and you will have the stark realisation that you are lost.

Completely and totally lost, being in the beautiful bush slowly becomes like a life-trapping ordeal that may never lift. A horrible entanglement of trees, saplings, and all types of eucalypts — the fallen logs and the hard ground will become a life-threatening disaster. As the sun goes down, your panic and fear will set in. That deep and lonely space is one you will need to overcome very, very quickly. There will be a feeling of nothing before and nothing in the future. You will need to assess everything in your reach speedily. Before the sun goes down and the darkness surrounds you with nothing but a cavernous blankness in front of your eyes. That complete blackness will hide all until that next sunrise. This is what you must do. You must think clearly about these five things: Water, shelter, warmth, signals, and food. Go to the muddy water and fill your shoe. To clear the mud, make a fine grass sift and slowly pour the water through the grass into your other shoe. If you cannot find water, do not worry because you can survive for a fair few days without water. You can always suck leaves from eucalypt seedlings because they have water vapour in their sessile. In fact, most fresh leaves will contain water. So, start sucking the leaves; they do hold moisture. To help you can always follow an ant trail up a tree and down the other side. Ants need water and you can often find a reservoir at the base of a tree.

Find the biggest boulder and feel which way the wind is blowing. The boulder will hold the day's warmth and you will need to position yourself away and out of the wind. Tear and gash away large pieces of bark from any trees. You will need a lot of bark to cover the ground, and also to use as a blanket. Then, find as much grass and soft foliage as you can. Place the bark down near to the rock and then cover it with the grass and foliage. Tuck your newly formed bed very close to the boulder. Now you need a cover. Go to the thickets and take off large pieces of leafy branches. Place the leafed branches over the grass and then put the rest of the bark on top. This top layer will be like your bedspread. This should suffice for the first night. The next day you can proceed with making a tent frame out of a middle-sized tree trunk and sticks, then covering it with bark and thick dense foliage. It is best to stay in one area, so the next day you can start to scan for food, make a fire, and work on a plan to signal for help'. 'Well Isobel', Elspeth sighed, becoming weary of all the advice. 'I am not planning on going down there to that abandoned hillside mine, to where they say people are lost forever, or if they do survive, they come back so disoriented or so forgetful they cannot recognise anyone. I actually do know this place so well Isobel, that I cannot see myself getting lost, I cannot see myself out in the wilderness with nowhere to go. I really have good bearings and am absolutely sure of myself.

There was a man who did get lost down there, though. He was our most experienced hand here at Seymour so nobody could believe that he disappeared and never returned home one summer's evening. There was confusion at first, as to what had happened to the 45-year-old man. He seemed to have stock of himself and his life — a perfectly good man. Why didn't he search for higher ground, or make a bed lined with soil and covered with a thick layer of leaf? The earth would have kept him insulated. Why was he found dead of dehydration when he knew how to find water at the lower points of the region? The story is one that has baffled those who knew him for years. This man knew how to kindle a fire from sticks without a match. He knew how to light a fire from spindle and a fire board, ensuring that the sparks from the friction glinted and lit the tinder nest that was made of light, dry grass and topped with small sticks and light bark. Something must have happened; he may have been drunk — but he never drank. It is strange that he just wandered down into that dreary, lost mine and never took any rations. There were no provisions found on his person. But, the strangest thing was the time of year — a still hot, windless summer's day — and he took not one drop of water. Months later, he was found at the back of the devil's mine.

It was just so very sad. Some actually say that the man may have actually went there to suffer a long and drawn out suicide. A long and terrible death seemed to be something that he had wanted. This way of dying was just so different to the way in which he had lived. He was the husband to a very pretty woman; with a five and an eight-year-old son. The funeral was a misery and everyone wondered just exactly what had happened to the local man. In the background of the shadowy trees that surrounded the cemetery, there was a man who stood right to the back of the shaded day. I felt that man held the key to what appeared to be a suicide. Dressed in mourning, everyone knew. Isobel's normally serene and gentle face went red with furry. 'Elspeth, are you implying that Homestead's best hand was a homosexual? Blasphemy child! You must wash all thoughts of this out or your mind, or for sure you will perish in hell or linger in purgatory'. Elspeth was quick to respond and sway the conversation, meanwhile Isobel ran to the washing room to get a piece of lux soap. Isobel screamed. 'Quickly Elle', as she sometimes loving called her. 'Wash your mouth, face, and hands with soap and go down on your knees immediately. Lift your face to the heavens and start praying'. 'No Isobel, don't worry, it is fine. The man was possessed by that damn nosy witch who has stalked me for years. I know he was good and kind. That other thought is absolutely preposterous! The man at the funeral was just one of the witch's many, many guises. Inside herself, Elspeth was very still. Yes, she had swayed the conversation. Elspeth was of modern thought and knew of many woman and men who lay with the same sex. She too was one of them and just had to have sexual experiences and had no intention of ever marrying. She knew God was not concerned with whom adult people had adult sex with, but was more interested in all people being good, kind, honest, and loving. These were things that many could just not ever talk about, and keeping private things secret would avoid shame that narrow-minded people would inflict. Obviously, the dead man found at the back of the mine had either been accidently exposed for being homosexual or he could not go on living a double life as a husband and father on one hand and a lover to a man on the other. The pain of being torn between two lives may have been just too much for him. Well, Elspeth guessed that the truth would never really be known and Isobel was best left with her rosary beads and church things because, although always wise with her advice, beyond bushland Australia, the world was changing. The world was opening up and immigration was bringing with it a multitude of changing values. The 1967 referendum had recognised both women and Aboriginal people as deserving equality in a society dominated by white men.

Life was sprucing up in the cities and, one day, Elspeth knew that same-sex relationships would be the norm — but not before literally thousands of suicides similar to the experienced good man's would occur. Isobel went straight onto the next topic of conversation. 'At the same time, the Prime Minister of the day, was also making great waves and transforming the White Australia Policy. The restraining laws came into effect way back when there was so much tension between the white miners and the early Chinese miners, particularly around these areas. The liberals, along with some labourers, opposed strict immigration laws. Now, in deep grief, we as a nation will never forget that our progressive thinking PM of 22 months has drowned at sea. At first, when announced missing, his wife said for us not to worry, that he often sat on rocks and looked out into the sunset. But, then he was gone. I know that some were very suspicious of the drowning of such a confident swimmer. However, there were many conspiracy stories about what had happened. I wondered if his strong and modern policies may have had a hand in him never returning to office; perhaps someone else was there by the seaside on that day. I guess we will never know now, but one day in the future, I feel the answers may come. A great thing to remember is that under his leadership a woman was appointed to be the Minister of Housing and is the first female to obtain a ministerial position. This is something for you to think about Elspeth'.

Isobel had so much to convey to Elspeth about promiscuity. 'I have seen promiscuity destroy many a man and woman. It is a seed that breeds rats and infests a person's soul with irreparable damage. It is the lowest form of human behaviour and steals real love and respect forever. I have seen women become so withdrawn into their bodies that their eyes literally bulge with bloody veins that sever the skin. I have seen people become contaminated with so much lust that it purges a toxic and putrid smell from every look that they give. They cannot see real beauty and the gentle essence of any person. They sniff around, like dogs in heat, trying to orgasm at any moment. A mere quick fix soon rises up again into a putty black smack, that needs to be quenched in the lowest ways. Promiscuity takes all that is good, wise, and wonderful and reduces it to a muddy scum of infected sores that cannot be treated. Bad luck follows the perverted mind; there is no escaping it. It is drenched in a bacterium that multiplies into rank circles of forgetfulness and faces that are hardened by its frothing wounds. A person's self-esteem is gutted, and slowly but surely, they begin to self-harm. A promiscuous man is one who is of such an ego that he believes all the world should fall at his feet.

He is a man who is only looking for the next woman's vagina to soak up his penis. This is a disgusting road to choose and a cancerous condition is bound to appear. It can only lead to great sorrow and pain. There is no real love in promiscuity and it cannot be justified by saying that boundaries are set and all is okay. Seeking to devour another person's body for carnal reasons quickly condemns all really lovely human attributes. It is wise to look at a person's face, and admire that person's individual personality, to see the gift of life given and to look beyond and into the purpose for life, the reason for living, caring, and sharing. To see people as purely sex objects is just so empty, just so bad. After so many similar experiences, both recipients will want to commit suicide. The people involved in a promiscuous life will end up in a living hell. They will fall into all sorts of medical ailments. They will have bad health and attract bad relationships. Bindings will continue to corrode everything good about being alive. A loss of memory is the first sign, and then either a dramatic weight loss or weight gain. Secondly, the skin becomes grey and with no personal care and no sexual dignity, a person can find themselves heading towards the haunted house the sits in the dark.

The haunted house draws them in closer and closer to its door. If those of promiscuity enter the house, they can never return to the light again. This is serious, Elspeth, and you must take heed of these words that I advise. The haunted house is filled with the lost and tormented souls of promiscuity — a place of rapes, poverty, and thick, dark, depressive thoughts which linger heavily in the dusty air — a place where dirty dark clown faces can appear. There is no light and the people there are full of badness. They sit behind screens that depict the worst of human degradation and afterwards nothing humane is left. Once there, a slow corrode of the spirit leaves an empty shallow shell of a being that cannot function and cannot find any door out of the oppressive black abuse. Sometimes, children are born, bought and sold up there — doomed and diseased before conception. They grow to become worse than their parents in that deprived place of immoral living. Who should sit at the helm of the table that is scratched with such a bad sign? Yes, it is her. A mixture of alcohol and urine seeps from the corner of every room and a paedophile is the caretaker. He's a bad man who is sometimes a pale-faced woman of no substance, corrupt and depraved in every way. There is no step that can lead to anything of goodness once the soul is permeated by promiscuity; the only road is the road to the sinister house'.

There was always a lot, yes, a lot of talk about the way that we should and should not raise children. Next to discussions about weather, sheep sales, food, and what time the pub opened and closed, raising children was high on the topic of conversation agenda in the house. Isobel, although not a mother, seemed to know so much about how to look after children properly. It was a shame that Isobel was not a mother as she had a mother-type figure and very motherly ways. But, she never had that one special relationship to actually conceive a baby. And, her life as a domestic did seem to take over most aspects of her world. Isobel did not believe in some of the old wives' tales that had been passed down from her mother about how to look after children.

Spanking as a form of chastisement and feeding at very specific times so that the baby went onto a strict sleeping and breast-feeding time cycle were a few of them. Also, rubbing rum or scotch into the inflamed gums of a teething baby seemed totally absurd. Isobel felt these babies were the drinkers of tomorrow. The loving, tender, and free approach was the method Isobel preferred. But, sometimes she did have to adhere to what the parents of the children would have her do. The Clarence children were young when they first arrived at Seymour Homestead but already seemed to have that embedded elitist way about them. They were not free to roam the hillsides like the country kids from the local area.

No, they were much more restricted in their nature and, from the beginning, were unsure of their new bush lifestyle, tending to play inside, even on a bright, sunny day. They were aware of the outdoors only to the point of what lay directly in front of their exact footsteps. It was this unawareness that took Aidan to the dam and never home again. Also, the parents were not that open to having their children learn that much about the bush and all its miraculous playground opportunities for their children to enjoy. Skipping, hopscotch, noughts and crosses, shove ha'penny, housey-housey, and quoits, the throwing game, were Isobel's favourite ways to enjoy an afternoon of relaxation with kiddies from the neighbouring farms. The best fun for the youngsters she would say, could be found sitting around a wintery camp fire, enjoying a good old Aussie sing-a-long such as Valderi, Valdera, Kumbaya and She'll be Comin Round the Mountain. These were Isobel's favourite fireside tunes. Their glowing rosy cheeks, alight by the fire, warm and smiles, told the stories of the notorious bush - ranger; and the like, who, in the imaginations of the children were still out the back of bush, working for the downtrodden poor and rising up against the force of the law and government dictation.

Isobel reflected on her early life in service. At first, it was very difficult being treated like a nobody and not knowing anyone. I coped by working very hard. And in every instance, I worked long hours and did more than requested of me. I coped by never questioning anyone and I did not get involved with any gossip or say one bad word against anyone. In fact, I just kept to myself, night and day and day and night. I felt that my life would turn one day, but not back then. Slowly and surely, my courteous nature was noticed by Mr Clarence, and he began to give me responsibility and trust beyond some of the others. I needed to be self-aware and would draw on some of the things that mother's aunt showed me when I was very young. That caring aunt showed me things like how to iron a shirt properly. Firstly, lay the collar on both sides and iron flat, then take the shirt and hold it at both shoulders, putting one shoulder over the end of the board and then ironing, reaching the area along the back of the neck. Then, iron the other side. Prepare the cuffs similarly to the collar, pressing on both sides. Then, place the full shirt back first on the board, neck to the left. Open the shirt and iron one side of the back, close the shirt and iron that part of the front, do the same on the other side. Lastly, the sleeves, iron the sleeves with a cool crispy seam. Mrs Clarence noticed that I could iron a shirt meticulously well and promoted me to head supervisor of the house. She was also impressed with the way in which I folded socks and towels. I was actually taught some very neat things by my sweet aunt. Character was another really big topic that I learnt a lot about, and this time from my mother. This education about a person's character helped me very much, not just in my early days, but right throughout my service life at the Seymour Homestead. These words of advice echoed in my mind for many years to come.

'Beware of some women, they can be cunning and cruel and vicious with their tongues. Some women can be very, very calculated and often have an underlying driven purpose to all their interactions. Mostly, you will find these women have come from very affluent families and are used to getting exactly what they want in life. They are spoilt little things that find it hard when, unexpectedly, life knocks up a ' big no' to something they really want. For the first time in their lives, they cannot get what they want. It may be a man they desire, or a holiday destination is all booked up, or their financial situation may take a sudden downturn and their rich father cannot pay their monthly bills. Or, maybe her husband failed at a job. There are other situations to be really aware of too.

These are women often from the most abusive circumstances, They can be totally cut throat, and watch out if you go up against one of them. They seem to have an extra sense of knowing how to cause underlying harm to other women, particularly those who they become jealous of. They are the worst. Never trust a woman who comes from such a bad place. Often, the badness of their upbringing has permeated their soul to a very evil point. They have never experienced real love and they have never been shown respect, and do not understand good wholesome values, like the ones that I was handed down by my own grandmother. Often with these women, they lead you to think that they are living and acting in a certain way, looking for pity and understanding at every drop of a hat. But, for sure, their personalities are nothing like you think they are. I did see one girl turn her life around, but it took her many, many years to do so. And, after all that she went through, she spent most of her time alone and forlorn, without friends or family. I heard that in the end she did a lot of community work but died alone and without recognition. Mainly, these women have plans of their own and very advanced survival skills. Against the odds, they had to survive whatever life dished out as they were growing up, and they are only ever thinking about themselves.

It could be such that a woman may have a simple job in a dress shop looking after the customers and being extremely helpful all day, every day. But, when she goes home, behind closed doors, instantly she has forgotten about the people at the shop, and is continually planning how to become rich, thinking up ways to overtake the store and wear all the silken and cotton garments. Not one person who she ever serves would guess that the sweet, caring, divine face at the counter is actually a mastermind — a person looking to improve her own position, no matter what she must do. Certainly, she would not care how long it would take, or who she needed to push out of the way. To get to the top of the fashion world and own every fine garment, she would be a very cunning player indeed.

'Your approach to this issue seems to be very hard Isobel,' replied Elspeth 'because when I was growing up I had a friend who lived on the way to Yaouk. When I met her, she was right off the rails. I always felt sorry for her, and if such a bad hand was turned in my life, I would probably be dead by now. I would have killed myself one thousand times over. Poppy was her name. Poppy had been raped when she was five and her mother had been killed; circumstances were horrific to say the least. She was left to look after her younger brother as her father of no education was never around to watch his kids. That father was also a mean, silly blotto.

Poppy was totally and completely uncared for and became an adult child. Nobody in the district liked her because she had bad behaviour, No sexual boundaries and poor hygiene, she was always off with some boy from around town. Appearing to be angry in herself, some of us other girls were a bit frightened of the way in which she sounded and looked older than what she was. But, one day, on the way home from our little local school house, I decided to stop and take the time to try and really get to know Poppy. It was in that one single piece of conversation that I could see right into the girl who none of us wanted to know. Poppy was a really cool girl, who because of all her difficult days, actually had some really very nice and sincere qualities. I have heard recently that she is now the head of a Welfare Agency and works tirelessly for people who she really understands. Quiet and a brilliant woman too, she has outstripped a lot of the girls who never wanted a thing to do with her. Poppy now owns a great, big, open-plan young women's recovery prayer retreat. None of the others can believe what she has done with her life'.

'Just be careful Elspeth', replied Isobel hesitantly. 'If possible in instances, protect your soul and heart to nourish your life's journey. Try and find women who offer honesty and don't play games. Find women who are of a graceful nature, and have their hearts in the right place. Look for the special qualities of purity, kindness, and caring. Know in your heart, that the women you choose to be your friends will never set you up, and will always show consideration towards you as a real person. A real girl friend is trustworthy and reliable, and will always speak the truth to you. A real friend will always include you in her friendship circle. No matter what, a true friend is reliable and integral towards your personal life. A true friend never plays pecking order and never deliberately tries to make you feel left out or on the outer.

A true friendship is easy to discern through feelings of peace and love you feel after being in their company. A real friendship weathers the highs and lows of life, and understands boundaries. If you can, give yourself time to give trust to another person. Do look for the goodness in others, but do not give completely of yourself, as it does take time to really get to know another person. As I have pointed out, not everyone has your best interests at heart and some will take what they can from you and run. They will run with your best things and claim them as their own, they will adopt your personal qualities and pretend. The best advice I can give is that no matter what happens when you eventually own your own hut, try and stay well, as being well in yourself will attract other well people. Perhaps you may consider becoming a specialist dietician yourself. You could then meet others who have a similar personal value system to yours and people who will add branches of song to your most beautified and magnificent outdoor world'.

Branches of Song

There were people who came from away, moving to the area. They were keen to leave a congested and busy city life to establish themselves as farmers. Although, without the traditional passed down methods of knowing how to read the weather patterns and actually live on a farm, day in and day out from childhood, many failed. Unless they had a helping hand and some good sound advice from a neighbouring farmer, it was nearly impossible for an outsider to work the countryside and to know the important decisions to make when looking after the sheep and cattle. This included knowing how to keep the land at its best yielding capacity, growing wool to its potential and being aware of the daily life happenings in the shearing shed and cattle yards. Often, they would graze the wrong type of sheep. Instead of Merinos for wool, putting cross-breeds on land of shallow soil that had no carrying capacity at all. They would not understand the cyclic pattern to looking after sheep. The ewes have their lambs in spring when the meadows are richly green and the sunshine, bright and warm follows after a long freezing cold winter. They are joined with a ram between March to May for lambing in Spring time. Or, later in October for pre-summer births. But, this timing also depends a lot on the rains.

Buying a lot of old, broken-mouth sheep meant they needed to be culled by the farmer because their teeth were breaking, warn or missing and putting them out to shallow soils with questionable hope of rain in the middle of summer was a gamble, with the added risk of sale yard sheep carrying foot and mouth disease, scabby mouth, fluke, worms or lice. This approach was not a good idea. The poor, aged sheep were tired and already dejected and rejected. Basically, the good, knowing farmer discarded them because they were of no use to his purpose of growing wool. These sheep could be seen dying on the land, all fly blown, on the newcomers', hopeful but hopeless rural enterprises. Most people from the land knew that being a real farmer takes skill and knowledge. Different mobs of sheep have different purposes and it is a shame that people do not understand that the man on the land's life is connected to the daily and traditionally handed down ways of how to manage the sheep. They need to understand that the genetic makeup of a sheep's constitution is very important in being able to produce the best wool. Although this all sounds like basic things to understand. Repeatable traits need to be constantly assessed, including greasy and clean fleece weight, the yield of the wool, including both the fibres' diameter and staple wool length, and the body weight of the sheep. These are just the first few steps in being able to run a sheep farm.

All of these important factors need to be taken into consideration by the grazier and the genetics of the mob needs to be continually developed, firstly by the purchase and care of the best rams. A good eye at the sale is needed to ensure the best ram at the stud sales. You need a good nourishing ram paddock and in the future will need to know just when to cull those that are not producing good, healthy sperm. A farmer needed to ensure shade in the paddocks because it is important, especially in the hot climate, as heat effects sperm. Also, vitamin A is essential for healthy sperm and is found in green hay.

Elspeth would take in every conversation that she ever overheard, both in and around the homestead. The farmers that came to visit never realised that Elspeth was setting herself up to become self-sufficient. Early on, Elspeth decided that if she ever did have children, she would pass down all that she had learnt about farming in her early days at

Seymour. Inside herself, she felt only a need to expand her own poetic visions of farming, which were embedded in stories of Jack, Jill, and Dora. Elspeth's love of the countryside meant she tended to naturally see the sheep as a gestation of poetic inference that seemingly appeared by way of just being there. But, one day, as she was cleaning the small, cold office, she noticed the dusty large leather-bound ledgers and registers that noted all the information about the sheep.

This information was taken from the farmer's Cooper Note Book for Stockowners. The pocket book was carried by farmers. It was where shearing tallies, ear marking reference, and importantly, memoranda pages to make notes like the date, name of paddock, numbers of sheep, type of sheep and what they had done on that day like drenched, shorn, or if they were diseased were all written down. It was a quick reference for disease, pests, and other safety precautions. The book, which newcomers to farming would not know about, was a must to use every day, and the best way to confidently manage the sheep. The trucks and sheep sales would come and go, and the huge homestead prospered in the 1950s. It was then that Elspeth thought to herself that it was very important to eavesdrop on the conversations of those station hands, seasonal contractors and farm hands, to learn more than just what she saw with her own eyes as poetic daydreams and notions.

One dream she had was when the poplars and deep green, rich, flourishing patches of lush grass looked to be natural realms of trees and grass, surrounded by sheep that huddled together in the shade of the trees. There were more to these groups of sheep than just following each other down the sheep trail to places of togetherness, much more than Elspeth's romantic, pretty, painterly landscape in her mind's imagery. The farmers had a small mob of sheep that were determined as the killers; these would be killed for household consumption. Others, if they were not deemed fit enough for mating, like cross-breeds, were then readied for the 'fat lamb' market. They were fattened on good pasture for sale. All the mustering was done on horseback, with dogs running around at the directions shouted by the horseman or those mustering on foot. Later on, every farmer owned a land rover to move the sheep from one end of the property or after shearing into the shelter sheds when there were blizzards and snow. This made for a hard day's work. The average number of a mob was about 350. The ewes' ovulation cycle was also so very important for the farmer to understand and discern. The ewes would be shorn in the middle of winter, moved into sheds in bad weather, and about two to four weeks later put through the sheep dip to ensure hygiene and no mycotic dermatitis or cheesy gland. Other sheep were also put through the chemically-infused dips.

Elspeth found out that all the sheep were inspected for cuts after shearing, after which, they were dunked twice through the long sheep dip run — the swim — which, according to the farmers, most sheep did not enjoy. They needed to be thoroughly wet, particularly behind the neck, which was the hardest place to ensure wetness. Therefore, the entry slash into the run was very important as a commencement to the almost 10 yard swim and the other 2 dunks. 'So much to consider when sheep dipping,' thought Elspeth, after thinking about all she had overheard the men talking about. Between 315 to 870 pints of chemical would be premixed in a large water container and the sheep would need to fast for a day beforehand, to reduce waste. The dermatitis was reduced by letting the wet sheep out of the holding pens and back into the paddock as soon as possible. When the lambs arrived in spring, if they were male, they would all be desexed, castrated or marked in preparation for becoming a weather. Merinos were the type of sheep grazed at the Seymour Homestead and a good stud ram was often purchased by the property, to bring a different and stronger blood to the breeding. The ewes were drenched and ear marked at the same time, drenching for liver fluke and worms, ear marking for identification and registration of the particular sheep. After this, the lambs were placed back with the ewes until such a time that they were ready for weaning when they were then mustered back into the yard. The known saying that Australia was built on the sheep's back was definitely true and much happened in and around the 1950s which brought forward modernisation. At the time, wool was fetching a pound note for a pound of wool.

'A few weeks into my work at Seymour a kind boy arrived', whispered Elspeth to the Swallowtail butterfly, who she confided many of her feelings after everyone, including Mannus, had left. 'I know he was sort of attracted to me. It was a windy day and I had been working at the clothes line, which was a long piece of thin rope tied between the veranda beams. I could see that he was good looking, almost too good looking. He had a very softly spoken soul, and seemed to be a bit lost in himself and looking for friendship. The wind was at my back that day and hurried me along the veranda where he was waiting. A very slender figure, dressed in a denim jacket with a line of badges across the top pocket and a faded pair of jeans. I remember looking down from his clean and unscathed face to his brown boots that were tied with red boot laces and a bit muddy. Initially, all he really wanted to do was just talk about what his life was like growing up living in the shearer's quarters next to a busy shearing shed. The harsh, loud wind, was the only reason why I decided to let him come inside the house. The door of the wood room was already pushed open by the force of the gust, and we hurriedly ran inside before the winds were to push us onto the ground.

This was a regular occurrence and the winds were a normal part of our everyday mountain existence. I boiled the kettle in the small kitchenette at the back of the wood room, and we sat at the table that was situated up against the window. We sat down, looked at each other, and began to be moved by the conversation of the weather designs and the warmth of the tea. It was then that the boy who called himself

Devine, a name that did not fit in around here at all, began to ramble on about the shearing shed and all the happenings in and it, characterised by the folks who did work the sheds. 'My earliest recollections of the sheds are the greasy, dusty, steamy, wool and cow dung everywhere. The dog's too, they were always barking. There was a strong smell all about, but those in the shed did not seem to notice. They were continually running over the backs of the sheep. The rhythmical sound of the shed engine, turning the belt that connects to the shearing rods at each stand, then to the shears, when engaged by the shearer, who shorn the fleece in an industrial wine of the comb. For my board, I had to work in the yards, branding, drenching, and drafting off the old ewes. We would shear about 100 to 130 sheep per day, and I sometimes worked as the rouse about, sweeping up all the extra wool and doing odd jobs for hours on end. I would try not to look at the clock because that seemed to make time go more slowly'.

Devine seemed to go on and on and on, talking life in the shed, when all I had on my mind was getting the washing folded and attending to the Clarences' evening meal. The meal was crumbed liver in gravy sauce, and by this stage, it was already close to 3pm. I just sat there and thought to myself, 'If he is trying to impress me, then he isn't and those red shoe laces are of no interest to me'.

Devine raved on. 'The head shearer, the gun shearer, became my best friend. Often, late at night, we would share a bottle of beer sitting near the run, a place where we could be away from everyone. It was a big deal to be the good mate of the gun shearer, as absolutely everyone wanted to know him. At first, I was not sure what to say to him as he was 10 years older and the quickest at fleecing a sheep I had ever witnessed. I was not sure if he would want to talk to the shed rouse about, but he did. Some winter mornings, the iced-up puddles and freezing cold would bring about a swearing rage from a shearer who had a hangover. One in particular, was a man who drank far too much. I remember his jealousy and contempt for all the other shearers and the Clarences also, for owning the shearing shed. It was so clear that he would never own his own property, farm, or even small plot of land. In fear of becoming like him, I never went too far into alcohol', finished Devine.

'I really tried to stay interested in what Devine was telling me', sighed Elspeth, 'but did yawn once or twice as he went on to explain the rest of what he knew and believed might let him into my secret life. Eventually, I had to ask the other kitchen hand to get the meal under way, handing her the fresh rosemary to garnish and cook into the meat. Devine said that he wanted to be a good spirited shearer and work towards becoming a wool classer. 'I want to get my certificate in wool classing, and then, well, maybe settle down with a gorgeous country girl who can cook meat in tender swelling.'

Outside in the yards, the good neighbouring farmer's sons would keep the sheep up to the shed. Sometimes, visitors or the next-door farmer's wife and kids would visit. As soon as a woman was spotted on her way to the shed a voice could be heard. 'Ducks on the pond!' This was the saying used by all shearers, and a sign that they had to watch their swearing and be well behaved in front of the women. A lot of cooking was done by either the farmer's wife or the homestead cook. In the case of this kitchen, Mrs Clarence has probably never even met a shearer let alone cooked for one'. 'You are right, Devine', sighed Elspeth, 'I am the one that helps Isobel cook lunch for the shearers. But, I have never been allowed to go to the old shed. On the other hand, I have heard a lot of shed stories from the visiting farmers who drop in here from time to time to talk about the weather and who has the best wool in the district'. The farmers gave all sorts of information about all sorts of things that happened in the shed after the shearing was finished. In the future, these types of shed stories may have related to a shearer having a bad back from bending over all day, and not wearing a stomach sling. The slings came much later on in time. This would be a problem because the shearer would not be able to work at the next shed. They may talk about whether or not the tar-boy or rouse about had done a good job with dubbing a tar stick on the hind of the sheep that were smelly, fly blown, and full of maggots.

Some graziers would be very angry to think that a fly blown sheep had mixed with the good wool, and all would have to be thrown into the dags section of the wool stall. They would also talk about the size of the shearing combs, with only 100 sheep being shorn before the introduction of wide combs. There were cute stories also of the little kiddies jumping in and out of the wool pens, and mischievously distracting the wool classer, as he was carefully considering and assessing a good fleece that was thrown on the table.

There was a bit of a show off, a young shearer in the shed one day. He was a fill in because one of the shearers had accidentally cut his hand with the shears and could not work the shed that afternoon. It seemed like he got everything wrong, bragging about being the best in the district, and pretending that he had won the Golden Shearing International Shearing Competition in New Zealand. The head gun shearer had to put a stop to the bragging. At first, he threw a bucket of cold water over a sheep, but everyone knows that sheep are supposed to be shorn dry. He also said that he had let a group of sheep out of the holding pens the night before because they seemed hungry.

The head shearer let him have it right there and then and pretty much swore his head off at the young, puffed up man. 'You are a liar and the sheep need to fast for a day before being shorn. Where did you come from you louse about?' The shearer stormed out of the shed to segregate the just-fed sheep. The preparation for shearing was so important and that boy knew nothing at all about shearing sheep. The young shearer took no notice of the head man in the shed and began to shear a sheep. He wore no moccasins to cover and protect his feet. And, instead of turning the sheep over to commence clipping the sheep's belly, the silly lad started his first blow from the rare of the sheep's back, moving up towards the neck. All the shearers were horrified at his poor attitude and lack of knowledge. He was thrown out of the shed and told to get off the property, never to return again. Tending to sheep and preparing them for shearing takes a great deal of knowledge, skill, and work. Sheep are shorn for their wool, to give comfort, and also for important health reasons like ensuring that the wool does not become matted and full of lice.

Especially good for ewes before lambing, shearing is ideal to help with cleanliness whilst giving birth and helps make it less difficult for the baby lambs to find their mother's teats when they do feed. To increase nutritional intake, the ewes will eat more grass to warm their body, and, as such, will have more nutrients for herself and the lamb. The timing of shearing is important for various reasons. 'All this information, I will one day convey to my own child or children and hopefully in his or her adult life, it may even lead to us owning our own farm and running livestock', said Elspeth in a determined stance.

'Aside from the practicalities of learning so much about how to graze sheep, the schedule of shearing, and good wool growth, I learned as much as I could about how to look after livestock. One of my favourite times of the day was at about 5pm on a still, winter afternoon. The very bright sun would stream across the landscape. The Angus cattle and hoggets would be feeding, as would the kangaroos. On the other side of the paddocks, the deer would appear on the horizon and also begin to feed. There did seem to be an unspoken communication between the beasts, sheep, and wildlife. I could almost hear them humming contentedly as they munched on the lush grasses that were grown in the rich, thick black alluvial top soils. To use a pertinent cliché in this conversation: 'Quiet to the contrary'. This particular part of the high country was not barren and desolate. The sun's brightest shine that drew close to the ground was very dazzling, in contrast, the deep blue shadowy and mysterious stream of mountainous ranges spread the bright and darkest skies at exactly the same time. The strong light made the trees' shadows standout, as the vivid brightness surrounding the depths made for a contrast on the ground.

There is a slowness out here, a slowness connected to the farming way of life and hard, steady, good work. It's a place where time seems to creep by ever so gradually, and life takes on a different meaning in a place where people can simply enjoy being people and the homey things in life like good long conversations about the cloud coverage or the priest's sermon at mass'.

Elspeth had clear and good intentions to observe all the pastoral care and management ways. She would pop all the ideas into her apron pocket, for future times and, perhaps, execution.

'There are no facades or pretences when working in the sheds or the house. People never try to outdo each other — to be better than each other. Out here, people only come together to help each other. People need to stand together for company, to break down the isolation and because of a genuine interest in each other and the families respectively. After the shearing, which occurred once or twice a year, the shed appeared to have an abandoned feel about it. On the occasion and even after dark, there may have been just one busy hand doing a bit of a clean-up or preparation for the next round of shearing. Otherwise, there was nobody in or around the shed for some long months at a time. The corrugated iron roof, pointing to the sky and the windows small and dark, still glazed in the shine and creaked in the high bustling air. The cast iron water tank heated in the hot sun and froze across the surface in winter's long nights and shorter days. The old shed took on a creepy feeling when being unused, the feeling that perhaps that some not-so-good things may be happening inside. However, this was just a figment of my imagination. When sliding open the door at the top of the ramp, there was nothing inside except for the oily lanoline smell of the fleece, a few tea cups, broken beer bottles, and a couple of rickety kitchen chairs.

There were a couple of things that happened in the shed. Pushed up against the left over an open bale of wool with a fleece of AAA placed up against it with a grading slot was a hideaway place for lovers who knew it to be a place for, well, good sex, knowing nobody would bother them there. This feeling of abandonment was only temporary because we all knew that the shed would be alive and happening again.

The men, the clippers, the stories, the hangovers, and, of course, the sheep would return to be shorn. The sheds would sometimes be cleaned and made ready for a special function, like a birthday party or even a wedding reception. Brian Clarence declined the suggestion made by a farming friend that he could hold his daughter's 16th birthday party in his 10-pen shed, saying he had planned to take her back to Lavender Bay and that the idea of holding a party in his shearing shed for Bessie would be absurd. Brian's friend explained that having a special function in a shearing shed was an authentic Aussie way that country folk celebrated the days that marked an important turning point in their lives. These events connected the work life of the station to the family traditions of the generations. The shed was a sturdy place for those who drank and may vomit could not do much damage to it. The parties were a way to bond siblings and would steer the younger people into a life of farming. It was a good feeling to remember a celebrated birthday party in the family shearing shed.

Then, the farmer's wife, who had been listening diligently to the conversation, went on to explain that she had heard of a special wedding celebration that had been held in a shed a few hours away. The shed had been decorated with hundreds and hundreds of wildflowers of all colours, shapes, and so many differing species. The bouquets, head dresses, men's lapels and mother's accessories were all of the same flowery style, which complemented the arrangement on the church altar, pews and wedding cake'.

✧ ✧ ✧

There were many hilarious conversations between the shearers and the Clarences. One lunch time, Augustina was tending to her special herb plot. She was particularly fond of sage. The herbal aromas were fanning all around her and she was deep in thought when a loud, deep, rough and intrusive voice penetrated her private thoughts. 'How do ya like it out here at the back of woop, woop Mrs.' Augustina was a bit annoyed to think of her magnificent homestead being located at woop, woop. 'Thank you', she responded reservedly. Going on to explain his current daily position, the shearer had decided to stop and give Augustina a full account of why he had a hangover. 'I am cactus taday, but might feel better by the arvo. I had a bit of a bingle and it was all over red rover. I now feel like a bit of a deadhead. I did chuck a bit of a woobly and had to get a coober to give me a hand. Being a long way from the black stump, I thought you might understand. But I suppose you have been flat out like a lizard. Dead set, I got a shock when it happened. Ya see, I was on the way to give the ace joolaroo a bit of a burl and couldn't hangon. Just between you and me, I sort of had in mind more than just a yarn, ya know, a bangaroo. But ended up a drongo and late for the show. I asked me mate to give her a hooroo from me and then gave meself a smoko. Anyway, I think he was interested in havin a yarn with her too. Anyways, Mrs Clarence, me a true blue Aussie and had a top drop to give her.

A hoon, this local lad with tickets on himself, was drivin like a rat up a drain pipe, down the main street and smashed his ute into me land rover. Stone the crows, there was a crowd on the scene and the accident will now end up in the local rag. Lucky, I had me swag with me and a bickie too. Later in the night, I became a cot case and felt that I might cark it. I probably have buckleys with that girl now. Even though I was dinky di, the boys in blue did question if I had a pint too many, I said no, only a chop sanger'.

Augustina just stood in her herb patch and wondered if the man speaking to her was of a different language. It seemed that he was totally unaware that his speech was extremely difficult to decipher for anyone, who say, had learnt English overseas and came to visit. They would have absolutely no idea what he was saying. Just in that moment, another shearer who was on his way back to the shed stopped to join the conversation. 'Fair crack of the whip Jack, it is time to and stop givin Mrs Clarence a burl, she'll be zonked out after all your yobbo talk. Come on, it's time to nick off and let the lady get back to her garden, she's probably had a gutful of you. You are such a mug, and nobody wants a drongo around. Not today anyway. Why don't you thank the woman for a good nosh up, because she is startin to look a bit cheesed off with ya. Paying a compliment, the second man, on what felt like a mad chapter in a book, said to Augustina, 'You are a real bona love, and you don't want to hear no more from this deadhead'.

Then they left to get back into their shearing. The two men left Augustina in total dismay at the reality of their language patterns and expressions, which they were completely oblivious to. Off they staggered along her nestled and well-kept garden path, smelling of sweat and greasy wool. To them, she was the strange one. Always getting around in the bush with her hair done, lipstick on, and wearing Sunday skirts and blouses, Augustina was a bit of a snobby wowser in their eyes, and they would not be looking to give her a burl again.

To her they sounded like larrikins, but interestingly, Augustina had a great interest in the development of language systems, in particular the indigenous language groups of early Australia and the Australian vernacular as a whole. She felt that the entrenched slang needed to be experienced to really fully grasp. it. So, she thought to herself, 'Well, I do feel a bit bonzer now'. Laughing, she bent down picked a big bunch of sorrel and ate a pretty pink flower. 'Compared to those two blokes, I look like a fine piece of bone china'. Back down at the shed, the men were laughin at themselves for boggin in at the table and not mindin their own bizzo by stoppin to try and have a naughty with the tall poppy, Mrs Wowser, as they now quietly referred to her as being. 'Bloody oath mate', said one shearer to the next, do you reckon that she boozers on a bit. Or is she just up for a cuppa'? The next responded, 'Well, she always looks a corker to me, so I dun know. Anyway you yabba a lot.

One thing that I do think about a lot when shearin up here at Seymour, is another beaut lookin sheila who visits and sometimes sleeps down the cottage there. I would like to give her a chokkie or two'. As he nudged the other shearer, the next went on to say, that he was a bit frightened of lookin like a dill, so he would keep his doodle to himself and then he let out a big yawn. The woman he was referring to was none other than Rosanna. The other lad just looked down and said, 'Me father, God bless his soul, told me not to gander at those types of women. Dad said that I would be made a mug of, and that me soul would perish in hell. Me parents were God fearin people whose own parents suffered the great depression. I was taught good values like waste not, want not, and to find a good decent joolaroo to marry, someone who would know how important it is to say grace before every meal. Anyway, I end up lookin like a bit of a wuss around those types of women, so you can give her a go and she might even cook up a good nosh'. The neighbouring cockie who managed the shearing for the Clarences overheard the two yobbos and said, 'scuse me, you two bodgies will be bloody cactus if you don't stop muttering and will come a gutser if you don't get back to crutchin and stop thinkin about crackin onto her'. It was that time of year again as crutching the sheep only occurred between main shearing times. The sheep, mostly female, needed to be shorn all over and especially around the udder to help when feeding their lambs.

The tiring and sweaty job was left up to the two young shearers who were told, in no uncertain fashion, to stop thinking about Rosanna. Just then, a flock of white cockies flew past the shed and the three decided that they had best get to work because they did not want to run late for the bush telegraph that was being built by the farm hand near the outdoor dunny. 'Don't ya start tellin porkies about Mrs Clarence now. She may get cranky and chuck us off her station. The bush telegraph runs riot around these parts and it would be hard to get any more work if we keep pervin on her ase'. The youngest shearer decided to voice his opinion on how he did not want to lose his job and was worried that his family would find out. They could be disgraced in the community. They were people of high standing, people who said grace before each and every meal and wanted their son to be spiffy in every situation. 'Fair suck of the sav, everyone has their situation,' said the cockie to the two larrikins. 'Beggars can't be chosers, so get back to work, ya yakk dakka's. Fair crack of the whip, back into it'.

Across from the shed, there was a swift fox, darting around. At first, he did not see Elspeth looking at him, who very sneakily moved in toward him. Until, in a flick, he was off and she was left standing in his scent, knowing that he would not sprint back her way. By now, all Elspeth could see in the distance were specks of colours, red and brown across the far-away hill that reflected so many different aspects of the ever-changing mountainous light. That morning, Elspeth had risen very early, before the sun rose. Up she got, to go to the top of the hill which was positioned away from the house and boosted a view across the ranges and above the gully that seemed to stretch way out to the sea. Elspeth had been told that the top of the hill was above the cloud line and that a spectacular site could be seen right at sunrise. Devine had described the view and, in his conversation about the sheep, had convinced her to rise early to experience the romantic and haunting view. Devine was right. The thick greys clouds hung out over the escarpment and below an open clear sky, closing the whole bush and winding river below. Soon after her arrival, the sun began to rise from behind the cloud mass and streams of pink and mauve painted the picture that could only be captured for about 15 minutes at that time of the day. Then, after a while, the clouds moved towards the hill and Elspeth was showered in a light fog.

Nobody was there on that day, except for Cain's voice that rang gentle from below the thickened and dense clouds. Without hesitation and without thinking, Elspeth slowly removed her clothes, a pair of jeans and a long orange jumper that was knitted by a woman with a bad tongue who was also a friend of her biggest enemy. Kicking off her boots, Elspeth slipped her silks onto the hard, hilly ground and stood in the thick, crisp morning air. It felt nice to let the fog cleanse every pore of her skin. For a while, she stood hidden in the fog, and then, as the clearing came, she quickly dressed and ran back to her morning duties. When she arrived back in the kitchen, she felt a connection to something other than herself and the Clarences. It was then that she had made the decision to find out more about the early days at the sheep station and who had actually lived at Seymour before her time, wondering if they too had stood naked in the fog.

Old Bob often worked down in a small acreage called windy corner. Elspeth knew that he had a good knowledge of all the events and historical happenings of the place. Nothing changed and very few new people ever set up house anywhere near Seymour. What interested Elspeth now was who, in fact, were the original folk that had initially owned the Homestead before the Clarences. Old Bob, she knew, would have a good recollection of who they were and why they had left.

Old Bob was at the end of the line of those yesteryear people, and worked his small 250-acre plot of land that Elspeth heard was given to him by the Fennels. The Fennels were the original family who built the house that for a short time was owned by the Council. This was long before it was moved because the man-made lake was filled. The Fennels had four sons who were all farmers. The boys were raised as strict

Catholics and were hard working men of goodness and hardiness, but with very individual characters. Samuel was the eldest. He pretended to be interested in other people, but most of the time was rude and gruff to his brothers. He played footy every Saturday and was known for secretly punching the other boys in the face whilst their heads were in the scrum pack. David, the second eldest, was a very prayerful young man, but was also extremely ambitious to the point where he would stop at nothing to get what he desired. Michael, the second youngest, was full of jokes, but some people felt that his humour may have been covering up some other deep and strange issues. Joseph was the youngest. He was clever, polite, but sometimes distant. This was the first insight that Elspeth had into the family who had owned the homestead before her time. Old Bob had come into his cottage early that day, because the weather had changed from a fairly bright sunny morning to a gustily overcast type of afternoon.

Elspeth was there standing with a warm batch of scones and asked the man if he would be interested in filling her in on who the original family were and what they were like. Old Bob explained that the matriarch of the family was a woman known as Grandma Betsy, and her husband was Mr. Jersey who always smoked a pipe. When not puff, puff, puffing away on his smoke, he filled the house with his happy, but sometimes annoying, harmonica music. They insisted that when the boys grew up, they could marry when old enough, but would need to bring their wives back to Seymour so that Grandma Betsy could train each young wife how to care and manage a house, ironing, preserving fruits, rubbing salt into meat also for preservation, and cleaning of all sorts, including how to meet their son's individual Godly needs. At that time, the bustling station was a great roving, working machine, with over 50 station hands and mostly horseman employed by the Fennels. There were all sorts of shearing shed parties and shindigs happening all the time. There was lots of beer drinkin, and lots of horses galloping around everywhere. Although cars were in existence then, there were still a lot of horses and carts in use. A good family life was considered above and beyond all else, except being a Catholic. The boys were expected to marry into a Catholic family and to a good Catholic girl, preferably a girl from the local district and to a family known to the Fennels. The boys were close in age and all ended up marrying within a period of 18 months. The marriages changed life at Seymour dramatically. The four new young women initially hated each other and there were many fights. Arguments occurred that took the peaceful feeling of the house away.

The boys, although very different in nature, rarely wrangled against each other and mostly obeyed their parents' wishes for life at Seymour to hold a certain type of dignified, cooperative routine. Once the lasses arrived, the house became a hotbed of stones and everyone began to walk around as if stepping on eggshells for fear of the next nasty outburst. Stemming from totally different walks of life, and having to share the house as a young newlywed with three brother-in-laws and their wives, including the new parent-in-laws, was too much for each girl. One was particularly good at continually causing trouble. 'Before I properly fill you in on all this', said old Bob, 'I'll just be off to water the horse'. He disappeared to the outhouse. On his return, Bob went on, uninterrupted, to explain something of the Fennels, the first owners of Seymour. 'There is still a portrait of me sitting above the door between the dining room and hallway. It was drawn 50 years ago or more so you may not recognise me. There was a young jackaroo who was also an artist. That young boy did pencil drawings of everyone, and I think mine is the only remaining one. I was the caretaker of the Seymour Homestead for many a year, and I saw all sorts of happenings over there. Mostly now though, no one will ever remember exactly what went on.

The Fennels left, because in the end, they fell into deep financial trouble. The head man, who was initially a very shrewd businessman, sold his sheep at the cattle sales for the highest dollar, a yearly wool cheque in excess of any other price raised for wool in this area. But, over time, he seemed to somehow lose his thrifty ways. In the end, and before he sold up, he and Grandma Betsy were living week to week. All the station hands were gone and no one was left to run the station. The sons who were initially meant to inherit portions of the large estate had left years before. They had various marriage breakdowns and big family catastrophes, which, all in due course, I will tell you about. The family dream of holding the highest station in the Shire, including all the respect that went with the prestigious social position, is now all gone. After the Fennels sold up and went to town, they had to come down a 'pedestal or two' and moved into an ordinary one-bedroom cottage. I think the family are all passed away now. They treated me well, but, then again, I was just the help. It was my deceased uncle who gave me my windy corner, 250 - acre plot and not them. He and I were good mates and he was the kindest man I ever knew. In his will, he said that the gift of land was his reward to me for looking after everyone night and day, working with the sheep, and doing every odd job asked of me with no complaint, ever'.

Elspeth sat eagerly at the end of Bob's table and sipped her tea, waiting for the rest of the story to unfold. She hoped that the explanations would open her mind to the ways in which she viewed the house and its surroundings. Old Bob went on to explain the rest of his yarn not verbally, but by handing her a small hand-written notebook that his wife had written in. 'Read this lovie, these notes will give you all the answers you need. My deceased wife, Lil, who, when not playing Euchre or consuming dozens of Bex powders because she needed to lie down, was a bit of a writer and wrote this before she died. I have never showed it to anyone. My wife was a reasonably good writer, being taught be a strange nun who used to visit the station when we were first hitched. Lil wrote mostly on a Saturday arvo, after having her hair done at the kitchen table by a neighbouring farmer's wife. The large plastic-coloured curlers, covered by a thin net, helped her to concentrate on her note taking, or so she said'.

Samuel, the eldest son, did say in years to come that he wished he had never married Bethany, the stuck up girl who had travelled from England with her parents to study botany in Australia, and more specifically, in the high country of the NSW farming district. The two had met at a dinner party that was held by Bethany's father's friend who had lived on a small acreage outside of the township. This man, a scientist, had written many papers about the life of plants and shrubs in Australia, particularly in the Snowy Mountains. Samuel and Jersey were invited because they were known to have a very good knowledge of plant science in the district. At first sight, Samuel and Bethany wanted to be together, and soon enough Bethany, changed her faith, so that she could marry Samuel. They were married in Saint Mary's, as were the other three boys. Bethany was eager to move from London and said the weather was more agreeable with her in Australia. She had come to detest some of the cold days in England. Bethany appeared to have some very big ideas about taking over the ownership of Seymour and would stop at nothing to put her position forward. No matter what, Bethany had planned to take over the whole property, and nothing and no one, not even her own blood, was going to stand in her way. All she could do at first was read the latest edition of the Women's Weekly, copying the fashion covers by sewing similar garments, reading the beauty supplements, and applying far too much makeup. The special recipes she would cut out for Grandma Betsy, saving the colouring in books for a child that never came.

Bethany was a compulsive liar and would go to great lengths to stir up an argument and lead people's thoughts in the wrong direction, away from the actual truth of any given situation. Once, she deliberately tripped Joseph's wife, Domenica, over in the hallway, doing so by making sure the long rug was crumbled in the dark. Bethany had a premeditated way of being nasty, but seemed to be able to cover up her bad actions quickly by hiding behind her education and training as a nurse. Nobody would think that a nurse could be so cold, calculated, and unkind in everything that she did, thought, and said. Bethany had the Fennels wrapped around her little finger. In their eyes, she could do nothing wrong. They thought her to be just so perfect and the best out of the four wives. This was just not right, Bethany was a bad girl, greedy, self-centred, and an uncharitable person who had grown up being very spoilt by her rich father. Bethany would lie about the other three young women and set them up against each other. Domenica was her easiest target because she spoke very little English and had arrived in Australia from a small Island off the coast of Italy. Domenica only knew about how to cook fresh, homemade pasta. A little plump in her figure with a very sweet personality, Domenica did not realise just when Bethany was making fun of her body shape and cooking.

It was cruel for the others to watch and they tried to shield Domenica from Bethany's constant teasing by hiding her under a bed and saying that Domenica was out shopping for flour. It was that sharp look in Bethany's eyes and the smirk on her conceited face that really upset David's wife, Rosie, who was a quiet girl from a neighbouring property. Normally, Rosie would never say a word of her own private thoughts, but towards Bethany, she could only express her complete disgust. How could Bethany be almost like two different people? Her transgressions included sneaking out at night, rolling tobacco, and smoking behind the shed and then going off with Grandma Betsy to a Red Cross meeting and drinking tea with the group of unsuspecting women. After dark, Bethany would always help herself to Scotch whisky, slurring a straight nip from the bottle and then quietly replacing the lid. Often, Mr. Jersey could be heard saying that he did not remember drinking that much and would scold his sons who were forbidden to take alcohol until they left home. Sure enough, Mr. Jersey was convinced that one of the boys was lying and never for a moment suspected that Bethany, the daughter in-law he absolutely idolised, was developing a drinking problem by sneaking into his liquor cabinet every night. In years to come, when it became obvious that Bethany was a heavy drinker, it became very clear that she was destined to be an alcoholic. Over the years, many important things started to fall away from Bethany's life. Some said that, once she realised that Mr. Jersey was not going to give her and Samuel the old homestead, she totally lost interest in her life at the station. Very soon, after she made it public knowledge that she was not happy being married to Samuel and started tanking herself, with one spirit after the next at the local pub. In the lounge bar. The pub was also a part of the families' estate. Doomed Bethany became, for all her education, fine clothes, and whatnot. It all became such an irony and nobody could believe the prissy missy from England, who spoke as if she had a plum in her mouth, was washing it every day with not just a few nips, but a nice big flush of brandy. Bethany started to lose her looks and became unkempt, her hair became knotted and her clothes a bit smelly. Slowly, her language and voice started to change and her other words began to taint her sophisticated tongue. The worst thing, however, was that she began to smoke in public. With all this, Bethany started to act very, very manly. Samuel quickly lost interest in the girl he had met at the botany dinner party, and although by this they time had borne two children, Samuel had decided to try and find a new wife.

All the nasty stories about Bethany were now coming from his three sister in - laws. Samuel, who initially would not have a bad word said against Bethany, would gruff them off, finally had to stop being stubborn and listen to what had happened, particularly to Domenica, who could now speak English fairly well. Those two, Samuel and Bethany, had attracted each other and they deserved one another. Samuel was completely aloof and raised in a way that made him actually believe that he was superior to others. Some men sniggered in the end, because his wife, who was known as initially being a bit 'stuck up', ended up being the town drunk. 'There is only one thing worse than a snobby woman', said Old Bob, 'and that is a drunk, slurring scratchy cat'.

David, the second eldest boy, who was less good looking than Samuel, but the most prayerful of the Fennels' four sons, did pray for his sister-in-law to stop drinking. But, after a while, David lost all interest in praying because Bethany was always drunk morning, noon, and night. Her eyes were full of white and red pus and her body odour was always fairly off putting. David was very, very ambitious and aspired to become successful outside of Seymour. He had gone off to the Agricultural School, but was mainly interested in law. David was not a farmer and could not avail himself to the outside workings of the property. Disliking mud and the smell of the sheep yards, the only things David really loved about his country lifestyle were the hatching of the baby chicks and the suckling of the lambs.

David did not like the hard, manual farm work, and had to endure a lot of teasing from his brothers and other men on the station. David was suited to a more academic way of living and, at 16, had been told by his parents that he would not be going to Law School because every hand was needed on the farm. It was a blow to the Fennels to find that their second child had left Agricultural School and had run off to Sydney to study law. They finally accepted their second son's decision not to become a farmer, and immediately paid in full, up front for the whole Law course and the books. One weekend, on the train travelling on the way home from his rigorous study to the quiet downtown railway station which was the last stop on the line, a girl stood on the platform. She was a very demure girl, simply dressed in a blue and white cotton shift and wearing a dark blue satin ribbon around her long, blonde ponytail. Instantly, David fell in love with Rosie. Rosie, he remembered as being the daughter of a neighbouring farmer. But, she had grown now into a sumptuous and most beautiful innocent looking young woman. At that time, all Rosie could do was think about her early Marching Girl Days, the precision of each step and the rehearsal of the military procession group formations and patterns. She'd worn the dark blue pleated skirt, worn exactly two inches above the knee, the white linen, double-breasted jacket with six red buttons, including a matching cap and sash. The white, looped, laced boots sat on her shelf now, and were a memory of the stiff competitions held in Tamworth way back in 1947, where points would be deducted for stepping out of line or creases in costumes. The marching bands were all finished now, the thrill of carrying the flag over. Rosie's father's landholding was a lot smaller than the Fennels' but, was in ship shape. condition. It was at this time that the Fennels started to get lower prices at wool auctions, and Grandma Betsy, dressed as a man, began drinking the profits of the estate and sneakily gambling at the local men's card tables after hours in town. She claimed her actions had come about because she had gotten sick and tired of sitting in the Falcon, in the main street of town, looking after the kiddies every Saturday afternoon for years and years while Mr. Jersey drank beer after beer in the local. Sewing cotton stitches, knitting baby booties, and sometimes darning his socks was boring. Many women, back then all over Australia, knew this way of life all too well.

David's high ambitions paid off and he returned home to marry Rosie and became the local solicitor. In the end, it was David who supported his parents when the whole estate went bust. Rosie's parents were good too during the established family's downturn, and offered home cooked meals and prayer. Rosie was a very quiet girl and the least antagonistic of the four girls. It would take a lot for Rosie to become upset or angry. Rosie loved reading, cooking scones, and preserving fruits. Rosie did not mind learning the domestic jobs and household routine from Grandma Betsy. In fact, her own mother had taught her how to do many household duties very well. Rosie was the one who loved performing many outdoor tasks. Gardening and cleaning the horse stables were her two most favourite things to do. Rosie avoided Bethany at all costs, and escaped from her by spending as much time as possible outside and away from the often-quarrelling household.

Within 10 months of arriving at Seymour, Rosie was pregnant and she and David moved into town. It was a relief for them both to get away from the workings of everyday farm life. David had found it all very boring living on the grange and buried himself in his legal work. The best thing about being the local solicitor in a rural community was that, because he was raised within the confines of a sheep and cattle farm, he knew how to best give advice to his clients and this helped him establish himself independently of his father. Rosie was happy living a small-town girl country life and was relieved to be away from the competitive dynamics between the four girls. Besides, she and David now had their own family to consider. For sure, when they gave birth to their first son, he was also christened David, and the couple expected that he would follow in his father's footsteps and become a solicitor. Things really moved on for Rosie and, after a while, she was able to employ her own cleaner and cook on Sundays.

As David's business grew and grew and grew, Rosie's fairly good position turned from an already embellished lifestyle into one of total extravagances. She spent lots of time enjoying watercolour painting with the local society of painters and taking lots of time with her own personal care. Interestingly enough, when the four newly married young women first lived at Seymour, it was Bethany who took the initiative with trying to outdo the other three with her fancy dresses and swishy makeup. However, the irony of the story is that actually, in the end, Rosie was the one who had the most personal respect and good community presence. Imagine that.

David adorned Rosie with pieces of jewellery and loved seeing her blossom and grow into a woman of fine stature, being very affectionate to her in public. From the outside, the couple seemed to experience an ideal lifestyle with no money problems, lots of nice friends, beautiful parties, and they both glowed in health. Certainly, David's work as a solicitor was suitable to the land of gentry's upper style of activities and higher social classes. As her father was fairly affluent, Rosie did know how to associate with people from all walks of life. David was happy to leave the dusty farm life behind, and very much enjoyed the luxury of wearing the best and finest clothes. The solicitor continually went to the barber's shop and was always meticulously groomed. David gleamingly stood out in any photo that was taken of him, and nobody ever dare say a bad word against the man who performed the finest legal work in the whole country. Attracting other women was a common occurrence and over the course of their entire 42 years of marriage, many women made sexual advances towards the desirable and rich man. Firstly, there was a common woman, who under David's legal direction, had successfully divorced her husband Kevin, gaining a settlement that was talked about for years in the legal fraternity.

The second was a woman who was a potato digger and came into the office giving her spare spuds away. The spuds were always just freshly dug from out of the ground and she brought them into town on the back of her broken-down buggy car to sell to the local shop. The shop was incidentally called, The Seymour Store. This was a friendly woman with light brown, shoulder length hair who was not much of a conversationalist and who only spoke when spoken to. She was a slim woman who found it hard to hide her attraction to David. The problem was that David was horrified at the thought of a door to door sales woman bearing potatoes standing in front of his office. Coming time and time again, and asking each time to see David, the day finally came when the solicitor had to just say no to the woman of potatoes. For years, the woman of potatoes was brokenhearted and envied every move that Rosie made. One day, she became so distraught with jealousy over David and Rosie's marriage that she stood outside the community rooms where Rosie was meeting with a delegate of the Red Cross concerning an up and coming prize for a raffle. Suddenly, through the windows hurled dozens of potatoes. The two women ducked for cover under a table and were very frightened. The potato thrower screamed all sorts of really terrible words towards Rosie.

Finally, the coppers arrived and the woman was taken away and put into a mental hospital. After that, nobody ever saw the potato woman. Again said that David and his legal team made sure she never walked the main street again. It was rumoured that the woman was found stuffed into a large potato bag. But, that was just a small-town rumour.

The third woman to fall in love with the slick solicitor was a silly woman from the coast, an arty type of a woman, who came into town to visit her dying mother, Gwen. Or, that is what she told a few locals who were overcome by the strange way that she looked. One said that she had a bit of lust in her eye when David had walked past her in the street. Turning instantly, she began to follow him and the hunt went on for ages. In the end, Rosie was the one who told the coastal woman to get lost and leave her hubby alone. It was after a wedding one Saturday, when the outsider was spotted amongst the locals, who always gathered to see any happy couple leave the church after they were married.

David and Rosie were guests at an employee's daughter's wedding. It was too much for Rosie to see the coastal woman standing at the back of the small, but happy, crowd who were busy throwing confetti onto the veil and newly married couple. She went through the church gate and up to the woman. It was not clear just what Rosie had said to the uninvited guest, but, within a jiffy, she fled the crowd and ran down into the main street. There she escaped to a second room at the back of the pub and proceeded to get really, really drunk. Alone, she consumed a large bottle of vodka and then she began to swear and vomit. Nobody knows if she did actually survive the booze that, for sure, would have poisoned her. Wandering off, out of the town, the message was clear that the wanting women from the coast would have realised that David was completely and totally out of her reach, and very much in love with his wife.

Michael, the second youngest brother who was full of jokes no matter what, discovered just how bad Bethany had been treating his one and only love, Annie. The other two girls, whom he knew, did not find it easy to settle into the new marriage arrangements whilst living away in the unfamiliar surroundings. They had an early falling out with his eldest brother Samuel. The bad blood between the brothers would never bind again, and a certain hatred began to permeate between the two. Annie was a good girl and loved Michael with all her heart, and he would not tolerate Bethany's badness. Another aunt had spread a rumour that, since marrying Michael Fennel, Annie was always trying to be someone that she wasn't, and someone who she would never be, you know, 'a bit toffee - too good for other people.'

Michael was always a happy-go-lucky young lad, kind hearted and gentle by nature. Loving to laugh, he was fun to be around. Michael was always respectful of other people and never carried any 'airs and graces' about himself. A hard-working young man, Michael knew the importance of teamwork and had a knack for making all those who worked at the station feel good about themselves no matter how long or how hard the day was. The fight was a bad one and started at a public function for all to see. Nobody could believe that the two were standing close to each other, red face to red face and blasting each other at the top of their voices. Then, it got really heavy with the two brothers fist fighting, blood and beer flowing everywhere.

Annie was the prettiest girl of the four and Michael knew that Bethany detested her. Michael would never forgive Samuel for bringing such a greedy and self-centred girl home to Seymour. Annie was slightly uncultured, being raised in the closed, small country town community, she was not exposed to many things other than being taught how to be good, kind, and honest. These values were instilled in her by her parents, no matter what. This is the reason why Bethany was able to get away with being so cruel all the time. Annie would forgive her in an instant and the degrading abuse just seemed to continue. Until finally, the light-hearted Michael lost his temper and in front of a full family gathering, told Samuel to get out of the district and take his terrible wife with him.

Annie was a slim girl with short blonde hair. She was always helpful and never said a bad word against anyone. All her life, Annie's beauty had given her many problems, although she did have a few good friends. Annie did want to experience life outside of the country town, but some other things stopped her from leaving the safety of her nest. It was her hormones. They were so unpredictable that all her life she had such heavy menses that she needed the care and safety of her familiar environment. In an instant, she could be sobbing for no apparent reason or crippled over in pain without being able to stand up and walk. Annie was a gentle soul who had been cursed by her jealous aunt to the point where her hormones seemed to react to the slightest amount of discomfort.

Sometimes, blood was everywhere and she would have to stand in it and weep, knowing she was powerless over the curse of her cycle and the pain of her throbbing back, hips, and fluidic, heavy body cycle. Michael was so aware of these problems and treated Annie with kid gloves. He nourished and nurtured her in every way. Michael was determined to love every inch of Annie, no matter what. Even on the heavy days of her cycle, Michael would book the local restaurant on top of the hill that overlooked the town and take his forlorn wife out to enjoy a meal and the sights, helping her relax her uncomfortable state of affairs. For these reasons, Michael was most upset with Bethany for always trying to hurt Annie and the other girls. On the night of the argument, Michael told Samuel in a loud and booming voice, so that all the guests were able to hear the real truth about Bethany. He noted that the girl from England was nothing other than self-centred and undesirable to have at parties, that she was too sure of herself and over confident. Also, he clearly and succinctly said that Bethany was overpowering and put herself first in every instance. She was not patient and kind like Rosie, Annie, and Domenica.

In the early months of newly married life, and without knowing it, the four girls each had their own really special hideaway place, tucked away on the outskirts of Seymour. In their own way, it seemed as if they all needed to escape to an imaginary world, to be away from all that was happening in their early training to be a wife, mother, and long term house carer. It was a rigorous undertaking to learn the exact ways to shine the crystal, mop the floors, and brush the edges of all the mats in the house. Grandma Betsy, although a real ditsy, would make sure that the girls worked impeccably, without a stitch out of place, or a speck of dust left on the shelves or any smearing on the glass. Everything was done to perfection, including crispy, ironed linen and very clean windows and floors. Nothing, absolutely nothing, was left undone or to do the next day.

The girls had to make sure that they threw on a good, nice spread. Every meal had to be top-notch, ship-shape. The cups had to be sparkling, the tea spoons without a smudge, and the tablecloth crispy clean and starched. The spread had to be laid out in exactly the way Old Grandma Betsy instructed.

There is a green, grassy stream that, from cascading under the ground, slides down from the top of the first flat landing on the hill which hollers above the last outcrop of the station. This was Rosie's favourite habitation, and way back then, she would never have known that another girl sometime in the future would also love the heavenly spring as much as she did. The area just looked so unusual, a lush emerald that upwardly merged from within what appeared a fairly bland hill. Up came a refreshing smell of natural waters that seemed to bring first light to the bright wildflowers in early spring.

Rosie adored the secret fresh water spring that felt slushy and gooey under her bare feet. It was where the rich worms were healthy, long and thick, and other soil parasites thrived in the banks of the sinking boggy earth. The area seemed like a place of miracles to Rosie who was not attuned to the mysteries of the out bush. It was a wonder to see a creek so naturally embossed by the rich grasses and soggy underground flows. The big round green patch of grass looked out of place amongst the dried grasses and yellow-brown scape. It was an unusual sight to behold, and Rosie would often run away to that subversive spring, needing to smell the fresh earth water and to bathe herself at the bottom of the creek that meandered down the side of the hill and turned into a flowing creek that opened up to the cool gap.

Nobody was there and Rosie loved to splash herself in the pool, clear damp water hole that came from that green submerge of mineral water. The invigorating experience took her away from the other girls and gave her a sort of private way of coping with not being in town and learning to live, at least for a while, in the country. At first glance, nobody would have seen the underlying charms that the inert spring held. But Rosie, with her inquisitive imagination and thirst for something new to experience outside of hearing the demanding voice of Grandma Betsy's annoying and forever demanding work instruction, investigated every inch of the emerging water line and fell in love with the inner cascading domain.

Annie was always thought of as being too pretty to get her hands muddy, but she was starving, in herself, to do something different, something that did require her hands to get muddied, and not wear a pressed ribbon in her hair. As a child, she was kept like a pristine piece of crystal and it seemed that when she went to live at Seymour, Annie's yearning to get out of the house and be away from everyone who thought her too exquisite to actually work hard, lift a thing, or hear a swear word stemmed back her early childhood, where she felt denied of being young, spontaneous in action, and free in thought. So, in the misted morning, Annie found her place of solitude. Early in the morning, immediately after sunrise, and just to get a breath of fresh air, she would sneak away from Seymour, only to find herself moving into the freshness of the first day. Waiting for the fog to come in from across the mountain ranges, it was there that she would walk towards slow drifty thick fog and then disappear into it. Hurriedly, she found her way to the top of the range, where she was able to see the full fog scene set amidst the low, open ground, and leaving the top of the seven hills in total, to look like land islands protruding through the greyish, coursing pall. Though it was chiselled with jets of the first light, wading through the fog at that very early time of the day toward the brilliance of the sun and being surrounded by the mystery of the seven island hills, gave Annie a feeling of being in the most mysterious place in her world.

There was a tinge of fright associated with it, but that made it all the more exciting to be outside and free in the fog that had a voice of its own. The seemingly unknowing atmosphere became full of wonder, and was, in some places, a little bit eerie in presence and full of unusual noises. The noises were not natural. They were bottomless and deep, felt distant and sad. They were unreachable through the haze and were creepy, but this did not stop Annie from running away to enjoy the feelings that the foggy island hills gave her, as she had never encountered this before in her life. Perhaps, another girl would one day experience the same misty feeling.

Domenica could be found hiding in the herb garden that was planted by Grandma Betsy, which was to feed the many mouths of the early station life and was very sizeable. This is where the Italian girl felt most at home and she thrived on growing carrots, parsnips, and lots of basil. There was something about gardening that grounded Domenica's homesickness, and helped her to feel normal again after many hours of trying to learn how to speak English under the hard tutelage of the station's school master, Gloria. Gloria was not a personable woman and was emotionally stone cold hard towards Domenica, and all the children that she taught. Each morning, along with Domenica, the Seymour horse and cart would collect the children from all around the area for schooling. Those of wealth sat up in the front of the one class room that was located two paddocks away, and near the road that led into town. Those from the poorest families sat at the back and there were none in between. Domenica could see, even without speaking English, that there was never any coming together between the rich and the poor kids. But, even so, she was humiliated as an adult woman at having to attend the school house for two days a week to learn with the little kids. Bethany would sneer and laugh at Domenica's broken English. The garden was the only place where Domenica could find that wholesome peace of mind that she enjoyed so much across the seas in Italy. The garden was a place that Bethany paid no attention to and, when in full growth, was an easy place for Domenica to hide. Lines of fresh, crispy lettuce, the borage herb and the long-stemmed gladiola had dolled up the entrance to the plot. The yellow sunflowers reaching to the sky made the garden an enticing treasure trove of natural abundance by which to escape the drudgery of all that was expected of her in the new and varied roles as an Australian woman, wife, and mother.

After listening to Old Bob, and reading Lil's notes, Elspeth began to understand much more about the house that, for so long, she attended to, including the establishment of the whole station. Many questions and gaps in her mind about the early days in the mysterious house were now completely filled in. Elspeth, for the rest of her remaining days, could then see so much of the previous owners hand prints in and around Seymour Homestead.

Then, much to her delight, in the bush mail came the long-awaited correspondence from her long-lost childhood friend, Liza. The three informative and unexpected Letters entitled, *'The Ship'*, *'A Conversation between two new Australians'* and *' Little Brush Stroke Flower,'* went as follows:

Liza's Three Letters

The Ship

'I ain't no good at readin or writin and I neera did go for schoolin but I a pretty girl and no how to cooknclean and do most home chores real well. The seaman thinks I am real neice, and we had a bit a fn last nite, he told me I a 'little beauty' and it sounded real good. This old ship is smelly and the cool nites hard as a board. I can feel a bub comin and I am not sure how I will feed it and no marriage proposal will surely give me a bastard. Anyways, although I cannot write, sometime after many, many days and moons, someone, a woman, will write a story about me and tell the world that I am innocent and guilty of no crime. The tale will also tell about me sewin, me apprenticeship and journeyman to become a master embroiderer. I miss me own shop and am sad to leave me homeland. This old ship has made me sick and is dirty, not like me clean threads and cloth. I came to this job not through another, but because of me own mother and her mother before. We were poor people, but the finest of sewers and the profession is a good one for good people's, not for criminals.'

It was late one summer's night, and the sun had just lost its last shine. On her way home, she carried her best piece of embroidery. It was long pieces of mauve satin laced with a dark purple thread that had been worked with a very fine hook to give the appearance of a crochet chain stitch. The pieces were an inlay in a gown to be worn by an important woman of the aristocracy and the pattern for a dress reminiscent of a Tudor style gown, but only more elaborate. The satin laid across the tambour hoops which were tools of the trade. The larger ones needed to be balanced between the knees, and Joan was a master of her finesse art.

There came a man to Nightingale lane, drunk and pushy, somehow making his way into Joan's house and refusing to leave. 'Get out of my house', ordered Joan. 'I don't want ya ear and I mus go to sleep before the mornin comes again, I have work to do for import peoples'. 'Yeah, you best get out of our house', screamed Maryanne, 'we are good women here and you won't find any liquor in our beds, only our sewin'.

'If you give me a candle then love, I will be goin to find the money that someone stole from me pocket', slurred Bobby, stumbling and smirking and reeking of dishonesty, wearing shabby, smelly clothes. The presence of such a low life reminded the women that they were in servitude to people who, although wanted stitchin service, spoke and directed them with respect and courtesy, not like the bad man who urinated on their kitchen floor and stank of smoke. When he left the house, the women somehow knew it was not the last they would hear of the night. The night that was slowly losing its attachment to the beautiful lush satin purple thread. The sewing became horribly lost in the court case that did see both Joan and Maryanne transported to new world.

'Oh God', cried Joan, as she waited in Newgate prison, 'no release will ever come and the Judge was so hard and cruel, he never listened to a word of truth and he ain't aware of hard times in this hell hole of a dungeon. The prison keepers are so bad, the only way for fair treatment is if you pay em. Hangens outside in the street are rowdy and a dark death feeling always hangs over for weeks before and weeks after. I would never have thought that after consideration on me self that I would end up behind the walls of the grey prison.

I already knew in here was notorious for lice, infection and screamin and cryin. No food and no help and no love and bad people all around. I already knew of overcrowding, bad treatment, and death at every turn in here. No fresh water or clothin, no embroider and only pain, hate, and disgust on the chapel seats where we sit, us women, out of sight of the men, with the preacher high on a pew growling and snarling at us. Screamin us to repent our sins and wicked ways, or if not, we'd perish in the fires of hell.

It is hell on earth, Newgate Prison, and all I can do is sit in me small cell and wish I was dead. There is nothing in this cell, only walls close together, and a roll up bed and small desk on one side. There is natural light that shows a hard-bare floor, cockroaches, and mice. Sometimes when I open my eyes, I see big, dirty, smelly, grey rats. All is sick in ere, nobody well. The food is a cool, slushy, cold porridge and other stuffs leftovers from the local shops; there is no care here. I am waitin to move to the dorm which is full of women and kids and can only cover me ears at the sound of the execution outside on Old Baily St. They say, 'beggars can't be choosers', but, then, hidden in some beggars is somthin real special, like the giving of warm soup and bread. Sad enough though, even when they do find wealth they always still act like peasants'.

There was one particularly bad criminal executed on a windy cool dry day in the month of February 1787. He stole a St Christopher's medal from a young sailor with dark hair and blue eyes, a gentle sailing boy who was far away from his family and trying to get ahead in life by undertaking odd jobs on the wharf. Tinker White was his name, a pirate man who said that he came from Wellington. His cold footsteps are still heard along dead man's walk. There he had to step a diminishing number of brick arched doors that reduced along a closed narrow stone hallway. Eventually, the prisoner was on his knees, with no chance of turning back his life, and the inevitable fate of death rang in the cast iron execution bell, as his body hung above the ground where he had left the young sailor dead and still. The heavy, old, cast iron bell rang as a reminder to other criminals that they would be caught and face public execution if they committed craven crimes. The Judge ordered that the medal of protection be returned to the boy's mother. But, the desperate, dead feeling still lingered for months outside the wall. The terrible feeling stopped those who walked past the gallows for months and years to come.

The only solace that Joan found whilst awaiting her transportation was the unexpected garnishes that came only once during her prison sentence. Soap and candles were given to women who were poor. These were given to those who did not enter prison garnished and supported by their own wealth and prosperity. The degradation of the terrifying building was deliberately stamped by the architect's reinforced walls; no windows and huge carved stone chains were placed above the entrance gate as a clear symbol designed to instill terror in all those who passed under. Joan's soap soon disappeared and the candle burnt away. These were gifts from a kind woman who wanted to help the unfortunate incarcerated women and sort a permit from the Lord Mayor. Some years after arriving in Australia, Joan heard that the kind women carrying candles and soap went to parliament and made a lot of changes to help the women and children at Newgate.

For Joan, it was too late. The tears of the lost threads of her trade, the tears of her lost family and homeland were as big as the horrendous waves that she battled and endured for eight months on the overcrowded and mostly damp ship. Being on a ship that had never sailed before was absolutely terrifying in rough seas storms. The vessel felt as if it would sink to the bottom of the ocean.

To be on a ship and going somewhere, or nowhere, was to see people struggling. Although unkept, people tried to have a bit of fun by singing and laughing late at night, to wash away the fear and terror which was too much to cope with. A dear lady had died amongst 40 others on the ship. Overboard her body was thrown, and a bland and short blessing from the ship's Captain was given, as we all stood on deck that dreary morning. This lady had had been educated and tried to teach those down below who were illiterate to read some letters, to write down a note or two for their loved ones. Just before she died, she recited her homecoming poem, and finding her way back to Old England Town, the Captain breathed a deep low and voice. 'God be with the lost soul and her journey to the afterlife', he said as her corpse hardened in communion with the salt water. The last piece I remember, in her own crackled words, went like this.

'The lighthouse stands tall, white against the horizon. A grey gull glides close above sea green water. The sky lifts up, disappears in flight. A cool, misty sea spray settles. A salty smell lingers over an almost still closure, hazy afternoon. A painting embodied. A mauve sky streams across, a never-ending seascape. Drifting sunlight flickers through transient shadows, colouring to rich purple and deep blue. Waves crash loud to meet moving sands, inviting to a keen water lover. Holding ice cold mid-winter currents, a deep flow, and oceanic life. The still daunting rock formations, cast a setting picture. Towering high, steep. Greenery in the distance touched graceful, ambience, this my last homecoming, a pictorial resonance'.

Overhearing a conversation between the doctor and the captain, Joan learnt a lot more about the ship, although she did not understand all the words that they said, she understood, 'a very new ship built by the Thames Company, coming from the East India Company and part owned by the Captain, a good strong clean crew and a well-cared for ship 338 tons, 104' in length 6'4", afore, 6'2", midships and 6'3" abaft. A doctor, a surgeon, and a good captain who made sure that the cramped long, hard journey was made easy by the supply of fresh fruit, vegetables, and meat at every port, and scurvy avoided by the clean food and good sailin, which later came to the Lady Penrhyn after a while, becoming a good sailin boat'. This, Joan told all what she had heard to her friend Maryanne, who, after arriving in Australia, she had sadly lost contact with. Joan went on with her little girl to Norfolk and Maryanne went to the outback, far away from Sydney cove with a man who had dropped a handkerchief at her feet when she first got off the boat. The bush was a hard place for them; everything was so different. They tried to create a little bit of England in the things they did each day. Initially, there were no supplies until other ships arrived. The ground was dry and the trees were hard to fall.

There was fear amongst both the officers and the convicts that even though they had survived the harsh seas and the dangerous journey, that they would, in fact, either be killed by the natives or starve because the vegetation was strange and the ground was hard to cultivate. Some people spreading out into the scrub built shabby-looking slab-stone and bark houses. The daily routines followed copper washing or scrubbing in the river, educating the children with what people knew, some letters or practical jobs, like white washing the fireplace, sweeping the floor, and cleaning the pots with black charcoal from the fire. The land made people hard and, without homely comforts, it cultivated a certain type of endurance that was only about how to survive the next day. Clay ovens sufficed and potatoes were cooked most days. Preceding the daily lunchtime picnic, which was had under any shaded tree, flies and wind and cold and storms and every imaginable sufferable occurrence had to be managed. Everything was a long way away from the familiarities of England that were slowly, but surely, being forgotten for the new world of experience.

A Conversation between two new Australians

'One day and not long before I was to leave for Europe Elspeth, I was waitressing in a café on the other side of town, and I just happened to overhear a conversation between two European men. I knew it was rude to eavesdrop, but I did anyway, and it gave me a different perspective on how those of European backgrounds think, how they see those of us born in Australia, and I also felt an alliance, a glimpse of understanding into who they are and why I now see things through their eyes. They spoke for a long time in broken English whilst using elitist style expressions. These two men were clearly cultured and hued with steep ideas about what was normal and what was not'.

Arnost was born in Vienna in 1910 and was raised an only child in Prague, Czechoslovakia. Arnost was of Czechoslovakian origin. Istvan was a Hungarian man of a similar age. Both men smoked one cigarette after the other, and over the course of their dense and thickly worded conversation, their language moved between broken English, European slang, and words common to both countries of origin. They reminisced about their childhoods, the commonalities and fear stories of the war, and their new lives in Australia.

Istvan told Arnost that he did have a family, two brothers still in Europe and one younger sister who could not remember many things and lived with him. Each day, she dressed in traditional Hungarian costume, missing so much her White-Stag Kalocsa homeland, that she wore her lavishly embroidered, gathered, and ribboned pure Richelieu traditional scalloped style blouses, pleated shirts, knitted stockings, and mule clogs. Of course, her aprons made a statement about the perfection of her flowered craft, and although the clothing was not understood by other women, and appeared almost theatrical, the stitching was always admired. Eddie was her name, and she cried for her dead husband, wearing her white on white embroidered blouses, as a symbol of her special wedding dress; she dreamed always of the Magyar myths. The smoke filled the café and their conversation became more fractured as the morning went on. But, they seemed to enjoy their European compatibility. They could very well have been sitting in a café in any town or city in Europe. Although I could not understand all of their words and utterances, it became obvious that these men were from a world far beyond the 'tatoes and chops' that we know. These men knew travel and the deep unforgiving grief of loss and the confinement of being controlled during every step and move they made.

They sat smiling and laughing and almost smirking at the farmers that came into the café for a 'cup of tea and lemon meringue pie'. The land workers, perspiring from their morning toils out on the land, thought the men to be stranger than any old windy day, where the clouds were dark and low and the threat of sudden weather change would beat up the stock and drag them out of bed at any time during the night.

'Australia is a big country with seems to be only one pub here and there. When I first came here, all you could get was a steak, potatoes and a cup of tea. All pubs closed at six o'clock, that was it, only steak, potatoes, a cup of tea and a bit of damper'. Arnost told Istvan, who responded with a sigh, which suggested an understanding that life in Australia was only about steak, potatoes and cups of tea. 'Me, I came here to this country with nothing. I was a poor immigrant and did all sorts of odd jobs before starting my own business as an engineer. This was my training from my country. Most Aussies, my old uncle warned me, are affected convicts from the era of transportation. I escaped the control under the Iron Curtain, hidden below a truck with a seven-year-old Hungarian Jewish girl who had brown hair and white ribbons and no feeling left in her body strapped on my back. We went through to Austria.

The Vasfuggong was never to be deceived. It was the unspoken boundary between us and them. We were kept in the darkness of its heavy iron, and could not see even a shade of light onto the other side. But, we knew if we could escape then, freedom and life chance would show us a better way. Everyone wanted a better way. Many had tried and were shot, destroyed, and never seen again. The smell of the fumes and the heat of the engine were horrible. I had nothing but my papers in my socks and the girl on my back. Somehow, the truck kept going and I kept holding, and at the stop point they never suspected and we just drove straight through. Haya, the girl who perished through the inhalation of fumes, is a reminder that people here don't know anything like real fear, and what it means to sneak away from such control. That is real fear'. Both men were well dressed in cravats, tie pins, cuff links, and double-breasted, cream, continental-style suits. An expensive car sat out front of the café. They had a certain sophisticated confidence and, although they had come from a long way away, their homeland culture had in many ways followed them and made them successful — very, very successful. This success in their minds had risen them above and beyond steak, potatoes, and cups of tea, and it was amusing to them that the pubs all closed at 6pm. Arnost had two professions, he was a chef and a tailor. Unlike many who came to Australia, he was lucky enough to work in his profession.

Many immigrants were automatically either allocated jobs as labourers if they were male or domestics if they were women.

'I am a tailor by trade and worked to make uniforms for the German Army. I had no choice but to work for them, otherwise, I would be put in the concentration camp. I did have good pay and, after the war, left Czechoslovakia and got away to make a new life. I immigrated to Australia after the war in early 1950, and like many migrants, worked on the Snowy Mountains Scheme. Lucky for me, I was the head chef'. Arnost obviously loved his work and told Istvan that he had cooked for royalty and members of the royal family who had come to visit the scheme. Arnost said he was the head chef at that time and was honoured in their presence, cooking fish for them. It was Arnost's dream to become an Australian citizen. After that time, Arnost also owned his own tailoring business and said that was where he had met his wife Livey, an Australian woman. Together, they had two sons, but the war, the bombs, and the SS officers still haunted him.

'I have German friends, good people, loving kind people who were victims like us. They carry the weight of the war in their lives. Nobody talks to them and their children, stones get thrown at them, they are called names, and have to run and hide. It was one dictator, one man who led the destruction of the innocent Jews, not those children. One night, after work, I was walking and stopped by three SS officers. One pointed a gun at me. I stood still, and when asked my name, I said I was born in Vienna and he said, turn and walk. I thought maybe then he would shoot me but then I heard the sound of their boots marching away. Another night, I lay asleep in my bed on the third floor of a building and I see bombs dropping out from the window. Where it all started and why is of no interest to me, only that it would never happen again. One mad Nazi dictator radicalised so many. It was he and his accomplices who took the power of a nation into their own hands and destroyed many of the good people'.

Istvan agreed saying, 'The history is never to be forgotten. Countries must unite in peace and freedom, because under the truck, that seven-year-old Jewish girl never did see her mama or papa again, and dead she was after the journey'. Both men had tears in their eyes at that point. 'How, I asked myself, could any outsider like me ever really know the pain of war, and the story Elspeth, of the girl wearing ribbons in her hair, is only a small example of a horrendous tragedy that affected millions of real people. There was nothing historically legal in it, and while there is evidence to suggest early plans all over the world of the occupation, this mammoth tragedy is not a fictional story to taunt and play games with. And, after hearing this, continued writing Liza. All I could do was see myself swimming with the slippery platypus in the coolness of the open river, trying to wash away my disgust at the shallowness of one individual's desperate desire for fame, fortune, and power above all others. Both men obviously had the need to strive for a better life, and after a period of long silence and reflection, Istvan spoke a few words before they left. 'Me, I will work my way to the top of my trade. I won't ask the government for anything. I will make a good life for my sister and I, and bring my brothers here one day'. 'Good,' responded Arnost again, as he nodded his head and responded. 'Well me, I will make suits for the men around here and I will respect everyone in this country. Even if I am not respected, I will still plant fresh vegetables'.

Both men left with the sound of the bombs ringing in their ears, and memories of the saddest deaths of those prayerful Jews who, by their birth were promised to the place of the greatest God. Both men, deeply scarred, wished for peace and the inclusion of the good German people into their new lives. They despised the racial hunts and curses that they knew were the seeds of hatred. They knew that those types of attitudes would stop unity and hinder a new peaceful life in Australia. Both men, although they were not Jewish, wore engraved numbers of war on their hearts, and under their breath. This is a colossal human atrocity that cannot be forgotten. They left wishing they had eaten a piece of Black Forest Gateau and had never found the need to leave their homelands for 'steak, tatoes, cups of tea and a bit of damper'. They agreed to do their best to build a better life here in Australia, and that there are no winners in any war, only exterminations. 'All war is very bad', said Arnost, and they both agreed. 'War no good'.

Little Brush Stroke Flower

Little flower, cherry flower, how her flowers are silk and shower, soft like clouds, soft like silk, beautiful girl, so cheery sweet. Rich petal pink cheeks. Fallen petals, forever in peace. Little flower, cherry flower, how your sweet buds, bloom and flower. Then you're gone, so quickly gone. Life and death, here and gone. Good fortune, good fortune. Nature, love and respect.

All she could think of on the long sad journey was the royal woman of the great Song Dynasty. One day, she would return to her own country, and like a rich royal woman, be revered for her extraordinary work. Like the treasures of the Song Dynasty, she would be a great artist, a painter, a musician or both. Yes, her clothes would be without a crease or crinkle; they would be fine, the finest fabrics made especially for her body. Being driven by a driver, the girl from the orient would be highly educated and was already planning to find a husband with credentials. This husband would either be a doctor, lawyer, or architect. This husband would still carry all the traditional ways of their country, but life to the outside world would appear to be completely westernized.

Their house would be a replica of a Chinese palace, symmetrical and designed with the central open courtyard that would draw pigeons and doves, baring the three symbols of the stars — fu, lu, shou — and the symbols of bats and pomegranates for good fortune. The doors would always face to the front of the house and the low ceilings and wide rooms would enclose the flowing feel of all the water features, ponds, pools, and wells that would beautify the dwelling along with poignant Fu character. The red and silver diamond-shaped sign would be hung up-side down above the front doors. This would ward off bad luck, and with the blessing of good luck, happiness and much fortune would arrive. All the rooms would be set with an oriental sukaranbo motif. On that sweaty, smelly, humid journey. Her dreams as a little girl showed the way to riches on the Australian soil. Onto her new life ahead, all she dreamed about was the water feature. There was a photo on the wall of a graceful divinity that sat draped in pure cloth, denoting images of roses. Small oriental dishes and vases sat in front of him as he preached with arms above his head. Drums beneath his feet began to illuminate the rituals behind the pillars. The golden chariot filled with embossed leaves resembled the fields of golden dry grass on a hot summer's day.

Ancient whispers told of wise men who did not lament death, as they foretold that the soul never does die. The shadow of death shows glory in the body as the soul transfers through each life cycle. And, the humble sage at the foot of the photo could see all virtue, knowing when it was time to leave the body, that a simple husk of wheat would dispel all sorrow. The water feature and green slate floors were misted by the fall of a cracked death face. This one face represented so many that had been lost. Their lives had been cracked, broken, destroyed, and forgotten. The silence behind the eyes became a shell mask of

triangle on the pottery which was from all over the orient. The woven lamp basket, made for the rich and fastidious, was meshed at the bottom of the design with black leaves and bark set in orange clay, shining a light for those to find their way. There were new people all pictured sipping ginseng tea and feeling nurtured from the scented jonquils and donqui. The yin qualities in the mask were hidden in the cold of night, passive and calm in the solidity of mother earth and fluid under the fire of yang. The warm, masculine energy had revealed heaven and the excitement of the union was shown in six flows. The feature — communion, zest, demure, unyielding, and softly textured — like the one that headed the mirrored gate between her and her future husband.

There were tea rooms where people also murmured and whispered stories of the silken jewels. Precious stones at the bottom of the water feature were a metaphor for the gold that many mined in the new land. They were red, yellow, and blue. The green one was on the other side of a pond, and, like him in the dream, seemed out of sight, out of touch, and not real. The jewels were placed only at night by the kind woman and could awaken the sight of the newcomers. Out of all the jewels, it was the green one that held the silk woven magic. This could be seen in the dark, and would lead all towards golden love.

In the dream, each of the water flows needed to be discerned against the green stone, and could only be seen when the moon was full. At that point, the gold would be revealed and their lives would be made rich in the strange and foreign land. All she would need to do would be to enter the feature, which, once there, would open up to a riverbed of silk and satin rushes. To do this, she would need to turn herself into a fish. At that point, the green stone was at the other side of the bank, basking and waiting, like him. Then, her feet felt the cool earth and the water was coldish. At that point, she would need to place the green stone at the center of her eye brow and the transformation into a fish would occur.

The silk river had other layers of life, washing the poor Chinese people away from the long, difficult, and painstaking journey, making them ready for the Sydney Dragon Flag Parade. The water brought a peaceful flow of communion to the new surroundings and the softly textured gemstones held the moral of the crossing. Even as a small girl, she seemed to know the stories of discrimination towards her Chinese country men and women. These were bad, sad stories. These tales were embedded in her psyche. They were stories that had been told to warn people that the finding of gold was not without suffering, and that it was not easy to settle in Australia. Riots, killings, and protests against the Chinese race began in 1861 and drove 3,000 people off a place called Lambing Flat. The tents were destroyed and everyone's possessions were stolen. It was then that the Chinese fled to Currawang Sheep Station, only to face further stigma and violence. There was never any thought of the four gentlemen or the literati of spiritual brush painting that depicted so well the orchid spring, the bamboo summer, the chrysanthemum autumn, and the blossom winter. The Chinese were referred to as 'coolies'. The word came from Southeast Asia and described the lowest of labour, only to be laughed and sneered at by a bunch of lousy grog-breathed and unaware colonials.

The flower girl had intended not to let racism stop her from being successful and making a new prosperous life. I now ask myself how could a small seven-year-old Asian girl, who was probably bullied in Australia by being called bad names, have such grand ideas. But, good for her, she did, and nothing and no one would stop her from raising up and out of the dangerous and flimsy, overcrowded, rank situation, into the slipstream of affluence. Raw silk and designer brooches, she would have everything modern that a rich, western woman would need and want. At times, she would also be reminded of the early days when her hair was full of bird nest knots, and in need of a bamboo comb. Today they say, her hair is once again is a lustrous sheen of heavy black, perfectly cut satin.

✧ ✧ ✧

It is true that most new people coming to Australia found it hard. Like those forgotten Japanese dolls — sweet, dainty, elegant war brides. Six hundred and fifty of them arrived to Australia in 1952 under hardship and difficult emigration laws. They found it so hard to be accepted in the homespun of their much loved silk, they too should never move away from their ability to contemplate the mirror water reflection of trees that are often painted in light strokes in origami flowered patterns on the Izumo Taisha. And forget not, that the floral oriental design and palmistry of the white sapphire praised and turned heavens cool mists, like the inscription of haiku that gave snippet images of graceful natural moments in time. Again, no one wants war, but this is also another story. And, we are now all just wanting to move towards the breakdown of national borders and live in a free and peaceful global world. The future holds the key.

With Love, and my kindest regards to you dear Elspeth,
Liza of Letters

The Wind Queen

Looking down at the once pretty lace tablecloth, Elspeth's best apricot dress hanging in the dusty wardrobe was alight with daisies and the room was filled with the remembrance of golden words from the past. As he always did, Cain whispered to her through the cracks in the walls and floor about the unchanging and shallow greys in the scented haze of the bush day and the calm, quiet space between his and her face. The feelings were similar to the stones that she threw to the wind after he had gone — empty, lost, hard, and forgotten.

However, from behind, the curtain moved slightly by the breath of the didgeridoo, and from across the mountains of time, there came a feeling of inner peace. The feelings were smoothed by pearl prayer beads and the sound of the open, natural wood instrument played her hands and heart. Elspeth's emotions were laced in notes, beads, and the beautiful divine knowing of the ancient songs, which made the space between the ethereal and the present seem to disappear into the grey and white atmosphere. Now, there seemed to be nothing to worry about or be afraid of at all.

Small splashes of what looked like translucent paint made the patterns of the early sky look sheer. Elspeth also needed to see the hand of the man she could have married, and could almost feel him standing next to her. And, then, he spoke for the last time. Cain whispered carefully and slowly, gently and with respect. 'Another thing Elspeth, that I feel you should now know. Right throughout the pages and chapters of your life, this women, by distant relation only, is cognate to you. A distant relative who hated you from the day you were born; her crooked finger and hooked nose were features that she bore and you did not. This is why when you were very young she wanted you dead and gone. Not one of her off-spring possessed even one of your special qualities; inside or out. I am sorry for this late news. But, in the end – you did win'. Next to the granite rock, again, she hovered above looking for him and not flinching at the cold, hard pain strung to her chest. There was blood red across the horizon and a chime bell that tingled a sweet song, a love song for the ages of regret, sorrow, and elation. The sky reddened the waters, and later in the day, when the sun went down, slowly it took with it all the muck and slime and dead rodents, which had habituated in the hut for many years now.

The angel of death was still there, placing a crown upon her golden wings and playing the strings of a harp that opened the clouds to heaven's gate. Elspeth's last thoughts were now fading, 'There is a saviour in the wind chime of hope and love'. The other gentle colours of the changing day gave Elspeth an extra sense of knowing, that beyond the sadness of death is a promise of tender doves and that the descent and ascent of life is only an expression of the divine casting away darkness and moving forward towards the light of life in absolute freedom of flowers — fresh and blissful grace. Elspeth's death was now only a slight whisper amongst the light winds of the wilderness.

It was only a small regret that she had not married Cain, thinking that a marriage may have given her more company later in life. She thought about her own private experiences of living in the secluded terrain, being swept up by the beauty of nature and the full enjoyment of the snow gums. All this gave a smile to the now old woman's face. She looked back on the places the Clarences had asked her to perform tasks, such as cleaning the windows, touching up the paint work, making beds, and sweeping the mats for them to wipe their feet upon. At the same time, Elspeth seemed to slip in and out consciousness, and began to see the light streaming from the other world above the cloud line. Elspeth could also see the memories of back lanes, smelly rubbish, and the sickness of vomit dissipate into golden stars. Red, yellow, and green balloons made the dreams of the earth in summer sweep away the fear of an unwanted sickness in the region. The many regrets and sour things, in her final hour of life, seemed to sweep away. In the corner of the hut, there it was, the beautiful Swallowtail butterfly. The butterfly seemed to lovingly flutter between the silver spider webs and lucky bamboo shoots. The bamboo was a gift from an Asian man who had told Elspeth that she reminded him of a character in a book. It was a long jargon about a first fleeter, by the name of Joan Lang. The Asian man was right, Elspeth was a blood relative of the wrongly convicted woman.

The story went that although the voyage of life was long and hard, in the end, the gift of the good luck bamboo would take her to a life full of delights, such as paper dolls, golden castles, and tall ships. The man had also told Elspeth in a palm reading, that one day she would help educate the poor, those who had been isolated through many difficult circumstances. There was a difference between kangaroo paw flowers and long stemmed red roses, enveloped in papers from Europe. The butterfly had also known this very well. The abstract looking kangaroo paw was beautiful in the natural, dense bush scrub and roses were a backdrop for something else. Elspeth did know many beautiful words, and was responsible for many of the comforting epigraphs placed on the graves of dead babies and saintly people alike, helping many in the local area who could not read or write, but who sincerely sought her poetic inference in times of sorrow and loss.

Soon, it would be her own name inscribed on a headstone. Elspeth's favourite rendition came wafting to her last thoughts. It was about an instrumentalist who played ethereal musical notes up and down the ovulation cycles of many women, leaving bleeding hearts, unclaimed children, unpaid bills, and running from his responsibilities.

The famous musician had also stowed away on the first fleet to start his new life. Wine, song, and no money were his main attributes. The man's music was that of a romantic poet, detached from the real world and leaving behind the many mothers of his children. The music he wrote was an incantation of free love making, spiritual spells, and magical charms. This approach disguised the pain that he would inflict on those who were drawn to him unknowingly, like a magnetic force. The end called for open conversation, drafting words of expressive kindness. A harp he played.

Elspeth could now feel the clouds speaking to her inner life, in the world that she was leaving. So special it had been for her to live so close to the earth. The treed, open skied, mysterious, and almost ritualistic landscape that she had always worshipped, and where many of her ancestors were buried, was now lit with prayer. From what she could see, her life now appeared to be a series of changing supernatural events. It was no longer a secret that the sun stone Elspeth had placed near her hut and stepped on each day was a powerful sign that all her life, she had, in fact, been a woman living a life similar to the ancient women of the earth. She was a woman who faced every life obstacle with courage and faith in her own self and life direction. In the all-encompassing directional seasons and storms, unchangeable was Elspeth, unbreakable and a monument higher than the sky line that willed her to survive the scratchy thickets, hollow boondocks, and the gnarl on her own.

With the sky light flickering through the trees, and the sun shining through the wilderness, it carved an image in the ending scene of what may have been mistaken as only a light shifting. But it was really two swans gliding to heaven's gate, showing Elspeth the way through. The woman of black dogs, debaseness, cruel ways, and arrogant thinking and behaviours was now gone into the depths of distant time on earth, never to return, never to set foot near Elspeth again. Kendra's piano gently played and there was now thunder roaring, as the two contrasting elements painted nature and life. The angel of death sung. Elspeth again felt refined and beautiful. It was love, like soft rain water, gentle rose petals, and the strings of the harp calling her to the renewed day.

Although an old woman now, Elspeth, in herself, was renewed from the days when she had left her own difficult, but sometimes sort of happy, family situation, to work for the Clarences. The dying woman was just so glad to forget them. It took many years for her to adapt to the way in which they viewed the world, their strange interests and out of place ideas about life in the country. All of that was also very tiring. For all that time, she was a good, hard-working girl, and showed respect in every instance to her employers, no matter how bad they had treated her. She was grateful now that she had left the Seymour Homestead with grace and dignity.

Elspeth had risen right to the very tip of the mountain, where she was respected by the people who knew her as the woman from the landscape of out back beauty. She was known for having conquered every bad thing that had come her way. It was the grey shapes of the mountain mists that she could now see. It was a skull, sword, book, vase, and half burnt candle that brought the last feelings of life to the hut's table. Elspeth could feel death in her bones and up through the muscles in the back of her neck. It was a strange sensation that she could not fathom and had never known before. Elspeth now realised that sad distance she was now experiencing, was because she would now never return to her hut again. The glimpses of her life still resonated within her visions like the red sap in the bark and the wet flower beds on a heavy rainy afternoon. The grasses whispering in the flowery scents now seemed to say goodbye to every day, month, and year. The sky, earth, wind, and rain could be like the togetherness of souls mingled by passion and natural yearnings, a path Elspeth knew we all have to take. The imagery of the rhythm, a harmony of the musical notes, and angelic voice depicted a certain sombre, but also surreal mood. Becoming refreshed in the realms of heaven had conjured up a sensitive warmth of elated euphoria. They were similar to those ecstatic moments that drifted into every crevice of her body, after the orgasms she experienced in the gully with Cain.

It was empowering, even in death, to reflect on the different phases of her life, knowing that, although she was unprepared for all the different events that would and did happen, Isobel was there with her many words of wisdom. Isobel, with her staunch ideals and unfaltering moral values, had actually helped Elspeth in so many ways. Elspeth carried so much in herself of Isobel's advice and sincere wishes for her deep happiness. At times, she wished that she may have taken the resolute road of total commitment and religious faithfulness. The promise of faithfulness was something that Elspeth struggled with for most of her life. Total personal peace she could only find, in total personal freedom. Elspeth was sorry that her and Isobel never had any contact after she left the Seymour Homestead. Those conflicting values did put distance between the two women, a divide that could never come together again.

Elspeth did happen to hear, just through passing, that Isobel had slipped away from her post one afternoon in the dead of winter to be with the Irish man. The two were both found dead the next morning. Fully clothed and asleep on his bed, there was blood all over the walls and a high-powered rifle aside the window sill. People said it may have been a suicide. Elspeth never forgave herself for not trying to heal the rift between her and her good friend Isobel who always dreamed of being a school teacher and who worked day and night for the Clarences without a word of complaint about her poor working conditions and low rate of pay. Isobel, she knew, was not far away now, and had found the needle amongst the hay.

Stepping in time with the music, she was feeling joy open her heart, open her mind, and open her body. It was a play between light and dark, between him and her, between the end and the beginning, between the ether, starlight, and golden flame flickering on the altar of flowered sacramental hosts. There were pears, golden peaches, dried cherries, plums, natural wood doors, leaves red, brown and sunlight crossed the time of idle hours. The printed roses and her delicate soft hands were alight in the burnt amber colours of the seasons of change. Standing tall, standing fine, standing elegant in the bush of laced apricot satin and silk dress, Elspeth held a concertina book that contained poems of time and seasonal changes. It brought with it the urge to unearth the quiet sleeping prince, to once again bring down the waterfall of lustful desire between him and her. Like the tall tree and the hut, they had a place together and apart. Time was now transparent. Some many moons after the last horse ride, in the clear open sky, just before she slipped across into paradise, the Prince and Elspeth did what they were always going to do, exchange a subtle vow of eternal everlasting.

Then, in an instant, the memory of the witch's jealousy came overwhelmingly flooding back. The feelings were thick and dense and Elspeth felt them sharp and cold. 'Let the jealousy eat her up', commanded The Wind Queen from the top of the ridge that overlooked the longest, deepest, and most difficult gully to access. There, the snake circled at the bottom of the gorge. It awaited her last command to defeat the jealous witch and her coven. Again, the Queen of Winds spoke. 'When they least expected you to do so, you did rise up'. The winds spoke of the power that Elspeth displayed in leaving the service of the Clarences, independently and with her own bare hands rebuilding the hut. Out in the back of sticks, this was a very brave undertaking for such a young woman. It was a time of strength, when, as a young girl, she braced herself and carried on not only self-determined and self reliant country style living, but also, independent mothering. In those days, a woman alone with a child did not receive the respect or much support from the general community.

'All praises to you dear Elspeth', gently whispered the angel. Elspeth responded with her last, dying breath that was full of that same fresh spirit and youthful glee, similar to when she wore her yellow smock with the embroidered strawberry applique. 'I, yes, I, Elspeth Abney, formally of James Creek, reclaim myself back from her and their jealousies. The bad coven did, throughout each chapter of my life, show their true colours. These true colours were dark, merciless, debauched, immoral, shameful, and cruel — and will all be realised by the great counsel. The bad woman's small conceited ways and dead spiritual essence will never be present again in the sight of the omnipresent great eagle. And, in that moment, the witch and her rank companions will once again be all cast down'.

The bird quickly moved the snake from within the gorge, as Mannus carefully placed his tired mother's body deep in the ravine of the gully. The witch's old patterns of jealousy that were there from the first breath of Elspeth's life, now finished. The witchy woman and her cruel friends were no match for Elspeth's shrewdness, her all mighty eagle's prayer, and the gentle qualities of the guiding Swallowtail butterfly.

After all this, it was only a simple hut that Elspeth truly desired. And, like her, it was everything to write home about.